PRIZE STORIES 1979
The O. Henry Awards

DATE DUE	
GAYLORD	PRINTED IN U.S.A.

PRIZE STORIES 1979
The O. Henry Awards

EDITED AND
WITH AN INTRODUCTION
BY WILLIAM ABRAHAMS

DOUBLEDAY & COMPANY, INC.
GARDEN CITY, NEW YORK
1979

ISBN: 0-385-14219-6
Library of Congress Catalog Card Number 21-9372
Copyright © 1979 by Doubleday & Company, Inc.
Printed in the United States of America
First Edition

CONTENTS

PUBLISHER'S NOTE

This volume is the fifty-ninth in the O. Henry Memorial Award series.

In 1918, the Society of Arts and Sciences met to vote upon a monument to the master of the short story, O. Henry. They decided that this memorial should be in the form of two prizes for the best short stories published by American authors in American magazines during the year 1919. From this beginning, the memorial developed into an annual anthology of outstanding short stories by American authors, published, with the exception of the years 1952 and 1953, by Doubleday & Company, Inc.

Blanche Colton Williams, one of the founders of the awards, was editor from 1919 to 1932; Harry Hansen from 1933 to 1940; Herschel Brickell from 1941 to 1951. The annual collection did not appear in 1952 and 1953, when the continuity of the series was interrupted by the death of Herschel Brickell. Paul Engle was editor from 1954 to 1959 with Hanson Martin coeditor in the years 1954 to 1960; Mary Stegner in 1960; Richard Poirier from 1961 to 1966, with assistance from and coeditorship with William Abrahams from 1964 to 1966. William Abrahams became editor of the series in 1967.

Doubleday also publishes *First-Prize Stories from the O. Henry Memorial Awards* in editions that are brought up to date at intervals. In 1970 Doubleday also published under Mr. Abrahams' editorship *Fifty Years of the American Short Story*, a collection of stories selected from the series.

The stories chosen for this volume were published in the period from the summer of 1977 to the summer of 1978. A list of the magazines consulted appears at the back of the book. The choice of stories and the selection of prize winners are exclusively the responsibility of the editor. Biographical material is based on information provided by the contributors and obtained from standard works of reference.

INTRODUCTION

One must be wary, especially in an annual collection such as this, of attaching too much weight to statistics, of generalizing from them too freely: the certainties of one year have a disconcerting way of reversing themselves in the next. And yet, this year—for reasons that I trust will become apparent—I feel even more strongly than usual that conviction must take precedence over caution in discussing the splendid and precarious state of the contemporary short story. Splendid, because the best of the stories, taken together, represent so considerable an achievement. Precarious, because of the paradox inherent in their publication: an abundance of excellent stories; an insufficiency of readers to welcome them.

Why should this odd pairing have come to pass?

In this year's collection are twenty-one stories, a larger number than usual. Sixteen were first published in the pages of little magazines, quarterly reviews, irregularly issued periodicals reaching a small, a very small, readership. (*Shenandoah*, for example, one of the best of these magazines from which I have taken two stories, prints approximately one thousand copies of each quarterly issue.) And the number of their readers, in total, is rather less than one might hastily conclude. It seems fair to assume that any reader who is prepared to take the trouble to look out for one such little magazine (not, alas, always to be found at the local public library) more likely than not reads another such magazine and another. . . . The overlap has to be considerable. In short, one can safely imagine a small number of dedicated readers discovering a large number of excellent stories by dedicated authors at the time of their publication. Just as safely, one can imagine (and regret) a much larger audience of potential readers who would welcome these stories if they were aware of their existence.

Consider now that larger audience of readers in their natural habitat. I am speaking here of readers who want stories of genuine excellence for whom the world of the little magazine is *terra incognita* or only to be tracked down with considerable difficulty.

Such readers will turn by choice to the aptly named quality magazines which are distributed in relatively large quantities, and there, though in decreasing numbers, they are likely to find stories that will fulfill their expectations. But what is disheartening is to discover how few such magazines remain that turn out still to be positively, rather than reluctantly, receptive to the short story. This year I have chosen five stories from these magazines—five out of twenty-one!—a disproportion that in itself is alarming and becomes even more so when one realizes that the five stories were chosen from only three magazines: *The New Yorker*, *The Atlantic*, and *Harper's*.

At this point I feel I must make clear what regular readers of this series will know already, that preconceptions, or a thesis decided upon in advance ("The Superiority of Little Magazines"), play no part in determining each year's selections. The O. Henry Awards are not intended to *prove* anything except the continuing excellence and vitality of the American short story. The extraordinary disproportion this year between stories from little magazines and those from magazines of wide circulation is precisely that, extraordinary—since in recent years the division has been fairly even—and therefore the more discouraging for what it may portend.

The signs suggest that we are entering a bleak period, after a relative and extended heyday, for the short story in magazines that aim at reaching a wide public. The most striking example of the change is in *Esquire*, a magazine justly admired for the fiction it has regularly published in the past decade (and before that), which now only intermittently opens its pages to the short story. No doubt a question of careful editorial choice is involved; no doubt, either, that the tastes of the majority of the magazine's readers have been considered and their evident preference for "fact" over fiction taken into account; but for readers who welcomed in *Esquire* the stories by Harold Brodkey and Cynthia Ozick that were afterwards First Prize winners in this series, the new policy represents a considerable loss.

I feel that I should add (though I wish that I did not have to) that *Esquire* is not alone in this turn against fiction. It has made the most dramatic countermove, and so is the most immediately noticeable. But perhaps in the long run what is more to be regretted is the gradual relaxing of standards—away from a brief, brave venture into serious fiction—in the former "women's magazines" that have transformed themselves into magazines for young home-makers, young suburbanites, and young swingers. But where are the young readers who want serious fiction to turn?

Perhaps they will follow the young writers (and their elders, too) who have come to recognize the little magazines as among the few remaining places where they can write truthfully, authentically, and imaginatively about contemporary life. Indeed, it is this quality of truthfulness—however painful—that so distinguishes the stories gathered here and accounts, I think, for the great number of them that are told in the first person: as though only "I" can be trusted to tell us what has happened, or is happening, in a life. Looking back to the end of the Second World War (as Gordon Weaver does in "Getting Serious"), do we not remember the bright future waiting for us as we entered the post-war world and recognize how little of it remains to us now, in the post-Watergate world? Is it any wonder that in an age of well-paid liars, when lying has become common currency among public figures who ask to be rewarded for telling their ghost writers an improved "true version" of their lives—is it any wonder, then, that writers, in the privacy of art, should catch at those moments, those events, which reveal the deeper, sadder, as some would say, the more depressing aspects of life? The storytellers, the truth-tellers, are the least welcome guests at the feast of liars; they have no choice but to go their own way, writing the story.

But it is precisely at that point that the precariousness of the present situation becomes most evident. Traditionally, and by choice, little magazines have played a marginal, though not an insignificant, role: in their pages have appeared experimental stories, avant-garde stories, difficult stories, unconventional stories, and first stories. Historically, they have served as a starting place for writers who have gone on, graduated, so to speak, from the little to the large. But now it would seem, as the larger magazines begrudge their expensive pages to fiction, that they are being thrust into a more central position: the survival of the short story may depend, more than was ever anticipated, on the survival of the little magazines. A luxury once, they have become a necessity. Given the financial difficulties under which they perennially suffer, and which are sure to worsen in an inflationary economy, one can only hope that one or other of our great Foundations may be persuaded to help them survive. The stories in the present collection seem to me evidence enough of the splendid writing they encourage in precarious circumstances.

I would like to take this occasion—and it seems particularly appropriate that I do so in the light of what I have written above—to pay tribute to the late Martha Foley for her outstanding services to the short story, beginning in the early 1930s with the historic little magazine, *Story*, of which she was a cofounder, and continuing through the many years (until her death in 1977) that she was editor and friend of *The Best American Short Stories*.

WILLIAM ABRAHAMS

PRIZE STORIES 1979
The O. Henry Awards

GETTING SERIOUS

GORDON WEAVER

Gordon Weaver, married and the father of three daughters, lives in Stillwater, Oklahoma, where he is Professor of English and chairman of the department at Oklahoma State University. Born in Moline, Illinois, he grew up in Milwaukee, Wisconsin. Author of two novels and two collections of stories, he has won the St. Lawrence Award for Fiction and the *Quarterly West* short story prize for his work. A third collection of his stories, *Morality Play: Fictions,* will be published in 1979.

When Captain Guy Roland of the Army Air Corps came home from the war, he drove his Lincoln Zephyr coupe right up to the edge of the bluff above Silver Lake, and blew the horn again and again to tell the world he was back. He leaned on it, long blasts that echoed out over Silver Lake, rolled through the pine trees, stopped us all where we stood, like an air-raid siren.

"What the goddamn hell!" my father said.

My mother ceased priming the kitchen pump with lake water, the pitcher in one hand, the other resting on the pump handle. "I think the Roland boy is back," she said, turning to see through the screened window.

"Where are you going?" my father said to me.

"I want to see."

"Let him go," my mother said.

"Far be it from me to insist on a damn thing," I heard my father say before the screen door slapped shut behind me.

Captain Guy Roland honked the horn of his Lincoln Zephyr, and his parents closed the bar and restaurant of the Silvercryst Resort and came outside. People came out of the bar and restau-

rant carrying glasses and bottles. Somebody gave him a bottle of
beer he waved and pointed with while he dug things out of his
duffel with his free hand. Everyone shook hands with everyone
else.

The sun came through the swaying tops of the tall Norway
pines, dappling us where we stood on the bluff above the lake. A
light breeze rose off the water, stirring the surface of Silver Lake
to glisten in the sun like chips of diamond or glass, lighting Captain Guy Roland's return. Mrs. Peaches Roland kissed her son on
his cheek, his ear, his neck, stretching up to put one arm carefully
around his neck, keeping her cigarette away from his face. She
carried a frosted Collins glass in her other hand. She said, "Baby,
baby," to her son and kissed him again. I could see lipstick she left
on his neck and jaw. He shook hands with everyone while his
mother kissed him.

Mr. Roland shook hands with his son, shook hands with all the
people who had come from the bar and dining room, then
stepped back to some shade and smiled, squinting at it all, twirl-
ing the melting ice in the bottom of the glass he carried with him
from the bar. Captain Guy Roland shook my hand.

"Our summer house is right next door to your resort," I said. I
think he said that was keen, or swell, something like that, and
then he was being kissed again by his mother and shaking hands
with more people. The sun dappled us, the breeze swayed the tops
of the Norway pines, shook the varicolored heads of the zinnias
and marigolds and hollyhocks Mrs. Peaches Roland cultivated in
tiered rock gardens on the slope below the bluff. The wind on Silver Lake shot the sun back up to us like the scraps of tinfoil that I
saved to aid the war effort.

Captain Guy Roland gave his mother a ring in a wooden box.
The ring was silver, set with pale stones, the box a dark, reddish
wood, lined with purple silk. "That comes from Manila," he said.
"Diamonds go there for a fraction what they're worth."

"Baby," Mrs. Peaches Roland said, kissing him with cigarette
smoke coming out of her mouth. She carried the open box around
for everyone to see, tried to make it sparkle by turning it to the
light, clutching the box and her leather cigarette case and her
empty Collins glass in her frail hands.

He gave his father a short Japanese sword. There were braided
cords with tassels tied to the lacquered scabbard, and Guy showed

us how the haft opened to reveal a piece of sheer rice paper, spidery calligraphy. "You commit harakiri with it," he said. Prayers to your ancestors were written on the rice paper to get you to heaven after you stabbed yourself.

"Wicked," Mr. Roland said when he unsheathed the sword and put the ball of his thumb to its edge. The cigarette in his mouth made him squint and cough while he handled his son's gift.

"You hang that up over the fireplace," Guy said. He gave me a Japanese army forage cap and a wad of occupation money that also came from the Philippines. "In Manila you could buy a hot time with that," he told me. I stayed there and watched until Mr. and Mrs. Roland opened up the bar again and everyone went back inside the Silvercryst Resort.

These are not *living* details for me. Rather, after thirty years, it is a kind of tableau, a group of people frozen in my memory like statues, like a memorial to the people, the place, the world war. I can look at it whenever I wish, but it does not *live* for me.

We are set in place on the lawn next to the huge Lincoln Zephyr, outside the Silvercryst Resort bar and restaurant, dappled by the sun that penetrates the tops of the pine trees. We are frozen in place by the edge of the bluff above Silver Lake. On the slope descending to the beach, Mrs. Peaches Roland's bright flowers bloom. The water slaps at the dock and the moored boats, laps the sandy shore, lights our pageant with reflected sun that blares brilliant as an air-raid siren. I am part of it, this picture, yet outside it. It is my vision of the time and place of my beginning, but after thirty years it is no more than that.

Captain Guy Roland is the center of this picture. His hat, bent in a fifty-mission crush, is cocked back on his head, his blond pompadour ruffled as if by design. His captain's bars gleam, his pilot's wings a duller silver. On the left breast of his officer's dress-uniform jacket are the muted plots of color of his campaign ribbons and citations; the flat gold bars of his combat service track his sleeve. His uniform trousers, a faintest suggestion of pink, are sharply creased; the toes of his cordovan shoes glisten, spitshined to the hardness of mirrors. *You can get diamonds for a fraction what they're worth*, he says, and *You hang that over the fireplace*, and *You can buy a hot time in Manila with that*.

My world, in this time of my beginning, is no more nor less

than my vision of it, and this picture is my vision, this time and place, these people.

"Look," I said to my father when I came back to our summer home, "it's invasion money."

"That and a nickel gets you a cup of coffee," he said.

"He was a *pilot*, I think," I said.

"I flew a Spad at Fort Sill, Oklahoma," my father said. "You didn't know that, did you."

"You flew back and forth to Texas because you couldn't get whiskey in Oklahoma," my mother said.

"Another precinct heard from," he said.

"You should see that sword!"

"Any luck, some night in his cups the son of a bitch'll cut his throat with it and bleed to death," my father said.

"*Will* you stop!" my mother said.

"Not unless I'm asked nicely."

"He gave her a ring from Manila," I said.

"Know why they call her *Peaches?*" he said. "Ripe for the picking."

"Do you care at all what you say to him?" my mother said. My father did not answer her.

"In Manila you can spend this just like real money," I said.

"Get that nasty thing off your head," my mother said. "God only knows where it's been before now."

"And He ain't telling," my father said.

After their divorce, my father moved to Minneapolis and remarried. He wrote me regular letters I answered whenever I could not resist my mother's urging. He was, after all, she would say, still my father, even if he had abandoned us both. In my letters I told him yes, I was working hard and doing well in school, I was behaving myself, I was a help, not a hindrance, to my mother, I was enjoying the summer on Silver Lake. It was not lying, just something I had to say to please both my parents.

I remember it as my summer spent hanging about, lurking in some shade of pine tree or off to one corner of the beach, smoking cigarettes, watching, savoring my boredom and bitter envy.

In 1950 Guy Roland drove a custom Ford convertible. It was the summer I affected tee shirts, my cigarettes rolled in one sleeve —hidden in the top of my sock when I had to go home to eat or sleep—wore Levi's slung low on my hips, black shoes with spade toes, my hair long on the sides and back, short on top. It was the summer season I gave over to hating myself for my boredom and resentment, detesting anything that chanced to come to my attention—except Guy Roland.

His father still ran the Silvercryst Resort, was still to be seen on the restaurant veranda, drink in hand, talking real estate with people who came to buy parcels of the lake frontage he had to sell. He was an immaculate man, his hair a spun white meringue, crisp shirts and casual slacks creased like knife blades. He wore two-tone brown-and-white shoes. He often stood on the bluff above the lake, jingling the change in his pocket, squinting against the glare of the sun off the water, as if counting the heads of vacationers who paid for beach privileges along with the cabins he rented. When he noticed me, he squinted a little harder, as if that was the closest to a smile of recognition he could muster. I would nod or shrug or blow cigarette smoke defiantly, flip butts into his wife's flowerbeds on the slope.

Mrs. Peaches Roland still came out late mornings to tend her zinnias and hollyhocks and daisies. Still light and colorful as the flowers she loved, she wore garden-party hats, the broad brims waving slowly in the lake breezes, tied under her chin with swaths of filmy gauze. She carried her cigarettes and lighter in the patch pockets of her pastel smocks, one hand free to carry a trowel. Eyes shaded by opaque aviator's sunglasses, she teetered as she stepped among the blossoms on platform shoes with open toes. The flaming reds of her lips, fingernails, and toenails always matched. When I slouched close enough, I heard the popular songs she hummed to herself, caught the wall of scent that surrounded her like a sweet cloud.

Guy Roland came and went all summer. I remember it as his perfect summer, the season I would have signed away my future to share the smallest part of—one week, a day, an afternoon.

Like the summer he came and went. He always had friends. From where I brooded, some shaded corner of the resort I do not recall, I heard the crunch of the Ford's white-walls on the gravel parking lot. The convertible's radio carried through the pines, played all the way up so they could hear it through the wind whipping them as they drove—from wherever to wherever. He pulled his car right up on the grass and pine needles at the edge of the bluff, always honked the horn in some rhythm as his friends climbed out without opening the doors. *Watch the paint, watch the paint!* he would say. He and his friends would laugh.

He drove barefoot. He and his friends were barefooted, wearing swimming suits, carrying bath towels and beach blankets, a big portable radio, cigarettes and bottles of suntan lotion, sunglasses, unbuttoned shirts with tails that hung down over their swimsuits.

The girls were always beautiful—long legs, skin tan-gold, hair pulled up off graceful necks, pouty lips, full breasts bound in halters or swim tops. Some of the men wore sweatshirts with the sleeves cuff off raggedly, faded Greek letters on their chests. His friends started down the slope to the beach while Guy went to the bar for their beer.

I put myself in his way whenever I could do it without awkwardness. If he saw me, he would nod or wink, or say hello, and I would nod, smile, wave my cigarette at him, make that do for the day.

"So what's the program plan?" Mr. Roland would say if he could catch Guy before he got away from the bar with paper cups and the cooler of beer.

"Busy, Popper, busy," Guy said to his father. "Hello there, Miss Peaches!" he would shout to his mother among the flowers as he passed her on the way to his friends. His mother waved, blew a kiss to his back as he disappeared down the slope. I followed no sooner than I had to.

Guy Roland and his friends spread their blankets on the sand, extended the radio's antenna to bring in the music of Chicago and Milwaukee, popped caps off bottles of beer, rubbed lotion into each other's shoulders. The beautiful tan-gold girls untied their halters, lay down on their stomachs to brown the whole of their broad glazed backs. I could get near enough to smell the tang of the oil. Guy Roland sat up on one elbow, squinting at the harsh sunlight reflected off Silver Lake. The breeze flipped his blond hair. He smoked cigarettes and drank beer, kept time to the radio music with one foot, the vision of a man in his perfect summer, a perfect life awaiting him in the distances not quite visible beyond the far shore of the lake.

They lay, soaking in the sun, seldom touching, never swimming, paying no attention to the children who dabbled in the shallows, the boats that docked and left—never noticing me, squatting at the base of the slope, souring my mouth with cigarettes, almost content with nothing more than my vision of them—static, impervious, unconcerned. It is a picture, but I am never in this one.

Guy Roland came and went, from Memorial Day through Labor Day, this summer I call the season of my rage at myself for being what I was without even the right to claim that I had made myself what I had become. His father ran the Silvercryst Resort and sold what remained of the lake frontage that he owned. Peaches Roland babied her flowers late mornings, drank away afternoons and evenings in the resort bar. What I hated most was my conviction that nothing would ever change.

"Where have you been so long?" my mother asked me when I returned.

"Nowhere. Down by the beach."

"I smell cigarette smoke."

"Cut it out," I said.

"You've been smoking!" she said. "What would your father say if I wrote and told him you smoke?"

"Come on, cut it out."

"I give up," my mother said to me. "You don't listen to me. When are you going to be serious about anything?"

"I'm serious," I said. I was.

The truce had been signed for two years by the time I came back from Korea. I was hospitalized a long time in Japan, a long time in Fitzsimmons Hospital in Denver, and a long time in outpatient rehabilitation at Fort Sheridan, Illinois, while I tried out my rebuilt knee in what they called *real-life situations*. They rebuilt my knee with steel and wires and plastic, and it worked fine. I only used a cane because I was afraid it might give way at any moment. They said that was psychological. I thought I could hear my rebuilt knee make a clicking noise when I walked, but that was psychological too. My mother was very nervous about it.

"You're being silly," I told her. "It's the strongest part of my body. It's like a spotweld, the last thing that's going to break."

"I'm sorry," she said, "I can't help worrying." She had not changed while I was away. She looked just a little older. She was really upset only when we happened to talk about my father, who had died suddenly in Minneapolis just before I came back from Japan.

"It's nice," I said. "Seriously, nothing's any different." She had not changed, except to look, naturally, a little older, and of course my father was dead, but he had gone out of my life years before.

It was night, so I picked my way slowly with my cane across the patches of moonlight breaking through the pine trees. I stopped to rest on the bluff, watched the moonlight ripple on the surface of Silver Lake. The lake stretched out below me, shimmering with the moon haze that drifted over the pines above and behind me. Dock lights defined the far shore, and I could hear the same lapping of the water against the beach, the wind swish in the tops of the pines, the rustle of insects in the grass and ferns at my feet. I could hear the music of the jukebox in the bar of the Silvercryst Resort.

I knew what I would not find. Mr. Roland was also dead, my mother told me, a suicide. He shot himself about the time I was in Denver. She did not know the story. Business, perhaps, or his wife. He drove out on a dirt road, put the barrel of a pistol in his mouth, killed himself. Maybe it was his wife.

Peaches Roland had begun to need long stays at a downstate sanitarium, drying out. Now, my mother said, her mind was gone and she was committed forever to the sanitarium. "You ought to see how he's let her rock garden go," my mother said. Guy owned and operated the Silvercryst Resort, but he was no businessman, my mother said.

I expected at least a small crowd on a Friday night before Labor Day weekend, but the bar was empty except for Guy and a woman. The jukebox glowed, played loudly, and the fluorescents lit the back bar softly, but there were only the two of them, sitting on stools at the end of the bar as if they were customers, the bartender on a short break.

I smiled, put my weight on my cane, held my hand out to him. Guy Roland stared at me for a moment—the woman with him did not raise her head until we were introduced—then squinted, recognized me, smiled, took my hand.

"You don't have to wear your war suit," Guy said. "I'll serve you even if you're not of age. Hell, we're old folks, you and me."

"I'm old enough," I said, "just. I haven't had much chance to buy something that fits."

"Meet Sue," he said. The woman smiled at me as if I were going to take her picture. She was a good-looking woman. "This is my old buddy what's-his-name," Guy said to her, and "Sue is a personal guest here. I stress *personal*," he said, "because I hear rumors she favors men in uniform." She laughed and lowered her face to her drink—she drank bottled beer, liked to peel the labels off the bottles, pile the scraps on the bar. I said hello, and she laughed but never, I think, spoke to me all the time I sat talking with Guy.

She was fine-looking. I imagined her one of the girls who came and went with Guy through the summers before I went away. I could see her as one of those girls on the beach, gold-tan skin glossed with lotion, unfastening her swimsuit top to get the sun evenly across her back while she napped away the season's afternoons on a blanket, the portable radio playing music from Chicago and Milwaukee.

She was old enough to have been one of those girls, paled now because she spent her time indoors, wearing dangle earrings and chain bracelets that slid and rattled on her bare white arms as she picked at the label on her beer bottle. In the lulls of the lake breeze coming through the screened windows facing the bluff, her heavy scent reminded me of Mrs. Peaches Roland drying out forever in a downstate sanitarium.

"Drinks on the house!" Guy said. "You name it, you got it," he said, "just so I can get to it without moving, that is." Sue laughed and tinkled her bracelets. Guy stretched across the bar, pulled up a bottle, splashed a refill in his glass—he did not bother with ice and water or soda. He spoke clearly, weaved a little when he tried to stand or walk, but did not stumble or stagger. When Sue wanted another bottle of beer to tear at, she got up and went behind the bar for it herself. She looked fine walking, too, her jewelry glinting and ringing, her skin very white under the fluorescents. Guy grunted, stretched far enough to find me a shotglass.

"I'm not used to taking it straight," I said, but he paid no attention.

"Happy happy," he said, and we all drank. He closed his eyes when he drank, as if he needed to concentrate to get the full taste of it, touched his lips lightly with his forefinger after he swallowed, sighed like a man falling into a long deep sleep. "So what the hell's with the walking stick?" he said. I told Guy and Sue about the mortar shell that fell near me. "You're crapping me," he said.

He leaned close to me, squinted, as if the campaign ribbons I wore contained fine print. "Real?" he said. "This is a *real* Purple Heart?" he said, pointing.

"That's the Syngman Rhee Citation. This one's the Purple Heart."

"You got to be crapping, buddy," Guy said. He made me pull up my trouser leg, show him the swollen, pink-stitched seams. I told him how it was rebuilt with steel and wire and plastic, that I imagined at times I could hear it click when I walked.

When he stopped laughing he said, "Six bits in the PX and you go off and get yourself the *real* thing!" Then he told me how he spent his war at Pensacola, Florida, some kind of air corps liaison with the navy's flight-training school. The work called for a captain, so they made him a captain. When Sue laughed, she was laughing to herself. His campaign ribbons had all come from the Pensacola Naval Air Station PX, bought the day he got his separation papers.

"Why the hell not? My folks got a bang out of it."

"You bought those souvenirs at the PX too?" I tried to see into the darkened dining room, see if a Japanese sword hung over the natural stone fireplace.

"I could get all that crap I wanted from the swabbies passing through flight school. You forget that was a *big* war, son," he said.

We talked, and we drank from Guy's bottle; and when I was feeling the whiskey, I told him my father was dead. When he only nodded, I said, "I was sorry as hell to hear about your father."

"That's a whole long story itself" is all he said, drinking, pressing his finger to his lips to dry them. Sue kept the jukebox playing, reaching into his pocket for quarters whenever it stopped.

"I'm sorry about your mother."

"She just needed a rest," he said. "You can understand a person needing a rest. Like yourself," he said. And: "So what the hell you figuring on now?"

"Home and sleep it off. If I can keep from going over the bluff with this cane." Sue thought that was funny, laughed with us.

"Smartass," Guy Roland said, "I mean your damn life."

"College, I think," I said, and told him what the GI Bill plus my permanent disability pension came to every month. He squinted at college, like it was a book he tried to recall reading, then smiled as if remembering it was amusing, but not serious. He had tried college, a couple of those winters that hit so quickly after Labor Day, upstate in Wisconsin.

"Don't break your fanny on my property," he called to me as I went out the door, keeping my cane out carefully in front of me— I believed my knee was going to collapse somewhere in the dark.

"Hey," I said, looking back at them from the doorway, "where's everybody? Is this Labor Day weekend or not?" He put his arm around Sue, rocked her as he laughed.

"He must think this is a business or something!" he whooped. "Close the screen door, you'll let mosquitos in," he said, and got up to stretch for his bottle again.

My mother waited up for me. "What did you find to do all night?" she asked.

"Talking with Guy." I did not kiss her, did not want her to talk about the dangers of drinking so much when I could so easily fall and really hurt myself. "It's like a tomb at Silvercryst," I said to be saying something as I went toward the porch where I always slept at Silver Lake.

"He'll finish the ruin his father started," she said. "He takes no care at all."

"It's sad," I said, but my mother had no sympathy to spare for Guy Roland or his parents. I lay on my bed on the sleeping porch, waiting for the spinning whiskey to slow so I could sleep. When I could clear my mind, I stayed awake a while to plan my life. I felt very good about it, as if my life was something I just discovered that I owned, mine to do with as I wished. I was pleased to discover that I was so mature.

I went to college and I got married. I studied nothing in particular in college, but I was graduated. The girl I married came from a very good Winnetka family. I learned the construction business from my father-in-law. I did not marry the boss's daughter and take over his business; I worked very hard, and the business was better for my work. First I lived in a fine home in Winnetka, near my wife's parents. After my children were born, I built a wonderful new home for us out in Skokie, where we lived close to wealthy Chicago doctors and lawyers and a few men who, like myself, were very serious about what they did for a living.

We built luxury condominium-developments that sold as fast as we built them, and I had first a son, then a daughter, and a special wing on our wonderful home in Skokie where my mother lived with us the last two and a half years of her life. I had no trouble at all in my life, and even my marriage was as good as most marriages—most of the time.

When my mother died, in the late spring of 1965, I used that as an excuse to go up to Silver Lake. "We can all go," I told my wife. "The kids would love it. You might even like it. Mix pleasure with business," I said.

"That's your story," she said.

"I can't sell it out without being there," I said. "Those country real-estate boys will rob me blind."

"I'm *not* packing us all up and hauling all the way up there," she said.

"I have to go," I told my wife. "I can't handle it long distance."

"You do what you think you have to."

"I always have," I told her. "That's why I'm so good at it. Or didn't you notice?"

My wife and I never talked about our failing marriage, because it was too serious and depressing a topic and because, I suppose, we thought our failure would heal itself if we left it undisturbed long enough.

A lake, something in nature, does not change. The water level goes up or down a little from year to year, but as I stood on the bluff above Silver Lake, the moon still shimmered coldly on the surface, the breeze shushed in the tops of the pines above and behind me, the far shore was steady with dock lights. I did not see the fading paint on the summer home in the dark that first night, did not notice the pine needles banked up against the house by the winter, the remains of our pier heaved and broken by the winter ice; but inside, the walls held the musty damp of the closed winter that I remembered from opening the house each season after Memorial Day, years ago. Inside, everything was in place, clammy to the touch after several years undisturbed, but whole and unworn. The music still came through the air from the Silvercryst Resort, higher and stronger than ever, drowning out the lapping of the water at the beach below the bluff.

The resort was very crowded—the bar, the dining room, the new wing that held a second small bar and a sandwich shop and a souvenir counter. The music was a man in a tuxedo jacket and bowtie, playing a piano bar. He had a machine he worked with a foot treadle. When people shouted requests from the dining room or the bar, or a woman at the piano bar bent close to his ear to whisper a request, he riffled the keyboard, smiled, nodded that he knew the song. With his foot treadle he flashed a slide of the lyrics on a white screen mounted on the far wall. The projector was built into the piano bar. The projector light also illuminated a name plate on the piano bar that said *Little Freddie Kay*.

The bartender was a man my age. The crowd kept him busy, but not too busy to take the drinks he was offered when someone ordered a round. He was a thin man with very black hair, long sideburns, a black mustache, a goatee so black it looked pasted on his chin. He wore a white shirt with ruffles, a red satin vest, frilly red garters on his sleeves to keep his cuffs out of the wet. He wore a colonel's string tie, trying for a western or 1890s idea in his costume. "Where's the boss?" I asked him. I had to speak loudly to be heard—Little Freddie Kay worked the projector treadle, and the crowd sang along with him. "On the Road to Mandalay." "K-K-K-Katy." "Down by the Riverside."

"Me myself and I," he said, grinning at me. He had very small and deep-set eyes, as black as his goatee, always lively, as if lit indirectly, like his back bar.

"Guy Roland?"

He grinned again. "He'll be along."

"You own this place now?"

"Since many moons back," he said, and went away from me in a hurry because they were calling for another round at the far end of the bar, insisting that he have a drink with them.

"You a friend of Guy's?" the new owner of the Silvercryst Resort stopped later to say. When he grinned, his white teeth were very white against the black of his mustache and goatee. I wanted to reach out and pull his goatee off, but his white, pointed teeth were like a dog's when the dog snarls.

"I used to know him a long time back."

"Now Guy is a man can drink drink for drink with you," the new owner of the Silvercryst Resort said, "but he only puddle-jumps now," he said, and shook his head and changed his grin to a sad grin. Little Freddie Kay sang "Waltzing Matilda" and "Roll Me Over in the Clover," and the crowd roared along with him. I waited, wondering why I was not with my family in my wonderful

home in Skokie, and thought about my father who left me when I
was fourteen, my mother who had only recently died. From time
to time I tried to see through the reflections in the thermal panes
of the big picture window, see the opposite shore, but could not
make anything out clearly. Little Freddie Kay and the crowd sang
"There'll Be a Hot Time in the Old Town Tonight."

When Guy Roland came in they were all singing "Row, Row,
Row Your Boat." I remembered his drinking, but he was only a
puddle-jumper now. He sat among all the singers who were singing "Danny Boy" now, sat in the middle of the singers and big
drinkers, as quiet as if he were absolutely alone in the room. He
did not call out or wave for the bartender. He sat on his stool
looking straight ahead at nothing, somewhere in the reflecting
glass of the picture window that was supposed to frame the view
of Silver Lake. He stared like a man who sees only what he is
thinking about.

When the new owner of the Silvercryst Resort chanced to look
his way, Guy raised one finger, made a dry kissing motion with his
lips to order the beer he drank now that he was only a puddle-
jumper. I waited before going over to speak to him, to get two
things firm and clear for myself. One was that I could never again
truly imagine the past. The other was that I would have no
difficulty imagining the future.

I could no longer imagine Captain Guy Roland of the Army
Air Corps returning from the world war. I remembered it clearly,
had it as I would have a snapshot in an album, and I was in that
picture, but it was just something I remembered. I could no
longer imagine Guy Roland coming and going, coming and going
in his custom convertible through the long summers of my own
ripening season. I remember his sporty car, and the tan-gold skin
of the girls, his friends with their cutoff Greek-letter sweatshirts,
the smell of suntan lotion in the lake breeze, music on a portable
radio, but it is just another picture.

There were many fine-looking women in the new Silvercryst
Resort bar, types of the woman Sue who tore labels off bottles all
one night in that same room, ten years before, but I could not
imagine any of them Sue. I could not imagine Guy Roland anywhere before that moment, watching him drink his beer slowly
while Little Freddie Kay led the hoarse crowd in "Oh! Susannah."

What I got very clear for myself, watching him from my end of

the bar before I went over and spoke, was that time and change
are facts of life for all of us. Time and change are what we are
talking about when we talk about the future, about what we want
for ourselves in life. These are the facts of life.

He would have, I saw, the spun white meringue hair of his
father—already the blond was shot with silvery streaks that caught
highlights. He wore his hair longer, in the new fashion, slicked
with dressing to hold it all in hard and perfect order. His face had
thickened to hint of jowls and double chin—Guy would grow
heavier with the years. His cheeks, the tip of his nose, were lightly
flushed—the years, doubtless, when he had matched every drink.
Years of cautious puddle-jumping would not bring back the
fairness of his prime. His blue eyes were still bright, like the eyes
of a child after weeping, but ten years clung to him like a sad
chronicle laid down in sedimentary stone.

"It's my turn to buy a round," I said. He recognized me at
once.

"I'm double damned," Guy Roland said. His handshake was
still solid, his voice unbroken; it was like hearing a recording that
holds its fidelity after years in storage. "Your money's no good
here," he said, taking out a clip of bills.

"This puddle-jumper," the new owner said, "I seen the day he'd
drink you drink for drink, make you beg mercy."

"A real authentic shit," Guy Roland said when he left us.

"Why'd you sell out?" I asked. He had an easy laugh that had
been used too often and too easily to ever be able to mean anything is ever funny any more.

He said, "Six of one, half a dozen of the other. I took enough
out that I'll never have to work a day in my life. My old man always told me I had no head for business," he said. "All I needed
was a few seasons to prove it." I looked to the door, to be sure
there was a path I could maneuver with my stiff knee—in case I
wanted to get away in a hurry. "The sauce," he said, tipping his
glass to show me the beer in the bottom. "I was bombed for years.
The amazing thing is I lightened up once I cut this place loose. I
go three, four weeks at a crack without touching hard stuff. Keep
an eye on yourself," Guy said, squinting, laughing, nodding at my
drink; "a man can end up like Miss Peaches before he knows he's
halfway there."

"I'll stay alert," I said, meaning it.

He told me Mrs. Peaches Roland was still alive, still lived in the downstate sanitarium. I told him my mother was dead, that I had come up from Chicago to see about selling the summer home. "Sell, sell," Guy Roland told me. "All the lake frontage's gone. You can turn it over in a minute. Get smart. Get free of it while the getting's good."

I told him I would, deciding I would not. I told him I was married, about my wife and son and daughter in our wonderful home in Skokie, Illinois, about constructing condominiums that sold faster than my father-in-law and I could build them. He stared off at nothing as I talked, licked his lips, savored the beer he drank three or four weeks at a time before he jumped into another puddle of the hard stuff. He did not tell me he was not married, that he did nothing, because he did not have to. I could read him as clearly as if his life were projected for me on the screen by Little Freddie Kay, between the lines of song lyrics.

Before I left, I asked him, "Guy, do you remember that girl Sue?"

"The which?"

"Sue something. She used to hang in here with you. Years ago."

"Sue," he said, trying to see something in the empty air in front of his eyes. "Double damn me if I do," he said. Why should his memory have been any better than mine?

Another ten years passed, and things were very different. When my father-in-law died, there were problems with our construction business—he left less in it than I thought he would. The construction business went bad for everyone, and almost nobody could afford to buy condominiums. Then I could not get money from banks to build them any more. Still it was not so bad until my wife divorced me and took almost everything that was left. Then I was no longer in the construction business.

I did not live in the wonderful home in Skokie, and I did not see my former wife or my son or my daughter any more. I had to drive up to Silver Lake in the dead of winter to sell the summer home because I needed the money badly, in a hurry, because I had almost nothing left. Guy Roland had put me in touch with a real-estate agent named Harley Eagan who, Guy wrote, handled most of the lake frontage that was bought and sold on Silver Lake these days.

I was almost snowblind for a moment, my eyes running tears from the bitter wind, when I got inside the Silvercryst bar. I stomped my feet free of snow, brought the sting of feeling back into my toes, coughing on the sudden warm air. When I took off my coat it was like taking off the cold winter air, like the season had changed back suddenly to late spring. Harley Eagan and Guy and the new owner of Silvercryst and another man I did not know were waiting for me. I thought at first they had opened the resort especially for me.

"Check his ID card, members only," the fourth man said.

"Welcomewelcomewelcome!" the new owner said.

"There's my man!" said the man who was Harley Eagan the real-estate agent. I knew his voice from the telephone. "Give the man a glass," he said. "He's about to dry up and die from exposure."

"No havee membership card, no drinkie drinkie here," said the man I did not know.

"Lighten up, Major," Guy Roland said. "This man's a war hero. I saw the scars myself." It was some kind of club. I dried my eyes on my handkerchief and, shaking, drank whiskey with them to start warmth inside me. They were a club, of sorts, meeting daily through the long winter at the resort bar to drink themselves through the long off-season. I think they were close to madness, together like that all winter long.

"I'll be wanting to see those scars," the major said. I never got his name. He was a retired army major, and they called him Major, and almost never listened to him or answered when he spoke. He wore his pepper-salt hair crewcut, and he drank more than any of the rest of them.

"Stuff a bar rag in his mouth," Guy Roland said to the new owner of the Silvercryst Resort.

"Shut your face, Major," the new owner said. "Don't mind the major. The major's a good man. He'll drink you under the table with your little tootsies turned up to the sky." The new owner had not changed. In the dead gray light of winter that came in the frosted windows, the stark black of his hair and mustache and goatee was more obviously dyed than I remembered. He had put off his vest and colonel's tie because he had no clientele in winter. His small eyes were still lively, and his pale hands never shook when he poured drinks or lit a cigarette with a lighter that flamed

up high and made everyone laugh each time he lit it. "Flamethrower," he said, turning his head away and lighting it again.
"Hey, Major, flamethrower!"

"A little pleasure mixed in won't hurt our business, mister,"
Harley Eagan said when I tried to talk to him about his selling
the summer home quickly for me. "Put the next one on my chit,
pal," he told the new owner. He reminded me of my ex-father-in-
law, who was dead. My dead ex-father-in-law was not an alcoholic,
but like Harley Eagan he smelled of aftershave and cologne and
the lozenges that a successful alcoholic sucks to cover the drink on
his breath. He dressed carefully, tweed jacket and vest, heavy gold
cufflinks and tietack, thick digital wrist watch, big Masonic ring.
He wore an old-fashioned hairpiece—when I got close I could see
the delicate net pasted to his forehead, the artificial brown of the
hairpiece marked off sharply from the washy gray of the hair
above his ears, at the back of his head.

"I *need* to sell," I told him.

"Get too eager, mister, you'll take a beating. I know."

"Pay heed," the new owner said. "You're talking to the richest
booze hound in this and three counties. And a charter member of
the Silver Lake Drunks, Incorporated," he said of Harley Eagan.

"You see me in what I'd call my element," Guy Roland said.
Past fifty now, he was different, yet the very same. He was exactly
as I would have imagined him, if I had bothered, over the years.
His hair was now exactly his father's spun white. He wore it sculp-
tor-cut, over his ears, sprayed to hold a sweep low across his brow.
He had gained a lot of weight, but covered it with a loose peasant
smock—like his mother, Peaches Roland, used to wear to tend her
flowers. He wore a bead choker, denim trousers, tan moccasins.

"How's your mother doing?"

"She goes on like time itself," he said.

"I thought you only jumped from puddle to puddle," I said.

"This is the puddle. Get it?" the new owner said.

"I'd go insane if I tried to dry out," Guy said.

"This puddle's so deep we grow gills just to keep breathing,"
the new owner said.

"I confess I never shed blood for our flag," the major was
saying.

"Winters I lie low," Harley Eagan said, tapping his temple with
his forefinger, as if there was a delicate mechanism there he might

set right with the proper nudge. "It's spring I get hustling. I turn over lake property like a one-armed paperhanger. I'd be afraid to tell the tax man the commissions I rake in, mister," he said.

"Jesus wept," I said to nobody there.

"So," Guy Roland said, "how's it feel to get up in your old stomping grounds again?"

Through the frosted thermal window the sky crept lower and darker with the snow it promised. I tried to see through to the lake, but had to imagine the sweep of the blowing snow over the ice, vehicle tracks, a few ice-fishing shanties, the exact line of the opposite shore hidden under the snow cover, the stark trees. The dining room was closed off, the piano bar draped with a cloth —what happened to Little Freddie Kay? I wondered.

"I'll be damned if I'll try to stay sober through a winter here," Guy said.

"I could sell cheese boxes sitting on postage stamps if it had some lake frontage, come spring, mister," Harley Eagan said.

"Military life requires a special breed of man to stick it out," the major was saying.

"What if I next year locked myself in here alone and reduced the inventory all by my lonesome," the new owner of the Silvercryst Resort said. "What'll you booze hounds do for laughs then? Major, you'll go completely nuts, won't you!"

Jesus wept, I thought. I thought about all the people I had known in my life who were dead, and I thought of my ex-wife and my son and my daughter who were gone from me, and how when I saw them next they would be so different, so changed they would be like new people I did not know. The people who were gone from me were like all the people who were dead.

I thought about all the summer homes on Silver Lake, closed up for winter, dark, empty, how the frozen lake was like the flat expanse of a cemetery, given up to cold and wind and snow. It was getting dark outside already. The four of them—five counting myself—were like last survivors, mourners huddling for the last warmth of the last fire, praying on our stools for the hope of springs and summers we have almost forgotten, that we remember only in the way feverish dreams are remembered. I closed my eyes, tried to forget everything about everything I ever knew. I must have said something, because Guy Roland heard me.

"Don't take life so serious," he told me. "It ain't even permanent." I opened my eyes, breathed very deeply, shook my head to be sure it was not the whiskey making me talk.

"Oh, it's serious," I said.

"No, it's not," he said, finishing his drink, setting the glass on the bar for a refill.

"I know better," I said.

"No, you don't," he said. He held up his fresh drink, squinted to see through the whiskey to the window, out the window into the winter dark.

I said, "Even if it's not, it used to be." He drank, puckered his lips, shook his head as he held the drink in his mouth, rolled it on his tongue. No. It was not. "At least for me it was, once," I said. He looked out the window, drank again, shook his head. No, not even for me. "Then what are we even talking about it for?" I said. He shrugged.

I left as quickly as I could. I settled the picture of them together there, half-mad, and I was in it, and not in it, and then I left. Thinking, I sat a long while in my car, letting the engine warm, the heater going. I thought about it all the way back to Chicago on the superhighway made treacherous by swirling snow and patches of ice. I could wait for spring to sell the summer home, a better market.

I thought about all the dead and living people I knew, and about the living people like Guy Roland, who were dead, and about all the living people who had gone from me, like the dead. I thought about all the living people I knew who were all going to die, when they died, or before they died.

I drove slowly so I would not worry about the road. I did not play the radio, tried not to read the green and silver signboards with the names of all the small Wisconsin towns, so I could think about all this, and about myself.

I tried to decide if I was living or dead. If I was living, would I wait to die to be dead, or if I was already dead, when had it happened? How long had I lived? These are serious questions. I do not ask them lightly, and I continue to work on the answers.

TRAVEL STORIES

HENRY BROMELL

Henry Bromell is the author of *The Slightest Distance*
(Houghton Mifflin, 1974) and *I Know Your Heart, Marco
Polo* (Knopf, 1979). He presently lives in Northampton,
Massachusetts.

For a moment, after delivery, Susan had felt herself sliding down
a long tunnel of darkness, Dr. Crawford's voice still singing,
"Push, *push*." When she awoke, Scobie was there, at the foot of
her bed. And in his arms he held their child. "Sammy," he cooed.
"Sammy my boy." She had made him a father——that was her
first thought. Remembering, she wondered why. Loving Scobie
was too much her life, she knew it would hurt her someday.

"Swish!" he cried, feigning a jump shot as he hurried into the
living room. "Off to the gym."

"Have fun," she said.

"Thanks." He kissed her. "I'll be back in a couple of hours."

"Don't kill yourself."

"I won't."

The screen door slammed behind him. She watched him cross
their short lawn. Shadows followed. Butterflies? Robins? And was
that a crow perched on a telephone wire? Solemn Sammy, three
now, sat with Tommy Delano behind their lemonade stand, Mrs.
Delano's card table, and waited for customers. Scobie stopped and
bought a cup. They stared in amazement as he finished it in one
swallow. Then he waved goodbye and disappeared down Johnson
Street, too thin, his hair long, wearing jeans, yet carrying himself
with a considered air. My fragile, stubborn husband. She looked
at her garden, careful rows of tomatoes and zucchini, peas and

squash, lettuce and spinach. Just to the left, her pear tree spun a web of light across the green grass. With her help it had survived the winter, something it was not supposed to do, something her friends had said was impossible in Iowa. Would it survive another? Yes, she thought. Or we'll move to California. Scobie could teach at Berkeley, or Stanford, or UCLA. She used to believe, as a child, that when she closed her eyes at night people as small as her dolls would slip from the dark hedges and dance in circles around the trees outside.

"Mommy! Mommy!" Sammy nearly pulled the screen door off its hinges as he charged into the living room. "Come see!" He tugged her to the door. "Look!"

A parade was passing along Johnson Street, about twenty beautiful women wearing white wedding dresses and carrying signs. "I Am Who I Am," one sign read. "Let Me Be," another read. Taking Sammy's hand, Susan stepped out onto the front stoop. One of the women played a guitar and sang. Neighbors clustered at their doors and smiled curiously. The women danced, taking small dainty steps. A few carried umbrellas, also white, open against the heat. One of them crossed the lawn to the stoop and handed Sammy a rose, the wilting yellow flower pinched between square dirty fingers—a man's fingers, Susan realized, looking closer and seeing the bristles of a beard behind the rouge. She quickly pulled Sammy away, holding him.

"Mommy, what's wrong?"

"Nothing, sweetheart."

"I wanna see!"

"Of course." She kissed the top of his head and let him go. "I'm sorry."

She stood still for a second, trying to steady her breathing. Sammy obviously did not know that the beautiful women were men. He just liked the parade. She could see him back behind the lemonade stand with Tommy. The parade had turned the corner and vanished. Some vision, she thought, crossing the living room and walking into the kitchen. Here the sunlight was brilliant, shining directly into the room, and as she moved between the sink and the shelves, stacking clean plates and glasses, she felt she lived in a tree house. She wiped the counter and table with a sponge, then swept the floor. Sammy should be taking his nap now. But if she let him stay up he would fall asleep earlier tonight. She bent

down into the cool breeze of the refrigerator, throwing away old
vegetables, a soggy salad, a yogurt gone bad. What could you say
to a man who wanted to be a woman? Or a woman who wanted
to be a man? What could you say to someone who wanted to
change herself that much?

Sammy came in through the back door. "Mommy, where's
Daddy?"

"Playing basketball."

"Why?"

"Sammy, please don't ask so many questions. I'm trying to
work. Have you seen the bucket?"

"When's he coming home?"

"Soon." She searched among the bottles and paper bags under
the sink. "Would you please go into the living room?"

"Why?"

"*Sammy.*"

He stared at her helplessly from the middle of the kitchen floor,
then turned and walked away, sneakers squeaking on the linoleum, shoulders stooped, head hanging.

"Sammy, what're you doing?"

"Nothing."

"Nothing what?" She peered around the corner. He was sitting
cross-legged by the couch, his back to her. "Come on, let's work in
the garden."

He reluctantly joined her, already anxious to grow up, escape. If
only you knew, she thought, watching his green eyes, speckled
gold out here in the sunlight. She handed him a spade. "Can you
dig a little ditch for me? Right along the edge. Like this. It's for
the water."

He studiously set to work, the spade unwieldy in his small
hands. She pulled weeds. The soil was dark and damp, the best
outside someplace in Russia. The Ukraine, maybe. She could
smell her body, the slight scent of her sweat. A few cars passed,
sounding imperative, going somewhere. A bicycle clattered over
the curb. She stopped working and stared intently at the view: the
Delanos' cluttered back yard, the corner grocery store with its
bright-red Coke machine by the door, the sandstone Catholic
church across the street. Downtown in the bars, she knew, men
and women her age were already drinking beer and watching base-
ball on television as they collapsed drunkenly into fitful camara-

derie, pounding each other's backs and rivalling to pay for rounds. It'll hit a hundred tomorrow, she thought, bending back to work, trying to ignore the thickness of the air. Surrounding downtown were these frame houses, porch swings, cobbled alleys, these streets quiet as Sunday. She had taught third grade until Sammy was born, the sinking fear she had felt as a child in school returning every time she passed through that heavy green door and heard her footsteps tap-tap-tapping along the hallway, the children's voices squealing and shrieking no matter what they said, because they assumed no one was listening, no one cared. Even remembering, it made her sick. Motherhood had come as something of a relief. Last night, she had asked Scobie if he thought she was stupid. Now why did I do that? It's just the kind of question he hates. "Sammy, be careful. Don't cut those roots. See?"

"When's Daddy coming home?"

"Soon. You can stop now, if you want. Why don't you go play in your sandbox?"

"O.K."

He trudged off. Poor kid. She was always suggesting things for him to do. She stood and squinted dizzily into the sun.

Walking home, Scobie passed under the concrete railroad bridge—a blur of moss and graffiti, short echo, darkness—and started the slow climb past the library. The wide blue sky was brilliant, electric, behind the darkening buildings. Starlings darted like bats in the shrinking light. That light, almost liquid, reminded him of something else. What? He turned, startled by a burst of rock and roll, early-evening excess obscure in the receding blackness of Peter's Tavern—a jukebox, gleaming. Suddenly church bells rang, soft and steady in the stillness. Scobie stopped and blessed the Catholics. They rang their bells with papal regularity, even here, in the heart of nowhere. Keeping step, he continued west, past the drugstore, across a parking lot, down a gravel driveway. Mothers called their children in to dinner. Screen doors slammed, springs pinging. A girl in a yellow dress skipped rope in front of the hospital, counting monotonously, dreamily. He stepped across the stretch of grass and into the kitchen. Susan was at the sink, slicing onions. He kissed the back of her neck. She turned and smiled and touched his cheek, her fingers wet. Her eyes went on forever. He held her tight, frightened, as always, by the smallness of her bones. "The good guys won."

"Congratulations."

The kitchen window was open. A warm sweet breeze rustled some papers on the table. He smelled lilac, cut grass, smoking hamburgers. "Let's cook out tonight."

"Wonderful! Sammy would love that."

"Where is he?"

"In his sandbox. Talking to himself." She grinned, crying—the onions.

"I'll start the charcoal," Scobie said, touched by her false tears.

He opened the screen door and paused on the concrete step, looking over the grass—he would have to mow it tomorrow—at the thick wall of bushes and drooping willows that obscured the Delanos' yard. Three white wooden chairs and a white table turned pale purple in the changing light. He inhaled noisily, closing his eyes and trying to relax his arms, his shoulders, his tight aching neck. When he opened his eyes, the lawn, the bushes and trees, the chairs and table all seemed to have just stopped laughing. He walked around the corner of the house. Sammy sat in the middle of his sandbox, moving toy trucks through a wilderness of collapsing mountains. "Hello, Sammy," Scobie said, so quietly he could barely hear himself. "Sammy?"

Those pink fingers, the delicate moons, waved in delight above the cooling sand. "Daddy!" A brief, imaginary embrace: "Daddy!" Or was he merely including Scobie in his secret world, the cause of all that pensive seriousness, so intense for a child so young? Scobie crossed to the red sandbox, bent down. "How're things?"

Sammy looked into the sand, puzzled, his eyes partially Susan's, partially Scobie's father's, partially no one's. "Daddy?"

"Yes."

"Tommy's father makes trucks."

"I know." Scobie laughed.

Their mouths moving slowly and silently, Scobie and Sammy looked to Susan like two men discussing the weather, war, something serious. Sammy, trying to imitate his father, leaned with his weight on one leg, his hip slightly cocked, his hands in his pockets. She quickly concentrated on the salad, humming an old hymn as she moved about the kitchen. She carried the salad out to the wooden table in the back yard.

"Hi, Mommy," Sammy greeted her. "Look what we're doing."

"What's that?" She unwrapped the paper plates, distributed the paper napkins.

"Trying not to burn supper is what we're doing," Scobie said, banging at the grill.

"How much longer?" she asked, heading back toward the screen door.

"Five minutes."

The house was already dark. She turned on a few lights as she made her way to the bedroom and changed, remembering nights like this when her father, splendid in his white tuxedo, would prance about the kitchen playing Louis Armstrong on his trumpet. Then off he would go to a club where his band entertained strangers until one in the morning. She stared at herself in the mirror, brushing her hair. Susan, where have you gone? Away. College. Europe. Marriage. Motherhood. She looked deeper into her eyes and saw a young girl sitting on a bed, rain sliding down the windowpanes behind her. Too much dope. She resumed brushing. Susan, where have you gone? Dancing, crazy, to the movies, nowhere, *I don't know*. It was an impossible question, a voice speaking from her worst fears, and she resolutely ignored it, dropping her brush onto the bureau, next to Scobie's watch, and leaving the bedroom. Yet the words, like a jingle, ran through her head, nightmarishly persistent. She pushed open the screen door and stepped out onto the grass. Scobie was seasoning the hamburgers. Sammy pushed toy trucks toward an inevitable and colossal collision.

"Mommy, I'm *hungry*."

"Dinner's ready," Scobie called. "Come and get it."

They carried their paper plates to the grill, then sat together at the wooden table, passing potato chips and ketchup while around them the shadows lengthened and the birds gradually grew quiet.

"Hi," Scobie said, grinning at her.

"Hi."

"What do you think?"

"About what?"

"This." He laughed. "Our future. It's here."

"I think it's fine," she said.

"Me, too."

"But weird."

He nodded, his eyes moving to the closing circle of darkness. Susan leaned back and stared at the pink and purple sky. Soon it would be drained black. The air's so clean out here, she thought, breathing deeply. Yet she missed the ocean, the strong salt breeze rolling in with the waves, the fog, the dampness, the sweet brackish stink of low tide, those long slow days on the beach. At night the lights exploded along the old boardwalk, the casino burned at the edge of the sea, thousands of kids strolled back and forth, eating cotton candy, smoking joints, trading albums on the steps of the bandstand where her father once played afternoon concerts. She had been one of those kids, one of too many. Where she came from, fathers worked in factories or for the government, mothers raised children, and everyone went to church on Sunday. She thought of her mother, smiling, rueful and scrutinizing as she turned from the kitchen sink, the slender white lighthouse balanced in the window behind her, an obsolete warning rising from a cluster of rocks and seaweed half a mile offshore.

"Daddy, how come I don't have a brother?" Sammy asked.

Susan jumped. "What?"

"Tommy has a brother."

"Virgil Smith has a sister," Scobie said, peering into his salad.

"How come I don't have a sister?"

"Most kids get jealous when they have a brother or sister," Susan said.

Sammy shrugged. "How come we're not going anywhere this summer? Tommy's going to Florida."

She reached across the table and wiped his mouth with her napkin.

"We can't go anywhere," Scobie said. "We don't have enough money. But maybe next summer. How'd you like to go to New Hampshire? See your grandparents?"

"Oh, boy."

"Really?" Susan asked.

"Sure. Why not? If we've got the bread."

"That would be lovely," she said. "I miss them."

"I know you do."

Sammy had pulled his hamburger from the bun and was now holding it above him and nibbling at the edges.

"Eat that thing right or don't eat it at all," Scobie scolded.

"Hey, folks." It was Joey, crossing the grass with Clara, Susan's oldest friend in Iowa City and an interne at the nearby hospital. She and Susan had met at a party, Susan immediately liking Clara's wide, welcoming face and big-boned softness, the enthusiasm in her gray eyes. Joey was as angular as she was curved, as dark as she was fair, a silent nodding elf with a habit of smiling before he asked you a question, pleased by its appropriateness, the possibilities of the answer. He played drums for a local band. Clara's red hair bounced at her shoulders, and when she smiled she positively beamed. "Happy Fourth of July!"

"So what's happening?" Joey smiled, a wrinkle of his rabbinical beard.

"Not much," Scobie said. "Just a nice suburban scene here. Want a beer?"

"Sure. Hey, Sammy." Joey bent and touched Sammy's dirty cheek. "When're you going to learn how to play the drums?"

Sammy thought. "Soon."

Susan loved parties, the quick rush of excitement she felt when friends or strangers arrived at the door or when she first walked into someone else's room and realized that within the next few hours anything at all could happen. A party, like sex, was organized around the simple principle of pleasure. Of course, sex had not always been that way. Her parents thought it was a command to have children, a necessary and rather embarrassing technicality. At least, that was what they seemed to believe. Who could tell? Not me, she thought. Scobie made love with the sad precision and distant thoughtfulness of a priest administering last rites. Afterward, they curled together like children, their small protected space something to defend from the outside world, the attacking forces—time and loss, disbelief, fear, the sure knowledge that pleasure seeks oblivion, annihilation, escape. Susan moved into the kitchen, compulsively wrapping vegetables in waxed paper and pushing them into the refrigerator. Clara kept her company, leaning against the counter, the screen door behind her neatly dividing the summer night into small square mosaics. Susan could hear Sammy laughing happily as he sat on Scobie's chest in the living room, miming attack while Scobie mimed horror, neither of them speaking, only the Beatles' ironic, nervous music accompanying their struggle.

"Sammy, bedtime!" Susan called.

"Aw, Mommy," he groaned, breaking the spell.

"Authority speaks." Scobie laughed.

"Do I have to?"

"Yes, you do. I'll take you up. Tell you a story. O.K.?"

"Yes, sir."

"So let's go." Scobie stood. "Say good night."

Sammy, slipping his hand from Scobie's, ran to Susan. Did he love her more? Scobie remembered his own father's threatening power, that silent shape refusing softness. He stared at the ghostly green aquarium, the flicking, darting fish, the mother-of-pearl cigarette box he had inherited from his grandmother, his wall of books. Two black speakers, large as coffins, stood upright in the corners.

"Good night," Sammy said to Joey, returning and taking Scobie's hand again. They climbed the stairs together, the music muffling behind them. Susan looked up as Joey hesitated in the kitchen doorway. "Hi," she said. "We're just talking."

He entered warily. "Any more beer?"

"Of course. I'm sorry. In the fridge."

He leaned down into the cold green light. "So what's up?" he asked, straightening and pulling the beer tab.

"Nothing," Susan said. "We were just wondering what it would be like to all sleep together."

"Are you serious?"

Even before they started laughing Susan wondered what it *would* be like. Scobie would never do it, he was too conservative. She could almost hear him: *Fathers don't do that sort of thing.* He and Sammy would often sit up there for hours, Sammy transfixed as Scobie told him about trees that talked and oceans that thought, her own voice reaching them as a reassuring murmur. "Would you be scared, Joey?" she asked.

"Disgusted."

"Why?"

"All that flesh."

Following him back into the living room, Susan sat on the floor, resting on one of the large bright pillows, and rolled a joint. Scobie would not smoke anymore. She wondered what reveries did to a surreal imagination, then wondered what they had already done to hers. Clara held her chin high, a touch of stubbornness in the stance. Susan stared at the soft shape of her loose breasts beneath her dress, her thin hands smoothing her lap. Clara took the joint from Susan and puffed delicately, her little finger cocked, as if the joint were a cup of tea, her eyes squinting in concentration. Scobie returned, smiled at them, and made himself a scotch. For a few seconds Susan resented his overview.

"Sammy O.K.?" she asked.

"Oh yeah, he's fine." Scobie shook his head, refusing the joint, as he stretched out beside her. "You know, he thinks I made all those stories up. He thinks all the myths I tell him are mine."

Susan laughed, clapping her hands, that girlish, delighted gesture she knew he loved.

Scobie grinned at the ceiling. "He probably thinks I'm a lunatic and just listens to humor me."

"Scobie, I have a big favor to ask you," Joey said.

"Change the record," Scobie said.

"Thank you."

Clara nodded vigorously, red curls dancing around her temples, the imaginary teacup still balanced in her hand. Scobie crawled to the stereo. "I first saw the Beatles in 1964," he said. "Twelve years ago. Incredible, huh? Any requests?"

"Something cheerful."

"Something bouncy."

"Aretha Franklin?"

"Let's dance," Susan said, clapping her hands again.

"Dancing it is." Scobie stood, pulled her to her feet, and led her around the room in an exaggerated waltz to the pure round notes of "Dr. Feelgood." Energy's the rush that comes with rock and roll, everything private made public, celebrated. He swirled Susan under his arm, dancing awkwardly, self-consciously, his eyes on Clara, a pleading gaze. He trusts me, Susan thought. But I can't trust him, not completely. There's the difference. Then she wondered if she also loved him more, if her lack of trust were the result of that difference. Scobie, needing her less, trusted her more? Did that make sense? One thought and Scobie lost the rhythm. He watched Susan to catch it again. Slowly he was back in the music. Clara saw him looking and smiled. He smiled, too, more with his eyes than his mouth, a secret message sent over Susan's shoulder. Or was Susan imagining things? Was he just being friendly? She glanced around the room. The fish in the aquarium seemed to swim to the music. Even the air bubbles were synchronized. Everything works that way, if you can see what's happening. She looked at Scobie. We're a beautiful couple, she thought. Friends said it, parents said it, employers said it, she had even heard strangers saying it: "What a beautiful couple." Beautiful couples don't have problems. Why had she ever believed that? Neither of them was really beautiful, she knew. They were pretty and graceful. They moved well. They gave pleasure when they walked into a room. They seemed to know what they were doing. She almost laughed, watching him now, gangly as a tourist trying to belly dance, his serious face concentrating on the impossible task of gyrating elegantly. "Won't the music wake Sammy?"

Scobie turned it down. "I don't think so."

"It might," she said. "Maybe we should wait awhile."

The song ended. They were left staring at each other in silence, kids again at their first dance, wondering what to say, how to stand. They all sat down.

"We're irresponsible parents," Susan said.

"No, we're not," Scobie said. "Children like to hear music. I can remember lying in bed and hearing my parents having parties. They played Frank Sinatra, that's the only difference."

"A little less loudly," she said.

"Maybe. I felt very secure hearing all that noise. And the laughter. They sounded happy."

Susan was watching him, the way his mother had once watched him try to flirt. There's no escape from familiarity. He had to live with it, as he lived with bad weather, his own depression, failure, the power of stupid and spiteful people. Only when love is a duty are we eternally secure against despair. He let himself really look at Clara for the first time since they had met, though he remembered that night, her slow movement toward him through the laughing couples, a smile ready on her face. She was dressed in jeans and a red silk shirt open low enough on the neck to expose the smooth white beginnings of her breasts, so much larger than Susan's and swaying as she leaned forward to tap her cigarette ash into an empty paper cup. She was very beautiful, a northern star, pale as breath on a cold window. He had always imagined her life as a series of outings. To football games, snug in plaid blankets.

To picnics and parties. To the coast in a crowded station wagon.

"Scobie?" She was offering him the joint.

He shook his head.

"How come you don't smoke?" she asked.

"I lose control."

"Of what?"

"Whatever it is that convinces me I'm only one person."

Taking the joint, Susan let her fingers brush Clara's, then quickly looked toward Joey, as if she were interested in what he was saying, or the smile on his face, that dreamy, tranquil expression he assumed when stoned or happy. Even my fantasies are clichés, Scobie thought, changing the record again. Two women tongue to tongue, nipple to nipple. He had once dreamed of singing with a rock band, prancing obliviously as his own voice boomed back at him, finally finding a beat indistinguishable from the heart's. That would be happiness. Smoking dope and listening to music always reminded Susan of college, those four fast years when she had almost escaped her entire childhood. Now that freedom seemed as ephemeral as any other. Nothing's in control because it all comes rushing at you a million miles a minute, nameless, contorted, laughing like God: What do *you* know, Miss La-Di-Da? Not much, she thought.

"Are you going to teach again?" Clara was asking her.

"Soon as Sammy gets a little older."

"What if you have another kid?" Joey asked.

"We'll deal with that when and if it happens," Scobie said and solicitously drew Susan closer. He smelled of sweat, tobacco, an old smell she loved, man smell, father smell.

"I'm not sure I want to have another kid," she said.

"I *know* we can't afford it," Scobie said. "But it'd be a shame for Sammy not to have a brother or sister, don't you think?"

"Yes," she admitted.

"He'd be very lonely. It's a trap," he continued, explaining to Clara. "You have one kid, then you feel morally obliged to have another to keep the first one company, and the next thing you know you're fulfilling all your statistical expectations. Gotcha."

The truth being, of course, that Scobie wanted to have another child but thought Susan wanted to be able to walk into a room and tell people she was more than a mother. "I don't resent being a mother," she said. "There'd be no point to that."

"It doesn't really make much sense, though," Scobie said. "Why put kids through all the crap you've just been through? They're not going to help you run the farm, or maintain your membership in the House of Lords. Right? If you have children, you've got to admit you're having them for your own pleasure. There's no other reason anymore."

"Propagating the species."

"Propagating the class, you mean. Or the race. What's the point?"

"So why did you have Sammy?" Clara asked.

"I'm sentimental."

Bliss, that's what he wants, and that's why he loves children, they seem so much closer to the source. Susan had always found it strange that someone who loved language so much should consider silence truth, but he did. She could never be sure what he was feeling.

"My father wanted me to marry and settle down," Clara said. "The whole thing."

"And now you're a hot-shot doctor," Scobie said. "I like that."

This time Susan was sure he exchanged a look with Clara, a quick, sheepish grin.

"It's dark enough," he said. "We should go out."

"I can't move," Joey said.

"Pothead."

"Moralist." Joey rolled over and looked at Scobie.

"Come on," Susan said. "Let's go out."

They stood and went together to the back yard, where they lay on their backs, staring at the sky and talking while beyond the trees a fierce red streak grew thinner and slowly sputtered away, leaving behind the sudden night. Then a Roman candle shot hissing high above them and exploded, showering down a soft umbrella of smaller stars. Susan flinched when the next explosion hit the sky. It was spectacular, terrifying. She could feel Scobie's arm touching her elbow.

"Napalm," he said.

"Oh, Scobie. Don't be disgusting."

"Sorry. Just free-associating."

"Do you think it'll wake Sammy?"

"It might," he said. "Jesus, can you imagine? He'd probably think it was World War III."

"Scobie, he doesn't even know what war is."

"You know what I mean. The end of the world. Cataclysm. Holocaust. Apocalypse. I'd better go check."

He rose and disappeared into the house. Joey lit another joint and passed it around. Susan took it all the way in, holding her breath until it hurt. The explosions vibrated, painfully explicit.

"Clara, do you ever wish you had kids?" Susan giggled. "Tell me the grass is always greener."

"I envy you sometimes, sure."

"We ought to start a mutual-admiration society. You've got freedom. You're making something of yourself."

"You sound like my father," Joey said. "Clara's just trying to get along, like everyone else."

"Clara's a woman who hasn't let her entire life be determined by what a woman's expected to be," Susan said. "In case you hadn't noticed."

"I'd noticed."

"I don't particularly like being a doctor," Clara said. "Not all the time."

"Excuse me while I slit my wrists," Joey said.

"You don't understand, Joey," Susan said. "We're having a conversation."

Upstairs, Scobie bent above Sammy and whispered, "Sh-h-h, it's all right." He picked him up and stroked the fine hair on his soft head. "It's just fireworks, that's all. Look." He pointed through the window. The sky was burning, lighting their faces, Sammy's round eyes staring in stunned wonder at the spectacle. And then he fell asleep again, his eyelids fluttering, closing, opening quickly, gently closing. His head rested against Scobie's shoulder, his hands clenched Scobie's shirt. Carefully, Scobie lowered him back into his bed, covered his legs with the sheet, tucked his frayed toy giraffe under his arm, and tiptoed from the room. Susan rolled over onto her stomach and lay with her head resting in the cradle of her arm, waiting for him to appear through the screen door. Blades of grass, so close, looked like giant trees. How she missed the sea! Here he was.

"Hello." He settled beside her. "Sammy's O.K."

"Thank you."

He touched her cheek. "My joy."

"You're a good father," she said.

"I'm learning."

"No, you've always been good."

"Hey, Joey," he said, changing the subject. "Did I ever tell you I once met John Lennon?"

"Hell you met John Lennon."

"I did, really. In London. Nineteen-sixty-six. I was on my way to see my parents. You know, for vacation, Christmas vacation. And there he was."

"Where?"

"At the airport bar. Disguised."

"Is he making all this up?" Joey asked Susan.

"I don't know."

"Disguised as what?" Clara asked.

"A tweedy literary type. His hair was slicked back, he was wearing a sort of gray sleeveless sweater. Thick glasses. Elbow patches. Those brown shoes that look like hiking boots, you know? We talked."

"I don't believe a word of this," Joey said.

"We talked about how we were both scared of flying. He was very nervous. Drinking."

For all Susan knew, he was telling the truth. Stranger things had happened to him. On the other hand, he invented half his life. Which part of him did she love? He touched her knee affectionately. Why wouldn't she respond? Why was she so cold? It angered him, briefly. He looked into the shaking light and saw Clara's hair, her round soft shoulders.

A Roman candle sizzled and died. Susan felt like an old woman, some friendly but irritating third person. The sky was dark again, still and moist and starless. "That was quick," she said.

"Actually, we've been out here six hours," Scobie said. "It's tomorrow."

"Seriously, wasn't that quick?" Susan asked.

"Yes," Clara said. "It was. I think."

"No, I'm on Scobie's side," Joey said. "Years have passed."

"Joey, stop it. You're making me nervous," Susan said.

High up, far, far away, a small light moved through the sky.

Scobie made himself another scotch.

"You're drinking too much," Susan said.

"Spare me." He raised his glass. "Quiet."

"What?"

"I thought I heard Sammy."

They both listened.

"No, he's all right," she said.

Scobie's arm had fallen asleep, a numb and prickly pain, but he did not move. "When you met me, what did you think?"

"That you were funny-looking."

"Thanks."

"It was your haircut."

"I cut it myself."

"That was apparent." She looked at him, shy and slightly angry. "I *chased* you, Scobie. You should feel flattered."

The aquarium glowed, a green light through which the iridescent fish slowly circled the wavering seaweed and rising bubbles.

"Did you have a good time tonight?" she asked.

"O.K."

"I wish it would rain."

"Me, too." He traced her arm with a finger. "How come you're so skinny?"

"I have a pot belly," she said.

"The size of a walnut. You're skinny, Susan."

"You don't like me skinny?"

"I love you skinny."

"Is this true?"

"Yes," he said.

Her fingers stroked his skull as the room ticked around them. There's always someplace we're trying to get to, he thought. Something we're trying to remember or imagine. "Once, when we were little and wanted to have an adventure, Dad invented a spy game," he said. "The whole family played. Mom and I just missed catching him pass a secret message to Matthew at the drugstore soda fountain."

"You romanticize your past."

"No, I don't. It happened. I know. I was there."

"You like it better there."

"Oh, Susan. Don't exaggerate. I don't *like* it better."

"Yes, you do."

He pulled her closer. "What's the matter, baby?"

"Nothing."

"Susan?"

"You're itching to get away."

"Not me. I do all my travelling up here." He tapped his forehead, an absurd gesture.

Cold as a sudden draft, her hand touched his face. "I'm sorry," she said. "I'm just jealous of Clara, I guess."

"What?" He felt himself blinking stupidly.

"I saw you tonight."

"What did you see tonight?"

"The way you looked at her."

"How did I look at her?"

"If you have feelings, you have feelings."

"Sweetheart, I love *you*." He realized he was slightly drunk.

"You can't avoid your guilt by not actually sleeping with Clara, then drive me crazy by making sure I know you'd like to. That's not fair, Scobie. I'm not stopping you."

He put "Nashville Skyline" on the turntable and sat back down beside her.

She sighed. "You really are going to leave me someday, aren't you?"

"I don't believe this. What's the matter with you?"

"I'm scared. Oh, Scobie, is this what you wanted?"

"Yes."

"Are you sure?"

"Yes," he said, though he was afraid of failure, afraid he might stop loving her.

"Let's go to bed," she said. "O.K.?"

"I'm not sleepy."

"Well, I am." She stood, stretching her arms above her head. "Don't stay up too late."

"I won't."

She bent down and kissed him, her mouth soft and wide. "Good night."

"I love you."

"And I love you, Scobie."

She turned to climb the stairs, leaving behind an aura of desertion. Scobie lit a cigarette, saw his own face in the window, the flare of the small flame briefly burning away his eyes. The walls were too white. He could not fill the space. He almost closed his eyes, but darkness seemed more frightening, an endless fall. The room taunted him, a parody of the rooms he had watched his parents soften and familiarize with their furniture, their habits, their laughter, their paintings. He missed them tonight. He wanted to ask them how they did it, how they made it through, for his own marriage now seemed as terrifying as their blank room. Why did he always feel he was doing something he had already done in another, more accurate life? He held on to his knees, trying to believe this version of reality. He could hear Susan upstairs as she moved toward the bathroom. Water ran through the pipes. The sound reminded him of his grandparents' house, the small corner bedroom, his father's old room—the flowered wallpaper, the musty scent of rain, the desk by the window. He remembered winter nights returning from that house after Christmas, he and his brothers wrapped in blankets in the back seat, his mother and father talking quietly in front, the red glow of their cigarettes and the dim light of the dashboard, the sense of their world, small and self-contained, moving through the unfamiliar darkness, each gas station and motel a separate star, alien but no longer threatening, placed by distance as they sped home. He rose and walked into the kitchen. He swallowed more scotch. A copy of Kafka's stories lay on the kitchen table. He picked it up and stared at the photograph, Kafka's soft animal eyes, his complicated animal sadness. Upstairs, in the bedroom, Susan turned on the television, then flapped the sheets, smoothing all the wrinkles, before climbing into bed. Someone was talking about Jimmy Carter. Would he really be the next President?

"Scobie, come see!" Susan called.

"What?" He ran up the stairs.

"The news, the news. It's incredible."

"What's incredible?" he asked, hurrying into the bedroom.

Susan had pulled the sheets up to her chin. "Too late. You missed it."

"Missed what?" He looked at the television.

"Nothing." She blushed. "It was a trick. To get you up here."

"Why?"

"So we can make love."

"Oh, Susan." He laughed. "You're so strange."

Later, he thought he heard his father calling his name. He sat up in bed and stared into the darkness. There was nobody there.

"What's wrong?" Susan asked.

"I thought I heard something," Scobie said.

"You've been hearing things all night."

He lay back down next to her. "Susan, let's have another kid. Sammy needs a sister. O.K.?"

"Fine." She hugged him.

But he was already breathing deeply, his cheek resting on her shoulder. She stared at the trees outside caught by the corner street light, branches waving gently across the edges of her world. The soft weight of Scobie's body held her down, kept her from flying away. She could still remember the dark rooms in which she lay awake all night because the nuns had told her Heaven was a hospital, eternity a white room with no windows, one soul to each room. Her parents, superstitious as peasants, had taught her the power of prayer. Order was the will to believe. Chaos was faithlessness. Out there beyond this room, this house, this family, a completely different way of thinking ruled the universe. Scobie was dreaming, twitching like a dog. She woke him. He grunted, rolled over, and soon she heard his quiet snore again. What had his parents taught him? Elegance, she thought. Elegance and desire. He had once told her he felt a moral obligation to disappoint them: "Every freedom has its costs." She rolled over and curled to the shape of his body, her breasts to his smooth back. She remembered a spot of light dancing across her eyes and her father's hands under her arms, teaching her to walk. Impossible. I can't remember that far back. She tightened her arms around Scobie. He moved vaguely, slept. Sometimes they woke in the middle of the night making love. Midnight plunder, he called it. She wished they had enough money to visit her parents this summer. Why can't I sleep? What's wrong with me? Scobie's religion amounted to a fairy tale, a wistful disbelieving love for the power of wonder. She slipped her arm out from under him. Marriage was a compromise with terror. She arched her back, smoothing more wrinkles, the princess and the pea. Scobie snorted. She stroked his forehead. He wanted answers, not compromises. He *believed* in answers. But no mortal can give them, she thought. People invent ways to pass the time between birth and death, then invest them with absolute meaning. Yet all over America, right now, as heads sank softly into pillows, the same question rose in every imagination. Why? And the same black silence answered, no answer at all, just silence, the single separate person trapped inside the walls of her skull, no way out, no way to hear another voice and not suspect it's your own. What bright beauty could counter that? None. Facts were facts: the wrinkles around Scobie's eyes, the sadness at the corners of his mouth, his sudden, always unexpected ebullience as his long fingers and flat wide palms lifted Sammy—squealing, delighted—into the air. Sweet, serious Sammy. His father's son. Her own love made visible. What would become of him? She slowly, carefully slipped from the bed. In a narrow shaft of light from the street she saw Scobie's sleeping face. A faint frown puzzled his forehead. Even in sleep he could not relax. She pulled the sheet to his chin. He curled, hands folded between his thighs.

Tiptoeing, she left the room, still naked. Sammy's door was open, his room almost bleached by the light from the street. He lay on his stomach, a small pool of wetness by his mouth, his hands clenched into fists, subdued fury, his sheet kicked back and tangled at his feet. She covered him, brushed his damp hair from his forehead. Now what? She stood for a moment in the middle of the room, pondering a mysterious winking light—the glass eye of Sammy's toy giraffe.

Quietly, she returned to her own bed. All was well. Strange, she thought, how late at night your room becomes every room of your life. She lay flat on her back, her hands at her sides, and closed her eyes. There was Scobie, only nineteen, smiling awkwardly from the dark dance floor, afraid, she later learned, to reveal his crooked teeth. He asked her to dance. His hands, she remembered, were damp, nervous, practically trembling as he held her at a respectful distance and spun her in a long slow waltz, or his version of one, a simple repetitive circle. Afterward, sweat cooling on her face, she walked with him through the sharp autumn night and he told her of his wandering childhood, his dream of becoming a writer, the cities he had seen. Time, too—he talked of time. On and on he went, talking, talking. She had never met anyone like him. So self-absorbed, so self-confident. All lies, she now knew. But then she could only see him bravely, her heart warming fast to this gloomy gentle stranger. From that night on she was addicted. She called it love, though she suspected that was only half the truth. The rest was recognition, finding someone so much like you he seems a brother, a shadow, an old, old friend. I could sleep with Joey, she thought. Then Scobie would know how it feels to see your lover made happy by someone else. As if you weren't there, as if you didn't exist.

She also remembered the day Sammy was born. She had just come in from the garden, a basket of squash and zucchini on her arm, when the pangs began, slowly at first, then gathering speed, urgency. She called Scobie. The moment had come. He gently led her to the car, helped her in, and moved around to the driver's seat, slowly and deliberately. Nor did he speed, he kept to the limit, cautiously maneuvering between other cars. Once, he turned and asked, "How are you?" Otherwise he was silent. Susan thought, This is happening much too fast, it isn't right, will I lose the child? She closed her eyes and counted, recited the alphabet, spelled ten-syllable words, imagined the time when this would be a memory, reminded herself that a million million women had already passed through this moment and come out laughing. She raised and identified each finger. *Scobie, it hurts.* Had she said that or merely thought it? When she opened her eyes Scobie was pulling into a hospital parking lot. Calmly he turned off the motor and guided her toward the swinging glass doors. Suddenly she felt fine. No pains. I panicked, she thought. It's not time yet. Silly fool. Then, direct as a rebuke, a line of searing heat severed her body. She nearly fainted. Scobie shouted something. He was holding her now, his arm around her shoulders. She heard running footsteps, a metallic rattling, the suck of soft shoes on tile. Hands rested her onto a cold hard surface. She was wheeled away, down hollow white hallways, into a room where Dr. Crawford appeared, efficiently giving orders. He bent and asked, "Ready?" Someone was trying to pull out all her teeth. *Where's Scobie?* "Here," his voice said. Then she felt his hands smoothing her face, closing her eyes. "I'm right here, Susan. Everything's O.K." He spoke from the bottom of an empty well. Someone else was drying her forehead with something cool. Scobie's hand kept her eyes closed, thumb caressing her cheekbone. The pains were so close together now they merged into one pulsing roar. There was nothing left to count. "Push!" Dr. Crawford called. "Push, Susan." His hand massaged her belly. She heaved, slamming down, Scobie whispering into her ear, "I'm right here, I'm right here." Surely her stomach had started to tear, ripped like a fat pillow? And was that blood on her legs, dribbling, warm? The pain, a solid mass, began to move. She felt it, alive, her child swimming for the entrance through which half his consciousness had entered eight months earlier. She heard Scobie hiss, "Jesus Christ." Invisible hands pulled her legs apart, farther than they could spread. "Push!" Dr. Crawford sang. "*Push!*" She did, with all her might, every muscle she had, arching her back again. What happened next she really could not remember, except for the easing relief and the horrible fear her child might be dead. Then she started falling.

She opened her eyes. The darkness had the quality of cloth. Where was she? Which room? When? "Scobie?" she whispered. But she and Sammy were back in New Hampshire. This was her sister's old room. Scobie had left her to live with Clara.

I WANT YOU, I NEED YOU, I LOVE YOU

JULIE HECHT

Julie Hecht was born in New York City. She attended
Antioch College in Yellow Springs, Ohio, and Columbia
University in New York. Her work has been previously
published in *Harper's Magazine*. At present, she is working
on a novel; she makes her home in New York City's Greenwich Village.

Thank God I got to save Elvis Presley in time. When I think
what might have happened if I hadn't gotten to him . . . well, it
makes me sick to think of it. Yes, sick, so sick and desperate that I
feel I might lose my mind. If anything ever happened to Elvis I'd
die—I mean my life would be over. The best part would be over,
that's for sure. That's why when I heard what bad shape he was in
I knew it was my mission to get to him, to reach that sweet shy
soul underneath that beautiful face and beautiful body, it was my
divine purpose to save him.

I was only eleven or twelve when I first found out about him,
but don't worry dear reader, this will not be a trip down that particular memory lane. Who cares how I first heard of him, just like
who cares where everybody was when they heard President Kennedy was killed? It's always a boring story when they want to tell
where they were on November Twenty-second. I happened to be
looking at my skin in the mirror when they interrupted Haydn's
Ninety-ninth Symphony, so the first thing I saw was my own
horrified face. That's the only reason I mention it. I'm not going
to say what I did next and what I was wearing, who I saw that day
and what my friends said and did. Who cares anyway? We're all
specks in the universe, aren't we? Not even specks, probably. Oh
God it makes me sick to think about infinity. I'm not going to

then. Why should I face things that will drive me insane? We must all get on with the business of life, mustn't we? Eat, sleep, buy groceries, ride buses, get old, and drop dead. That's what life is all about anyway, isn't it?

Just let me say one or two things though about the beginnings of Elvis Presley. They will be redeemed by their slight humor.

A thuggish girl named Karen from my sixth-grade class was visiting me one afternoon with a silly, giggling, chubby girl named Elinor. This tough, thuggish girl who had just moved to Long Island from a tough part of Brooklyn knew all about rock and roll. Her older brother had black wavy hair and blue eyes, was a poor student, and dressed to look like a hood. Instead of trying to be Ivy League, as was done in our little suburb, he wore tight black pegged pants and a black leather jacket. In no time he became all the rage. Karen was bored at my house and kept asking where my records were and I told her that all I had in rock and roll were "Seventeen" and "Rock Around the Clock." "Come on," she said, "What about 'Heartbreak Hotel'?"

"What is a heartbreak hotel?"

"Come on, you've heard of 'Heartbreak Hotel.' It's the big thing. It's number one."

"I never have heard of it and I don't even know what it is."

"What? And you're supposed to be so popular."

"Come on, don't tell me you never heard of Elvis Presley? *Elllllvis?*"

"What is it?"

"WHAT IS IT? *What is it?*" Karen was screaming and Elinor was giggling.

"It's *him*, not it!"

"You mean it's the name of a person?"

"Yes, stupid, it's the name of a gorgeous handsome singer! Everyone has his record in Brooklyn! You're gonna faint when you see him!"

Karen got her loose-leaf book and opened it up, and inside, instead of having notes and assignments, she had pictures of this person Elvis Presley. I didn't expect that a girl like Karen would have a picture of anyone I would be interested in. She got C's in spelling and D's in reading and conduct, she had a pool table in her finished basement and her parents owned a beauty parlor. But when I saw the picture I was stunned, and I immediately admit-

ted that Elvis Presley really was the cutest I had ever seen. It was
the clearest truth, he was the cutest, although maybe too much of
a hood for me. I wasn't sure what that hood look meant and I
thought it might mean something bad.

When we went back with Karen to her house so we could hear
the record I was surprised to see that it was not a real record. "It's
a forty-five, dopey!" she said. It was a tiny, thin record with a big
hole in the middle and it had to be played with a big red plastic
cylinder on the phonograph spindle. " 'Rock Around the Clock'
is on a normal record," I said.

"Seventy-eights are out now," Karen said. "Nobody knows anything in this town."

I didn't really understand "Heartbreak Hotel." I thought it
must be about a sleazy rooming house in some slummy part of
town down South or somewhere. And I didn't know why such an
adorable-looking boy would sing about such a thing. It frightened
me to picture the hotel, dark and gloomy, with peeling yellowed
wallpaper and bare light bulbs swinging in the long hallways on
the way to the public bathroom. But then there was something
about that special voice and the way it went down to those low
gasps, crying, "lonely, lonely" all of a sudden from the high sweet
voice of pure youth on the "heartbreak hotel," and the way he
breathed those heavy deep breaths, moaning, "be so *lonely*, baby,
make you so *lonely*, baby, be so *lonely*, baby." There was something frightening and exciting in that line but I didn't know what
it was.

I guess we listened to the record over and over that day about
ten or fifteen times. To see pictures of his sweet yearning face was
one thing, and to hear the song was another, but to watch him
sing that song was something else. I now know that it was sex. I
didn't know what sex was at the time; I'd heard of it and knew
the facts, but I didn't know the feeling. It was when I got to see
Elvis Presley on television that I learned the feeling. I'm afraid I
thought it was love. But it *was* love. Elvis Presley was the first
male I loved and I'll never love anybody the way I love him. I'm
intelligent, I'm high class, I have degrees in higher learning, I
have a trained mind, I'm an original thinker, I wear horn-rimmed
glasses (for driving and movies), I buy designer clothes from
Bloomingdale's and antique clothes from all over. I'm thin and
flat-chested, I'm a modern young woman, and I love Elvis Presley,

I always have. I love him harder than I love my husband and harder than I loved John Kennedy. I love him so hard it makes me sick to think of him, makes me cry to hear him sing.

It was "Don't Be Cruel" that pushed my excitement to an unbearable pitch. It was the, what they call "the beat," the beat, the voice and the way he said, "*Baby*, I really love you, baby. *Baby*, it's still you I'm thinking of." I wanted to hear him sing it again and again but instead there was a commercial and some stupid comedy act that wasn't a bit funny. When I heard "I Want You, I Need You, I Love You," I left the world of reality. I could feel myself slipping on the "Ho-ho-hold" of the "Hold me close hold me tight," slipping and drifting quickly under his spell. When he sang, "I thought I could live without romance uh-uh-un-til you came to me," I knew that he was just kidding around on the "until." "Ho-ho-hold me close" was serious, though, so serious that as soon as I'd hear the few bars of guitar that preceded it, the excitement would sweep over me—a soft dark velvet wave in my brain rolling over everything else that had ever been there. "You're like Pavlov's dog," my sister said.

Yes, the members of my family were harsh with Elvis, they were cruel. My father had never had patience for any kind of emotional singing, or any emotion, for that matter. When he'd come into the room and a female singer was emoting and moving and twisting intensely out of feeling for some love song, usually pretty bad, I have to admit, he would just stand there holding his pipe and say to the TV, "Is something wrong with you, miss? Are you in some kind of pain?" And then he would not let us watch "The Hit Parade" in peace. "Snooky Lanson?" he would say. "*Snooky Lanson?* Am I hearing correctly? What kind of human being, for any price, would allow himself the indignity of being called Snooky? A grown man, Snooky. Why don't you turn the goddamned thing off?"

You can imagine what he had to say for himself when he saw Elvis. "I guess he has one of those spastic conditions, poor fellow." "He has the Saint Vitus dance disease," said my mother. If they dared to speak while he sang I said "Shhhh!" and "Wait!" a few times and then I'd scream, "Shut up everybody!" They were a good-natured bunch in those days so they did shut up, but they all stayed around to watch. I'd look around at my mother and my fa-

ther and my older sister—my family; and my home—American an-
tiques and paintings and oriental rugs—and I'd think what a
worthless bunch they were, how wrong and out of place they
were, how dull were my family and our home compared with
Elvis Presley. They were just nothing. In pain, I'd go up to my
pink room and lie on my bed and think about him.

I'd spent the summer of 1956 lying on the floor of the front
porch playing "Don't Be Cruel" and "I Want You, I Need You, I
Love You" over and over. My sister would be lying on the couch,
reading, and my mother would be in the kitchen, cooking. "You
know, I can't even understand the words of these songs," my sister
would say. "It's ridiculous, don't you think? What is he saying
after 'Baby, it's still you'—'um blub blubblub'? or 'Baby, it's still
you um glub glub glub'?"

"I think it's 'Baby, it's still you, dig it up.' "

" 'Dig it all,' not 'dig it up.' "

When I looked on Karen's album cover I found all the words
printed: "Baby, it's still you—I'm thinkin' of."

"Well, at least that makes sense," my sister said.

At night in our room at our summer house my sister and I
would occasionally talk before we fell asleep. We had very narrow
beds in a tiny room, and a big chest of drawers was between the
beds so that I couldn't see her face, just the shape of her body in
the dark under the white summer blanket. There were two book-
shelves over our heads, and I had pasted some color pictures of
Elvis to the bottom shelf on my side so I could look at his face at
any time before I fell asleep or when I woke up. My sister liked to
tease me about these pictures. "He's just a cheap, vulgar, greasy
hood," she'd say. "He's ignorant and low class and cheap."

"I bet he's sweet and kind and he's just kidding about being a
hood."

"I'm sure he's lacking in intelligence also."

"I read in a fan magazine that there's a contest to win a date
with him. You write an essay on why you want a date with him
and the best essay wins. You know, in school I always win for the
best composition."

"A twelve-year-old girl does not win a date with a twenty-two-
year-old."

"Why not? I look fourteen. I could wear make-up."

"I'd tell them your age."

"Why? Why couldn't I have one date with him?"

"Look, even if you did, by some chance, win, out of all the millions of girls, mostly mature teenagers, millions all over America, which is very unlikely with all that competition, you couldn't go. Daddy would forbid you."

"Why?" I cried.

"Because Elvis Presley is just a low cheap hood. You know what? If I were walking down a dark street alone at night, and I saw him, without knowing it was Elvis Presley, coming toward me, I'd have to cross to the other side."

"Why?"

"I'd be afraid of him, that's why. I'm afraid of hoods and so are you!"

"I'm going to enter in secret."

"What would you do on the date? What would you talk about to a twenty-two-year-old low-class hood?"

"I can't think of anything right now."

"Oh, this is just so stupid, there'll probably be a chaperone anyway. They're not letting any young innocent girls be alone with a sex fiend like that. He's not your type, you know. He likes cheap slutty girls like those stupid baton-twirlers and he wouldn't understand you. You'd have to cut off your long blond hair and get a pageboy fluff. You'd have to wear lipstick, pink lipstick."

"Don't you have any man you admire from afar?"

"Yes, I do. Senator Kennedy. But you've never heard of him. I'm saving his picture in a book. He's being carried out of the hospital on a stretcher and he's so cute."

She switched on the light and took out her book with the newspaper clippings. "Who's the beautiful woman?" I said.

"Well, that's the drawback. He's married. And here's a picture of them with their new-born baby, Caroline. See, he's more our type."

"He is really cute but in a different way."

"It's more subtle, it's not just raw sex."

When *Love Me Tender* came to town my friends and I decided to be first on line. We got there at 10 A.M. for the twelve o'clock show and we planned to stay all day. Actually the movie did not come to our town but to Far Rockaway, a shabby town near our richer, cleaner suburb. As it turned out we were second in line. Some tough older girls, natives of Far Rockaway, were ahead of us. It was winter, January 11th, and my mother kept saying to take hot soup, more sweaters, more food, more of all those kinds of things. We knew that food intake was not possible on such an occasion. My mother also said we were going much too early. "You'll freeze out there for two hours. Take turns, let Daddy wait with you in the car until the time." That was out of the question. What would one want with a father at a time like that?

By eleven the line was long, going all the way around the block, and we were cold and tired. I was surprised to see my father drive up in his dark green Buick. "Oh God, what does he want?" I said. "Mommy sent this blanket," he said. He had with him a small dark-blue plaid blanket with a fringe around the edge. It was the blanket that covered my baby carriage in my baby pictures in our album. I couldn't bear to see it there at the opening of *Love Me Tender*. I just looked at it in revulsion, although it was a beautiful thing and I wish my mother would let me have it now, and I couldn't believe what a stupid bungling thing it was to do, to send that blanket. It was just completely out of place. From age one to twelve is a whole lifetime, I thought, and I was right because it was my whole life. But now, twelve years ago I was twenty. At twenty, almost two twelves had gone by. Twelve years is not so long ago now; I was almost the same as I am today. I guess my parents thought they had just gotten the blanket twelve years ago and had been using it for this or that purpose ever since. Too bad I didn't understand anything then. "Oh, Daddy," I said, "I don't want *that*."

"Mommy says you'll catch cold."

"I'm not cold. Nobody here has a blanket."

"They take blankets to football games, don't they?"

"This isn't like a football game."

"Just take it, so I can say I gave it to you. You don't have to use it."

"Oh, Daddy!"

"Oh, Daddy, oh, Daddy—just fold it up and hold it," he said. I took it and watched him walk off in his brown felt hat and his black-and-green-checked reversible lumber jacket. I thought he was some alien being.

When he had driven away, Karen and Elinor did some stupid

things with the blanket. They put it over their heads, they wrapped it around their hips, they did a bullfight with it. After a while we sat down on the sidewalk and when we got cold we covered our legs with it.

We sat in the first row and we could hardly see his face. Then we moved to the fifth row and finally to the tenth. Too bad it was a Western. Wasn't everything a Western in those days? Or half the things anyway? He didn't fit into a Western and I didn't see why they couldn't make a movie of him as his own self. The movie was really disappointing. The song, though, was so beautiful, to this day I can't stand to hear it. I always cry. What am I crying for, for him or for me? For my childhood or his youth, I can't be sure. I guess they go together. There was something so frustrating about that movie. We got to see him and stare at him up close and in detail but it wasn't enough. It just made me want more of him, the real Elvis in flesh and blood.

"Would you be one of those girls who tears his clothes and touches his skin?" my sister asked when I got home.

"I don't like to be in big wild crowds," I said.

"Then you'll never get close enough to meet him."

"*Fan*," my father said, "comes from the word *fanatic*. Do you realize that?"

"How could you sit through it for eight hours?" my mother asked. "That's how people get sick, breathing in all those germs in dark movies. Go drink some orange juice."

It was nighttime and I drank juice only for breakfast. The whole day was gone, it was so dark when we came out of the theater. It was a lost empty day of my life. I saw him and I saw him but I didn't really see him.

For my thirteenth birthday my sister gave me an album called *Elvis*. One thing about her is that she always gets people exactly what they want even if she hates it herself. It was the best present I've ever gotten and I still have it. He looked beautiful on the cover, in profile—in color—mouth opened, head back singing, and wearing a lavender shirt. He was holding his guitar and his forehead was wrinkled so earnestly.

"My God," my sister said, examining the picture. "He has light-brown hair, not black! See for yourself. He must dye his hair black."

My sister always knows the inside story about people before everyone figures it out, but nobody believes her. She's the one who told me, "Jacqueline Kennedy has naturally kinky hair. She has it straightened. I can see it always growing out frizzy, like a Negro's."

Next she told me that John Kennedy had many girl friends, some of them college age, and one of them Marilyn Monroe. I didn't believe any of these things.

When my sister was in college I read a page in her college humor magazine with a long list of awards to famous people. "To Elvis Presley: The Most Odious Bellow of Puberty."

"What does pooberty mean?" I asked.

"Pewberty, silly. *Pewberty*. I can't wait to tell everybody how you pronounced it. It means age of sexual maturity. Adolescence. Teenage."

"Oh, how disgusting."

The next summer at night in our bedroom, she said, "I have a confession to make to you."

"Yeah, what?"

"Remember you used to tell me how sexy Elvis Presley was?"

"I never said 'sexy.' "

"But it's what you meant."

"I did not."

"Well, 'cute,' 'adorable,' 'beautiful,' 'handsome,' how you thought he was just so great?"

"Yeah, so?"

"Well, I've thought it over and I've listened to a lot of his records and I've come to the conclusion that you were right. Some kids at school got me to rethink my position and now I understand."

"What? They like him in colleges?"

"The best colleges have a group of intellectuals and beats who understand him in a way."

"Not the real way though, I bet."

"I do. I really am getting to love him."

Who needed her to love him? was what I thought. Who needed all these intellectual college kids adding themselves to his first true fans? I tried to talk her out of it, but just for spite, I felt, she was insisting on joining up with me and my friends. She knew I didn't like it and she persisted. There was something I didn't un-

derstand in the way she was talking about him; it was a kind of secret private savoring of his qualities in a way that seemed too en-
joyable and even bad. She and her intellectual college friends
must have all done some sex by then and talked about how sexy
he was and how he just exuuuuuded sex from every pore, every
note, every expression, everything, sex, sex, sex. That's what they
did in those best colleges at the end of the fifties I guess.

When Elvis got married, in 1967, my sister's roommate, an intellectual filmmaker, said to me, "Have you seen his wife? I can't
believe it. She looks exactly like him." She said this in a mean
way, although by then I was advanced far enough along in life not
to be bothered. What did it matter to me anyway whether Elvis
Presley's wife looked just like him? I was old enough to get married myself by then and did marry a few years after he did. I knew
he was in another world, wore white satin suits, jeweled capes,
black leather suits, ate thick steaks and drank Coca-Cola. There
was no future for us together, I was sure. I had read the year before that when asked why he didn't marry, he had said, "Why
buy the cow if you can get milk through the fence?" Now I'm sure
he didn't say that, but at the time I thought it was true. I was going
through a cynical and bitter phase I guess.

I'd already met John Kennedy by 1960 and that was keeping
Elvis off my mind. Not just met, but met and exchanged pleasantries with.

"Pleasantries indeed," said my sister's boyfriend. "Everyone in
Cambridge tells me what he's like. I want you to see it was more
exciting than you thought."

It *was* more exciting than I thought. Mainly because he's not
around anymore, old and gray, divorced and scandalized, to com-
pare the golden moment with. The John F. Kennedy moment. I
spent one of his half dollars today. I had to use all my change to
buy an Elvis Presley record, what could I do?

That's right! We're not to dwell morbidly on those days, are
we? People are simply marching forward with the 1970s now, expecting the very worst. Though they cannot imagine them because their imaginations fall far short of the task, as things happen they take them in stride, knowing our present times are
composed of a series of dreadful events. Go forth, men of the
world, lead your own little lives; work, fail, succeed, buy a Harris

tweed sports jacket, discover new restaurants, grow your hair long, cut it short, and come home, sit back, and watch the news.

I was lucky, though, because I listen to the news so much and so hard that I happened to hear all the little warnings and reports of Elvis Presley's health problems. From time to time we hear of this or that famous person being hospitalized for an "undisclosed ailment," and we have learned to expect that soon it will be announced that that person is dead. Of course if it were a harmless ailment it would be disclosed. Yes, there is only one ailment that is not disclosed, but no one need worry for fear it will be mentioned here. No, we have gotten together for a good time, for an old-fashioned tale with a happy ending. That's why when I heard Elvis Presley was in trouble I moved fast. I was lying on the oriental rug doing my exercises when I heard that he was "hospitalized with intestinal difficulties." I quickly got up. I looked at the announcer's face to see if he knew more than he was saying, but it was Rolland Smith on CBS and he didn't even care.

The next time I heard a report they said something even worse —"intestinal blockage." Now I have listened to enough of these news stories to know that one or two things follow that—one is surgery, and the other is death. In this case they said nothing about surgery, only that he'd be released the next day. That is always a bad sign, as we all know. I wondered whether someone like Elvis Presley did not have people around him who were smart enough to keep the hospital from giving out such information. How dare they discuss his digestive system on national TV? I thought that perhaps since Elvis is such a completely honest and innocent boy he might have just said, "Tell 'em the truth." He might not be sophisticated enough to be thinking of how things sound and how they will be interpreted. This is an ugly world, Elvis, I wanted to tell him, especially the world of newscasters. But he must have known all about that, mustn't he?

After these two health reports I heard a critic give a review of an Elvis Presley concert and he said many bad things about Elvis, how awful he looked and how he didn't look himself, and then he topped it all with, "Come on, Elvis, YOU ARE FAT. Shape up, be the idol you once were, you're just fat now." Does anyone ever wonder how Elvis Presley might feel hearing something like that, that particular thing, YOU ARE FAT, announced to him over

the airwaves for millions of people to hear? Isn't there any compassion for him anywhere, and doesn't it occur to anybody that he
needs help?

The next night a movie was on television showing him on tour
in 1970. What could I have been doing in 1970 that was so important that I had missed this film? I never even knew he looked like
that, that he'd let his thick straight hair fall forward into his face
and that he was so thin the dimples in his cheeks had become
huge deep dents. I didn't know his lean hard body slipped around
underneath his white jumpsuit, which was loose and tight in
different places and opened bare down to his waist. Why did I
give up on him just because he wore white jeweled jumpsuits and
capes that weren't 100 per cent cotton or probably any part cotton
at all? Surely his underwear was cotton, but it looked as if he
wasn't wearing any.

He was a scared sweet boy who was nervous and breathless before he went on stage. He took songs that I hated, songs from
Tom Jones and junk like "You Don't Have to Say You Love Me,"
he took these songs and put them through himself, through his
mind and through his body and through his voice, and they came
out beautiful. He was magic. He was a god, not just a king. What
could ever have been more important to me than Elvis Presley?

I don't know why I wasted my time in college reading existen-
tialism when there was Elvis. I should have put all my energy into
meeting him. Why didn't I?

I can't be blamed for the 1960s, when they had poor Elvis making all those terrible movies, and neither can he. But it's no wonder I had to take some brief respite from my adoration of him. I
can't help it if at age fifteen I didn't know what to do about Elvis
Presley. Couldn't I have learned? . . . no, all was forbidden to
teenagers in 1960. I believed it was anyway. Believing and truth-
telling are the bad habits of youth, they lead nowhere. They've led
me here, sitting in an old flannel nightgown with a crocheted
blanket around me as I stare at him in black-and-white TV when
I'm just two years over thirty. The time was here and now it's
gone. You see, that's the trick of life, isn't it cruel? The Time Is
Past. Touch them while you can, Elvis Presley and John Kennedy
too.

I went into the bedroom when the film was over and I said to
my husband, "I have to help get Elvis on a better diet." But he

didn't hear me because he was sleeping. Snoring too. My husband watches football and drinks beer, I went to Radcliffe and I love Elvis Presley. We come from Alabama and we sell apples. He didn't apply to Harvard but he went to Yale. What good does any of it do us, if I cannot get to Elvis? That he might die and John Denver should live; why should a rat, a snail, a roach have life and he no breath at all?

The next day I said to my husband, "I have got to meet Elvis Presley now."

"Don't you think you're going too far?"

"John Davidson is healthy but Elvis Presley is ailing in Tennessee."

"I thought it was John Denver you hated."

"Aren't they the same person?"

"Your wit is intact anyway."

"They might as well be the same person. No, one is a natural ass and the other works at it."

"So what?"

"I have to meet Elvis Presley. My sister wishes so hard she had met John Kennedy."

"So you're both nuts. The doom and gloom sisters."

I wanted Elvis to take me seriously, I wanted him to respect my mind. I didn't want to be just some annoying crazy fan. Even though I knew those fans were treated well by him. I saw cheap slutty women, young and old, being touched and kissed by him at his concert tours. That meant he didn't have such high standards, he'd kiss anyone. These girls and women with their breasts pushed up high out the tops and sides of their dresses would tell reporters how they had seen every concert, how they had traveled thousands of miles, how they had met him twice or three times, and how it was the most exciting moment of their lives. Perhaps these cheap low-class women knew something I didn't know.

"You have plenty of time to meet Elvis," my husband said. "He's young and you're even younger."

He was lying in bed in the style known as glued to the television, and he didn't even look away from his sports event as he spoke.

"Look, I'm in a hurry," I said. "It sounds as if he's really in trouble."

"Someone else can get to him."

"Who? I can get him a juicer, he'll go on a juice fast, I'll convert him to vegetarianism and exercise. Who else can save him?"

"Well, certainly not you. How could you get to him?"

"I could get famous. Fast."

"Fine. Go write pornography. I've been telling you that for six years."

"I'm sure he doesn't read pornography."

"Sure he does. Everybody does now."

"We don't."

"I have to get around to it."

"That's not how people feel about pornography."

"I want to keep it from you."

"Look, why can't I write the way I write?"

"It'll take too long to get famous that way. You have to be shocking. Be mean. Be the goddess of meanness."

"That wouldn't appeal to Elvis Presley."

"No, but you'd get on TV."

"But he wouldn't know how much I love him."

"Johnny Carson could introduce you."

"Elvis probably wouldn't want to meet me because he's so kind."

"He wouldn't want to meet you because you're not cheap. He likes his women cheap."

"He would have a different compartment for me."

"Why should he? What's in it for him?"

"Curiosity. He likes to know what's going on in the world."

"Not your kind of world."

"Well, maybe I could get cheap."

"You could never be cheap enough."

"I could wear a gold bikini."

"Now you're talking. And while you're wearing it go to your desk and write some pornography."

"Why won't you take this seriously?"

"Shhh. This is the most exciting moment of the game."

"Well?"

"Well what?"

"Why won't you take this seriously?"

"Hmmm? What? Take what seriously? Oh, Elvis? Because it's not really serious."

Some nights after my husband falls asleep I creep out of bed and float into the living room so I can hear Elvis sing. I'm wearing my long flannel nightgown that's soft and faded light blue and I sink down into the wicker armchair at the end of the big room where the sound from the speakers is intended to be best. I sit, just sit and listen. Sometimes I put my head back and I can feel the hard wicker edge digging into my head, but I don't care. It doesn't bother me. There's a window right behind me, and across the street there's a rundown welfare hotel filled with junkies and drunks and loonies of every kind. I never used to sit in that chair because I know that at any moment one of these hotel guests might take a shotgun and begin blowing out the windows of my apartment building. But I don't worry anymore. It wouldn't be a bad way to go, to get my head blown off listening to Elvis Presley sing. Why sleep when I can hear his voice, deep and hoarse and wild with energy, calling to me, "One Night With You"? Why sleep when I can hear that voice, and how can I sleep if I hear it when it isn't even playing?

Until recently I had never heard "Are You Lonesome Tonight?" I had never been to King Karol Records or Discorama or Discomania, and I made sure to cross to the other side of the street when I got near Crazy Eddie's. But now I've been everywhere and bought everything. I have all his songs. I've talked to the salespersons at Crazy Eddie's, who must be from another planet, and I've bought a new needle from someone who hadn't even been born when I first heard Elvis sing in 1956. She didn't exist in 1956 and I had to ask her when they'd be getting "Live From Las Vegas". I was stunned when I heard "Are You Lonesome Tonight?" and I had to cry as I listened. I had lived all these years without hearing him sing "Are You Lonesome Tonight?"

My husband has dared to dance around and snap his fingers to Elvis singing while I am listening alone in my room. I just look away quickly, but I've felt a terrible hatred for him and even a desire to stab him. I must control my anger for I know I am a crazy bitch with a violent temper to boot. WOMAN, 32, KILLS MATE FOR DANCING TO ELVIS.

Either I devote myself completely to Elvis Presley's music, give myself over entirely to it, or I never listen to it again. I know it has got to be one or the other. Either I let his voice sweep me

away with him to a deep dark faraway place from which there will
be no return or I shut my ears and eyes completely.

In August I took the cue from my husband. We had to proceed, and go to our vacation house because it was costing so much
to rent. I could have wasted the money. I could have stopped
everything—gone to my room with my records and gone insane
right then. But it was summer, and we owe it to ourselves to get
the most out of summer. Fall too. In spring we may all flip out. In
winter deep depressions are permitted for everyone. But not in
August. I had to buy corn. Slice tomatoes. Cut basil. Bake peach
pie. Ride a bike. Swim in the waves. Give the human body its
chance at a healthy life.

When I got back to the city I took out that record my sister
had given me many years before and I listened to it a few times.
Or a few hundred times. What difference does it make? There
was no getting enough of him, especially now that I understood
sex and it was all out in the open to the degree that I had lost all
interest in it, I saw what a genius Elvis was. I'd always known he
was the King, that he was the Greatest, but I'd never known why.
It was the feeling in his voice, in his sweet voice, the combination
of sexiness and sweetness and fun—it was all in good fun. Except
when he sang "Love Me Tender"—then he was sincere, sweetly
sincere, but his deep sweet voice still had the promise of fun and
sex. Sex, not as we all know it today, but as we imagined it at age
twelve in 1956. That's the beauty of Elvis Presley, when I tried at
age twelve to have a fantasy about him it was too confusing. It
was a vague hazy picture of a kiss, an embrace—a long intense embrace, maybe a fifteen-minute embrace—it was his voice, his face,
his beautiful long tall body, his smile, his wonderful special voice
that held everything in every note. There had never been a voice
like that. I didn't know what came after the kiss, it went on forever. I think I was wearing a long white chiffon nightgown that
blew in the breeze, but what was he wearing? Black chino pants,
and that lavender shirt, I think. The collar was not turned up.

I have tried to live a normal life. I've tried, I've tried to blot it
out, shut it away, but something pulls me to him. He pulls me to
him, his voice, his face, his eyes, his hands, his legs, his body, his

sweet smile. I'm his. He's mine. He's ours and he's no one's. He's here and he's gone.

But I live in the real world. Who are the people of the world? What are the things in the world and how are they connected to the brain? The brain, in part, is composed of metal spokes, and immediately upon arising the spokes begin whirling.

None of the things they said about Elvis Presley were true. I mean none of the bad things were true, not true at all. He did not dye his hair. It was light brown but he did not dye it; it just photographed black. He was very tall and not fat, but weighed a trifle more than he should have. Those pictures of a bloated puffy person were not him, they were not even a person at all, they were those inflatable dummies that you pump up, it was a cruel trick of his many rivals and detractors.

Elvis Presley is alive. I did save his life. He did get a juicer and he juiced organically grown apples and carrots and spinach and wheat grass and he got thin and healthy. He grew his own vegetables, went jogging and bike-riding and swimming. He remarried his one true love, his wife Priscilla, he swooped down with his long lean body, down to the green grass, and lifted up his little girl into the blue sky and swung her around as they all three laughed and jumped for joy. They had two more babies, a boy and a girl. Priscilla went to art school and became a great primitive painter, and they lived happily ever after. It's a wonderful world. My wish came true.

I did get to touch him. I touched his hands, I touched his face, we hugged, we kissed, I kissed his hands, I kissed his face, I touched his face, I touched his arms, I touched his eyes, I touched his hair, I saw his smile, I heard his voice, I saw him move, I heard him laugh, I heard him sing.

We're the best of friends now and he sometimes tells me that I saved his life, but I know it wasn't just me. It was all of us, all his fans, his crazy teenage fans. I was just one of millions. We wanted to save him, we needed him, we loved him so much. I was just a little crazier than most, smarter too, and because I understood his greatness I knew he had to live, to last, to be happy, to thrill millions, and I couldn't let anything stop me.

SHY BEARERS

LESTER GOLDBERG

Lester Goldberg has published thirty short stories and a
play-in-progress in such magazines as *Transatlantic Review*,
Epoch, *Literary Review*, and *Iowa Review*; the University
of Illinois Press published a collection of short stories, *One
More River*, in 1978. Five stories have appeared in *The Best
American Short Stories*. A 1978 Yaddo Fellow, he lives with
his wife in Cranford, New Jersey, and manages a housing
project in Manhattan's East Village.

The church bells are in full cry as Krueger bicycles up the main
road rising out of Moreton-Hampstead. He winces when a holiday
car comes too close and swerves around him. The road steepens
gradually, and after a few last leg strokes, toes trapped in the clips,
he dismounts and walks, pushing the new black bike up the hill.
Now he can search the fields for the red and yellow poppies he
remembers; the day sharpens and stands poised. His old World
War II billet wasn't far away—a glance at the map and he could
find his way in a long day's ride, and he will do it, he decides—if
only to make the bells stop ringing in his ears.

Those other chimes had given him no rest the first few nights at
Evelyn Kiley's. Outside his little upstairs room that overlooked
the rear garden, the church bells played a tune every fifteen minutes. On the half hour picked up the first tune and added a few
bars; at three quarters, the bells replayed the first and second bars
and added a third part, and on the hour—the reprise of 'Come All
Ye Faithful.' He had asked Evelyn for another room or could she
stop the bells. No chance, Evelyn said, they'd been off all during
the blackout and blitz and now after V-E day on they went, and
they might ring on for the next five hundred years. Krueger real-

ized he had arrived too late. The danger past. Wrong-way Krueger: all the others are on their way home and Sergeant Krueger had been left behind to sit in the office all day and stamp discharge papers. Flight mechanics, bombardiers, pilots; majors no older than Krueger passed through his hands and back to the States.

Krueger had washed out of flight training in Big Springs, Texas, after one month. He dropped out of college to fly into it. Whirled and spun around in the training cockpit, and afterwards, the officer said, you'll never make it son, you're a fine specimen but your equilibrium is off. A Staten Island girl had comforted him (I may never come back, he warned her, half-believing it), comforted him several times in a copse near Miller Field. Only it was actually a woodlot; Krueger transformed it into a copse and one could imagine it so, on a warm June day, sniffing the wild honeysuckle. Krueger didn't ship out. He stayed. He overstayed.

Then she continued to write long letters to him in England, and she made plans. Krueger, in the full knowledge that once, this once, he was unmaking plans that had been ordained for him, shucked her when he returned across 3,000 miles; crossing the Hudson, this time, he married a New Jersey girl. His wife is waiting now in London. She doesn't write, can't write. He's left no itinerary. Krueger, when he thought about it, which wasn't often, imagined her visiting the Tower of London. It had escaped damage during the war, but last week the IRA provisional wing set off a bomb in the Tower. In the Tower, Krueger envisioned a small bare room with rough rock walls. His wife, after viewing the crown jewels (step lively now, keep moving), looked through a slit in the wall and saw him strapped to a stone bench. One waited while the ceiling descended and the walls moved closer. If one closed one's eyes, it didn't help. Then double-chinned Robert Morley came in, crooning, we'll take good care of you. You don't look comfortable, my boy. Would you be happier not staring up at the ceiling? I could see to it that you're strapped facing down, so you could look at the floor. Krueger waved him away.

A long uphill slog to reach the first Dartmoor plateau and as Krueger climbs higher, leaning on the handlebars, the purple moor grass and scrawny hawthorns disappear, until at the top only cairns of granite and yellow-flowered gorse and bracken survive;

four grazing ponies disappear into the fog settling over the moors; the passing cars turn headlights on and as Krueger remounts, a cold drizzle begins. It turns into a steady, pelting rain, and a pool of water fills the fold in Krueger's cape, draped over the handle-bars.

Krueger flips the puddle out of his lap. Can see about five feet ahead in the swirling fog. Several cars stop and pull over. Others move slowly, no faster than he pedals. A gray wraith cuts across his path and turns into a sheep which leaps the rock fence and runs off bleating into the fog. He wonders if Evelyn is still alive. Christmas cards for twenty-seven years but none last year. A tall woman, no extra flesh on her, wide forehead, pale blue eyes, ma-tronly bosom, a pink sweater pushed up from the wrists exposing roughened elbows, and muscular calves you sometimes see on an older waitress. A deer tapestry in rust and brown hung over the fireplace. She spoke more quickly than the local people.

"I had two little girls from London staying here during the blitz and neither wore knickers under their frocks, poor dears. Now I have you young sojers. And Marla, I took her in when she was three months old. My cousin's child. I wasn't married then, still at home, taking care of my old dad. She doesn't look eight-een, does she? You don't talk much, Sergeant." Krueger re-members the troll-girl's thick neck, how her head always tilted to one side and her heavy shoulders set on a blocky body.

One morning, Krueger, walking past the dining room, saw Marla clearing the tables and Evelyn Kiley on the floor, wearing a green exercise suit that ended in a pair of flapping, pleated bloomers, halfway down her lean thighs. He paused and heard the radio: Hello dears. This is Penelope Snedeker and her morning ex-ercise class. Evelyn stretched and thrust right hand to left toe and left hand to right toe but not quite in time to the radio's com-mands.

"Hello, Krueger," she panted, reaching deliberately and ignor-ing the radio's—On your feet. She stretched right, "Krueger, my husband, Victor, six years in the German camps," stretched left, "should be home soon. You're the oldest man here, Krueger (al-ready old at twenty-three, Krueger thought), and you're a sergeant and carry a book under your arm." She reached negligently and more slowly, "So it's you I'm looking to for advice. Marla's a dear girl, and plays the accordion, and helps with the cleaning and can tell colors. That's all, Krueger! She can't make change, can't shop, can't cook. I had to take her out of school after three years. They said she'd never learn to read. The girl's never peeled a banana, I can hardly remember the last one I've tasted. She's never tasted pepper. There's no elastic so it's hard to fix a pair of drawers. She's never owned a pair of nylons. She's got a boyfriend, Sergeant. A twenty-year-old farm laborer. He has no home and he's no smarter than she is. He wants to marry her. Can I deny her love, Krueger, can I? What do you think?"

"It's not my affair," and he turned his back and walked out.

Krueger yawned his day away stamping discharges: aircraft mechanics, clerks, heroes, majors (back to the hospital for the major with four oak leaf clusters and excess albumin), captains, mad bombers, gunners, a colonel. He picked up another blue V-Mail from Staten Island and stuffed it into his shirt pocket. Bought a carton of cigarettes at the PX and, impulsively, he grabbed four pairs of nylons, a neutral shade, and a set of pick-up-sticks.

Krueger lingered over tea that evening. After the other three soldiers left, he called out, "Another cuppa, please, Marla." She poured, her stubby fingers curled over the bunny ears of the pink and green wool tea cozy. "Sit down, Marla, have a cup with me." She sat heavily, gazing straight ahead, her hand still clutching the teapot handle. He laid some change on the table: sixpence, a few shillings, two florins, a half crown, "Let's play a game. Can you guess how many shillings I have?" and he covered the shillings with his cupped hand.

She shook her head, dipping it toward her right shoulder and upright again.

"Just guess?"

"I can't. Your hand is on them."

He withdrew his hand. Krueger saw Evelyn watching from the kitchen doorway.

"Four?"

"That's right. Just grand. Now suppose you went into a store to buy a pair of nylons."

"There aren't any."

"Just pretend. The man asks you for six shillings and . . ."

"But there aren't any nylons!"

"Stay put, right here." Krueger jumped up and took the staircase to his room, two steps at a time. He came down with his gifts

and gave Marla and Evelyn two pairs of nylons each, and to
Marla the box of pick-up-sticks.

Evelyn pecked him high on one cheek. Marla, clutching the
box, ran up to her room. Evelyn poured more tea and brought out
a piece of fruitcake she had been saving; "Not enough for the
crowd," she said. It tasted good after the salty mackerel dinner.
Marla returned, without her apron, and wearing a new yellow
blouse. She held the box in her hand.

"Sit near me," Krueger said, "and I'll show you how to play."
He showered the colored slivers on the table, picked up four or
five and soon missed. He held Marla's hand around the bundle
and let them fall again. With her stubby fingers, she picked up
more sticks than Krueger on the first attempt. Krueger found
later, he didn't have to let her win. She usually beat him easily
and wanted to play every evening after tea. If he said, "Wait until
I finish my tea," she circled the table with the sticks in her fist,
peering over his shoulder into the tea cup. One day, he borrowed
Evelyn's husband's wheel and, with Marla on her bike, rode to the
grocery. Turning daredevil, he rode without hands, and then
placed his feet on the handlebars. Marla applauded wildly. Soon
he was skipping the pub more often and sat around in front of the
peat fire, reading *Sons and Lovers* that, until now, he'd only carried under his arm.

The wind lashes Krueger as the fog begins to lift.

"We're celebrating, Evelyn, you and Marla and I, three tickets
on the bus tour to Land's End. Hard to get, too. Now you've no
excuse not to wear those stockings. Pull those nylons up around
those good looking legs and let's go."

"You're sure you want an old lady along," Evelyn sniffed,
"what with all the time you've been spending with poor Marla."

In front of Krueger, sat Evelyn; never a beauty, today she had
achieved majesty. Too short notice to get her brown hair frizzed
by a new perm, her hair looked better this way; she must have
found a new bra, creating a promontory under her white satin
blouse tucked into a grassy-green skirt, plus the nylons and tan
pumps. Marla sat next to her, in the yellow blouse, blond hair
brushed and gleaming, and combed down to one side to cover the
thicker part of her neck. She clasped the accordion case tightly in
her lap.

The bus sped past fields of barley, the wind pressing the golden, bearded stalks almost to the earth, the wind soughing past Krueger's window, a rock fence and a field of blue alfalfa, a small woods. Nothing stayed very long in his view. He counted six pollarded oaks, like sturdy old men whose heads had been lopped off, and from whose necks sprouted three or four new arms. The bus driver tipped the blue cap back on his head. Swaying as he swept the wheel from side to side, and the bus climbed and rocked harmoniously, he sang songs about sons sailing o'er the seas, mothers mourning and sweethearts pining. He urged the passengers, "Sing along now, don't let the old Singing Bus Driver down." Stony silence. The passengers stared out the windows.

The bus rolled through the moorlands, honking sheep off the road, past a wire-fenced area, restricted zone sign up and, within, two soldiers carrying long metal wands and searching the fields.

"There's a beautiful little girl back there with an accordion on her lap. How about a song from the little duckling?"

Marla blushed and hugged her accordion case. Krueger leaned forward, touching her shoulder, "Go ahead, Marla, give them a song." She took the accordion from its case and bending over it, played a few chords. Then she launched into "Galway Bay," and without resting played "Lord Randal" and when she played "Bawbee Allen," a cracked voice in the rear picked up the refrain—"O, mither dear, you'll mak' my bed / Ye'll mak' it saft and narrow." A clapping of hands that grew louder. Krueger touched her heavy shoulder; she shuddered, bowed her head. "Lovely music, Marla. You have the gift." He wanted to kiss the back of her head.

Going up the hill, the driver shifted gears, the motor coughed and choked and, just below the crest, the bus stopped. It slid back and the driver jammed the footbrake, pulled the emergency and opened the door. He tramped on the gas, ground the starter, but the motor wouldn't turn over. Again the screech of the starter and no ignition. "Ducks and ducklings—let's hear "God Save the King." They finally sang. "Step up front, Sergeant. The American Army gets out first. Stand below those steps and help the English ladies down. Don't let them walk over the cliff. Stay away from the edge of the road, mates, over the hill and it's a short walk to the inn below."

Krueger hopped off and stationed himself below the steps, his back to the bluff that dropped one hundred feet and then the

land leveled off. Slowly the passengers alighted and Krueger aided
the women; Evelyn tendered her hand, wrist bent, like Queen
Mary giving her hand to an Indian sepoy. The men, except for the
very old, disdained his outstretched hand, and in a long straggling
line, they walked up the hill.

Krueger reached toward Marla who had trouble closing her accordion case. As she stepped off, she threw herself on him, both
hands encircling his neck, her accordion smacked against his ribs,
and he staggered back, grabbed her wrists; she was choking him,
hanging from him, feet off the ground. Her thrust made him stumble, his back felt naked; he heard Evelyn scream and a cry—watch
out, mate! He steadied, planted his feet firmly and embraced her,
felt her pulsing in his arms, like a pigeon he'd once held against
his chest, all of her bursting and beating against him in one mad
flight.

Ahead, North Hessary Tor rises to the west. Behind him lies a
hill, perhaps the same hill. Bearing down on both handbrakes,
Krueger starts the long downhill run. He might find at the bottom
an inn on the left hand side, and a bridge crossing the river. He
sweeps the yellow hood off his head and snaps a look left, the bike
picks up speed, and down he flies, the hood flapping and pulling
like a sail, holding his head taut with the pressure of the wind—
the inn flashes by. He glimpses the inn sign—TWO RIVERS and
underneath, the ever-present motto HAVE COURAGE. He
wants to shout back at the hill, the fog—COURAGE, COUR-
AGE for Richard, the Lion-Hearted, COURAGE. Mustn't jar
the English, he thinks; and now when the bike hits the flat and
crosses the bridge, he wants to place his feet on the handlebars or
ride without hands. Instead, he applies the brakes, stops and pulls
over to the side. Krueger, his legs shaky, turns the bike around and
walks back toward the inn.

Krueger orders a double whiskey at the bar and takes it into the
lounge. Standing in front of the stone fireplace, he turns his back
and like Robert Donat in an old film, toasts his backside, swaying
back and forth. He kneads his right thigh. Then he takes the map
from his windbreaker's zipper pocket and spreads it on the table
that smells of beer spillings. Drowsy, he knuckles his eyes, and
studies the scribble of roads that run north-south between the inn
and Horrabridge. The bartender sticks his head into the lounge

crying, Last Call, and Krueger determined to get off the heavily traveled A384, traces a squiggle of yellow-marked roads to his destination.

Aided by a tail wind, he journeys south. Krueger almost turned back when the wind tore at him as he opened the pub door, but no, he'd stay with the impulse, ride with it and drop in at the Kileys'. He could have phoned from the inn, forewarned them, the polite thing to do; it had been twenty-eight years and Evelyn (if alive, she'd be sixty-seven), he remembered, had acted strangely the night they returned from the bus tour.

Krueger, reading in his tiny room under the high small window, so badly cut out of the thick walls that he had stuffed old torn underwear into the chinks around the ill-fitting casement, heard Evelyn running a bath in the round high tub. Restless, he stepped out of his room, thinking he might go down and brew some tea. He heard splashing sounds from the bathroom, feminine and awkward and vigorous. A crack of light along the edge of the door.

"Victor always scrubbed my back, Krueger." He stood breathing deeply at the head of the staircase. "That's why I'm faithful to him after six years. Do you hear me, Krueger? Krueger! I've had my chances."

"I hear you, Evelyn," and his voice resounded in the narrow hallway. No sound of splashing but from the far end of the hall the accordion played a few bars of "Bawbee Allen," then it went berserk and repeated the same chord—a siren.

"Get dressed, Evelyn. I'll take you down to the pub."

"You never asked me before."

"I'm asking you now." The accordion shrieked.

"People will talk. Go yourself. In fact, go to hell, Krueger."

He left a month later and although he asked her twice more, she never went down to the pub.

It has rained forever for Krueger: pedal, dismount and walk, pedal again. The lane forks, uphill to the right, and he gets off and starts the half-mile trek up an even narrower hunchbacked lane. Twist and turn, always the impenetrable hedgerows alongside, shoulder-high banks of earth topped by beech saplings and hawthorn, interlaced with brambles; then the gray sky opens at a pasture entrance, the red earth churned by cattle crossing.

A milk truck, cans jouncing, comes down the lane and Krueger presses against the unyielding hedgerows; the brambles catch his jeans and make scratchy plastic noises against his rain cape.

The thick-walled cob house with its overhanging thatched roof sits broadside facing the road. Krueger looks up at the small, higher window at the left corner of the house. It had been cut through not long before he arrived when the room was partitioned to make extra bedrooms. No smoke rising from the side stone chimney.

He leans his bike under the roof overhang. Knocks softly, then louder, his old signal—three knocks, pause, two knocks.

Evelyn opens the door. "Come in, Krueger. You'll catch your death. Come on, don't stand in the rain, staring at me, just hang your cape on that hook." She backs up a few steps, still looking at him and when he crosses the threshold and hangs his cape, she says, "You're quite gray after all these years but still lean." She pats her hips with both hands.

Krueger tries to recognize her. He wants to. Brown frizzled hair mixed with gray, and her angularity, the sharp chin and bony shoulders now all filled in—a tall heavy woman, and it is only when she turns away, saying, "I'll put the kettle on," and walks across the dining room to the kitchen, that her long, determined stride brings back the younger woman.

He sits at the table while she fills the kettle and sets out the tea things. "I feel at home here because your pictures still hang crookedly."

"You must still like cucumber sandwiches," she says, slicing the long green cucumber. She places two sandwiches cut in triangles in front of him. Two apple tarts, the juice running out of them, one onto each white bowl. A large bowl of thick Devon cream.

Krueger methodically eats the four sandwich halves while Evelyn watches. He spoons the cream onto one tart. He cuts off a yawn by taking a deep breath. "How's your sister?"

"You mean Charlotte? She didn't take care and quite lost her figger." Evelyn drew herself up.

"Your husband, Victor?"

"Victor? I gave him a very good life when he came back. He was busy caring for his peonies and got his old job back digging graves. He died peacefully, sitting right on the old couch in the lounge," and she waves toward the sitting room. "He was lacing up his boots."

What could he tell her about himself? She asks no questions. "How is Marla?"

"She had a lovely concert at the church before she died. The whole town came. That kind dies young."

"Ah—that lovely child—"

She pours more tea. "That kind dies young. Do you remember, Krueger, the night before the bus trip, your lovely treat, and Marla wanted to eat by candlelight like during the blitz."

He nodded, recalling how their faces shone, dancing suspended in the dark, all blemishes vanished.

"And I made that special trifle you loved, rainbow colored with heavy cream."

"How did you get cream in those days, Evelyn?"

"I have my ways."

Krueger closes his eyes and snaps them open. Closes them again.

"You cut a fine figure of a soldier, Krueger. That you did."

"And you're still a very handsome woman yourself, Evelyn."

"Why don't you make yourself comfortable on the couch in the lounge? Take off those wet shoes."

"I'll help you clear—"

"No, no. Go ahead and get your rest."

Krueger enters the lounge and sits on the couch facing the deer tapestry that hangs to the right of the fireplace. On the left side of the mantel, a light green elephant on a gray onyx stand; to the right, just below the fringed edge of the tapestry, stand three translucent glass mice, a red, a yellow and a blue one. He stands and looks at the pictures: Victor Kiley in his woolen army uniform, Victor with his hand throttling the neck of a giant peony—third prize, Victor and Evelyn, just married—two defiant chins. Krueger gazes at Evelyn holding Marla, in a knit suit, looking like any normal, rosy-cheeked English baby. He straightens the picture. Then sits down again. He tosses the pink-faced kewpie doll to the other end of the couch and wonders if its smaller sister is still upstairs in the toilet, its crinkled skirt coyly covering the spare roll of toilet tissue. He can't keep his eyes open.

Evelyn walks in and switches on the electric heater that stands in the fireplace recess. A warm glow. As good as the old coal or peat fire.

He hears the sound of running water in the kitchen. A sharp noise, of a dish dropped. Broken? It thrusts him awake. Warmth creeps from the soles of his feet, up his toes, to his calves. Evelyn walks in and throws a blanket over him. He drowses, sitting upright. She goes out. He slides lower on the couch. She returns and with his eyes half-closed, he can sense her watching over him.

She lifts the blanket stealthily and eases herself down onto the center of the couch, drawing the blanket over both of them. Wide-awake now, he watches through veiled lids. She shifts closer. Three inches separate them. He smells the scent of violets. He tucks his legs under him. His wallet, clasped to the folder of the traveler's checks by a rubber band, digs into his pelvis.

Sitting upright, he stretches both hands in the air, dropping the blanket from around his neck and letting it fall on his lap. "I must be moving on. I'm all dried out now."

She sits up, back straight. "I thought you'd stay the night. It's still raining ducks and drakes."

"No, I can't. Awfully sorry. Must get back to London."

"Whatever is your first name, Krueger? I have it written down some place but for all the world, I can't remember."

"I'm called Henry." Although he'd signed his cards Sergeant Krueger for many years and in the old days everyone called him Krueger, he was certain she hadn't forgotten. He stands, picks up his shoes and slips a hand inside one—still wet. He sits on a chair and draws them on. Hard to tie wet laces. He stamps his feet several times and rises. Leaning over Evelyn, he tucks the blanket around her shoulders, and kisses her on one cheek. With a twist of her body, she shrugs the blanket off. She doesn't stir. Nor move, when he walks through the archway into the little hall and puts on his rain cape. He closes the door softly.

He steps off into the rain and wheels his bike into place, back to the house. One foot on the left pedal, starts down the path, throws his right leg over, in the saddle, a glance back at the closed door.

The lane tumbles down and away with the aimlessness of a horse's stream. Winding around the third bend, Krueger eases up on the handbrakes, then on a sharp pitch, he squeezes the brake;

the bike will not slow down, the wet brakes don't grab and in seconds he is hurtling down the hill. An S curve ahead, he's hidden by the cloistral hedgerows, and if a car comes up the lane—he takes his feet off the pedals—perhaps stop by braking with his shoetips, impossible now at this speed and deliberately, before it's too late—he turns the handlebars left and slams into the bank. Dazed, he's lying in the road; can't see his bike. The cold rain strikes the back of his neck. He gets to his knees, hands propping him, tries to get up, falls back and strikes one knee on the ground. Stays put, on his knees.

He'd come through, pierced the other side, and Krueger, Krueger, he tells himself, you're an old hand, you missed a connection, Krueger—why didn't your head tell you to walk down that hill? Finally, he gets up and straightens his rain cape, looks at his torn left sleeve, slashed from elbow to wrist and flapping open. The back of his hand is gashed, earth-blackened and bleeding, and his fingers feel sticky. He flexes wrists and elbows. He sees the bicycle lying behind him and reaching down into the rear pack pulls out his shaving kit and a towel. A knife pain strikes his ribs. He shakes out the shaving kit, toothbrush, razor, soap falls to the ground, and taking the wet soapy washcloth, he ties it around his wrist. He sucks in a deep good gulp of rare air. Again the knife pain. Ties a handkerchief to hold the cloth in place. He bends to pick up the bike. Dizzy, he almost pitches forward. The hell with the bike! Now, breathe delicately, breathe with care. He straightens and sees the handkerchief, dyed dark crimson. He'll not go back to the house, not ever again.

Krueger starts to walk down the lane, taking slow halting steps, breathing shallowly, and carefully measuring every breath of bestowed air.

THE SUMMER GAME

STEVE HELLER

Steve Heller teaches in the College of Education at Oklahoma State University in Stillwater. His fiction has appeared in *The Chariton Review*, *U. S. Catholic*, *Intro* 9, and *Cimarron Review*. He is working on a collection of short stories.

Warren liked to watch them burn the cane fields. He liked to watch the runners race along the edge of the field after the backfire had been set, pausing only to lay their flaming brands at selected points along the base of the thirty-foot green wall of cane. Today the wind had whipped the flames quickly through the field, raising clouds of heavy gray-brown smoke well above the dark outline of the Waianea Mountains rising in the distance beyond the plain. The red flames consumed the green, licking away everything but the bamboolike stalks encasing the sweet juicy brown sugar pulp.

It would all be quite beautiful, Warren thought as he watched, if it weren't for the acrid smell of burning cane.

The fire was nearly out now; Warren could see blue sky beneath the dissipating cloud of smoke. He smiled. After three months on Ewa Plantation, Warren appreciated how the burning was an integral part of the sugar harvest in Hawaii. He knew how the fire cleared away the dry tangled mass of leaf trash, leaving the juice-laden stalks unharmed and ready to be cut. He gripped his machete expectantly.

Lately Warren had been trying to take it all in—the sights, sounds, and smells of the cane fields—trying to savor his last few days at Ewa. He was summer help, and summer was nearly over. He'd had lots of other summer jobs, ever since he was thirteen. But this was the first one he would miss. Ewa was special.

He didn't really know what made it so. As summer help, Warren was many things on Ewa Plantation, and today he was a cane cutter. It was his job to enter the charred reddish-brown field and chop off the exposed cane stalks protruding from the ground in thick twisted rows. The stackers would follow behind, piling the cane into bundles to be picked up by the tall red tractor crane waiting to load the harvest onto the giant cane-hauling trucks lined up at the edge of the field.

A machine would normally handle the cutting too, but last week Ewa Plantation's tractor push-rake had thrown a rod and parts had not yet arrived from Honolulu. So now ten men with machetes lined up one to a row at the field's edge to harvest the cane in the old way.

The cane-cutting crews were makeshift. Most of the cutters were Japanese, but there were always a few Filipinos, maybe one Korean, and even a *haole* or two on hand as well. This time there were five men Warren knew.

Down at the far end of the line was dumpy old Henry Sakagawa. Henry could have named everybody in line for Warren; the pudgy Japanese had lived and worked at Ewa for nearly forty years. In the middle of the line were three boys roughly Warren's age: Kenji and Yoshiro, a couple of full-time guys from Wahiawa; then tall, brash Kelsey, another summer laborer. Finally, next to Warren at the very end of the line was Santos, the old Filipino who was Ewa Plantation's master cane cutter.

"Go! Go!" Demattos the *luna* shouted, and they charged into the field shouting, the younger voices sounding above the rest.

"Banzai!" Kelsey yelled, baring his teeth at the two Japanese boys next to him and brandishing his machete above his head like a crazed samurai.

"Watch out you don't commit *hara-kiri* with that knife!" Kenji shot back.

"Kelsey don't need a knife for the cane," Yoshiro added. "He should just *bite* it off!"

Other shouts and threats echoed along the edge of the field.

Warren did not participate in the ceremonial bantering as they began to attack the cane, but he did not ignore it either. Warren wasn't very good at kidding around with the rest of the crew. He could never think of the right thing to say. So usually he just smiled or nodded and went along with the rest. It was better that way.

He liked to stay on the edge of things, where he could see what was going on. Now, as he sliced through the first stalk with a quick fluid stroke, Warren could see the entire line of cutters advancing on the tangled rows like eager athletes taking the field. He could see Yoshiro's grimace and Kelsey's square jaw thrust out as both boys slashed at the first stalks protruding from the cane bunched in front of them. And Warren knew it was Henry Sakagawa's high piercing voice he heard shouting "Ey, give 'em!" to goad on the younger men around him.

Everything was easy, everything as it should be, as Warren lifted back the cut stalk with the hooked end of his machete, lopped off the soft sugarless top, and tossed the cane behind him. He worked swiftly, as he always did.

But the broad scene, the sights and sounds around Warren, narrowed quickly today, because today he was intent on something else. Tomorrow afternoon they would lay off the summer help. That meant today was the last chance he had to finish his rows ahead of Santos, the old Filipino working next to him.

In the corner of his right eye, Warren could see the thin spidery figure in the wide-brimmed straw hat and checkered work shirt laboring silently on the next row, wielding his blade with an easy grace that always amazed Warren. Always, when they were this close, he would watch the old man's hands. Like most of the men who handled cane, Warren wore heavy cotton gloves for protection. Not Santos. He swung his machete and grabbed the splintered cane barehanded. His hands were like claws, thin and leathery, with dark scaly calluses on each palm.

Henry Sakagawa said that when Santos was younger his hands would bleed every day. But Warren had seen the Filipino dig long slivers of cane out of his dry cracked palms without drawing a drop of blood.

Crazy Santos. "Santos *pupule*," they had warned him the first time Warren saw the old man sharpening the long hooked blade of his black machete in the tool shed. "Don't worry about Santos," DeMattos said reassuringly the day he handed Warren a hoe and sent him into the fields with Santos to irrigate furrows. "Santos never talks to nobody. Just watch where he points and stay out of his way."

Kelsey, who had started to work a week before Warren, had other advice. "Don't make any sudden moves," he warned with a sly grin. "They say he chopped up a man on the big island once."

Warren hewed a twenty-foot stalk with a firm flat stroke. Santos was different from the rest of DeMattos' crew. The *luna* was right—Santos never spoke. Anyone who worked with the old Filipino had to learn strictly by imitation. Except when the cane had to be cut by hand, Santos was a ditch-man, controlling the flow of water to growing crops with his hoe. He was the best at letting just the right amount of water from the irrigation ditch into each furrow.

But it was as a cane cutter that Santos was renowned. "Never be anybody like him again," DeMattos liked to say. It was understood that no one could finish a field ahead of Santos and do as good a job. Of course, there was no precise way to tell who finished first or cut the most. The "rows" of charred cane were tangled and overlapping. But still it was obvious that even the younger men had to push themselves to keep up with the old Filipino.

Despite all the taunting, the cutters didn't really compete with each other. The fields were marked off by the numerous cane-hauling roads that crisscrossed the Ewa sugar plain. In an average burnt-over field, everyone would have to cut three or four rows apiece, and it didn't really matter who finished his part first. All the year-round guys had pride in their work, especially old Henry Sakagawa, who usually went back along all the rows to make sure that each stalk had been cut and properly topped off.

But why did Santos always finish first? Warren had to admit he would take a certain secret pleasure in beating Santos just once. It was a little game he played to get through the hot summer days in the cane fields. Of course, he would never push himself just to win. That would be pointless. It meant something only if he could do it working as usual.

Kelsey had finished first once. But he hurried and missed several stalks and left the sugarless tops on others. Santos said nothing, of course, but Henry Sakagawa had to go back along each of Kelsey's rows, cutting and tossing.

"Well, what the hell," was all Kelsey said.

Warren separated two twisted stalks and chopped them both off near the ground. An ache was already developing between his shoulder blades. He glanced over at Santos. Despite his exertions, Warren still felt as if he were a spectator watching an expert at work. Santos was a technician, examining rather than attacking his work, and yet the cut cane piled up behind him.

Warren liked to work next to Santos, so that he could pick up the rhythm, the natural movement of the old man's hands as he swung the blade and grabbed the cane. And although the Filipino was always absorbed in his work, it seemed that sometimes, for just an instant, the old man's eyes would flicker and he would take notice of Warren. But the younger man could never be sure, for they had never spoken, though Warren always wondered about Santos' opinion of him as a cane cutter.

Warren stepped up the pace—it was a small field, only three rows apiece for the cutters, and they could afford to work just a bit faster in the late afternoon sun. But it made no difference to Santos; he kept his regular rhythm: chop, grab, chop, toss—and drew steadily ahead. By the time Warren started his second row, Santos was already several yards in front.

As the afternoon wore on, sweat dripped off Warren's nose, tasting salty and bitter with the acrid smell of the burnt cane. Gradually, Warren recovered his wide view of the field. He saw them all moving across the scorched landscape: Kelsey with wide sweeping slashes, Kenji and Yoshiro in short hacking bursts, Henry Sakagawa with relaxed steady strokes.

The last row was the toughest. Warren could feel the pace slowing, the line of cutters becoming more and more crooked, as they neared the edge of the field. Warren narrowed his view again only at the end, when Santos tossed the last stalk over his shoulder and turned for an instant to view with hawklike eyes the littered field and the other cutters advancing toward him. There was only this momentary recognition in the old man's eyes; immediately he began to chop stray stalks along the edge of the road.

Warren had looked up purposely at that instant. Unless they cut cane again tomorrow, this was probably the last time he would see Santos finish a field.

The red tractor crane had already begun to lift dirty piles of cane onto the waiting trucks when the cutters finally finished. The stacking and loading would continue until the field was cleared, because sugar sap in a burnt-over field deteriorated rapidly. But the cutters were through for the day; an old rusty yellow Ford truck with wooden slat sides waited on a wide road to take them back to Ewa.

"You ready to go or what?" Kenji, who was already aboard, shouted at the rest of the crew.

They needed no additional prodding in the late afternoon heat. Wiping dirt and sweat off his forehead, Warren climbed in back with the rest, settling down in a corner next to the cab. Santos climbed aboard last, moving all the way up to the opposite corner and squatting down in the space always left for him. He said nothing, just took off his straw hat, looked down, and began to rub his hands together, peeling the dirt off his palms in tiny rolls. Warren tried to relax.

DeMattos poked his head back through the glassless rear window of the cab. "Everybody on?"

"Ey, when you going to reupholster?" cracked Yoshiro, patting the splintered wooden floor.

DeMattos shrugged.

"Wait for me!"

Warren leaned around and looked through a space between slats and saw stumpy-legged Henry Sakagawa run out from behind a tall clump of sugar cane in the next field amid catcalls from the truck.

"Ey, this bus don't stop for that!"

"Supposed to shake the leaves so we know you're there, man!"

"You sure you're *pau*? Don't hurry your business!"

Henry puffed up to the truck. "Got enough room for me?" he said red-faced, and reached for the wooden railing. But before he could grab hold to pull himself aboard, the truck lurched forward.

"Hey!"

"Go for broke, man!"

"Faster! Faster!"

Warren laughed with the others as Henry ran along just behind the truck in quick jerky steps, until Kelsey extended his long muscular arm and pulled the older man up. The old Japanese swayed a bit unsteadily and clung to Kelsey as the truck picked up speed.

"You need to grow a couple more legs before you start chasing cars," Kelsey grinned as he helped Henry hunch down against the railing. Warren could see them all settling back now, the heat and the dirt forgotten as they began to rib each other.

"Henry runs faster on payday," Yoshiro explained.

"Used to be so," Henry admitted, catching his breath. "Used to be Wahiawa ladies come to Ewa first of every month. Everybody rich a couple days; get all you want. No more." He shook his head sadly.

"What's the matter with Honolulu girls?" Kelsey objected. "Only thirty minutes to Hotel Street, you know."

"Honolulu girls all *haoles* now. Business women. Got to have reservations and credit cards. Better to stay home with my wife."

One of the older guys laughed and slapped his knee.

"Well, don't sell *haole* girls short," Kelsey warned. "They've got good taste. I had to work in this godforsaken place all summer because they like their men rich as well as damn good-looking."

"Aw, man! Getting deep in here," said Yoshiro, raising his feet.

Henry chuckled. "Tomorrow your last day, eh?" He was talking to Kelsey, but his eyes wandered back to Warren for just a moment. Kenji and Yoshiro also looked back.

They were doing it again—giving him the opportunity to jump in, to say something amusing or silly. But Warren could think of nothing, so he just nodded and smiled.

"Yeah, you clowns will be on your own after tomorrow. . . ." Kelsey went on.

Warren could see them all clearly from the corner. Henry and Santos, Kenji and Yoshiro, and the rest of them. All were looking at Kelsey now: "You know, you guys all look alike to us *haoles*, but I'll tell you what—I'll never forget how ugly this crew was."

Warren laughed. It was comfortable to be here and to laugh. He didn't like to be in the center anyway. That was the nice thing about summer; you could pick your own place in things. In school he was stuck—always the new kid, the Williams boy. The family had moved a dozen times since he was ten. Commander Williams was always being transferred—from Boston to San Diego to Pearl Harbor.

Sound faded as Warren watched the dust boil up into swirling red clouds behind them as the truck rumbled along the cane-hauling road. The dust obscured everything—the cane, the voices. . . .

It was a luxury to be able to watch like this. You could do it if you weren't in the middle. It was better to stay on the edge of things where you could relax and see the whole picture. The same principle applied everywhere. Warren tried not to draw attention to himself at school. He was no scholar; on the football team he played offensive guard.

Summer was better. He could design his own summers, and since he liked to work, that's what he did. Last summer he worked at the Hawaiian Holiday Macadamia Nut Factory on the big island. In a way, it was a lot like Ewa. He wasn't really close to any of the other workers. But on the last day they gave him a present —a tie-dyed T-shirt that said "Nuts to You" on the front. They gave it to him in the glassed-in lobby, where Jack Lord's saddle was mounted above a display of Macadamia Nut Brittle.

He could still remember how embarrassing it was—smiling faces of coworkers, many whose names he had never learned, but who had nevertheless judged him worthy of a gift. You could never tell how it was going to be when they picked you out.

Warren looked over at Santos, still staring down at his callused palms. The old Filipino stayed on the edge of things too, never joining in the heckling with the rest of the crew. It bothered Warren a little that they were alike in that way, because everyone thought Santos was crazy. They would have to put up with him only another year or so, however; Warren had overheard DeMattos saying they were getting ready to retire Santos. Warren wondered what would happen to the Filipino after that. . . .

The truck hit a bump and Henry Sakagawa's voice faded back in above the rumbling noise.

"Yeah, I know that guy long time ago. Used to cure pain with a needle—practiced acupuncture, you know? He come over here from Molokai back before statehood. Come into my place one day and say his name was Bluebell. Has to be same one. Has to be only one Bluebell from Molokai." He paused amid smiles. A couple of the older guys nodded their assent.

"He come in with his wife. *Big* wahine—three hundred pounds, at least. She had a big gallon jug of opihi in her arms. Hooo-*boy* that woman smelled bad! She say 'give him a haircut.' I was the barber then, you know. Anybody in Ewa cut hair in those days. We didn't have the electric clipper, just the hand clipper. . . ."

"Why didn't you just let Santos skin him with that big black knife?" Kelsey interrupted, grinning.

Henry glanced quickly at Santos, who sat up straight, glaring at Kelsey. Santos' eyes were hawklike. Kelsey seemed surprised by the confrontation, but regarded the old man steadily. Warren felt his stomach muscles tighten.

"The guy wanted to pay me with needles!" Henry pounded the

floor for emphasis. "Wanted to stick pins all over my leg! Said I feel better later." Yoshiro and a couple of others turned back around toward Henry and laughed uneasily.

"I tell him I feel better *now* when I get my money. . . ."

The truck shuddered to a stop in the dirt yard outside the Ewa Plantation Sugar Mill. The trailing cloud of dust swept over the passengers, choking off the rest of his words. When it had passed, Kelsey and half the crew had already dismounted, heading for the showers. Warren was the next to last to get off. Santos remained behind.

Warren didn't look back. He knew Santos would wait until everyone was out of sight.

One of the best things about Ewa Plantation was the shower at the end of the day. The water always soothed Warren while it rinsed away the incredible layer of grime compacted on his body from a day in the sugar fields. Only the younger workers who didn't live in Ewa used the mill showers; most of the men went home to their own small wooden-frame houses just a short walk from the mill.

As Warren emerged wet but refreshed, he saw several other workers gathered around a bench in the locker room. Kelsey, the reigning arm-wrestling champion, was straining against Yoshiro, who was about twenty pounds lighter.

"Hmmmph!" Kelsey snorted, and plunked his opponent's arm flat on the bench. There were scattered claps and a few dramatic hisses. Kenji shielded his eyes in mock amazement.

"And still champion!" Kelsey boasted, rubbing his arm. Sweat coated his skin, making the hard muscle shine. He tossed back his head and laughed. "Any of the rest of you wimps want to see what a man's grip feels like? How about you, Warren? Last chance!"

All eyes were on Warren as he dragged a towel across his own bulky arms and shoulders. He looked back at Kelsey and the others gathered around the bench. In his father's basement Warren had once bench-pressed two hundred fifty pounds. He figured he might be able to take Kelsey.

"I pass," he said and shoved the towel into his locker.

"All right, what about the rest of you panty-waists?" Kelsey grinned around the room triumphantly. "Well, what do you say, girls?"

When he had dressed, Warren headed for his blue Chevy Nova parked in the oil and grease-stained dirt lot next to the mill. He was about to climb in when DeMattos the *luna* came out of the mill:

"Your check will be ready tomorrow, Warren," he said, walking up to the Nova.

"Thanks."

"There's something else, though. The boss says we're going to hire some new guys full-time next month. Strictly unskilled labor. I wondered if you'd be interested."

Warren hesitated. This was a new thing. Summers had always ended on time before. "I don't know. I'm supposed to enroll at the UH in a couple of weeks."

"Well, think it over." DeMattos cocked his head. "If you want to stay on permanent, I think I can arrange it." He turned to leave.

"Well, thanks—oh, hey! There *is* one thing I wanted to ask you about." Warren's eyebrows wrinkled as DeMattos turned back around to face him. "Today, in the truck . . . I was wondering . . . what's going to happen to Santos when they retire him next year?"

DeMattos threw up his hands. "Who knows? Probably sit around his house and drink *La Copa* all day."

Warren pictured Santos sitting alone on the steps of his tiny iron-roofed house, watching from the shadows beneath the bright red and green branches of his flaming poinciana tree.

"Santos doesn't make sense," DeMattos went on. "Santos *pupule*. Ask Henry Sakagawa; he talks the best stories about Santos." He gestured toward the pudgy Japanese just emerging from under the huge gray sliding door of the mill garage.

"Thanks," Warren said as the *luna* turned to leave again.

"Henry!"

Warren watched him change direction in the middle of a step. "You got car trouble?" Henry asked, approaching the Nova.

"No, I just wanted to talk to you," Warren replied, leaning back against a fender. "DeMattos said you could tell me about Santos—what's going to happen to him next year, I mean."

Warren watched the older man hesitate a moment. Warren seldom asked questions like this, but he also had never seen Henry Sakagawa refuse to talk about anything. Warren felt a secret satisfaction as he watched the puzzlement in the older man's eyes quickly disappear.

"Nobody knows about Santos," the Japanese began, shaking his head. "Teofilo was here when I first come to Ewa back before the war. Not too many Filipino guys at Ewa back then, but everybody say to me, 'Stay away from that one, Henry. Stay away from Santos.' Used to be every Saturday night we watch Filipino guys get crazy drunk and get in the truck and go Wahiawa and bet on cockfights. But Santos don't like to socialize like that. Always stay home, except for one night when the fields too wet for work all week. 'Ey, too boring to stay at home and drink,' they say and they take Santos along that time—how, I don't know. That night there's one big fight in Wahiawa, and Lui Mendoza come back without his thumb."

Henry paused and ran his hand through stiff black hair streaked with gray.

"Santos should have got him a wife, you know? Then he could just sit back and watch the cane grow and get soft and fat like me!" Henry patted his stomach proudly.

Warren smiled.

"But Teofilo stay away from everybody most the time. You ever watch him cut down a field? Whack! Whack! Out there he's the master. Out there he can be proud. But next year he has to stay in town with old Masaru and Eduardo-guys. Sit around and wait for the check, you know? Who can say what Santos will do then? Maybe stay, maybe go someplace else—who knows?"

Henry looked off toward the green Waianea Mountains.

Both men were silent for a few moments. Then Warren looked directly into the older man's eyes.

"Do you think Santos is crazy?"

Henry looked away from Warren toward the rows of tiny wooden-frame houses spreading away from the mill.

He shrugged.

Warren took a last look, as he did every morning, at the blue stripe of the Pacific Ocean on the horizon just before he turned off the freeway, coasting down the ramp onto Highway Seventy-six into Ewa. He would not see the ocean again until evening; thousands of acres of sugar cane would block his view.

Highway Seventy-six was still hardly more than a paved cane-hauling road. Along most of it, the narrow strip of asphalt was flanked by twenty- and thirty-foot green walls of growing sugar plants. There was barely enough room for him to avoid the giant trucks that rumbled by.

Warren liked this road; it gave him a sense of place, a feeling for what the land here had always been. He'd never lived long enough in one spot to feel like he really knew it, so he looked for signs, place markers, wherever he went.

He leaned forward against the wheel as the Nova passed beneath an old wooden railway trestle left over from the days when the cane was always harvested by hand and the planters used tiny steam engines on narrow-gauge tracks to transport it to the mill. Ewa was like that, he thought. Old things out of place among the new. You could never tell what was going to last.

Warren stepped on the accelerator. He was late today, the first time all summer. He had overslept after lying in a fitful daze most of the night. He hadn't bothered to speak to his parents about DeMattos' offer to stay on. There was really no decision to make; as much as he liked Ewa, he certainly didn't want to make a career out of cutting cane. It was good for a summer, no more. It occurred to him that he wouldn't look forward to summer nearly as much after he took a year-round job. And he didn't want Ewa to become just another job.

The Nova's tires squealed as Warren turned onto the short connecting road into Ewa. The twin rust-colored smoke stacks of the sugar mill appeared over the green canopy of monkeypod trees ahead. Warren realized this was probably the last time he would ever see that sight. He began to develop that peculiar prickly feeling he always had on last days.

The men were already standing around the truck when Warren pulled into the dirt lot. He parked next to the mill, where Yoshiro was filling the five-gallon water jug with a hose.

"Better get your knife," he said as Warren got out. "Going to burn another field today and the tractor's still broke. Same crew."

Warren went into the long metal tool shed attached to the mill and picked up his machete. When he came out there was some commotion around the truck.

Kenji came running out of the crowd.

"Get DeMattos!" he shouted. "He's going to kill him!" He ran past Warren into the mill.

Warren looked back toward the truck instead. The crowd had parted around two figures facing each other. Santos was brandishing his machete at Kelsey, both edges of the black blade gleaming in the sun. Weaponless, Kelsey stood tense, towering above the Filipino. The crowd moved back, every eye on the two men.

Warren stood frozen by the shed.

"Teofilo!" Henry Sakagawa came running out of the mill. "Teofilo! Stop!"

He ran up just to the length of Santos' reach and halted.

"Teofilo, let him go! Tomorrow he's gone anyway!"

Santos continued to glare at Kelsey, who was watching the knife.

"Let him go, Teofilo!"

Santos glanced at Henry, then back at the younger man in front of him. Finally, he lowered the knife.

"What the hell's going on?" DeMattos shouted, rushing out of the mill with Kenji behind him. "All right, what is it?" His voice fell just a bit as he reached the truck and realized the emergency was over.

"Hell, I was just trying to apologize to the bastard!" Kelsey complained.

Warren didn't hear much of the rest of it, though it must have been a good thirty minutes before they all finally climbed into the truck. DeMattos was talking very quickly and threatening everyone before they got aboard. Then his voice fell and he spoke in soothing tones.

The ride to the fields was silent. Warren didn't watch the crew this time. He looked down at his own feet and thought about how different the last day had always been. He didn't want to remember Ewa this way.

When they reached the field, the cutters lined up along the edge as usual. But there were no jokes, no challenges this time as the runners set the field aflame and the acrid smell of the burning drifted back over them. The cutters remained silent.

Warren didn't see the whole line this time as he stood with the rest. Only Santos—down at the end, holding his machete with both hands and watching the fire intently.

For a few minutes, Warren just stared. Then he began to walk slowly toward the old man. They were all watching him—he knew it. They would single him out. It didn't matter now.

The Filipino turned sharply as he approached.

"This is my last day, Santos. I wanted to say goodbye." That was it. He turned to leave when Santos' voice stopped him.

"Better you work hard today. Maybe you finish first one time."

Warren turned back around, but the Filipino had already moved away, watching the fire devour the field.

Maybe you'll finish first. . . . Warren stood motionless as it sunk in. . . .

He absorbed it silently. The rhythm, the speed he thought was natural. . . . He looked at Santos standing there in his wide-brimmed straw hat, gripping his machete with both hands. The Filipino glanced quickly, almost imperceptibly, at the younger man, but Warren caught a tiny flicker in the old man's eyes as his clawlike hands tightened around the knife and pointed it very slowly toward the row of twisted cane before him.

It hit Warren. He was being challenged. For a moment he just stood there, watching the smoke curl up above the field. Then he shook his head slowly and returned to his place in line.

"What did he say?" Yoshiro, who was standing next to Warren, asked.

"Yeah, what did he say?" Kenji echoed. They began to gather around Warren now. The field would take a few more minutes to burn.

Warren hesitated, looking around at the faces.

"Nothing," he said finally.

"That figures. I never understand that guy," Kenji remarked, shaking his head.

"Yeah, Santos *pupule*," Yoshiro added.

Henry Sakagawa looked suspiciously at Warren, then shook his head. "Well, we going to cut cane or what?"

"Just stand back so you don't lose a leg, boys!" Kelsey boomed.

"Ha—just don't cut off your head!"

"Is that you I smell burning?"

Shouts sounded all along the edge of the smoldering field now as the line reformed. Someone slapped Warren on the back.

Warren just stood there for a moment, then looked over at Santos, watching the fire burn low. Warren could detect no movement at all in the old man now. He seemed fixed there, like the trestle across Highway Seventy-six.

Warren turned away. He listened to the shouts, the boasts and threats sounding along the edge of the field, and his mind slowly cleared. He took a deep breath.

"Let's get it!" Warren shouted suddenly and gripped his machete with both hands.

"Yeah, let's get it!"

"All right!"

The voices echoed all along the line.

Warren had no idea what would happen when he entered the field this last time. He didn't know what it would feel like, as he stood there watching the last clouds of gray-brown smoke swell up above the charred field.

But the smell was exhilarating—pungent, aromatic, and bitterly sweet.

THE QUALITY OF LIGHT IN MAINE

FRED PFEIL

Fred Pfeil was born in Port Allegany, Pennsylvania, in 1949; he now lives in Columbia, Missouri, where he is fiction writer-in-residence at Stephens College. Other stories have appeared in *The Minnesota Review, New Letters,* and various other literary magazines; presently he is at work on a novel set in the near future, featuring a professional friend.

It was spring in the end of the sixties; Scott, Annie, and the Narrator were driving from Amherst, Mass., to Old Orchard Beach in Maine. The morning was somewhat overcast, and the towns slid by more and more sullenly—gray New England factory towns, factory removed to Hong Kong. Yet the three companions were more or less unaffected by the scenery, these possible hints of the seventies outside the car. Classes were over at our schools; we were graduating in ten days. We were playing Botticelli with the funds of knowledge we had gained. It was a G, someone in the arts. We were getting near Lowell.

"Are you the famous Spanish painter?"

Scott laughed. From the back seat it looked to the Narrator as though he drove with a little less grace than he did almost everything else; his thin shoulders hunched forward, head set straight ahead, as if locked in the effort to will the car on. "You're trying to trap me," he said. "I need more."

"Famous Spanish religious painter."

"I'm not El Greco." His gray keen eyes never flickered. That was all the Narrator could tell in the mirror. Ahead of me Annie was tossing around in her seat; I could feel her restlessness.

"Is it a contemporary Polish playwright?" Her head jerked to the side, toward Scott. I could see the sharp lines of her profile,

brow slanting to straight small nose, rounded cheeks, skin tinged
with a kind of warm brown. "Five seconds," she said, raising
fingers, starting to grin.

"Not Grombrowicz," Scott said.

"The eighteenth-century composer of the opera *Orfeo?*" I said.

"No," Scott said, "not Gluck."

"Are you the author of *Elective Affinities?*" I said.

"I am not Goethe."

I waited a few seconds, looked out the window. Stunted countryside, gray grass, crust of billboards over everything, the only
bright colors BUY, SELL, HAVE A. Annie said nothing, but I could
sense the spreading of her discontent; so could Scott, I thought. I
waited another minute to see if he would say something to her or
touch her, hoping he would. We were almost to the North Shore
now, and the New Hampshire line.

"Are you the famous evil conservative nineteenth-century
French minister of state?"

"Under whom?"

"Louis Napoleon, I think."

Far off, the sky seemed to lighten: the ocean. The traffic grew
heavier; Scott leaned forward more. "All right, you got me."

I flopped back in my seat. "Guizot. What question should I
ask, Annie, what do you want to know?"

"Who cares?" she said, looking at Scott, not me, talking almost
in singsong. "Who cares about this boring game anyway? We'll
never get it. You're too smart for us."

She turned her head over the seat to me and grinned wide, her
face rounding and its heat moving over the seat until I was grinning too; but looking away, out the window at the Coppertone
girl and dog, giant-size. "I want to smoke some dope. You want to
smoke some dope, Marty?"

The billboard was past; I turned back and curled my lip at her,
mock-tough. "Could be. You want to smoke, Scott?"

Scott smiled: a long mouth, fine white teeth. His eyes were still
square on the road. "Good idea. Let's get stoned and listen to
some groovy tunes off this here new car radio of ours."

"Some boss music," Annie said.

"Gear, man," I said.

"Right arm," somebody said, we laughed, Annie rolled the
joint, we smoked it, heading north. Rain pellets struck the wind-

shield, and Scott told us it was Fulke Greville, seventeenth-century poet complete with a sonnet cycle starting with lust for his love, ending with vows to God. He quoted us some lines, they were nice, and then we were in Maine.

The Narrator is quite stoned by the time they pull the car off the short gravel street; he is not much used to getting stoned in daylight, and their two voices from the front seat, gestures moving out of the car, lugging tote bags, seem invested with an oblique magic he does not understand. His own movements are heavy, books loose in his hands, one topples to the needlestrewn ground of the front yard: *Beethoven: His Spiritual Development.* The needles, brown, thin, half-rotten, drop from the larches nestling the darker brown-shingled cottage and dripping the morning's cold rain.

Annie and Scott were in the kitchen out back. She was putting the groceries in the fridge, on the white wooden shelves, while he bent over the old stove striking up pilot lights. I must have stood in the doorway and looked at them, stoned, arms full of books and my decrepit gym bag, for a full minute.

"Just dump your stuff," she said, and I spilled it over the yellow linoleum table where their bags sat. "We've got to get this place cleaned and opened up before anything else." She liked giving orders; they gave her voice a hard but not unpleasant edge, her mouth and brow a small scowl. "There's a broom by the back door, you can take it and sweep the needles off the porch while you"—her eyes flicked Scott leaning against the stove—"start the pump."

Then he is alone again: the Narrator, narrating to himself. His feet in moccasins pad over the needles, the gray chipping paint of the porch. Between the broom's scratches he can hear the soft sound of the water still falling from the trees on the porch roof and, more crisply, on the ground outside. He can hear soft talk of birds in the woods across the street, a film of dull green through the screens. He is still stoned enough to wonder how the needles, so many of them, get through; then he sees the slit, perhaps two inches high, that runs from beam to beam around the porch. Air moves cool across his fingers when he puts his hand down: for extra coolness in the summertime? He tries to place a set of parents, Scott's, whom he has never met, upon the red porch swing.

It is a humid night in July, bugs tap the screens. Scott, his face already complete, carved out, plays on the floor: a game of chess. Birds shout from the woods. He places Scott and Annie on the swing, slowly rocking. What are they talking about, are they kissing, do they kiss with any heat? Annie stands before him in the kitchen, between him and the refrigerator, with a Gioconda smile: she crosses her arms around her waist, brown arms, and lifts and peels the black turtleneck off: her round breasts appear, move toward him. Off in the woods the birds coo. He is very happy; here, at this time of his life, in Maine, in this house of Scott's unknown family, with Annie and Scott, life seems to have the potential to be a work of art.

Minneapolis, in the seventies, a hot day in June. Scott and Annie's apartment is so near the Pillsbury plant that the air on the street outside clouds with the sweet, choking scent of grains, a smell of glut. We walk down the old sidewalk, shrouded by elms, and Annie talks.

"I met him through some friends, people I have classes with at the university. There was a party, Scott didn't want to go—no, he had to work that night, that's right."

She pauses; and I am aware of her masked face under the speckles of sweet green light, held still as a small hunting or hunted animal's. I think: she has caught herself trying to blame Scott.

She smiles and tosses her head; her eyes glance to the side at me. "I danced with him a few times, talked to him some, even met his wife at one point. He told me about his life. It was an amazing story. Do you know he started out with nothing? His parents are dirt farmers in Oklahoma. He ran away when he was sixteen with this woman he married, and went to L.A. to learn film."

"No," I say, with a smile I hope shows precise amounts of sympathy and ironic wisdom. "No, I don't know that." Then, with apparent casualness, watching her closely: "Do you love him?"

She frowns; her brown eyes flatten and lose their light, as though struggling over a sum. "Maybe I do." Then she grabs my bare arm and, while the shudder thrills up it, down my back, sending my gaze away from her face down to her leather sandals: "Oh, Marty, *you* know what it's like when it starts though, the way you want to be in bed with them all the time and talk and eat with them and you can't get them out of your head. Is that love? I don't know. But that's how it is."

"I don't know either," I say, "but I know what you mean." And so I do, but not so well or often as she thinks. I understand her fantasies of me as Don Juan, her fictions on the subject of my life in California, when I am not with them: the life a part of herself would have. My own opinion of my few affairs is that they are modest, scrupulously limited, and a little tired; though there are many reasons why I would just as soon Annie never found that opinion out. "How is Scott taking all this?" I say.

We have broken out into a sunlight so dense it dulls the green of the park to our left and burns my eyes. "Scott," she says, as if his name were itself a statement, and turns and plops down on the browning grass. Against the ground and in this light, the blacks, blues, purples of her batiked shift smear further and seem to bleed her back into the lawn. "Well, he's doing just what you'd expect. When I told him about it, he cried a little but not for very long. Then he asked me if I wanted a divorce."

"Do you?" I say, easing down next to her. Already sweat sticks my white T-shirt to my back, lies on my arms and hands like a thin paste.

"No," she says and bites her lip before starting again. "Anyway, he told me that he loved me. And that if this was what I wanted, he wanted it for me too. And now he's just the same"—she turns her head to me, her open, hungry face—"I mean, you've been with him the last few days, isn't he just the same?"

I try to see through the heat Scott's face during the last two days of my visit, his movements through the shady apartment, his talk. "I don't know," I say, watching my hands grope to say it for me, "maybe I'm projecting. But when I think about it, he doesn't seem to"—the fingers try to shape something, I smile lamely— "well, *move* the same way. I mean, he leans back into chairs, he talks slower. The other day, he was telling me something about Pound, what it was like reading the *Cantos*—"

"Oh yeah, Pound," she says tonelessly, her face hidden downward.

"Yeah, right," I say; but the image of the lean face startled, haggard, figure sagged into the beanbag chair, hands fumbling like mine now is too strong. "Still, the thing is, it was like he forgot what he was saying, he had put it on automatic pilot without even knowing it and it ran out on him. And I've never seen Scott at a loss before."

Even through the heat, we both can feel the same image of him hanging, floating: Scott, different from us. Scott like a deer.

Then Annie looks earthward again. "Sometimes, even when we were first going together I used to think, 'He's so smart but he doesn't know anything. Nothing's ever happened to him.'" Out of the corner of my eye, like a distortion from the heat, I can see the twist of her mouth. "Well, now something has, but he doesn't want to admit it. Doesn't want to admit he's mad or he wants me, or it hurts him, doesn't want to fight for me at all, no, he's too good for that. Then, when we do sleep together?"

She hesitates; does she want to tell me this, is she a bitch? And me, do I want to see it, her rich body listless on the sheets, some shame spreading from him, old lust fogging my eyes like heat? "Yes?" I say. "Yes, what?"

Her fingers make claws held out in the sun. "He clutches. The way he clutches and holds on so to me."

Then her face is turned up and open, sweat dotting her forehead too, set lips like rage, sun glaring the face as bright as in my sweaty dreams and "You know me," she is saying almost fiercely, "you and I, we know each other, we're alike, that's why I love you so much. You know he *has* to be mad somewhere, but he won't show it. Tell him he is. Get it out of him. It can't go on like this, he's got to get it out."

Her hot eyes close to mine as any lover's, the sick scent of the grain as if from her breath on my face, and sweat breaking finally down my brow and cheeks: "Okay," I say, "I'll try. If you think it'll do him some good."

"So do you," she whispers, almost hissing.

"Yeah, right," I say, getting up. "So do I."

On the way back to the apartment, then, we talk about our fathers; hers still scratching out a living on a Pennsylvania farm, mine still trying to be happy as a foreman at the tire plant back in Akron. We laugh at and feel miserable about them at the same time, and for a moment neither one of us is thinking about Scott. She's right, of course; we are alike. But even in the shade now, the heat seems unbearable.

They walk, the three of them, through the town of Old Orchard, two blocks on their way to the beach, deserted as a stage set. A stage set, thinks the Narrator, passing the brown little bank, church of weathered white clapboards, neat green of the tiny square: as if there were nothing behind these fronts so clean in their particularity, as if you could poke through them, push them over. But he is too stoned to understand this as a function of the quality of light in Maine; and besides, Scott is pointing and talking, his face stamped out clean against the sky. "Here's where I work in the summer," he says, waving his hand to the left.

I look at the stores, the green, the two tennis courts, the flag-pole. "Where?"

"The courts," Annie says softly, and winds her arm around Scott's waist, moving against him. "Scott's the Old Orchard tennis pro, gives lessons and everything."

"Slight misrepresentation," he says, grinning at both of us. "This was back in high school. And I had to sweep the courts down after rain and mend the nets. You don't have to be Rod Laver to be the Old Orchard tennis pro."

A few steps more and the giggles rise like someone else's pumped into my mouth. They start to laugh too. "What's funny?" one of them says.

"A minute ago, when you said there's where you worked?" I say, gasping it out. "I was looking around the place, looking for where it could be. I was looking for some kind of plant." And they both laugh harder too.

Then the sidewalk becomes planks set in the dunes and they run out and we are on the beach for the first time. The sky is still overcast and it is cold. The goddamn Atlantic Ocean, thinks the Narrator, it really is slate-gray. While he has been watching it, the other two have moved away, farther down, and now he turns to watch them: the young man in his orange trunks, woman in her lime two-piece. They are settling their blanket. They are putting their books, their radio on it. They are holding and kissing each other against the sky while gulls wheel overhead, everything in a tight, perfect composition of Lovers, Sea, Sky he will not disturb until it breaks, they break apart. Then he goes running over the beach to them without taking off his sneakers, so that they fill up quickly with gritty wet sand.

"You know what?" he says when he gets there. "This goddamn sea really is slate-gray. This is the slate-gray sea."

"Klutz," Annie says, scowling, shaking her head. "You got sand all over the blanket, good Christ."

"But it is also," Scott says, lifting a finger, "wine-dark."

"And froth-chained," I say, pointing back.

"Yet leaden," he says with a long horsey face.

"Incessant," I say, "yet somehow—imperturbable."

Annie is belly down on the blanket already, her halter strap unhitched, the radio on. "Primeval," she mutters. "The cradle of life. Why don't you two hacks run along? Go swimming, see if that gives you any new clichés."

The Narrator watches Scott bend down and move his hand over Annie's bare brown back. The Narrator notes that the hair of Scott's head and body, quivering slightly in the breeze, is the same color as the sand. "Warm down here," Scott says, "you're under the wind." The Narrator watches Annie stir under Scott's hand. "Yes," Annie says. "Don't fall asleep or forget to roll over," Scott says. "Cloudy days up here, people get burned before they know it." "I know," she says. "I've sunbathed before, I'll be fine."

Scott rises. As a backdrop, behind the faunlike face, the Narrator finds a chain of cliffs stretching off to the south. And the quality of light in Maine is such that their distance from him makes itself known only by spatial perspective; for the jagged shape of the farthest cliff stands as clear as the one that is only a hundred yards away.

When Scott gets off his shift I pick him up at the hospital and take him to a bar. While I ply him first with pitchers of beer, then with manhattans, Irish whiskey, Old Grand-Dads to crack him apart, he sits across a wooden table still in his orderly's smock, and tells me funny stories about his work.

"Then there's Callahan, another old-timer," he says, eyes gleaming, head starting to weave. "The nurses told me he was crazy, you had to watch for him. Nobody ever knew what he was talking about. I couldn't either at first, but I liked it. He spun out these strings of incredible images, one after another, and they didn't make the least bit of rational, linear sense. Then"—he opens his hands on the table, leans forward his thin, smiling face—"I realized that he was talking poetry. He had gotten tired of ordinary discourse, he made metaphor instead. When he was going to get a barium treatment, he'd say he wanted a pearl-handled revolver with a silver bullet in it, he was going to shoot his stomach from his mouth. See what I mean?"

Then, again, the moment: his eyes flee mine, he looks up as if someone had called to him and his face collapses into shadows. It is just a second, but enough; it is time now. "Let me think," he says, "what were some other ones?"

I raise a hand from the table and prop my forehead with it and make myself look straight at him. "Annie told me today she has a lover."

He smiles in a thin-lipped way that, in my own drunkenness perhaps, could be almost, almost taken as snide; then it breaks genuine, generous, soft. "Yes, I know," he says.

"I know you do," I say. "She told me that too." And now I have my arms out on the table, palms up, and am leaning toward the floating wooden face, darkened eyes. "Scott," I say, "I'm not trying to hurt you or taunt you or anything. I just want to know what you're doing about it and how you feel."

The caving in of his cheeks, twist in his lips are definite now; though I am too drunk to know exactly how it makes me feel. Now it's going to come out, I think, he'll purge himself. And also I think: you dirty shithead, you're hunting the deer.

"I'm doing nothing about it," he says very neutrally. "I want her to be able to do anything she wants. What she wants right now makes me sad. I don't feel very good about it. But it's what she wants to do. And besides," he says with the same lack of any tone, "I still have a decent life. The job is all right, I only have a year to go before the C-O's done and I can go back to school. I have my books, I even have Annie most of the time, you know. She still spends more time with me than with him."

This last without the slightest trace of pride or boastfulness; without the slightest trace of anything. He picks up his glass and drinks from it as if washing down his throat after a speech delivered too many times. Just to Annie, or himself too? I wonder, and cannot find the end of the thought for the rush of feelings in me, the same she must have when he tells her the same damn thing. "Goddamn it, Scott," I say, bringing my fist down on the table, grateful for the cover of the alcohol, "but goddamn it, don't you ever get mad? Don't you ever want to kick the guy's face in? Or hers?"

He smiles; a smile that turns his face radiant, as if with gentle victory. "I'll tell you something that may sound silly to you, but it's true. When I was very small—eight, maybe—I decided I was never going to be angry again. Anger never seemed to solve anything, I could never control it, and it was unpleasant. Then, later, I thought of another reason; people should always be able to do what they want, especially the people you love." He stood up then, his white coat bright and clean in the bar's dark, like a cassock, like an icon of some damn saint. "Now maybe we better go home," he said, smiling. "I've got to work tomorrow. Here, let me help you pay for some of this."

But by the time we are in the car and on our way home, my mind is flooded again with an image too much stronger than his thin, studied composure, his smile in the bar and now; the picture of him covered with sweat and tears, clinging to Annie's body in the middle of these humid Minnesota nights.

The Narrator is in Maine, seated on one end of an old leather couch, its brown slick surface webbed with tiny cracks. The Narrator is reading *Beethoven: His Spiritual Development* by J. W. N. Sullivan, the chapter on Art and Reality. He reads: "It is characteristic of the greatest art that the attitude it communicates to us is felt by us to be valid, to be the reaction to a more subtle and comprehensive contact with reality than we can normally make." He has read this sentence three times slowly, trying to decide if it is stupid or if it makes a sense beyond what he can know. But he cannot decide.

He looks up. Though it is night and the lamps glow orange off the pine walls, there is still an almost crystal quality about the scene: Annie curled up at the other end of the couch, frowning over *Washington Square*, Scott in the stuffed chair across from him, focused effortlessly on Wallace Stevens. "Stop," the Narrator says.

They look up, their reading expressions still on. "What's the last sentence you read?"

Scott says: "The ever-hooded, tragic-gestured sea was merely the place by which she chose to sing."

Annie says: "Love demands certain things as a right; but Catherine had no sense of her rights; she had only a consciousness of immense and unexpected favors." She fidgets and frowns. "My back is driving me crazy. Will you rub some Noxema on it for me?"

"Sure," I say.

When she is down on the brown and green braided rug, in sunbathing position, blue blouse rolled up over the slightly pink skin, and I am astraddle her ass, dipping fingers into the cool white paste, Scott looks up from his book again and says: "Why'd you ask?"

Off the fingers, onto the firm flesh, the paste warms, becomes cream. "Ahhh," Annie sighs; it is hard to be the Narrator, detach myself from this warmth, rubbing, watch her and answer Scott myself at the same time. "I don't know," I say as the Narrator smooths over the rise of scapulae, softness at the edge of the shoulder, reddening brown. "I was reading this sentence about art, what it can do, and thinking about all of us sitting around reading art. And I wondered"—rubbing the sheen into the flesh until it disappears, she keeps moaning softly Oh that's good, the Narrator listens to her—"I've had this funny sense ever since we got here, and maybe before, ever since, you know, we've been friends"— feeling silly saying it, while the Narrator watches the fingers stroke the slippery ridge of spine, pressing for bone Oh that's nice please don't stop—"that everything's fitted together in some very clean way, if you can just see it that way. So the thing about the quotes just now was a kind of a test."

"God, that's wonderful," Annie murmurs. "You've got a genius pair of hands." The Narrator watches hands move in wide circles, press the hot skin.

"And did they fit with your quote?" Scott says.

"I'm not sure. Maybe so. And remember anyway, I said if you can see it that way."

"And even if you could," Scott says, smiling slightly, enjoying himself, "who could tell if that was art or life?"

The Narrator stopped moving, stopped watching; I looked very closely at Scott. "Which is it for you?"

"Either," he says, grinning wide and friendly. "Both. I'm reading Wallace Stevens."

"Stop talking," Annie said. "Frost said Stevens wrote on bric-a-brac and Frost was right. All just surfaces. Rub me."

And I did. I rubbed cool cream into her broad firm back until I could no longer be the Narrator watching it or even fully myself, even the weightless ache of my loins somewhere behind, all that was happening that melting touch of hands and skin, that smooth slick pressure. While Scott read on in his Wallace Stevens the only sound was from her an occasional murmur or groan, the light thickened to golden heat, until I was rubbing the very skin of her back off in tiny curds my motion rolled into small balls on her smooth back when she said: "Oh, that was so nice. I know I'll sleep just great now. Coming, Scott?"

It was hard to remember that moment clearly, or to fit it in later on, while I took off my clothes in Scott's brother's room upstairs, where the wood was darker and the air was cool. On a shelf across from the bed were swimming ribbons, tennis awards, and some books: *Lost Horizon*, *The Yearling*, *Wild Animals I Have Known*. There were no pictures of the boy; so it was easy for me to imagine, for a long moment on the edge of sleep, growing up myself that way, the way of Scott and Scott's brother, summering in Maine and learning tennis and swimming and reading the right books for a thirteen year old, learning a life as clean and cool, as composed as the air and light in Maine: being Scott's brother. As I thought of these things, my groin stopped aching, and I fell asleep.

After that visit, I went back to California; but Scott and I kept in touch with letters. His told me of his reading, the weather, his job, with an occasional reference to Annie and her lover, who were fine. For a while, the three of them moved in a house together, close to the river, with a beautiful view, Scott said.

But when the C-O ended, Scott wrote to say the two of them had said goodbye to the film editor and were moving to Cambridge, where he'd been accepted into Harvard's Ph.D. program; again, I could detect no malice or triumph between the lines. After that, our letters passed less frequently. His became less witty and less careful, trains of mild observations on classes and books. I wondered whether graduate school had ground his edges down; I wondered what psychic price he had to pay to win Annie back with exemplary behavior, and what price she had had to pay to lose. But she never wrote.

Six months ago I saw them again. I had finally got an agent, the agent had sold a story, and Scott had just accepted a job offer from Wesleyan; when I scraped up enough money to go see my agent in the flesh, we made plans to meet in New York. They knew a little bar, thought it was still there, in the East Village . . .

New York jars me. Downtown, near my agent's office, there are too many people with too much money, dressed like the ads in the *Times* Sunday Magazine and moving very quickly to get more, stay ahead, not get caught up in the random movements of the shabby desperadoes and wrecks they share the sidewalks with. My agent spoke despairingly of my lack of commercial sense; I was writing about the wrong people, she said. What with all this, the pigeons screaming doomed traffic reports, and a gray drizzle in the air, I knew I would not be seeing Scott and Annie with a very clear head. Besides, I had given up being a Narrator as a bad habit long ago.

The bar was tubular chrome, red vinyl, junior executive types, male and female, loudly displaying their charms. Scott and Annie have to come up and tap my arm. "Marty."

I turn and hug them before looking. Scott's body is still lean. Annie's feels softer, rounder; I feel no ache.

"Let's go sit down," Scott says, turning away. "Then you tell us how you broke into the Big Apple today."

While I make a story out of my agent's dire innuendoes, I look them over. My sense of touch was correct. Scott has grown a full, sandy mustache, though, and his face is narrower than ever: almost a ferret's now. And though Annie's figure in the green caftan does seem fleshed out, her brown eyes are harder than I remembered them. Then again, though, maybe it's just this place. "But you're the ones who've made it," I say as soon as I can. "What's with you? Tell me about the job."

"It's two classes a semester," Scott says while Annie leans forward, watching him, stroking her glass. "One Freshman Comp, one Survey English Lit, one Victorian Novel, and a graduate seminar in Victorian Studies."

"It's a beautiful job," Annie says, looking straight at me. "Nobody gets English jobs like this one any more. Four classes a year and tenure-track."

Scott glances at her and starts a smile that wavers on his face.

His eyes seem to lose their focus. "That's great," I say. "And your dissertation's in?"

His eyes snap back, but not quite; as if they look only inward, into himself. "And approved," he says and starts to pick with one hand at the cuff of his powder-gray suit. "But there's still something I don't like about it. It's not clear enough, it doesn't say exactly what I mean. What I was trying to do is make a case for a non-dramatic reading of Ruskin's aesthetics." He keeps on picking at the imaginary lint, he is not looking at me any more, and his words are coming rather fast. "You see, the way I think Ruskin must be read is with all his historicizing stripped, the story element, all the bombast peeled off, and only then can we see the clear, simple airy structure of the aesthetic itself. See Marty," he says, "I think—"

"It's a great dissertation," Annie says and backs fingers through her brown shagged hair. "His judges all told him it was publishable. One of Scott's professors has already sent it on to a press, with his recommendation attached."

"I'm sure it's all right," I say. "Scott, you've always been able to say exactly what you mean."

Scott smiles out of the side of his mouth, Annie fiddles with her glass, I chew my cherry. Nothing seems really terribly wrong. "So," I say, "when are you moving?"

"Next month," says Annie, with a trace of her old frown. "We're getting a place in a new development on the edge of town. It's two-story, brick, sort of colonial, right up next to the woods. We'll lease with an option to buy. You'll really have to come and see us more often, now that we're finally going to be in one place."

I picture the house a moment—almost like the old Narrator— then delete it. "That'd be nice," I say. "I'll try. But I really don't have much more money than I ever did."

"Why do you live in California anyway?" Scott says, tipping his head and leaning close to me, breathing a bitter smell. His stomach must be eating him alive. "We miss you, old friend. Why don't you come up to Cambridge right now and spend a few days?"

"I can't," I say. "I'd love to but I can't. The money's too tight. I have to be back day after tomorrow punching the clock at RayChem in Redwood City, CA."

Scott's mouth twists in a funny way, a way I have never seen before. "You can get jobs like that here too that'll keep you in touch with those people you write about," he says.

Those people. I think about what my agent has just told me; about the people I work with; the people I have lived with since I was born, except for my college days. "Those people," I say, looking back at him as neutrally as I can.

Scott rubs his nose and looks down at the table. "Well, we do miss you, don't we Annie?" he says, and pats her hand.

"Yes," she says, staring hard at me, "we do."

A minute later he excuses himself to go to the bathroom and I am left alone with Annie, still watching me sullenly. Her face *is* rounder, fuller though—

"Hey," I say suddenly, lunging forward in the chair, "are you pregnant?"

She smiles politely, reaches for her drink. "About three months," she says. "How'd you know?"

"Just something about you," I say; and can't help smiling. "You look filled out. But how do you feel about it? Are you glad?"

"It was planned," she says. "I'm glad."

"You two must be happy together then," I say.

She shrugs. "I suppose."

It makes me mad. She's pushed him, I think, she's molded him, she had kept him as her lover all along and she doesn't have the decency to be pleased. "Listen," I say, keeping my face quite still. "Did you get what you wanted from him out of that affair? Are you satisfied now?"

Her eyes narrow, lips press tight. "I don't know what you mean," she says and turns, and almost whispers: "Here he comes."

I turn my head too, and watch him moving through the thick expensive crowd, his gaze directed myopically to the match and the bowl of his briar pipe. He lights and puffs blue clouds of smoke: a few other people look on after him; and I watch Annie watching him with her own sour, defeated face.

The rest of the time we spent in Maine passed in the way I have described to you. But there is one incident I remember out of that time that stays so sharply in my mind that I am not sure if it happened or if I dreamed it. And if I dreamed, whether I dreamed it then or later on.

It is very simple, really. I was walking along the edge of the deserted beach at Old Orchard, close to the dunes. A crisp steady wind blew into me, filling my ears with a low roar. I passed a pocket in the sand dunes, and knew Scott and Annie were there. I turned and walked up into the dunes, at the edge of the pocket; and there they were, lying together on a bright striped towel. They lay on their bellies, completely still; he in his orange trunks, she in her lime two-piece, their beautiful faces close together, completely still, completely clear. The two of them together filled the space that framed them; and the quality of light in Maine that makes the surfaces of things so clean and complete, illumined them completely and made them both, on that towel and in that pocket of sand, a work of art.

I have walked into a work of art, I thought; and the thought both thrilled and frightened me so much that I stepped out of the dunes and turned back up the beach. But when I repassed that pocket they were awake, alive, standing up. Annie beating the sand off the towel with hard, slapping motions, her face swollen and angry; Scott squinting vaguely off at the darkening sky; the wind gone and, ahead of me, light falling dully on the sand that stretched off into haze.

THE PASSION OF MARCO Z——

ANNE LEATON

Anne Leaton was born in Texas, educated there and in Italy,
Vienna, and Berlin (on a Fulbright scholarship). She writes
stories and radioplays: the former have been published in
Esquire, the *Transatlantic Review*, and elsewhere; the latter
are produced by the BBC and U. S. National Public Radio.
She makes her home in Fort Worth, Texas.

"I think it's a lousy title," Janet said. "Where's the passion?"

"You simply don't understand," Edward said. "Passion doesn't
have to refer to jumping into bed with this or that person, as you
seem to construe. Marco's is intellectual passion, about which you
obviously know nothing."

"I know about intellectual passion," she said. "I knew somebody once who suffered from that."

"The hell you did," Edward said.

"George Wade. In Albuquerque."

"George Wade," he said, "was obsessed with Indian rugs. That
doesn't constitute intellectual passion, not by a long shot."

"He studied patterns. He could talk for hours about patterns.
He chased weavings the way some men chase blondes," Janet said.

"You just don't get it," Edward said.

"You ought to master A before you go on to W," Janet said.
"That's just common sense. This Marco guy is a eunuch. If what
he's got is passion, I'd hate to see a dead goose."

Edward felt faint with deprivation. For three years he had devoted himself to Marco Z——'s passion. He knew every wart in
Marco's delicate skull. When acquaintances asked, "and what do
you do for kicks?"—Edward smiled wearily, remembering the in-
tensity of ratiocination. He had 120 perfectly typed pages attest-

ing to the vigor of perception. To have married in a fit of error a woman who could not understand the subtlety of his exploration made him feel as isolate as a bear on an ice floe. What remedy could there be?

I was distracted, he explained to himself, by the demands of Marco Z——'s lucubrations, machinations and concatenations. My eye was wholly fixed then as now upon that singular behavior (is anything less required of the artist?). It was not surprising to him that he had failed to see Janet Staines in the fullness of her inadequacy. The wonder was he had noticed her at all.

Maybe, he said to himself, it will all work out, in the end.

"I see no reason for you to come home roaring drunk from the cantina," he said. "What is the reason for this excess?"

"I've always been a heavy drinker," Janet said. "My father's liver was cirrhosed before he was forty."

"Are you saying that drunkenness is hereditary?"

"He set me a good example," she said. "I don't like living alone on the Southern Anatolian seashore. I might as well be in Albuquerque. You knew about my father. You also knew about my mother, before you married me. You also knew chances were good I wouldn't like drawing water from a village well, in the company of women speaking an unknown tongue."

"Can't you learn a little Turkish?" he said. "Are you of such feeble intelligence that you cannot learn to say, that is my bucket you have there, in Turkish?"

"Why should I learn?" she said. "Someday I'll go back to Albuquerque. In Albuquerque the water runs out of a spigot in the wall."

He shook his head, defeated.

"You knew my mother was a person of easy virtue . . . I told you my father chased little girls, with gin on his breath . . . what made you think I could learn Turkish . . . ?"

"We'll work it out," he said, returning to Marco Z——.

How could he have been expected to perceive, in the early days (he asked himself while sharpening his pencils with a very fine penknife), that Janet Staines was neurotic? That she drank whiskey before breakfast? That she neither liked to draw water, nor to poach fish, nor to scrub tile floors from a kneeling position? That travel beyond the suburbs of Albuquerque was anathema? She might have been more explicit in her confessions. After all, she knew there was Marco Z——. The thing to do now was to hope for the best. The 120 typed pages had grown to 150.

Their sexual relationship was reasonably good, Edward thought one afternoon, as he rested between pyrotechnic chapters. He liked to make love about twice a week, preferably after a light supper. He didn't care for the more experimental aspects of the encounter. He thought there was very little that couldn't be satisfactorily expressed in the traditional postures. In his personal life (he smiled knowledgeably), he was a conservative; in Marco Z——, he was an icon-smasher, an idiosyncrast, an adumbrator of things to come. One should discriminate baby from bathwater, before opening the window to hurl something-or-other out.

"How can you join," he asked, "an amateur theatrical group in a country the language of which you speak not a word?"

"It's in Adebei, at the airbase," Janet said, looking slightly glazed. "They're English. We're doing *Death of a Salesman*."

He cleaned the keys of his Smith-Corona. "Well, it's the best of Miller," he said. "How will you get to Adebei?"

"On the People's Bus. Twice a week. We open in May."

"I'm glad you've found something to occupy yourself with," he said, digging sludge out of the E with a pin. "Who'll draw the water while you're away? Who'll poach the fish?"

"The pot is not my province," she said thickly. "I've never wanted to cook anything but fried tomatoes. I don't suppose you've noticed how often fried tomatoes are served here?"

"I've noticed," he said, replacing the top of the Smith-Corona. "I thought it would resolve itself, in time."

"It's probably because my father never drew a sober breath except for the sake of eating a fried tomato."

"I don't see what your father's got to do with it."

She wept, clutching a tomato not yet fried. Edward sighed with irritation. How had this happened? She was to have led distractions away from his door, as the Pied Piper fluted away the rats. As it was, she had sold out to the rats.

"Who is this man?" Edward said, flexing his tired fingers as he entered the sitting room in response to the random giggles and clinking of glasses he heard there, late one night.

"This is Reginald," Janet said, rising unsteadily from the carpet-swathed divan. "Reginald is a theatrical friend of mine."

"How'd you do . . ." Reginald said, prone.

"Theatrical?" Edward said, massaging his fingers.

"The Adebei Art Players?" Reginald said. "I believe you know of us. Your wife here's the crackerjack of our little group."

"You don't say," Edward said. "Are you rehearsing?"

"Rehearsing?" Reginald said.

"I gather Janet's playing the mother," Edward said. "I was trying to recall the scene in the play where the mother comforts one of the sons. I didn't remember it looking so incestuous."

"The mother?" Reginald said.

"We're doing *Streetcar Named Desire*," Janet said, refilling her glass. "I play Stella."

"She's a crackerjack Stella," Reginald said, patting Janet on the cheek. "I suppose I should be off. Getting late . . ."

"Playing Stella?" Edward said, cracking his knuckles to relax them. "What happened to *Death of a Salesman*?"

"It was too depressing," Janet said, seeing Reginald to the door. "I'll just be a minute."

Edward thought about drinking a little wine, to soothe his nerves, but he decided it wasn't worth the risk of a thick unproductive head the following day. He had to remain vigilant in these critical stages: Marco Z——'s passion had risen to its zenith. He sighed and crept up the ladder to his bed. Towards morning he thought he heard Janet come in. He supposed it was Janet. Someone, a female, was singing "The White Cliffs of Dover." He turned over again, to sleep.

"Little is asked of you, but you seem unable . . ." he began.

"You knew about my ginny father, my easy-virtued mother, when you married me."

Had she told him? She had talked a great deal in Albuquerque. But of course there was always the counterpointed monologue of Marco Z——, buzzing blissfully in his head. Perhaps she had spoken of the perpetual pursuit of the little girls by the gin-soaked father through the back streets of the city . . . But in the great ninth wave of female saying, who could discern a trickle here, a rivulet there? If only semaphores could be flung up to draw attention to some telling detail! Should he ask her, now, how easy was the virtue of her mother?

"I'm going away for the weekend," she said, swaying a little in the doorway.

Edward stiffened at his Smith-Corona. "This is very unwifely behavior."

"I know," she said, sadly. "But it's me, it's me. Didn't I tell you about my passion for fried tomatoes, my boozy father lurching after pigtails, my—"

"What has that got to do with your present unwifely behavior?"

She considered. "I wish I could get to the bottom of that. Maybe you could help. You're very clever sometimes."

He sighed again. The wish that she could understand the exigencies of his life passed through his head, as he listened to her footsteps leaving his house.

"I just don't understand how this happened," Edward said, to the Turkish official—caparisoned like a parade horse—who had caused him to be summoned to the Adebei Hospital and now stood next to him like a bright fiction in the gray foyer.

Parade Horse offered Edward a gold-tipped oval cigarette, which he took, to soothe his nerves. "The woman," he said, "drinks graceless the liquor. Allah alone know the reason to this."

Edward flopped down exhausted on a gray bench in the gray foyer. The drive to Adebei with a monolingual constable had been arduous. "Where is the doctor?" he said.

"Worry not," Parade Horse assured him. "Your spouse remain. There is the one arm only who dangle."

"Dangles?" Edward said. "Dangles?"

The doctor, when he appeared, said (through the graceful interpretation of Parade Horse) that the dangling arm dangled in fact because it was broken, at the shoulder. The other victim plucked from the inferno of the small Fiat which had pitched over a cliff near Adebei was in much more lamentable shape. "A man name Reginald Baldsworth," Parade Horse offered. "He, regrettable, remain not."

"What in hell were they doing in a Fiat, near a cliff!" Edward said.

Parade Horse cleared his throat noisily and looked knowingly at the doctor. The doctor put both hands into the large front pockets of his dingy white coat and left, discreetly. Parade Horse said: "While was take place some regrettable festivities in the Fiat—this little car is very small for do such regrettables, a foot unknown to us alas, maybe she foot, maybe he foot—ruin the brake and this little car progress over cliff. No person see this progress alas. Praise Allah, is very small cliff only. If she runned Fiat over close by cliff of my acquaintance, your spouse is be small stain only."

Edward felt dizzy. Nausea grew in him like mushrooms after rain. How long had she been away? "How long has she been here?" he asked Parade Horse.

"Since two weeks, I hear it say. She was be since two weeks by the Adebei Palas."

"My God," Edward said.

Parade Horse nodded piously. "Yes . . . thank the God, your spouse dangle only."

"I don't know what to do about her," he said, to Tom Barnes, an old friend on his first visit to Southern Anatolia. "I just despair of the situation."

Tom Barnes shook his head, closing his eyes a little in sympathy. He rotated the raki in his glass. The two men were sitting in one of the village's two earth-colored men's coffee houses. Three other men sat in a distant corner, playing a dice game and surreptitiously watching the two strangers in their tweed jackets and thick brogans. "It's a very difficult situation," Tom said. "I can see that. You certainly can't just go on as usual."

Edward grimaced. "I've done all I can," he said. "I can do no more."

"Perfectly natural," Tom Barnes said. "A woman like Janet—I mean, whatever a man does is the wrong thing, isn't it?"

"I simply can't *depend* on her for anything," Edward said. "Except the drinking. And the incoherence. And now of course it's come to this . . . running around with . . ." Edward couldn't go on.

Tom Barnes sighed. "Well, Edward, it's just as well this happened as it did, that's what I think. Just as well you found out the whole truth of the matter."

"I suppose so," Edward said.

"No one could blame you for getting out, you know. After all, you can't go on like this. You're getting nowhere, are you? How's the book coming along, by the way?"

"I would have finished this month, if it hadn't been for . . ."

Tom Barnes nodded understandingly.

"I can't help wondering what will happen to her, when she's all alone," Edward said.

"Well, you know," Tom Barnes said, "you can't be responsible for everybody else's life, now can you? No man is strong enough for that."

"I guess not," Edward said. "Would you like to go to Adebei to eat something? After all, we have to eat, tragedy or not."

I was glad (she wrote) to see the book in print—thanks for the autographed copy! I had never heard of the Oahu Tech Press before, but the dust jacket should help sales, although I don't remember any nude woman in old Marco Z——'s life! But then as you know I never got past page ten, since you tucked all the rest away after I failed the first test, you might say. Anyway, I've finished the whole thing now, and believe me it had to be a labor of love since my shoulder still twinges when I turn anything over, including pages. Maybe I overlooked something, but I still didn't find a woman in there even partially undressed. Are you sure Oahu Tech didn't pull a switcheroo on the dust jackets?

Albuquerque is the same as ever. I don't know why I'm so sad all the time, it's just me I guess. Pop had a little run-in with a pair of pigtails last week and he's out on bail now. Mom's out right now (he's a real sweet guy with the longest sideburns in Albuquerque!) but if she was here, I'm sure she'd send you a big hello.

How is Teheran? George Wade told me the other night that he'd heard from a guy in oil that it's a fascinating place. I know you don't think Albuquerque is fascinating, but in a funny kind of way it is to me, I wish I knew. Maybe I'll get to the bottom of it one of these days. If you ever get back here, look me up. For old time's sake. Sincerely, Janet.

"The Passion of Marco Z—— (*Publisher's Weekly*) is 175 pages of dense twaddle."

"If an author (*New York* Magazine) wants to write pornography, the least he can do is have the courage to come out with it (snicker)."

"What is Oahu Tech Press up to, anyway?" (Book Editor, New York *Times*—privately.)

"I've never read anything so unreadable." (Virginia Kirkus, at the beach.)

What do they want? Edward said. I give them complex perception. I give them close observation of singular behavior. I give them an anguish of awareness . . . Is anything more required of the artist?

COON HUNT

ANNABEL THOMAS

Annabel Thomas was born in Columbus, Ohio, in 1929. A graduate of Ohio State University, she worked briefly as a newspaper reporter and a teacher. Many of her stories and poems have appeared in such publications as *Prairie Schooner, Kansas Quarterly, Forum, Four Quarters,* and *South Dakota Review.* She resides in Ashley, Ohio, with her husband, a veterinarian; they have four grown children.

Nobody saw Quenby get out. Clara Fortune went to feed her and she was gone from the house, that was all.

"Quenby. You, Quenby!"

But you can't call a cat like you do a dog, can you?

"Kitty, kitty, kitty."

Pedigreed and not allowed to roam. Came into the house at six weeks old and never set foot out of it until now, seven years later. Why would she want to and her cushion so cozy and her food set out?

"Look under the porch," Mama had said, "and in the bushes."

Mama's voice was always warm and coaxing like a brood hen's.

Not in the bushes. Not in the long grass around the cistern top. The last light burst through cloud low in the west brightening the saltbox shape of the Fortune house.

A star showed through the top branch of the oak like a tear in an eyelid and the sunset wind moaned amongst its shaggy leaves. Booth's woods lay below, dark as deep water.

Clara threw herself on her back beside the porch steps. The day lilies around her were closed to shapes like fingers. The rising moon was white. There were moths on the screen.

Behind her breastbone all this summer there'd been flutterings like wings. She thought her soul was trying to come out but Mama said it was only her blood pounding because she ran too hard.

"Quenby?"

She crawled through the hole in the lattice and under the house, a tight squeeze. Only a year ago she'd darted in and out like a fish. Now her shoulders and breasts caught though the rest of her was skinny enough still. A beanpole, a stilt, a stepladder of a girl. Over her head she could hear Mama's quick light steps.

Clara found, not Quenby, but a nest with five eggs still warm from the hen. She put the eggs inside her blouse and slid out on her back. Coming around the house corner, she saw the end of the oak branch over the porch roof whip and set the leaves a-quiver. She put the eggs in the porch box.

Up it for sure and can't get down.

Clara swung herself onto the lowest limb. She climbed, scraping her knees and elbows, until she was on a level with the second-floor window. There sat Papa on his and Mama's bed with his galluses turned down. Across the hall she could see, in her own room, the chair with the red cushion on which Quenby usually dozed, purring, every afternoon.

Clara climbed higher to where the tree, still full of sun, swung in the breeze like a tolling bell. From this high she could see the complete round of the yard, already in shadow. There were Mama's flowerbeds, bright from the coming cold, round and square, triangle and rectangle with wire fencing at the edges. There was the woodshed and her bicycle leaning against it and the pear tree where her old swing drifted to and fro.

A scratching on the bark.

"Quenby?"

Clara climbed higher until her fingers closed on a warm smoothness. No cat. What, then? Clara tilted her head, staring up. A face looked back at her through the leaves. She held the branches aside and found Floyd Kilkinney perched in a crotch like a possum.

He opened his fist and showed her three locust skins sitting on the palm. Looking close, Clara saw locust skins everywhere clutched to the bark, staring back at her with empty eye bubbles.

She climbed up to where Floyd sat. He smelled of the fields, of dew and sumac and sassafras. He had locust shells stuck to his clothes and in his hair.

He moved his leg until it touched hers all along the calf. His face was in shadow but she felt his breath quicken against her neck.

She said, "I thought you was Quenby."

"That Quenby's gone off with some tom," he said.

He leaned down of a sudden and pushed his mouth hard against hers so that her lips puffed and stung and a strong pulsing began in her throat.

He settled back triumphant.

"I told you I'd do that before this day was done," he said.

All at once he lifted his head.

"Hark!"

They held their breath. Far off across Booth's woods came a thin piping. When Floyd said, "That's Uncle Garret's Liza up front," she knew it was hounds after a coon.

"Doesn't your uncle ever get lost hunting in Booth's woods?" she asked him. "Papa won't let me go in it because he says I'd never find my way out."

"Uncle Garret gets lost. So do I. That's half the fun."

Floyd dropped a locust skin into her lap. "There's one never made it," he said.

The shell felt heavy as a bullet. Sure enough there was the dead locust, greenish and dull-eyed, still inside. She shivered and let it fall, hearing it hit branches as it dropped. The sun was suddenly gone from the tree as if a lamp had been blown out.

Floyd wound his leg around hers and kissed her again. The kiss lasted so long they both gasped at the end of it.

"Let's get the hell out of this before we fall out," Floyd said.

They inched down the trunk, hung by their hands from the lowest branch and dropped into a pool of shadow.

Floyd flopped belly-down in the grass.

"Let's run off and get married, " he said.

Clara sat beside him, Indian-style. Till the day he came to help her papa make Fortune hay, she'd thought boys were silly. But his eyes, black and wild as sin, picked her out and picked her out wherever she stood. Soon he was talking to her every chance he got, she watching his soft, curving mouth shape the words.

All that summer he hung around her and on into autumn like a hummer at a blossom. Winter he came and waited in first light to walk her to school and waited by the school door to walk her home when last light was coming on.

The next spring he was still around her. Then the summer day she surprised him drinking at the Fortune well, he looked at her with water running down his chin and said, solemn as a sage, "This fall, we'uns 'll get married."

She didn't say no. He was her choice, same as she was his. But when fall came, she didn't feel ready so she said, "In six months." And when that was up, she said, "In six months more."

And now that was up and she said, "We ain't got a dollar be-twixt us, Floyd. We'd starve to death inside a week."

"I got the promise of a job at the sawmill down to Beloit on the river," he told her. "After we save some money, we'll go on down to New Orleans. I always wanted to look on the Gulf."

"I ain't going."

"Yo're scared to leave home, is all. Age you are, my ma'd been a wife two years. Yo're scared to let go of yore mama and papa. Chicken liver!"

Clara buried her fingers in Floyd's hair and gave a pull. It was so crisp and springy it started her fingertips tingling. Locust shells fell from it right and left. It was too lively to hold them.

He gripped her wrists one in each hand and bent her backward. They swayed, then toppled flat on the ground where he held her arms pinned wide, leaned his forehead against her neck and blew his breath down her blouse so that all of her skin prickled.

He was quick as a weasel and too strong for her. Sweat from his chin dropped into her eyes and her mouth. It had a tangy taste like ocean water.

Twisting sideways out of his grip, she grabbed up one of the eggs from the porchbox and pelted it against his chest. It broke, the yellow popping like a bubble and spattering him chin to knee.

"By god, you'll answer for that!" he said through his teeth.

Scooping up the other four eggs, he caught her in the back with one as she ran through the yard and on the shoulder with another as she went down the hill. At the edge of the woods, she stopped to look back and the third egg caught her on the thigh.

Still she'd outfox him. He'd never get her with the last one. She slipped in under the trees where it was dark as a cave. She walked until she stumbled over a rotten log by a run of water, then crouched behind it panting.

She didn't hear him coming but suddenly he swept back the bushes so the moon, gone yellow now, shone on her.

"You look good enough to fry for breakfast," he said. "Here, you can throw the last one so you won't hold me no grudge."

He held out the egg cupped on his palms ready to snatch it away when she reached for it. Quicker than thought she clapped his two hands together. He stood staring at his dripping fingers until she moved off, then, with one lunge, caught her by the skirt.

Pulling free, she gave him a push that sent him reeling backwards into the creek. He came out of the water shaking himself like a wet dog.

Floyd reached for her, bent on giving her a ducking, but she made off into the woods. He came after her, running. They ran until suddenly dogs were barking all around them and there stood Floyd's Uncle Garret with several other men beside a small campfire.

The flames lit a great tree around which dogs were leaping and yelping. One large yellow bitch was baying with a deep bell tone. Clara followed the raised noses of the dogs with her glance until she saw masked, bright eyes and a furry body on a high limb.

"Hold her, Liza!" the men whooped. "Hold her, girl."

They heaped dry leaves and light limbs on the fire and stood about it, staring up. Clara, too, couldn't take her eyes off the coon. When the fire brightened she saw black hands gripping the bark, heaving sides and the pricking of small pointed ears.

Floyd stepped into the firelight, kicking off his shoes. He shed his shirt like an old skin and stood for a moment gazing at the coon.

Then he was across the clearing and up the tree, pulling himself hand over hand up the grapevines that matted the trunk until he gripped the bare, curving lower limbs with his knees. The firelight shone on his dark skin as the muscles moved beneath it. The dogs leaped higher, yelping louder. The coon, immobile as a statue, watched Floyd climb toward her. Her lip was lifted from her teeth and her nose wrinkled in a snarl. As he drew nearer, her body quivered, her hands gripped tight to the bark and she crouched lower, gathering her feet under her. A rank, pungent odor coming from the coon filled the air.

As Floyd climbed higher, the coon backed away from the trunk, edging further out onto the limb.

"Keep a tight hold. Don't you slip," Uncle Garret shouted to Floyd. "Whatever falls from that tree, these here dogs is going to tear to pieces, boy or coon, don't matter which."

Clara looked at the hounds. Their long teeth were like knife blades and their tongues licked in and out.

Floyd reached the limb where the coon perched and began to shake it, bracing himself against the trunk and using both hands.

How tight the furry thing clung to her place! She must be dizzy from whipping up and down. Still she hung on. There on the branch, the coon looked like a cat. Like Quenby. But a wild Quenby. A Quenby gone mad.

"Fall, you goddamned varmint, fall!" the men shouted.

Floyd rested against the trunk, breathing hard. Through the leaves, Clara saw the coon's shiny eyes looking down at the dogs.

Floyd shook the limb mightily. Clara's mouth gaped open. The coon sprang out as though she would soar away, then fell on the dogs, limbs spread.

The hounds, in their scramble to get at the coon, scattered the fire so that the clearing fell into sudden darkness.

Clara could hear the snapping of the dogs' teeth, their yelps and their growling, the screeches of the coon and hoarse hollering of the hunters above the din.

Wild and sightless, the men ran this way and that, bumping into now one another, now the trees or bushes as they tried to keep from being bitten by the dogs or scratched and bitten by the coon.

The fight subsided. Silence fell on the woods. The men kicked the embers together and piled on dry leaves and branches until the fire blazed up once more.

The hounds, bleeding from torn ears and bitten muzzles, milled about whining while Floyd lifted up the dead coon, dripping blood and urine, from their midst and held her high above their heads. From her ripped and bloody face, the coon's half-closed eyes looked out with a dreamy stare.

Uncle Garret danced a jig and pounded Floyd on the back. All the men cheered and shouted and talked at once, relating the hunt to one another while they brought out fruit jars and passed them around. Floyd came up to Clara holding out a jar.

"Since you're a coon hunter now, you might as well finish up right with a drink of corn," he said.

He was laughing and panting, his shoulders heaving. Sweat glistened on his chest and in his hair.

Numb to the lips from the coon's drop, Clara took the jar in her hands and looked into it at the raw colorless liquid. All the men were smiling, watching her, the firelight flickering on their faces. She raised the jar and drank.

At once she began to gasp and to beat at her throat and her chest where she felt a thousand matches suddenly lit and flaming.

The men roared. Uncle Garret fell on the ground and rolled. Clara wheezed and sputtered. When at last her breath came easier, a glow began in her belly and spread to all her parts until her skin was a-blaze and her insides filled with heat and she thought she had fallen into the fire and herself become the flames, leaping, devouring the leaves and branches, giving off an astounding brightness.

Afterwards, she slipped to her knees and began to retch. She heaved and heaved again while Floyd held her forehead and the trees marched around and around them like soldiers. She ended, tired out and sobbing, and, weak as a day-old kitten, fell asleep against Floyd's chest.

When she woke, the fire had burned to a red ash and the men and dogs were gone. Floyd sat beside a lantern watching her.

"God a'mighty!" he burst out. "I thought you was poisoned and yore death coming on you."

Then he threw back his head and laughed until tears stood in his eyes.

"If yo're going to hunt coon, you got to learn to hold yore corn better than that," he said.

Clara stood up, mortified to the roots of her soul.

"I'm going home," she said and moved quickly off into the woods.

The blackness was full of briars and branches and night animals that started up under her feet with a great noise and ran off. She tripped over roots and walked into bushes. Behind her came Floyd swinging the lantern at his side, laughing to himself.

She began to walk faster, looking to come out on the road below the Fortune house. However, no way she turned seemed right. She went on and went on and still there was nothing but trees. In front, behind, to left, to right, only trees.

A few stars shone down through high branches. She stopped, started off to the right, then turned left. Floyd came behind her, laughing.

"Which way?" she asked him over her shoulder. "Why don't you tell me which way?"

She stopped so that he walked into her. Feeling his chest come against her, she pounded it with her fists until her face was hot and her breath came in gasps.

"Show me the right way to go," she said, almost crying. "Pretty soon you'll get lost yourself. Then we'll never get out. We'll die in Booth's woods."

He gripped her arms so she couldn't pound him and kissed her neck, then down onto her breasts. His mouth was everywhere, pressing against her from every direction, scattering her out into the dark.

She heard a screech owl cry close beside them, then again further off. The woods swelled full of murmurs and clicks, scrapes and calls, whistles and barks, rustles and sighs. Loudest of all were the tree frogs, buzzing like the locusts in the day only more shrill and not so loud.

Floyd laid his head on her shoulder and she felt his face hot through her sleeve. They stood without moving while the moon climbed over their heads and filtered down amongst the leaves.

When she tried to pull away, he held her fast.

"Clarie, meet me by the highway bridge tomorrow night," he whispered, muffled, into her hair. "We'll hitch to Kentucky and find a J.P. Come when the moon clears Booth's woods. Clarie, will you come?"

And wouldn't turn loose of her wrists until she'd nodded her head.

When Clara stepped out of the woods, the first sight she saw was Fortune Hill. On its top, the saltbox house stood out black with sharp edges like a cardboard cutout.

Mama's voice, faint and thin, was calling her name from the yard. By the time she started up the path, the calling had stopped and she heard the kitchen door closing.

VISITING THE POINT

THOMAS W. MOLYNEUX

Thomas Molyneux, who died in 1977 at the age of thirty-
four, was a native Philadelphian. He was Professor of English at the University of Delaware, as well as a writer whose
work appeared in such magazines as *Shenandoah*, *The Virginia Quarterly Review*, *The Sewanee Review*, and various
anthologies.

During the summer I was seventeen about five of us made frequent trips to a town near the beach in New Jersey called Somers
Point. Only two or three went at any one time, though we each
went often enough. The only person who made every trip was
Bob Wharton. He was older than the rest of us by several years,
just returned from three years in the Marines. He had more
money than the rest of us, who were still for the most part dependent upon our parents, and of course more freedom. The car
we used was almost always his.

It was a gray Dodge sedan, an utterly anonymous-looking car.
But it had air conditioning and push button windows even in
1959, and an oversized engine—one that had been designed for a
bigger, heavier car. Bob kept sandbags in the trunk to steady the
Dodge, but when he really put his foot to it, the car would veer
and shimmy at the start of acceleration; and cruising at high
speeds, you knew you were going too fast, but you knew too that
the car would go much faster, that the engine wasn't straining,
that whatever strain you felt came in fact from holding back.

Bob was an extraordinary driver, with quick reflexes that let
him drive a little faster, turn or stop a little later than other people, so that driving with him always had about it an unsettling un-
familiarity. He drove slouched in the seat, small hands cupped
loosely on the bottom of the wheel. He had a long flat face, the

Originally appeared in *The Virginia Quarterly Review*. Copyright © 1978 by
The Virginia Quarterly Review. Reprinted by permission.

hairline already receding in two sweeps, and, whether by calcula-
tion or nature, his eyes were held narrowed in a slight squint.

Even at the end of the summer, when I had begun finally to acknowledge that I was bored by him, I still occasionally found myself trying to follow his gaze, wondering what he was studying,
remembering only after I had puzzled the landscape for a time
that the look was merely habitual.

He drove the same way whether he was driving a hundred or
120 miles an hour, as he fairly often did on the trips to Somers
Point, or, as was more often the case, simply driving around. We
drove, it seems in retrospect, interminably that summer, occasionally going someplace new but for the most part going over
and over the same neighborhoods, the same streets, doubling end-
lessly back on ourselves in mesmeric, time-killing windings.

Occasionally someone peripheral to the immediate group would
reveal some fear of the speed or erraticism with which Bob drove,
say something, or begin to fidget. Such occasions were the only
ones on which Bob's eyes left the road. He would drive still
faster, glance across or back intermittently at the person.

"Fast enough?" he would say.

And then after a while perhaps: "Nervous?"

For the rest of us it had become a matter not so much of pride
as of simple stubbornness not to reveal such qualms. We knew
that speaking up would only goad Bob to go faster, for he was
quite open that ownership of the car carried with it control of
choices. One Saturday when all of us were at his parents', sitting
on a grassed incline that overlooked the pool, drinking beer, and
talking of girls we might call, Bob suddenly got to his feet. He
was not big, but he had the extraordinary quickness I had mentioned. None of us wanted to fight him and he knew that. Still,
off and on, out of the blue, he would issue a challenge. His legs
were splayed, and he was crouched in the steep crouch that karate
people use, arms lifted, hands rigid. The crouch tensed his muscles and, so, exaggerated the peculiar effect they had of seeming
grafted onto him.

"Hai," he called out. His right leg raised and kicked out, and he
stepped after it, hands slashing. He bounded into a crouch again,
swayed there for a moment, feet steady but body listing, kicked
out with the other foot, followed again. The patterned geometric
quality of the movements, his intentness, the contrasting torpor of

the summer afternoon lent the performance a quality of mime. The flashing and chopping of the hands seemed less the movements of violence than the signings of some obscure ritual.

"Anybody want to try me?" he said conversationally.

No one said anything.

"'Cause if you do," he said after a while, "I'm ready. You know? Like a battery. Ever ready."

There was some antipathy between Bob and myself which at such moments focused in open dislike. I believed that his eyes met mine particularly in those moments, that his taunting was addressed particularly to me. I did not know him well. I had moved to that section of Philadelphia only a couple of years before, after he had gone to the Marines. And then he seemed simply to have turned up, always ready to do something or to go somewhere. I do not even remember meeting him.

Perhaps in consequence, when he was not around, I occasionally made some remark about the incidents, was apt as well to take up comments others made about his driving. We were pretty generally agreed that it was dangerous and that Bob's insistence on it was unpleasant, but we needed a car to get to the places we went. To get anyplace for that matter. We lived spread out. There was no likely public transportation. Even driving around without specific goals, there was at least the possibility of coming upon one. Without a car, given the suburban distances between things, that seemed impossible, and we could not rely on parents' cars. Bob always had one. At any rate we all did go. I don't think any of us thought seriously of not going.

The trips to Somers Point were not to the beach. We went to the beach in Ocean City, across a bay from Somers Point, drawn there by its reputation for pretty girls who worked as summer waitresses. We went to Somers Point for the bars, which thrived on business from Ocean City because Ocean City was a dry town. The pretty girls of Ocean City, of course, were among those who frequented the bars. And we went to the bars, of course, to pick up those girls.

In retrospect it was an unlikely business. We didn't know the girls, had no place to take them, couldn't split up because we had only one car. Still we made a lot of trips that summer. We would leave Philadelphia shortly after dinner, around seven. It was about eighty miles to the Point and we would get there around nine-thirty or ten o'clock, having stopped at various bars along the way. Occasionally, if we arrived before nine-thirty, we would go across the bridge into Ocean City first and cruise from place to place in vague quest of girls.

There were about five of us including Bob who made the trips with some regularity. For a two-week period at the end of the summer a fellow named Fred Hunt, who had gone to school with Bob and then, like Bob but a year later, joined the Marines, also came along. He was home on leave. When he began to come along, something changed about the trips. Bob Wharton changed for one thing, those characteristics that bothered me in him becoming exaggerated. Some ugly things happened. Finally I didn't want to be around Bob or Fred anymore and stopped going places in Bob's car. But Fred didn't come, as I say, until the end of the summer.

The drinking age in New Jersey then was twenty-one so that, except for Bob and, when he was along, Fred Hunt, there was some tension about the trip for the rest of us. Most of us had false identification. But that served only to make the tension double-edged. We remained unsure about getting into the bars in the first place; then, once in, we were afraid of being caught in a raid or by an ABC man.

As it turned out, we got into the Somers Point bars that summer with rare difficulty. The ride down, however, was another story. The little bars in which we stopped—roadhouses really—tended to have a steady, largely local business. They didn't much want strangers or kids in the place. Sometimes they served us, and sometimes the bartender would simply tell us to get out. At other times he'd joke with us, tease us about the ABC, which of course paid little attention to such places, though we didn't know that then.

In some places, however, there was an antagonism; something in us offended the people in these places, something in our dress or youth or glib carriage perhaps; it is hard to say because I was only vaguely aware of it at the time; something perhaps in the possibilities that plainly remained for us, for they were mostly poor bars and we must have seemed to them rich kids.

One time Tommy Clark was in one of those bars with Bob. I was not along. They'd already stopped in several places. Tommy had had a few beers and started kidding the bartender, who refused to serve him. Meanwhile Bob was drinking his beer, listening with a smirk as he did in such situations. Bob ordered another beer. When the bartender brought it, Tommy said something else to him. Perhaps it was out of line, overstepped some boundary. At any rate a woman seated a little way along the bar turned to him and said, "Why don't you be quiet?"

She was in that bleary state that precedes real drunkenness, a thick woman about forty—or so I imagined her—in a housedress. Tommy, who after all was just trying to have a good time, hesitated for a moment. Then he turned to her.

"You think I'm twenty-one, don't you?" he said. He turned his profile to her and jutted his chin out. "Tell the man I'm twenty-one," he said. "He'll bow to woman's judgment."

"You," she said then with abrupt bitterness. She snorted. "I lived in New York when I was your age and I flushed better men than you into the Hudson."

Bob Wharton gloated about the incident for weeks. "Told you, didn't she?" he would say. "Good old broad, she was. Told you. Punk Kid."

I would think about it when we went into such bars or, as sometimes happened, while a couple of us waited in the parking lot, perhaps splitting a quart that Bob had brought out to us while he drank his two drafts unhurriedly inside. He was adamant about that: if he stopped at a bar, he drank in it. I would try to imagine what the woman had looked like, what her tone had been. I wasn't sure precisely what her phrase meant; its more general meanings were clear enough but about the technical details I was unsure; I thought she might have been talking about douching or disposing of contraceptives; I imagined the apartment and bathroom in which she'd done whatever she'd done as small and bare and streaked and yellowed light like glaze. Anyhow, though the technical aspects intrigued me, it was the abrupt access of brutality that baffled and haunted me, and the undercurrent of violence it suggested.

Different bars were popular at different hours. One, the Dunes, didn't get good until around three when the others were beginning to peter out. We would usually end up there. It was a large rectangular block building, like a warehouse, set in a large macadam parking lot, which in turn was set in a marsh. It had four service bars, but when the band went off and the crowd began to thin, three of them shut down. The only bar that stayed open then was the center one. It was immediately in front of the wide glass and entrance doors. We would stand and watch the sun rise —vivid and lovely, the effect dreamlike—through those doors across the marsh and the parking lot and then we'd get in the car and go home.

I remember the first trip on which Fred Hunt was along. I'd begun to talk to a stranger on my right. Bob and Fred were on my left, talking to a couple of fellows on leave from the Naval Academy. When I looked back after a while, all four had disappeared. Outside, the sun had begun to rise. An arc of it showed above the horizon, an orange sun so clearly demarcated that it seemed to belong in a cartoon, and the sky was streaked with extraordinary clarity. And then in the doorway I saw two figures. They were profiled to me. Their front legs angled forward so that their feet seemed to merge; their arms also came forward, as though they were shaking hands at an odd angle. One of them jerked almost spasmodically, and then they were still again. And then the one who had made the initial motion lifted off his feet and flipped in the air. The other figure stepped back, all the movements jumpy in the way of old movies.

It took me a moment to realize that the man who had stepped back was Fred Hunt and the man who had lifted into the air and flipped onto his back was one of the midshipmen. After a moment they repeated the scene, everything subtly speeded up though the jumpy mimed quality of old movies remained. The other midshipman stepped forward and then Bob Wharton. A new tableau formed momentarily, the four squared off. Then the second midshipman came back into the bar and gathered his change and his buddy's and went out. He looked angry. As he went out, he jerked his way between Bob and Fred, who were coming back into the bar laughing.

"I'm pretty good at judo," Bob was saying, apparently mocking the midshipman's voice. "Sure you are, buddy. Tell me about it. Why don't you show me?"

The midshipman, it turned out, had mentioned taking judo at the Naval Academy. The lessons had been only in basic principles. Fred had pretended to be curious, and they'd gone outside so that the midshipman could demonstrate. And then Fred, who'd had some judo of a less theoretical sort in the Marines, had blocked the midshipman's move and thrown him.

Bob and Fred thought the scene was hilarious. They kept repeating lines of dialogue from it on the way home. We'd been up all night, of course, and there was perhaps an edge of strung-out hysteria in their reactions.

I found it less amusing than they. Something bothered me about it. I felt separated from Bob and Fred in their raucousness, felt that that separation was in large part intended. Something in the incident itself also bothered me. I realized that such a thing would not have happened before Fred arrived. But I recalled the scene nonetheless, the sunrise, the startling freshness of the dawn sky framed in the blanched haze of the Dunes, the silhouetted body flipping through the air, getting up, flipping more suddenly. It seemed to me magical, strange, and compelling, somehow the most likely of all possible endings for the night.

In terms of their ostensible purpose, our trips to Somers Point were failures. All that summer I never picked a girl up at the Point, rarely even danced, came away only once that I recall with a name, address, and phone number. The only one of us, in fact, who did pick someone up was Fred Hunt. I was not along, but Tommy Clark was. Fred had some friends who were working that summer in Ocean City and had rented the upper floor of a big, run-down house there. When Fred met the girl, he talked Bob and Tommy into going back and spending the night at his friends' house so that he could take the girl there.

The girl was a fat girl.

"What do you mean *fat*?" I remember asking Tommy when he told me.

"I mean *fat*," he said.

All the way from the Point to the house in Ocean City Fred mauled at the girl in the back seat.

"Don't do that," she would say, "please don't. Not yet." And, "You're sure you care?" She breathed heavily, according to Tommy, in a way that had nothing to do with passion.

When finally they reached the house, Fred led the girl directly into a bedroom, leaving Bob and Tommy in the living room with a couple of quarts of beer they'd brought. The people who lived in the place, having jobs, were already asleep. One had shuffled groggily out to show Fred the room he could use. Bob and Tommy were to sleep in the living room.

Bob and Tommy drank beer. They began to sort about the room to figure who would sleep where and on what. The door to the bedroom into which Fred had taken the girl led directly off the living room. Suddenly it was tugged open, making a noise, which, falling away, seemed to leave the place momentarily stopped in time—preternaturally silent and still.

Then the girl half backed, half sidled through the doorway into the living room. She moved in a confused way, drifting. She was naked. She held her Bermuda shorts and panties and tennis shoes in one hand. With the other, she made a listless stuttered wiping motion before her face, as if the last swipe of a windshield wiper after it has been turned off were repeated over and over. She backed against a chair and made a startled mewing sound.

At that moment Fred appeared in the doorway. He, too, was naked and carried some of her clothes. The girl stopped when she saw him and again, her whimper abruptly truncated, the room seemed to still. Then Fred started across the room toward her.

"Go on," he was saying, his voice hoarse and his words only half-shaped. "Keep going. Go on, fat bitch."

He flung her blouse at her. As he spoke, she had begun to back away from him, again following a confused drifted path and now the hand with which she was swiping the air before her face began to swing more rapidly, perhaps to ward off the blouse. But the blouse opened in the air, hung there, drifted eerily toward the floor.

"Go on," he was still saying, "go on, fat bitch."

The apartment was reached from a flight of open exterior stairs which led to a small landing, also open, outside the door. Fred chased the girl out onto the landing. He went back through the room then, snatching her clothes from the floor. She must have begun to dress on the landing, to pull at least her panties and shorts on. Fred went back into the bedroom, got her pocketbook and returned to the door.

"Go on," he said. "You can't stay there. Go away you fat cow bitch."

He threw the rest of her things out across the landing and down the steps.

Fred and Bob told the story, when they returned, as though everything had happened very fast, the girl rushing out of the room and Fred storming behind her roaring and laughing and flinging clothes like confetti. Told in that way, it conjured up an image as much antic as awful. But that is not the way it happened. It was a slow, ragged process. Fred was not roaring but speaking almost in a whisper. He was not laughing at all. His face, rather, was strained, veins jumping at his temples. Tommy was insistent about that.

"Jesus," he said, "I thought he was going to push her off the landing."

"But Bob said he was laughing, that it was all a joke."

"He wasn't laughing," Tommy said. "He wasn't laughing. He was messed up. I never want to see something like that again."

"What about Bob?" I said.

Tommy shrugged. "What about him?"

The next weekend I made my last trip to Somers Point with Bob and Fred. And I took along a girl. She was not, I suppose, what would have then been called a date. She was plainly with me and not with Bob or Fred.

She was a girl who was around a lot that summer, though not much with us. She saw an older group. I suppose she was, like us, bored and uncertain about things, though we did not think of it that way at the time. There were three or four such girls that summer. Everyone knew who they were. This one's name was Anne Carnett. She had dark shoulder-length hair. Her eyebrows were straight rather than arched and grew low and close together on the bridge of her nose in a way that made exotic features otherwise regular. She was a good-sized girl, not fat but with solid arms, her back muscled so that the shoulder blades didn't pop from it like hookups for wings, already womanly in contrast to the stylish slender girls I then dated.

I wasn't aware of that distinction until the first time I put my arms around her on the Thursday night before the weekend. Anne and a friend turned up. I don't know how. I don't think anyone invited them. Though her name and her friend's and a couple of others cropped up pretty often in our talk that summer, this is the only night I can remember any one of them being present. We were swimming in Bob's parents' pool. (Bob's parents were away.) We came out of the pool together and started across the lawn to-

ward a cluster of towels and beers. Everyone else seemed to have
disappeared. We brushed against each other a couple of times as
we crossed the lawn. We bent for the towels at the same time and
when we straightened we were faced toward each other. She
stepped into me and I folded my arms around her and even before
I leaned my head back to kiss her I was aware that her body
against mine was solider than those of other girls I'd known. After
a while Anne Carnett and I went into the house and upstairs to
an empty bedroom.

She herself went across the room—preceding me as she had up
the short incline of lawn to the house, the strips of the white
bathing suit glowing in the stippled night—and turned back the
covers of the bed, sat up when I climbed in beside her and un-
hooked the suit's halter. But after a while when I reached for the
bottom of her suit she drew back.

"Not tonight," she said.

"Why not?"

"No reason, I guess. Couldn't we just not tonight?"

She had drawn back some, the lines and planes of her face, especially the slash of her brows, simplified toward abstraction in
the glimmer. Her eyes seemed unsure, the drawing in of the features forlorn.

"We don't have to do anything," I said. "Tonight or anytime."

"Just tonight," she said and ran her hand falteringly along the
length of my body. Her eyes, holding to mine, remained unsure.

She had, I knew even then, no expectation of my accepting her
demurral. My response, in consequence, surprised her and
changed her way of thinking of me. We both knew that, I think,
and it occurs to me, at least in retrospect, that such awareness
showed itself in the way we behaved toward each other. There
was some mooniness, I think, in her regard of me, some vague
responsive gallantry in my attitude toward her. Both attitudes
were quixotic and inappropriate in the circumstances and something about that no doubt grated on Bob Wharton.

Given Anne Carnett's implicit promise and my assumed goals,
it would, of course, have been simpler and more likely for us to
have stayed in Philadelphia the next night. Instead we went with
Bob and Fred to the beach. Someone had moved out of the
Ocean City apartment at which Fred, Bob, and Tommy had

stayed, leaving extra room. We planned to spend the night there and then go on the beach the next day. The trip was a spur of the moment thing and, although by this time the antipathy between Bob and myself had begun to grow open, I do not think that it occurred to me not to go.

From the first we made a point of doing things as we had done on other trips that summer. But the presence of a girl seemed to require something livelier than the desultory talk that had been characteristic of such trips. The strain, of course, is more apparent in retrospect. At the time we laughed a lot, struck poses substantially little different from those we had fallen into on other trips. The real trouble did not occur until we got back to the apartment in Ocean City, though from about one o'clock on an element of coercion entered into things, and some hostility. Anne Carnett and I, because we had brought less money than Bob and Fred and because we were looking forward to the beach the next day, wanted to return to the apartment earlier than Bob and Fred, and Bob, of course, refused in any way to accommodate us.

When we did get to the apartment, we discovered that all the bedrooms were occupied so that the four of us had to sleep in the living room. The door had been left open for us and two light blankets left out and a note, which made clear that only Bob and Fred were expected.

The room was dank and cool. A light had been left on in the small kitchen. It served to outline the heavy furniture of the place and to reveal occasional detail.

"There's only two blankets," Bob said.

"That's no problem," I said.

"Not for Fred and me it isn't," he said.

I laughed. "Give me a blanket," I said.

He cocked his head and lifted his brows, held the piled blankets back as well.

"You could take it from me if you wanted," he said.

"Hey, Bob, it's three o'clock. Just give me a blanket."

"The way I see it, there's two blankets. Fred and I know the people. We get first shot at the blankets."

"The way I see it, you and Fred get one blanket and Anne and I split the other and you're being a pain in the ass."

"Like I say, you can always take it away from me."

"We don't need a blanket," Anne said. "Let's just go to sleep."

Fred had gone into the bathroom. Now he came back into the room. He had taken his shirt off and as he started across the room he began ostentatiously to unbutton his pants. Anne passed him and went into the bathroom. Almost immediately he turned and rattled the handle there.

"Jesus, don't you start too," I said.

He turned and smiled at me, his boyish face dimpling. The top button of his pants was undone and his hands jutted into the waistband of the pants, his shoulders lifted and spread in consequence. His thick columnar body, long neck, long face seemed huge in the low ceilinged room. For the first time I could imagine him chasing the fat girl out of the apartment. Though it was his arrival that had precipitated the changes in Bob Wharton and our trips, I realized that, perhaps because of the antipathy I have mentioned, I had associated the changes with Bob, had never really credited Fred's role in Tommy Clark's story. As I had riding home from the Dunes after he had flipped the midshipman, though more sharply now, I felt cut off from Bob and Fred and realized that that separation was a thing intended. It seemed almost plotted.

"Hey, Bob," I said, "don't keep this up. It's late."

"What are you, Sir Galahad? We can all fuck her."

"C'mon," I said.

"C'mon yourself. I provide the car, Fred provides the place to stay. What do you provide? You're just along for the ride."

"This shit's not funny at this hour."

"I'm not trying to be funny."

"You want to fuck somebody, you call her. I don't want Anne bothered. Okay?"

"No, it's not okay. What are you going to do about it?"

Anne Carnett came out of the bathroom. As she did, Fred, the amused smile held, began again to strip. There was something menacing in the sharp sound of his zipper being tugged down. Hearing it, Anne seemed to step more quickly.

"Keep the blankets," I said then. "Where are you going to sleep?"

"Not tired," Bob said. "Night's young for us. Anne could help me sleep though."

"No," she said then. "I won't."

"Nobody's talking to you," Bob said.

"Dammit, Bob," I said.

But I wished that she would stay quiet. I knew—or thought I knew—that Bob finally would force nothing. But I knew too that anything Anne said would serve only to goad him. There seemed nothing I could do. Bob was stronger and faster than I. A fight seemed likely only to increase the stakes. I had no doubt now that if it came down to it, Fred would stand with Bob.

I chose a corner of the room out of line of the door and its drafts, one that also gave us some privacy by a couch. Anne and I settled there, using towels and bathing suits as pillows. The heavy tart smell of the sea which had lingered in my nostrils when I came into the apartment was run by now with dankness. Anne Carnett turned toward me, huddled herself. Her hair, pushed against my face, smelled thickly sweet.

"Think we ought to keep them company?" Bob said.

After a while we heard them settle for the night.

Anne Carnett gnarled her body close against mine so that my arms closed around her. She cried almost without noise, as though she realized that a sob would trigger more abuse, but her body in my arms shook and shook. All that I could do was hold her. Her hair pressed in my face, its smell sugary and muffling, the nip of its loose strands itching. I thought of the things that I thought I should want to do: cross the room and kick Bob Wharton bloody as he tried to stand; take my clothes off and Anne Carnett's and in that glimmering eerie light slowly explore the strangeness of her body. I could picture both possibilities clearly. But in truth I wanted only to be warm and to sleep. The antipathy I had felt toward Bob Wharton throughout the summer was open and clear now. I hated his bullying, his arbitrariness, the way that, not really wanting much of anything, he toyed with violence and pain.

Gradually Bob's comments ceased. I could hear then his breathing draw out and grow rough so that I knew he was asleep. I sensed that Fred was awake. Anne Carnett held tight against me, the curl of her body unsprung some by now. She too had heard Bob go to sleep. She leaned back on one side, lifted my hand into her breast and pressed it there. I left my hand there as long as I thought politeness demanded. I knew she was watching me and realized gradually that, like my acceptance of her demurral the night before, my behavior that night set me off and particularized me for her: while I had been shamed at my futility and coward-

ice, she had been surprised that I did not join with Bob and
Fred. Bob was right; I realized we all could have fucked her. I let
my hand drift down along her side, feeling obligated at least to
hold her. But I would not look up and see her. I feigned sleep
until I felt her lapse against me, then slept.

The next day when we reached the beach, as though by agreement, Anne Carnett and I spread our towels away from Bob's and
Fred's. Anne herself said little except to remark on the brightness
of the day. We slept intermittently on towels.

We had only about seven dollars between us. In the middle of
the day we went onto the boardwalk and spent almost three of
them on milkshakes and cheese steaks. When we returned to our
towels, she fell asleep again.

I went across and behind us then to where Bob and Fred sat
wearing sunglasses and vague smirks.

"When are you leaving?" I said.

"Not," Bob said.

I looked at him for a moment.

"Gonna stay till tomorrow," he said. "Maybe Monday."

"I don't have enough money," I said.

"That's your problem."

"How the hell am I supposed to get home?"

"Mooch a ride. Same way you got down."

Fred watched the ocean blandly.

"Are you serious?" I said.

"Don't I sound serious?"

"You might have said something before we left."

"Didn't know then. Changed my mind."

It occurred to me that I could at least borrow bus fare from
him.

"Up yours," I said instead.

He shrugged. "Anytime," he said.

I turned and walked back to where Anne Carnett was waking.

"They're not going back till tomorrow," I said. "We'll have to
thumb."

I did not see Fred Hunt again after that day. His leave must
have been nearly over. No doubt he returned to the Marines. I did
see Bob Wharton again, of course. I bumped into him only a couple of weeks later at a big party. He was slouched against a wall,

dangling a quart of beer in one hand, staring out across the mulling room with his thoughtful-seeming squint. As I went up to him, I realized for the first time that his eyes in fact were never really still, that all of his attention was peripheral. He watched everything from the edges. He rarely looked in the distant direction that his expression seemed to indicate.

"Get home okay?" he said conversationally.

"Wasn't bad."

"Should have stayed."

"Couldn't."

"So you said."

There was no difference in our tone from most of the rest of that summer. He did not turn toward me, though I realized now that his flickering eyes kept me in view. I swung around so that I was looking out at the party as he was. It was a big party, early in September, and a good many people were drifting in and out of the room. Some were beginning to dance.

"Look at them," Bob said in that same flat voice, shrewd and a little mocking for all its offhandedness. "Asses. Punks. Gonna get drunk. Gonna get laid. Sure y'are, buddy. Sure, kid. Tell me about it."

A slender blond girl whom I had dated a couple of times the previous spring came into the room at its far side in a group of three girls. She had spent the summer at a ranch in Colorado, and this was the first time I had seen her since her return. Her pale hair was pulled around in a French twist. She halted, gripping a drink in front of her with both hands, and stood with slightly awkward, expectant grace for a moment, her eyes big and clear in her thin face, shifting about. I caught her attention, and she smiled and I crossed the room to her.

"Hi," she said. "I hoped you'd be here."

Anne Carnett was also at the party. I did not see her until late in the evening. Even then I saw her only momentarily at a distance. I was dancing with the blond girl. Her name was Susie Harrison, and I spent most of the evening with her. As I danced, I came aware of someone watching me, and I looked up and met Anne Carnett's gaze. She was alone. It was a hot night, and her hair had plastered in a damp streak along her forehead. The solidity that I had taken two weeks earlier for womanliness seemed at that moment just too much damp flesh, like her breast as she

pressed my hand on it in the Ocean City apartment. She could, of
course, have been watching Susie Harrison, as girls do watch other
especially pretty, well-dressed girls, or could, for that matter, like
Bob Wharton, have been looking somewhere altogether different
from what her gaze indicated. But my impression was that she
was watching me and that there was something in her look of the
reaction she had had when I did not press her that Thursday
night, something of the look I had refused to see in the Ocean
City apartment after Bob Wharton had gone to sleep.

On the trip home from the beach, we had gotten a ride straight
through to Philadelphia. After a couple of questions, the two
fellows who provided the ride left us to ourselves, no doubt tired
themselves from the sun. They dropped us in a part of Philadelphia distant from our own and we took public buses to a point
about a mile from Anne Carnett's house and walked from there.

The car in which we got our ride was an old Ford. I don't think
we went over sixty the whole way to Philadelphia. As we drove,
the fellow who was not driving kept fiddling with the radio. The
same songs played over and over, and the flat dark piney scenery
repeated itself as though we had been moved into a nightmare.
And then in Philadelphia we had to wait three times for buses,
ten minutes, twenty minutes, I had no idea how long, stuck on a
corner in a strange part of the city, unable to do anything except
wait.

Anne Carnett sat beside me on the buses, her towel and pocketbook plumped together in her lap, cut offs and blouse bulked out
by her bathing suit beneath. We did not talk. She sagged on herself some with tiredness. She seemed passive and content, and
finally as a bus idled through two changes of a single light while a
fat woman trundled up the steps, rooted through her pocketbook,
finally started down the aisle to permit people behind her to
board, I turned and demanded, "Doesn't it even bother you?" She
looked over, smiled, flipped her hands. "I'm sorry things got
messed up," I said after a minute.

"It wasn't your fault," she said.

Walking the final mile to her house, on familiar streets now, I
walked ahead of her, stopped, waited, walked ahead again. We
reached her house. With the door half opened she looked up at
me. My hands were in my pant pockets. I grinned raggedly and
shrugged.

"No one's home," she said. "Do you want to come in?"

I shrugged again. "I guess not," I said.

"I'm sorry I was strange the other night," she said.

"I didn't mind," I said.

"You're sure you don't want to come in?"

"Thanks anyhow," I said. And even as I brushed past her and started down the couple of steps from the porch, I seemed to be walking in mechanical slow motion. It seemed forever until I heard the muffled closing of her door. I went back along her street with my hands still in my pockets in the summer evening. In the old Ford I had thought I was impatient to get to Philadelphia; then in the buses I had thought I was impatient to get to the section in which I lived; then walking from the bus to Anne Carnett's house I had thought I was impatient to be away from her. And now, alone in the night, the air quick and sweet with summer smells, I was still impatient. All summer I had thought I wanted a girl like Anne Carnett and then I had walked away from her offer, and I still wanted something.

Now Anne Carnett was watching me as I danced with Susie Harrison, and I was avoiding looking at her, all the while remembering the awful moment when I stopped at the end of her street, impatience and wanting so strong in me that they seemed physical, as though they might tear some emptiness inside me, realizing that I didn't know what I wanted or why I was impatient, starting back toward her house, then away again, my fists still clenched in my pockets.

IN THE AUTUMN OF THE YEAR

JOYCE CAROL OATES

> Joyce Carol Oates's most recent novel is *Son of the Morning*
> (Vanguard). This story, "In the Autumn of the Year," will
> appear in her next collection of stories, *Sunday Blues*. Visit-
> ing Professor at Princeton University during the academic
> year 1978–79, Ms. Oates is originally from the country out-
> side Lockport, New York.

One of them was her lover's son. Her dead lover's son. He had
turned out curiously: a balding young-old man with hairs in his
nostrils, an annoying habit of picking at his fingernails, a quick,
strained meager smile.

They were absurdly reverential. All this chatter about her comfort displeased her. No, it pleased her: she had grown petty about
such things over the years. Is there anything more we can do for
you, Miss Gerhardt. Is there anything you would like.

Graciously she smiled and told them no.

Graciously she looked from one to the other to the other, favor-
ing them equally. (She and her former lover's son had, of course,
exchanged certain furtive looks—at the airport he had stammered
his name, so nervous, so highly wrought, that Eleanor herself had
begun to stammer. What folly! But she was, as always, beautifully
in control of herself.) When she told them she preferred to rest,
since the plane from New York City had been delayed, and the
flight tiring, they seemed quite satisfied. Clearly her presence
made them uneasy: she was too famous; she was too old.

The Dean chattered as they prepared to leave. Was the guest
room suitable, had she noticed the antique furniture, if it was cold
tonight she might want a fire, the fieldstone fireplace was handsome, wasn't it?—the entire Alumni House a very attractive place.

He hoped she would like it here. He hoped the award presentation and the banquet wouldn't be too tiring, he could respect the fact that she did so much of this sort of thing, meeting people, being praised and congratulated and photographed, it must have come to seem rather familiar by now . . . which was why, he said, his face creasing with the effort of his smile, Linden College was especially grateful to her for accepting their invitation.

Though she was not in the least embarrassed, she murmured something that sounded embarrassed. A modest woman. Despite her fame she was modest; she was unpretentious. The Dean would tell his wife shortly that the visit wasn't going to be a difficult one after all—Eleanor Gerhardt appeared to be amiable, and approachable, and sober, and she was remarkably attractive for a woman of sixty-three. Her white hair was perfectly groomed, she was slender and light on her feet, her eyes were a fine pale green, calm and good-humored. Her throat was probably quite ravaged, though: she was wearing a pretty little pearl-gray and scarlet neck-scarf.

"Well," said the Dean. "We'll give you a little time to yourself now, Miss Gerhardt. One of us will come by at six to pick you up for dinner. Is that agreeable?"

"Perfectly agreeable," Eleanor said.

As they left, the man who was her lover's son looked back at her, half-smiling, his eyes narrowed as if he were staring into a strong light. Eleanor waved goodbye, wishing to put him at his ease. The poor man appeared to be so uncertain of himself—was it possible that he felt guilt, over his father's behavior?—his father's treatment of her? But it wasn't likely that he knew very much about Eleanor's relationship with Edwin Höller since he had been a mere child at the time.

Now he was Chairman of the Music Department at Linden College, and Director and Conductor of the Ellicott Civic Orchestra. He must have been, Eleanor guessed, in his mid-forties. It had been nearly three decades since they'd seen each other last.

Benjamin, his name was. Would she have remembered it?—probably not.

I don't want to hurt the boy, her lover had said. I don't want to hurt his mother either, but it's the boy I'm most concerned about. He's inherited my neurotic propensity toward making too much of things . . . and his mother's inclination toward despair.

I understand, Eleanor had said.

Sometimes she spoke angrily, sometimes ironically. Sometimes with perfect sincerity. At the end, with a studied lightness which she believed adequately masked her despair. I understand, she said. Stroking his face; pressing herself into his arms. But it wasn't true: she had not really understood.

In the autumn of the year she gave in to certain wearing, sentimental thoughts. She became shameless—allowing herself to dream for long moments of love, and of death, and of her girlhood, and of the only man she had loved: the only man she had seriously loved, that is. (Of course there had been many men.) In the autumn of the year she remembered vividly the emotions that were no longer hers, and the harsh, rich, merciless pleasures of the body. It must have had something to do with the slanted light, the acrid odor of burning leaves, children hurrying to school in the morning. There was an urgency to the days, a sense of quickened meaning that did not include her. Autumn was for other people, for younger people. She did not regret this fact. Her mood became elegiac, she played Beethoven's quartets on the phonograph, she labored over long, loosely-constructed poems celebrating the tragic necessity of loss.

It was true that she sometimes wept, unaccountably; she sometimes woke from dreams in which she wept, convulsed by a painful soundless wailing. That she had become an old woman. Old! It was a difficult concept to grasp. But most of the time she rather enjoyed her memories, she rather enjoyed the cleansing tears. Merely transforming certain experiences into language subdued them and allowed her a curious sort of triumph. She was a poet, after all. She was a highly disciplined craftsman in her art. Years ago she had emerged from that disastrous affair with Edwin Höller and had forced herself to survive it without self-pity, and had forced herself to write about the experience. Since that time she had never lost faith in her ability to withstand suffering.

My sincerest congratulations, Edwin had telegraphed, when her *Collected Poems* was awarded the Pulitzer Prize some years ago. *Admiration also. And a certain measure of envy.*

She had laughed, delighted; but had not replied.

In autumn she dwelt upon such memories. Her lover was dead —but still living; it wasn't difficult to hear his voice. Others whom she had loved and who had died—her father, her mother, one of her brothers, a favorite aunt—were dead but still accessible if she gave herself enough time.

For years, foolishly, she had believed she would not survive each winter. She anticipated a winter death—lightning-quick and brilliant as a January morning. She would not have minded; she would not have protested. (Pain frightened her, of course—she had always been a terrible coward about pain.) There was no intelligent reason for her to expect to die shortly, since she was in reasonably good health for a woman of her age, but she had supposed—halfway serious—that since Edwin had died at the age of fifty-eight, some ten years ago now, she would probably not live much beyond that. She had even caught herself planning on it, as if such a maudlin gesture would please him. The handsome shingleboard house she had inherited, in Chestnut Hill, Pennsylvania, would go to her niece, a junior high school teacher who had been renting the house for years now for a token $75 a month. Sally was a fine, industrious girl, not pretty, not even very charming, but she was Eleanor's favorite niece and she would be enormously grateful for the inheritance. The furnishings in Eleanor's apartment on East 85th Street would be sold, most of her books probably given away, and her records, and her motley assortment of clothes; the half-dozen pieces of good jewelry were to be divided among friends; the money in her savings account and in various investments—a considerable amount—was willed to several charities, including the American Cancer Association. At odd, idle times Eleanor found herself going through this list with a sense of satisfaction. She did not want to die, she really did enjoy life immensely, but at the same time . . . at the same time her life had come to seem strangely unreal, this past decade. Whether it was because of Edwin or not, she didn't know. (She hadn't seen the man in how many years?—twenty-nine?—so perhaps it had nothing to do with him at all.)

However. . . .

Still, she knew she wasn't superstitious; she might have made a few blunders in her lifetime but she wasn't an ignorant person. She had always taken pride in her intelligence. You know too much, Edwin used to say, laughing, drawing back from her as if frightened; not just about me but everything—everything! It's a fearful thing.

She investigated the room. Yes, it was attractive. Quite suitable. Silk wallpaper in blues and grays, a lovely old Queen Anne writing table, hardwood floor, oriental rug, a brass-framed bed. The field-stone fireplace drew her attention. It was very neat, dustless. There were two small birch logs in it, for show; it didn't look as if the fireplace was ever used. Eleanor had always liked the idea of a fireplace but, living alone, never married, she hadn't had the energy or the inspiration to use one. What if the smoke backed up into the room? She had no idea how a fireplace worked.

On the mantel was a brass hurricane lamp and a Wedgwood vase in blue and white and an oversized book, *A History of Linden College 1894–1964*. At one time in her life, when being honored by colleges, universities, and various institutions was a novelty, she would have read through the book, out of respect for her hosts; but no longer.

The bureau mirror reflected the afternoon sunshine so brilliantly that Eleanor's image was obscured and there was no need for her to peer anxiously at it. (Had the breeze at the airport disturbed her hair, were those soft, dark, mournful pouches beneath her eyes more pronounced than usual, was her mouth set in that grim line she sometimes noticed—none of it mattered, she refused to look, she was going to remain invisible until they came for her at six.) At the window she stood for a while in utter peace, staring at the unfamiliar countryside. Where was she?—the northwestern corner of Connecticut? She could not remember if she'd been in this part of the state before. No matter: it was lovely. The hills were graceful, the foliage was already turning color, there was an exquisite grave stillness to the horizon; the eternal solace of beauty without words.

Is there anything we can do for you, the strangers asked. Meaning only to be courteous. Meaning only to show their ceremonial reverence. One of them was her lover's son—her lover's child—and she could not keep from staring at him. He was far slighter than his father, and hadn't his father's busy, exuberant presence. But the eyes were the same—the broad forehead the same. She stared, smiling. He had tried to smile in return. Had the others noticed? Thank you, she said graciously, but I want to be alone for a while. I need to be alone.

It was now two-fifty. Suddenly she was tired: her legs felt the strain and began to go stiff. Well, it was her age. It was accountable. She drew the blind, and took off the scarf and her dress and shoes, and lay carefully on the bed, and closed her eyes. She would rest. She would sleep. She would prepare herself psychologically for the evening ahead—the fuss, the hyperbole, the confused affection these good people had for her, a stranger named Eleanor Gerhardt who seemed to them somehow familiar, perhaps because she was so old, she'd been prominent most of their adult lives, a likeable fixture, a comfortable sort of monument. . . . We are so grateful for your visit, they said.

She and Edwin Höller struggled on the narrow horsehair sofa. The study smelled of dust: of books. Hundreds of books. Somewhere behind and beneath her, beneath her straining head, a piano sounded—notes that were sometimes muffled and unclear, and other times remarkably precise. Two floors below a child practiced piano. For hours he kept at it, maddeningly patient. Edwin's son Benjamin, ten years old, said to be gifted. Very gifted. Eleanor heard a run of scales, and then fragments of compositions, and then an entire composition from start to finish. (It wasn't until years later that she found out the name of that particular piece—Satie's *Gymnopédie*.) Notes slid in and out of her hearing. She could not listen. She cried aloud, gnawing at her lip.

My beauty, Edwin said, delighted. My beautiful girl.

He kissed her hungrily, held her too tight, buried himself in her. Wildly he spoke of love. The very first time she came to his attic study he spoke of love, and even of marriage: of going to Europe together. Wasn't it possible? He half-sobbed, he ground his forehead against hers, he kissed her until her mouth ached. Wet, noisy, child-like, ungovernable. Edwin Höller. He had been born in Munich and he wanted to show her Munich. And then they would go to Turkey, and then to Afghanistan and India. He was writing a book on Bactria—ancient Bactria. The Greeks. A civilization and its destruction, its doom. It would be a great book: the most ambitious and comprehensive book on the subject. He would become famous as a scholar. He would be invited around the world to give lectures, and to be a visiting professor, and she would come with him: his lovely, lovely girl.

Eleanor laughed in despair.

She clutched at him, kissed him. Wasn't it possible?

She had been twenty-nine when they met, thirty-four when they parted. This was in the mid- and late forties, in Boston. Edwin Höller taught at a women's college and lived in Cambridge and Eleanor met him at a party and shortly afterward came to him, climbing the outside stairs to his attic study, anxious and silly as any bride. Are you shocked, she asked. I'm shocked myself. It must be disconcerting, when a woman is so relentless. . . .

He had not listened. My beauty, he said. My lovely girl.

Professor Höller was a noisy exuberant big-boned man who looked somewhat older than his age. (He was only thirty-eight when Eleanor met him). He was not handsome. At times he was rather ugly. A broad flat forehead, busy peering eyes, a too-prominent nose. Large, clumsy, stained fingers. A habit of muttering to himself in exasperation or triumph.

Where do the hours go was his constant refrain.

Life to Edwin was accelerated and melodramatic. He was not afraid to weep—he was not afraid to beg. Reading Eleanor's poetry (which was at that time fashionably difficult, a neo-metaphysical verse she later repudiated) he was not ashamed to admit that he understood very little of it and that, in a way, her imagination alarmed him.

I don't think I've ever known anyone quite like you, he said.

He had not lied. She was certain he had not lied.

She came to his study and it did not matter to him—amazingly, it did not matter at all—that his wife was in the house, or his young son, or that the neighbors might see her climbing the stairs. Of his wife he said nothing except that she was "difficult" and "selfish." They had been married a very, very long time, they'd both been too young, in their early twenties, they had grown apart, who was to blame? He did not think he was to blame. Anyway it did not matter that Eleanor came to him because students and friends dropped in all the time—they climbed the stairs and knocked and if he wasn't there or too absorbed in his work to answer they simply went away again, and came back later, or dropped over in the evening, or saw him at the college. (Several times when they were making love someone had knocked on the door and Eleanor's heart had leapt, not with fear of discovery so much as with simple jealousy. She did not want to share Edwin with anyone else—she did not even want to share his good-natured attention with anyone else.)

So she came to his attic study where it was necessary to make one's way past small mountains of books, and where their love was heightened, perhaps, by the presence of other people in the house—the always-invisible wife, the young son at the piano; or he came to her apartment in a charming old building at the very edge of Beacon Hill, always bringing presents—wine, brandy, roses, snapdragons, a potted azalea, an antique doll in gold brocade, a volume of German poetry, untranslated, by a poet Eleanor had never heard of who Edwin insisted was of "colossal genius." Sometimes they met in a downtown hotel, sometimes they drove in Edwin's station wagon up the coast to Swampscott or Marblehead; a few times they went to New York City together. He was a fussy, old-fashioned lover, self-dramatizing, exaggerated, rather comic.

She believed she was the first woman he had been involved with since his marriage; she was fairly certain she was the first woman he had genuinely loved.

They quarreled and he twisted her wrist to silence her. Good! Do it harder. I deserve it: hurt me. She was capricious, playful, reckless, perhaps a little stupid. At the start of their relationship it was she who appeared to be less involved than he, less passionate; it was her refrain that she did not want to marry, she never wanted to marry, the very idea of marriage struck her as stultifying and absurd. He warned her that she would bitterly regret this attitude. It was unnatural for a woman to want to remain unmarried, she would see. So they quarreled, half-seriously, and were reconciled, and Eleanor went away for several weeks one winter to test her feelings apart from her lover, and Edwin worked twelve and fourteen hours on his research, and they came together again, and again quarreled: and Eleanor realized that she was very much in love. She was twenty-nine years old. She was thirty. And then thirty-one.

Should I drown myself? she asked once, impulsively.

She gripped the bridge railing as if to throw herself in, even made a playful move with her leg, of course she wasn't serious, she was only joking, Eleanor Gerhardt would never do such a desperate thing. Nevertheless Edwin reacted as if she were serious. Stop! Are you mad! What is wrong with you! You will regret— The shock and disapproval in his voice made her laugh, for how could he believe his threats might have any meaning to a woman ready

to commit suicide?—though of course she wasn't serious and anyone but Edwin Höller would have known that. Afterward in her
apartment, in her bed, he told her she would be very sorry for
such foolishness—she would remember it when she was an old,
old woman and be very embarrassed.

That remark struck her as very curious indeed. He was such a
histrionic, silly person, where did he get his ideas from, were they
folk-sayings, were they part of German legend? She could not stop
laughing.

He slapped her, to quiet her.

Yes, that's right!—hurt me. Do whatever you like, you know I
deserve it.

She had never felt younger. She was never going to age.

In his arms she was immortal.

Her fingers in his thick, springy hair; his mouth gnawing against
hers; the taste of each other's bodies; the necessary rituals of love.
(After they parted, after Eleanor left Boston at the age of thirty-
four, she made it a point to seek out other men; especially, for a
while, large slovenly good-natured men, and married men; and
men who would probably hurt her. She wanted to exorcise his
memory, she wanted him gone. She had not forgiven him and
never would. She wanted him *dead*. But it was five or six years before she could bring herself to respond sexually to a man—after
Edwin her body had gone numb, she was always nervously distracted, preoccupied, embarrassed. That too was his fault and she
would never forgive him.)

The Edna and Walter G. Davison Award for Distinction in
American Letters carried with it a prize of $1,500, and Eleanor
Gerhardt smiled gratefully, as one must, and read the poem of
hers about autumn in New England, in an old churchyard, which
she knew would please her audience; and she made a brief, graceful speech which was well-received; and the most difficult part of
the evening was over.

They crowded about her to congratulate her and to shake her
small, frail hand. They backed away so that a photographer could
take her picture, standing alongside the smiling young Dean of
Humanities.

How honored I am to meet you, voices claimed.

How very honored.

She autographed books, in most cases the paperback edition of her *Collected Poems*. She was quite tired now but of course she didn't show it. If her hand began to tremble, why she had merely to lean against the podium and to steady one hand with another. If her hearing failed occasionally, she had only to smile intently and nod, and the speaker was usually satisfied; if she was forced to ask him to repeat his question it could be attributed to the noise in the auditorium. Fortunately she had been able to sleep for about forty-five minutes at the Alumni House—otherwise she would have been very tired indeed. It was quite possible she might have been unable to complete her little speech and the audience would have been disappointed; moreover, they would have been alarmed, they would have made a fuss. If there was anything Eleanor detested it was fuss.

At the reception in a quaint filigreed parlor called the Founders' Room she noted, and was grateful, that the Dean and his wife and Benjamin Höller stayed close by, to protect her from people who wanted to talk too long, or whose questions were inappropriate, or who might have requests to make of her. (Though in recent years very few young poets had asked her to read and comment on their work.) She accepted a scotch and soda. She heard herself laughing, a melodic girlish laughter. Who were these people? Who were these strangers? It was touching that they should wish to honor her, to single her out for an award. It could not be true, as they asserted, that her poetry meant a great deal to them, and that she had contributed something marvelous to American letters—what *were* American letters, she had always wondered—but it was very decent of them to behave as if this were so. Everywhere she went, in this phase of her life, she encountered good, generous, admiring people. They were all so adamant—so young.

Someone's voice broke through. "Would you like another drink, Miss Gerhardt?"

She turned and it was Edwin's son. Unnecessarily she put a hand on his arm; she squeezed the rough material of his coat. Yes. No. Well, perhaps. It crossed her mind that her pale, slender hand was still attractive—delicately blue-veined, fragile. The star sapphire edged with diamonds was lovely. It had the look of an antique ring, an inheritance, but in fact it was quite new—a gift

Eleanor had given herself, whimsically, for her fifty-ninth birth-day.

"Yes? Shall I get you another?" Benjamin asked.

"If you don't mind," Eleanor said.

While the Dean's wife talked to her about the radical changes at Vassar (where Eleanor and the Dean's wife had gone, at different times), Eleanor watched Edwin's son make his way to the bar. She hadn't known, had she, that Benjamin Höller was teaching at Linden . . . ? Or had she known and forgotten? Years ago, years ago, she had spied on the Höllers from a distance and she had known a great deal about them, but after Edwin divorced his wife and moved to California, and remarried, and then divorced again and remarried, and accepted a visiting professorship at the University of Hawaii, and never returned to the States, she had grown confused about what, exactly, she wished to know, and what it might be best for her to forget. Of course she had known that Benjamin Höller was studying music. He had gone to Juilliard, she believed, at a fairly young age—fifteen or sixteen. But by then Edwin had left Boston; his life had changed completely. Her life had changed completely.

For a while she had been bitter. Very badly hurt, and very bitter. He had professed to love her, he had courted her, had appeared to wish to marry her—but when their relationship began to alter, after a few years, and it was evident that Eleanor had become rather dependent upon him, and quite emotional at times, he spoke less of marriage and more of his responsibility to his family: he did not love his wife, of course, but he had a commitment to her and to his son. In those days Eleanor Gerhardt was a striking young woman, outspoken, even a little brazen, known in the Boston area for her piquant good looks and her sarcasm and her poetry, which appeared in magazines fairly often, enviably often; she had a wide circle of acquaintances and had accumulated, she scarcely knew how, a tight little band of detractors. At times she felt almost invincible: she intended to work very, very hard at her craft and she intended to take all the prizes by storm. (Her first book, a modest enough venture called *Nurturings*, had been awarded a prize from the National Council on the Arts and one of the Boston newspapers had published a very flattering interview with her.) At other times, weeping in Edwin's arms, she felt helpless as a child, grotesquely weak, contemptible. She did not want to marry him, but—but perhaps— Wasn't it possible for them to go away for a year, she asked, begged, hadn't he wanted that at the very first, why had he changed his mind . . . ? He didn't love her! He had never loved her! He comforted her, she raged at him, he told her to stop, to be still, she thrust him from her, would have liked to tear at him with her nails. It was obvious that he loved her when they were together. No man could pretend such love, such passion. His cries were torn from him; they were brutal, almost shameful to hear. And she in turn loved him—she could not help herself. (Afterward she recalled that she had been aware of her behavior all along, eerily conscious of herself even when transported by passion or rage. A distraught, weeping, reckless young woman who was nevertheless witnessing herself, as if from a distance, contemplating her own mad excesses. She had been an actress pronouncing certain difficult lines, working against them, laboring to master them, until the point at which the words overtook her and carried her along without her conscious will—and then, of course, it was too late.)

I'll leave, she cried. I'll be the one to go away.

My dear Eleanor, please—

I know what you want: what you've been maneuvering. I'll be the one to go away.

Even then the affair hadn't ended. It had dragged on for another year. There were telephone calls in the night, there were threats of suicide, there were outbursts, periods of lucidity and good humor and optimism, dinners together in Boston, weekends in New York, sessions of desperate love. During the five years of their relationship Edwin had changed very little; he was a little grayer, a little more shaggy; he had gained ten pounds, perhaps. But he had not changed in any substantial way. Eleanor, however, had changed a great deal. She was no longer really young—not *young*. She carried about in her imagination a vision of herself as a striking young girl and when she happened to see herself, mirrored when she did not expect it, the sight was distressing.

He's made me ugly, she said to anyone who would listen. Look what he's done to me.

They laughed at her, and denied that she was ugly, and whispered behind her back. She had many enemies; there was no one she could really trust.

I'll be the one to go away, she threatened.

He held her heated, pale face in his hands and kissed her; kissed her goodbye.

I'll be the one to go away—

They could see that the reception was tiring her, so, though it was only ten o'clock, they drove her back to the Alumni House. Benjamin Höller accompanied them, seated beside her in the back seat of the Dean's car.

They chattered happily about the lovely autumn weather, the lovely countryside, the college's endowment fund, the fact that the faculty was "young and vigorous and community-minded." Eleanor did not care in the least but she heard her voice with the others, and was pleased that she had acquitted herself so well and that the evening was coming to an end. If she chose, she could recall the admiration with which she had been received; she could hear again the warm, generous applause. But in a week or two the visit to Linden College would begin to fade, and within a month she would be confusing it with a visit to the University of Virginia, where she had been awarded an honorary degree the previous spring. Friendly people, generous applause, handshakes and photographs and a few strong drinks; then the flight home.

Except for Benjamin Höller. She would remember him.

At least it was a genuine love, she wanted to tell him suddenly. Your father and I hurt each other very much, we suffered, we were in misery much of the time—but we were alive, at least. I hated him for years and wanted him dead and then I stopped hating him and now I think of him with love, I can't help thinking of him with love; it's almost as if no time has passed at all. It's almost as if nothing has changed at all.

After leaving Boston Eleanor returned to her family's home in Chestnut Hill for a few months, but there were disagreements, misunderstandings, attempts to possess her (always made in the name of love), and many quarrels. She was thirty-five years old. She knew herself to be a wreck, a failure, an ugly haggard creature: whenever she thought of Edwin her throat constricted, as if to prevent her from crying aloud. She had no friends now. She wanted no friends. She moved to New York City, to a partly furnished room on the West Side, and there she lay in bed for days at a time, too lethargic to dress, too fatigued to write. She

believed she would never write again—what was the point of it, really? She had done quite well with her poetry; people envied her,
resented her modest success; she had worked hard and knew that,
if she worked hard again, she might be a very fine poet indeed.
But what was the point of it? Edwin had been impressed at first,
and then he had lost interest. He had loved her very much at first
and then he had stopped loving her. No matter what she wrote,
no matter how successful she became, it would not have the
power to make him love her again.

Her hatred for Edwin detached itself from him. It floated loose,
fouling the air. Once she drew a razor blade lightly across the inside of her arm, simply to see what would happen. She detested
herself: she was such a liar, such a coward. The razor blade hurt,
so of course she dropped it into the sink. Oh Christ, she cried, this
is such folly.

The razor blade hurt her sensitive skin, a comb drawn roughly
through her hair hurt her scalp, the cold bright ferocious winter
air hurt her lungs. This is such degradation, she thought. Surely
there is some mistake.

She wanted to telephone him. She wanted to write.

She was reasonably certain that if she approached him he would
take her back. He had loved her so much, after all—!

But she did not telephone or write. Instead she began to work:
haphazardly at first, with a rather cynical sense of direction. If she
loathed herself she might at least make a kind of poetry out of it;
it was preferable to love oneself, or to approve of oneself, but if
that was out of the question she would have to make do with
what was at hand. Months passed and she had nothing to show
for her effort except piles of notes. Raw emotions. Words. She
began another love affair, fully conscious of the fact that she neither loved the man nor felt desire for him—it was simply that she
needed someone between herself and Edwin Höller, so that she
would be able to deal with her experience. The emotions had
been transmuted into words, and now the words had to be given a
certain focus, a certain tone. She would have to create the exact
structure to contain these words: if she worked very hard she
might force them into perfection.

Two years later *A Season of Love* was published. It was an odd
book—less than one hundred pages of brief enigmatic pieces, some
of it poetry, some prose, in a terse, elliptical voice that was unlike

anything Eleanor Gerhardt had done in the past. It received a
very limited attention, like most books of poetry, and Eleanor had
not been especially disappointed—she had expected nothing
much, after all. She would have liked Edwin to read it, she would
have liked him to write to her, perhaps . . . But he never wrote. It
was highly unlikely that he had read the book; possibly he hadn't
even heard of it.

And then, several years later, when she was immersed in other
things, a director who had read *A Season of Love* and had been
very moved by it contacted her, and asked if she would like to
fashion the book into a play; if she would like to collaborate with
a playwright on it. At first she refused, thinking the idea ludicrous.
She knew nothing about the theatre and could not bear the
thought of working with other people. And wasn't the subject
simply too familiar?—a disastrous love affair, a great deal of suffering, a bitter farewell? But the director persisted and in the end
Eleanor gave in and the result was a surprisingly successful little
play. Since it required virtually no stage settings, and only two ac-
tors, it was easy to mount; since it involved a great deal of emotion it interested audiences, especially women; and the language
was deft, bitten-off, shrewd, cruelly precise, so that one came away
moved by respect for the articulate nature of the lovers, however
familiar the situation itself was. Eleanor forced herself to see the
play once and was not altogether ashamed. . . . And then the extraordinary thing happened: the play made money, it was taken
up by universities and summer stock theatres, there was even an
Off-Broadway "revival" in the early sixties. Eleanor Gerhardt, by
then an established poet, was lauded as a precursor of the
Women's Movement; she was praised for her unblinking honesty,
for the terseness of her language, for the violence with which she
condemned received ideas of male domination. She might have
written other plays, she might have attempted a novel, but, pru-
dently, she shied away from such risks; she did not want public acclaim, she was perfectly satisfied with poetry. At first she felt
guilty about the royalties she received—as a poet, she had grown
to believe that one was never paid for one's best work. Then as
the years passed and the royalties continued, and the sales of her
books, even increased, she came to take this income for granted:
at least she was not disturbed by it.

People who knew Eleanor knew that *A Season of Love* was

closely based upon her love affair with a man named Edwin Höller, and they might have known that Höller had published a single book, a scholarly study on some obscure facet of Greek civilization, but they didn't know Höller himself, and had only a mild curiosity about him. Had he minded the play, they asked Eleanor; what might a man feel about the fact that his personality had been publicly analyzed, his behavior as a lover so rigorously assessed? Eleanor said curtly that she hadn't any idea—no idea at all. What about the man's wife?—had she minded? It must have seemed ironic to her, that her husband's former mistress should fashion such a success out of their love affair. But Eleanor knew nothing about Höller's wife. Since she wasn't evidently much of a reader she had probably never heard of the book of poems, and possibly not the play either. She knew nothing about Eleanor herself, after all. She might have suspected something but she hadn't any proof. The woman was said to be a self-centered, vain, limited person, mainly interested in her household, and in her son; and in any case she was to lose her husband anyway, a few years after his affair with Eleanor ended—he'd divorced her to marry a woman in her mid-twenties, the wife of one of his colleagues.

I was only the first of his women, Eleanor said. She wondered if this was true. Probably not: but she liked the ironic, stoical sound of the words.

Would he like a cup of coffee? There were facilities in the next room, a small kitchen she could use; it would be no trouble at all to make coffee.

He declined, saying that a single cup would keep him awake all night. He'd always been a poor sleeper.

Eleanor murmured something sympathetic.

They smiled uneasily at each other.

Eleanor had seated herself in a wing-back chair beside the fireplace, conscious of sitting rather stiffly. A proper old lady. Her hands clasped in her lap. Benjamin Höller sat in a chintz-covered easy chair facing her. He was very nervous: Eleanor noted that his fingers moved almost constantly, as if picking out keys on the piano, marking a secret rhythm. She wanted to say that he had played beautifully as a child—she would never forget—there were certain melancholy, haunting melodies—she would never forget—

"We might as well—"

"I was thinking—"

They paused. Eleanor began by asking gently how his father
had been—had the last years of his life been happy?—he'd been in
Hawaii, hadn't he—

"I really wouldn't know," Benjamin said with a small hurt
smile. "We didn't keep in contact."

"I'm sorry to hear that," Eleanor said.

"I would have thought that—possibly—he'd have been in contact with *you*."

"No," Eleanor said, startled. "Not at all."

"I thought—"

"Just a telegram a few years ago—no, it must have been twelve,
fourteen years ago— Just a single television program, nothing
more."

Benjamin's fingers moved lightly. "He was always such a bastard, wasn't he," he said.

Taken by surprise Eleanor laughed. But it was a mirthless,
choking sound.

"He was a—an exceptional person— He couldn't help—"

"He was a bastard," Benjamin said flatly. Out of his drab tweed
coat he drew a manila envelope; for an instant his expression
shifted and Eleanor wondered in alarm if he was about to burst
into tears. "My mother used to say it was because he hadn't the
professional recognition he wanted—the fame he thought he deserved. He was so petty, you know, so jealous, he could be so
vicious—writing savage reviews of Eliade's books, for instance, and
sending them in duplicate to journals—anything to hurt an old
friend—anything to get published. I think she was wrong, though.
If he'd gotten the attention he wanted he would have been just as
miserable—just as much of a bastard."

"Would he?" Eleanor asked, surprised. She stared at Benjamin
and could see, now, nothing of her lover in that face: not his eyes,
certainly. This intense, balding young man was a complete
stranger. "I thought— I— But I thought," she said feebly, "that
you loved him—I mean, that you—"

Benjamin laughed harshly. "When?"

"What?"

"*When* did you think that?"

"When did I think—?"

"That I loved him?"

"I—I don't know— When you were a boy, I suppose."

"Yes, but when did *you* think that?"

Eleanor was quite confused. She started to speak, then stopped.

"Did you think that when you were sleeping with him?—or was it afterward, maybe?" Benjamin asked. He was tapping the manila envelope on his knee. Though he spoke harshly Eleanor realized that he was quite nervous. She herself had started to tremble; she felt a little faint. "How many years afterward?" he asked.

"I didn't realize that you knew," Eleanor said weakly.

"Knew *what?*"

"About your father and me— About—"

"Of course I knew. My mother and I both knew. I was ten years old when your affair with him began, and fifteen when it ended. I knew everything. Nearly everything. How could I not have known?" he laughed.

"But—"

"You were both pigs," Benjamin said.

For a few shocked seconds they sat in silence. Eleanor could not look away from him. Something pulsed in her throat, in her ears. Was she going to faint? What had happened? . . . She saw that the young man's lips were moving, she realized he was speaking again. "How could we not have known?" he said. "Everyone knew. It was no secret. One day my father threw a bottle of wine against the wall while we were at the dining room table, he began screaming at my mother, asking why she kept so quiet, why did she pretend nothing was wrong, was she scheming against him— calling her names, pounding on the table like a madman— He made no secret of it, he didn't believe in secrets. He believed in *passion,*" Benjamin said softly.

"I didn't know—"

"Of course you knew."

Eleanor half-closed her eyes. She heard herself denying it, she heard herself begging to be understood. If only this agitated young man would—

"You were both pigs," he said flatly, "but I'm willing to agree that *he* was the worst. He made a fool of you, he intimidated you, used you, it pleased him to taunt my mother with the fact that he had a mistress, a devoted, passionate, highly intelligent young woman—*Younger than you,* he used to say, *beautiful while you're ugly*—that sort of thing. He liked to shout, he liked to stamp around the house throwing his arms about. That was passion, that was the way passionate people behaved. Filled with life, you know —that sort of thing. He pretended to worship the instincts. His lectures were filled with that sort of crap. In fact he was in despair because he couldn't publish anything substantial, because ideas slipped through his fingers, he was getting old, he was a failure, he was inferior—he was viciously jealous of his colleagues and afraid they were all laughing at him. So he turned to you. So he tormented my mother and destroyed her life."

"But I wasn't the only woman," Eleanor stammered. "I—I wasn't the first, even— I don't think I was the first—"

"But you were the most faithful," Benjamin said. "You stuck like glue. Even when he wanted to get rid of you he couldn't—and that was pleasing to him too, that you were so idiotically in love with him, wanted to marry him, wanted to help finance a trip to India for him— He used to ask my mother for advice, and friends who dropped over: what was he to do, this unbalanced young woman was so madly in love with him, how was he to extricate himself from her, what was he to *do?* In front of my mother he talked like that. He got drunk, he bawled, he threw his arms about, he pretended to be sorry, to be ashamed. The filthy old bastard. The pig. *My God,* he'd croak, staring at me with this stupid, cruel, operatic expression, *what will happen to Benjamin?—to all of us?* He was afraid you would kill yourself, you see."

"Kill myself?" Eleanor said faintly. "But that's—that's preposterous—I was never going to kill myself— And I never wanted to marry him; I have never wanted to marry anyone. He must have been lying—"

"He wasn't lying," Benjamin interrupted. "He was too stupid to lie. The fact was that you *were* begging him to marry you and you *were* threatening suicide; and everyone knew it. He was frightened but at the same time euphoric—that a young woman should love him so desperately, so shamelessly, and if you had committed suicide—"

"This is ridiculous," Eleanor said faintly.

"Here are your letters," Benjamin said, holding the envelope out. "That last winter you wrote a dozen letters and I remember him reading parts of them aloud—to my mother, that is—in their bedroom—I listened at the door, I eavesdropped, I had to be close in case she needed protection; I believe I was ready to kill him if necessary. Yes, you wrote him long deranged letters, you certainly were begging him to marry you—and you *were* threatening suicide. If you don't believe me—"

"I didn't write any letters," Eleanor said. "I never wrote any letters."

"When he moved out he left an attic of books and papers and correspondence—and your letters were in all the mess, in a desk drawer. I wanted to throw everything out and my mother wanted to keep everything, so we kept most of the books, and some of the letters—just left them where they were. I would have liked to burn everything," Benjamin said lightly, "but I didn't get my way. My mother still loved him: that was part of her illness."

Eleanor stared at the manila envelope he was holding. She had written no letters; she was positive she had written no letters. Certainly she had never begged Edwin Höller to marry her—!

"I don't believe this," Eleanor whispered. "Any of this."

Benjamin waved her words aside. "Your beliefs don't interest me, Miss Gerhardt, any more than your emotions interest me. *You* don't interest me, in fact. I realize my father exploited you, you were stupid enough to fall in love with him, and at one time I did hate you—I hated you very much—but right now, tonight, whatever you think or feel doesn't interest me in the slightest. I want to hand these letters over to you, that's all."

Eleanor made no move to accept the envelope, so he laid it carefully on the table between them.

He was breathing hard. His expression was queerly bright and contemptuous. "If you had committed suicide I think he would have been pleased—though of course he would have put on a noisy display of grief. It was his *nature*, he used to say, to be demonstrative; he didn't believe in suppressing his emotions. He ruined my life and my mother's and he even liked to berate himself about that—saying he didn't know what to do next, he didn't know where to turn, life was a terrible mystery. My mother was half-crazy with shame, as you can imagine. She was from the Boston area, her father was a Presbyterian minister, she simply didn't know how to handle what was happening. It wasn't just that she loved him—it was also the fact that everyone knew about his betrayal of her. Word got back to her family, even. She was so ashamed, humiliated—she began to drink—she'd say to me *I'm just dirt, trash, I'm no good, I'm nothing*—when I came home from school she'd be in the kitchen, drunk—staggering drunk—I felt so sorry for her and I hated him but I didn't know what to do. I didn't know what to do. She and my father had these terrible fights—he'd scream at her, and after a while she began to scream at him, and they'd throw things at each other, and the next day I'd find her drunk again, and she'd hang onto me and say she was trash, garbage, she should be thrown out like garbage, she should be destroyed—should die. What could I do?" Benjamin said sharply. "She had been an intelligent woman at one time— she'd gone to Radcliffe, she had a bachelor's degree in French— she loved French literature—but when my father started being unfaithful to her she went to pieces: she lost everything. Then she did the most desperate thing. I wonder if you knew about it?— probably not, he would have been embarrassed to tell you. At the age of forty-one she got pregnant. Deliberately pregnant. Did you know? Did he ever tell you?"

"Pregnant—?" Eleanor said, blinking. She tried to think, tried to remember. There was Edwin whom she had loved, and Edwin's wife whom she had never known. She had met the woman a few times—or had she?—she couldn't remember. A frail vaporous face, an insubstantial body. "Your mother? Pregnant?"

"I suppose my father had you convinced that he made love only to *you*," Benjamin said with an ugly smile, "so he wouldn't have told you about it. But it's true: she got pregnant at the age of forty-one. I don't know why. And then she tried to abort the baby. She was hospitalized, and wanted to keep the baby, and she was released, and they had another of their fights, and he went to New York for a week—I think it was immediately after she was discharged from the hospital, in fact. She was still pregnant. She decided she wanted the baby. But she kept on drinking, she got worse, and in the end the baby was born prematurely—slightly deformed, it was, and brain-damaged from all the abuse, the drinking, the poor diet. You didn't know any of this? No? What a pity. I would have supposed your lover told you all his secrets," he said slyly.

"I didn't know—I had no idea," Eleanor whispered.

"So I had a baby sister. Have a baby sister," Benjamin said. "In fact she's still alive—she's very much alive. Twenty-nine years old, I believe."

"She's—?"

"Very much alive,," he repeated. "Can't you hear?"

"But—I had no idea—"

"How *could* you have had any idea, Miss Gerhardt?" he said. "My sister has been in the state hospital at Readsboro for a very long time. Even when my mother was living, she was too much for her—the brain damage was severe, she never learned to talk, can barely manage to walk. A six-month-old infant, really. But she's twenty-nine years old and in excellent physical health, the doctors say. . . . Would you like to meet her, Miss Gerhardt? Have you time for that?"

Eleanor pressed her hands against her face. Something caught in her throat; she could barely breathe. I didn't know, she wanted to cry, I didn't know, why are you saying these things, why don't you let me alone?—I didn't know. I am innocent.

"Never mind," Benjamin Höller said, getting to his feet. "I'll say goodbye now."

She stared wildly at him, cringing. For a moment she thought he was going to strike her.

Then he was leaving, backing away. The visit was over. His words swam and echoed and pulsed in her ears. She could not decipher them. She could not understand. He was leaving without shaking her hand; he did not seem to care for her.

"Good night, Miss Gerhardt," he said.

"But—"

She stared at the door and tried to think where she was. What time it was. He had been so angry, that man—that stranger. It was not her fault, surely. Why had he left without shaking her hand?

"I had no idea," she said shrilly. "I'm not to blame."

The fire flared up brightly. Then died down again.

She prodded it with a letter-opener she had found in the writing desk, grunting with the effort. Why didn't it burn, what was wrong? She heard herself sobbing with frustration.

Lining the bureau drawers were sheets of near-transparent paper that crumpled noisily in her hands. She made balls of them and arranged them in the fireplace, close about the letters. Stooping, breathing laboriously, she lit another match and held it against the paper. The flame caught at once; again it flared up, nearly touching her fingers.

She stood before the fireplace, panting, trembling. She stared at

the crumpled papers. Unread, the letters were starting to burn. At
last they were starting to burn.

Where do the hours go, she wondered.

She brushed at her eyes with the back of one hand, sniffing. She
was so tired. So very tired. It was unfair. He had not shaken her
hand. She was innocent, yet the letters burned so sluggishly.
What if they did not burn? But they would burn. She had all
night if necessary.

PASSION?

JONATHAN BAUMBACH

Jonathan Baumbach, who was born in Brooklyn, New York, is currently living in London on a Guggenheim Fellowship. He is a founder and former director of the Fiction Collective. His fifth novel, *Chez Charlotte and Emily*, and a book of stories, *The Return of Service*, will both be published in 1979.

> "Everything remains to be done."
>
> —*Jean Luc Godard*

1.

A man I know, a long-time sometime friend, recently left his wife and three children because he had fallen in love with another woman. Such news has a disquieting effect on our crowd. Henry is the most domesticated and repressed husband among us, the most devoted of fathers. If Henry, our moral light, is capable of such anarchic behavior, it strikes us that almost anything is possible. Surmise, however, is not the business of this report. What I mean to do here is to separate the knowable evidence from unwarranted conjecture. I mean to investigate the mystery of Henry's inexplicable act as though I were a detective tracking down a criminal.

2.

Henry was barely twenty-four when he married Illana. They had met at college, had started going together when Henry, who was a year or so older, was in his sophomore year, though they had known each other casually (or such is the story one pieces to-

gether) from childhood. There were times, says Illana, when each
was the other's only real friend. Her remark is not surprising.
Henry and Illana had always seemed, to those of us who thought
we knew them well, exceptionally close. They had grown over the
years of their marriage to seem like mirror images of one another.
One breathed in, we supposed, and the other breathed out. They
saw themselves, and we tended to confirm that view, as a perfect
couple.

3.

The year before he married Illana, Henry, then a Rhodes scholar,
started work on a novel about a young intellectual affianced to his
childhood sweetheart who falls in love during a summer abroad
with a French woman twelve years his senior. He wrote 126 pages
of this book before giving up and the manuscript apparently still
exists in its first and only draft. It was, insofar as anyone knows,
Henry's only attempt at prolonged fiction.

4.

In the second year of their marriage, their first daughter, Natalia,
was born. Henry and Illana were extremely serious about the responsibility. Shortly after that, Henry, an up and coming editor,
moved to a job in another publishing house that paid twenty dollars more a month. Illana also was working and they had a live-in
maid to look after the child. Henry announced, we all remember,
that Illana's working was a temporary arrangement, that it was
the preference of both of them that she stay home with the child.
Illana said that she and Henry on that matter were in thorough
agreement. She made this assertion, as I remember, with surprising passion.

5.

Henry was under a great deal of pressure at work and went into
therapy to avoid, as he said, breaking down altogether. He had a
dream—his therapist had been after him to write down his dreams
—in which his father, whom he hadn't seen in ten years, came to
him and said that there was evidence that someone was shooting

at him and he wondered if it were Henry. Henry said that he admitted to being angry at his father for having walked out on his mother but that he had no recollection of trying to kill him. The father said if thoughts could kill, Henry would have to be number one suspect. Thoughts don't kill, said Henry. Well, how do you explain the bullet in my stomach? said the father.

6.

About that time Henry reported to friends that he and Illana were reading to each other in bed at night. "We are going through the entire canon of Dickens," said Illana, "one chapter a night." "How long will it take to do all the novels?" someone asked. Henry, figuring to himself, a private smile on his face, said nothing. "We'll do it until we decide not to do it," said Illana.

7.

Illana had written a children's book in her spare time. Henry agented it for her, showing it to children's book editors at two other publishing houses, avoiding his own as a matter of moral discretion. Illana and Henry had always taken impeccable moral positions. And though they didn't presume to judge others, one sensed a certain discomfort with the unscrupulous or overweeningly ambitious. Illana withdrew the book at some point, indicating that she had no great desire to make her work public.

8.

I spoke to Henry at the hospital after the birth of his second daughter, Nara. He said, although he and Illana had wanted a boy, they were not in any way disappointed. Illana said the same thing to my wife in almost the same language, impressing on us (was it meant to?) how together they were, how intimately allied. A week later, when we visited them at home, Henry in Illana's presence made the same speech. When we got home my wife said, "Perhaps they protest too much," and I said, no, I thought they meant it. "It's the same thing," she said.

9.

We all admired the seeming ease with which Henry rose in his chosen profession. What was most impressive was that his ambition, which evidence suggests was considerable, was never aggressively displayed. He had never, not to our knowledge at least, advanced his career at the expense of someone else. We had almost never heard a bad word of him. Yet at the same time we felt that Henry's full capacities were not being realized. What we meant by that was not at all clear.

10.

What do we know about Illana? When friends of Henry's and Illana's get together, the question tends to come up. What has she had to say for herself in all the years we've known her? We thought of her as taciturn, though not unfriendly, a bit formal in manner, a woman who spoke her opinions as if they were national secrets. She had a way of looking after her children—this was when Henry was there to help—without making it seem, as do some mothers, that the job was overburdening her. We can enumerate her qualities with no strong sense of knowing the person who is the sum and substance of them.

11.

This is Henry's story mostly. It is Henry who announces one day, Illana sitting at the table with the baby on her lap, that he has fallen in love with someone else. "You have?" Illana is imagined to have asked. "What does that mean in terms of our marriage?"

"I don't know," said Henry. "It's too new to me."

"You don't know?" The question asked with some manner of skepticism. "What do you want to do?"

"What do you want me to do?"

"Well, naturally," Illana said softly, "I'd like you to break it off if you can."

"Out of the question," said Henry.

"I didn't realize that it . . ." said Illana, a small crack of panic in her usually impassive face, swallowing her words as though ashamed of their inadequacy.

"It happened," said Henry. "I didn't mean it to, but it did. I'm terribly sorry."

12.

After that first confession, Illana becomes a tacit partner, an accessory after the fact, in Henry's double life. Henry works out a regimen, accommodating both worlds. He has dinner with Illana and the children, helps put the children to bed, leaves afterwards to spend the night with Patricia, returning by taxi at 5 A.M. to be present when the children awake. It is important to him to have the children perceive their world as intact. (Also important perhaps to keep up appearances in front of himself and Illana, a way of deflecting awareness.) "I want you to do what's best for you," Illana is reported to have said to Henry. "I don't want to leave you and the children," said Henry, "and I can't give up Patricia." If this assertion wounds Illana, there is no visible evidence for it. After breakfast, Henry takes the oldest daughter, Natalia, to school, as he has always done before going off himself to work.

13.

The vice-president of the government foundation at which Henry now worked had been having an affair with the wife of one of the board of directors and word of it—one wondered why the news had taken so long—finally reached that lady's husband. Scandal ensued and the notorious administrator had no choice but to resign in favor of a slightly higher paying job at another foundation, leaving in his wake a vacancy at the top. It was rumored that Henry was in favored consideration for the post. Who knows where such rumors start? Henry, at the time, was the youngest and ablest associate director at the foundation, and it was more than possible that his well-wishers, wanting the rumor so, presumed its likelihood. Henry, taking nothing for granted, went to see the president of the foundation to indicate his interest and availability. Whatever Henry's boss said to him—the account given to me was notably short on specifics—Henry appeared hopeful in his guarded way. "Frankly," he said, "I have no reason to expect anything."

14.

Illana said, out of Henry's hearing, that she thought Henry was setting himself up for a fall. "You think he won't get the job?" asked her confidante, who in this case was my wife, Genevieve. "I think his chances are not as good as he thinks they are," said Illana, according to my source. "Of course he deserves the job," she added. "I just don't think he's in line for it." Something odd was going on between them, we thought. Why hadn't Illana, who was the epitome of loyalty, offered this perception to Henry?

15.

One day my wife asked me if I found Illana sexy? Sexy may not be the word she had used. "Attractive" or "beautiful" is more likely. I don't remember what I answered. "Uhnrr," perhaps. Something that canceled itself out, I suspect. What's that about? I thought, though let it slide by at the time. About a week later, something else bothering me, I asked her why she had asked about Illana. "Oh," she said, "someone else was saying, I don't remember who, that Illana was the most beautiful woman of his acquaintance and I wondered if you thought the same thing." I said I didn't even think Henry thought that. "That's an odd thing to say," she said. "Well, she's beautiful in a conventional way," I said, "but there's something glacial about her as if she weren't quite alive."

16.

Why do I remember my wife's question about Illana and my answer, and what do they have to do with the larger question under investigation in this study? I think we both felt that there was something invisibly wrong with Henry and Illana's perfect marriage, though we were not in touch with that perception. And why should we have been? Why should we have thought of Henry and Illana at all? I don't know the answers. I ask the questions merely to ask them. Illana was not the issue of my wife's question as it turned out, merely the displaced occasion. I had heard the question she had asked, but not the unspoken confession it contained.

17.

Two days after Henry's son was born, he got word that the job he had coveted, had come in fact to count on, had been given to someone else. The news arrived, as it tends to in government agencies, by way of rumor, and Henry, as angry as he ever remembers himself, went to see his boss to check it out. "Don," Henry said, "I've heard some disturbing news." Don took his glasses off to listen, lit a cigarette, though he had given up smoking a week ago this day. "Well, what have you heard?" he asked. (His tone suggested, Henry reported, that there wasn't any rumor around he wasn't prepared to deny.) "I had heard," said Henry, "that you had made a decision on Calvin's replacement." "Oh that," said Don. "You said you would let me know as soon as you came to a decision," said Henry. "Did I say that?" said Don. "Frankly, I don't remember making any such promise. The feeling was, and as you know I queried opinions from all directions, that you could have done the job adequately—no one had anything negative to say about your capabilities—but that . . ." Henry had no recollection of how the sentence was completed.

18.

Henry, it was reported, took his disappointment with extraordinary grace, which was our idea of Henry. "That's the way it goes," he said, defending the qualifications of the man chosen in his place. "What I have to do is re-evaluate my commitment to my job." Illana seemed emotionally drained. We perceived it as a form of loyalty to Henry and admired them both—this special couple—all the more.

19.

The following account has been confirmed by two sources and so it is included here despite my own tendency to disbelieve it. The time was about four weeks after Henry learned that he had been passed over for the promotion he had anticipated. The affair with

Patricia, if it had already started, was some two months shy of
becoming public news. Henry and Illana were at a party hosted by
Henry's employer. It was a cocktail party held in some east side
apartment to honor the grant recipients of that year and the living
room was crowded to the walls with the mostly uninvited. Some
bearded middle-aged composer, congenitally sour, took it into his
head to assail Henry over the granting policy of the foundation
which had just passed Henry over for promotion. Henry was polite at first, said he was not responsible for the choices of commit-
tees on which he hadn't served, then proceeded, which is typical
of Henry, to defend the foundation's policies unequivocally. The
composer kept after him, finding fault with one choice after another. When he could take no more—one can imagine the complication of his feelings—Henry turned his back on him. Illana, who
happened to be on the periphery of the small group listening in,
was heard to whisper to Henry, "Why didn't you answer him?"
Henry, usually under control, lost his temper and shouted at her,
"Why didn't I answer him? Why didn't I? I didn't answer him
because the son of a bitch is not listening to anything I say." It is
reported that Illana's face reddened and that she apologized to
Henry's adversary for her husband's behavior.

20.

Even after Henry moves in with Patricia, Illana continues to pretend to the children that she and Henry are together as before.
"Why are you doing it?" my wife says to her when she comes to
visit with the three children, who range in age from six months
to six years. "If I were you, I'd tell him to fuck off." Illana, who
rarely smiles, smiles at that. "I would if I felt that way," she says.
"I'm not angry at Henry. I want him to be happy and if he's
happy this way, then that's the way it has to be." When Illana is
gone my wife says to me: "One of these days she's going to realize
how angry she really is. And then . . ."

21.

A call from Henry this morning at work. He wants us, he says, to
be the first of his friends to meet Patricia. An appointment is
made for dinner at a Chinese restaurant called Hunan Feast. My

wife says, when she hears of the arrangement, that she won't go, that it is a disloyalty to Illana even to meet Patricia. I mention that Henry is also a friend and that there is no reason why we have to take sides. "I can't forgive him," she says. "He may be a friend of yours, but he's no friend of mine."

Patricia seems as nervous to meet us as we are to meet her, and the experience reminds me of the blind dates of my adolescence. None of us seems able to strike the right note. "What do you think?" Henry whispers out of earshot of the women. "I think she's . . . (I search for the word) fine," I say generously. My answer seems to disappoint him. "Is that all?" he asks.

22.

"What do you think of her?" my wife asks when we're in bed that night, the first either of us has risked the subject.

"She's different from what I imagined," I hear myself saying.

"I don't know what you mean by that." A note of irritation in her tone.

"Does that mean you don't like her?" I ask.

"It's not a question of liking or disliking her. She's nothing. She's a blank. Didn't you see that?"

My silence offers denial.

"My God, Joshua, I've never seen anyone with less personality. She's pathetic."

"Well, what do you think she has for Henry?"

"I haven't the faintest idea. What do you think?"

"Well, she's not unattractive," I say.

"Not unattractive? She's the most ordinary-looking woman I've ever seen in my life."

23.

Henry is on one of his periodic diets; we go to a health food restaurant for lunch and have a couple of shredded carrot sandwiches. Our conversation is correspondingly low on calories. "Patsy liked you and Genevieve," he says a few times, rephrasing the remark so as not to seem to repeat himself. "She felt the two of you accepted her." "She seemed extremely nice," I say. "Very . . ." The word eludes me. "Unconstrained," he says.

"Unconstrained," I repeat. "In that way, she's the opposite of Illana," he says. "Do you think you'll stay with her?" I ask. He becomes thoughtful, which is a form of reprimand with Henry, an indication that you've overstepped yourself. Then he says with a forgiving smile: "We take every day as it comes." It goes like that until later in the meal when Henry says, "Illana and I still love each other. The situation hasn't changed that."

"Then you are thinking of going back to her?"

"It's impossible," he says, smiling enigmatically. "We're both happier this way."

"Both of you?" My incredulousness seems to escape notice.

Henry eats his yogurt and nuts with a beatific smile.

"Is it sex?" I ask, expecting no answer.

"Never been so good," he says.

24.

"It's not sex," says my wife. We are still trying to understand our friend Henry. "Or sex is merely an excuse for something else."

"If Henry says their sex is good, why should you doubt him?"

"Henry," says Genevieve, "is trying something out. He wants to see how far he can go, how outrageous he can be, before Illana will say 'no more.' "

"That leaves out the implication of Patsy altogether," I say.

"Patsy doesn't count. Don't you see that?"

"If you ask Henry, Patsy is the only one who counts."

Our conflicting views of the reality abrade against one another, strain the limits of our friendship.

"Why are we fighting over Henry and Illana?" my wife asks.

The continuing argument becomes its own answer.

25.

Henry and Patricia have been living together for six months. Henry visits with the children on weekends and sometimes comes over in the evenings to put them to bed. Illana, although she sees other men, appears to work at it as if a recommended though pointless exercise, remains in her heart faithful to the Arrangement. How do I know this? Illana tells us or tells Genevieve, which comes to the same thing. Genevieve becomes increasingly impatient with Illana's stance, though talks to her almost every day on the phone, gauging her emotional temperature from the evidence of the unspoken. "She has no idea how angry she really is," says Genevieve. "Her calm is a form of self-oblivion. Meanwhile she won't allow herself to get interested in any of the men she sees. I can't stand it."

26.

My wife says, à propos of my arm around her, "You're behaving like Henry."

"What does that mean?"

"Henry and Patsy, as you know, behave like teenagers in public, but they have an excuse. They're new to each other."

Her rebuke turns into a fight. I recall my arm and take refuge in another room.

She follows after a moment. "Don't you see what you're doing?" she asks. "You're jealous that Henry has another woman."

"Maybe I am," I say.

27.

I overhear Genevieve complain to Illana on the phone about me, her way I think of criticizing Henry indirectly. All of our men are unreliable, says her tone. And what have I done? Whatever it is, she refuses to forgive me. "I am not Henry," I say to her.

"You wish you were," she says.

I call Henry from work, but he is not available for lunch that day, which is too bad. He is precisely the person I need to talk to in my present mood. An odd coincidence: I run into Illana at lunch; she is with another man, I am with another woman. We hail each other across the restaurant. At first I didn't recognize her —how absolutely smashing she looks!—was staring at her in admiration. "We'll have to talk some time," I say to her. She says, "Yes, yes."

28.

Have I drifted from the subject of this investigation? The subject itself drifts. To tell someone's story is to identify, to some extent, with the inner life of that person. In explaining Henry, I explain myself; in explaining myself, I explain Henry. Although not influenced by Henry's behavior—I am convinced that he is not my example—I have just split with my wife of ten years. My situation differs from Henry's in certain definitive ways. I haven't (at the time, at *this* time) fallen in love with anyone else. Genevieve and I weren't getting along, were fighting too much, were making each other unhappy. I realize this sounds evasive, but the disrepair of our marriage is too immediate for me to see it with any clarifying distance. It is easier, if not altogether more edifying, to talk about Henry and Illana. Henry continues to live joyfully, passionately, with Patsy, who is neither more nor less beautiful than his wife and who, despite apparent differences, resembles her more than not. Illana continues to make do and to accept her husband's manifest disaffection with public and private grace. I envy them both. My situation is neither pleasurable in itself nor might it engender the admiration of others.

29.

Tonight I have dinner with Illana and the two older children, sitting at the table with them in their makeshift living/dining room as I had times before in significantly different circumstances. Illana prefers, she says (the evening's arrangement is her idea), to eat with the children like a family. After dinner, I help her put them to bed, a chore of some complication. "How do you manage by yourself?" I ask. "Henry usually comes to help," she says. "But since you were coming I told him there was no need for him to bother." I indicate some surprise that she had mentioned it to Henry. "We have no secrets from each other," she says with that seriousness characteristic of them both.

"What now?" she asks.

The question is not meant to be answered. We sit on the sofa, holding hands, talking about nothing. At one point, she says—we have just kissed somewhat awkwardly—"Joshua, do you think of me as a cold person?" I reserve answer, kissing her again as if that urgent gesture (is it really as urgent as it seems?) were a response to her question. And yet what I think one moment ceases to be true the next. She is passionate yet remote as if her passion were a private wellspring separate from her day to day nature.

30.

I return to my hotel room at four in the morning and have barely
dropped off when the phone rings. "I want you back," the voice
says. It is odd that I am unable to identify or rather confuse the
identity of that voice. I finesse my confusion. "At this moment?"
I ask. "As soon as you can," says the voice. (I will know in a minute who it is, I think. Keep her talking and she will reveal herself.)
"Why do you want me back?" "Oh, God! Do you have to ask? If
you don't come to me, I'll come to you." She hangs up abruptly
though soundlessly, fitting the phone like a piece of a puzzle into
the base. Three hours later (all time is an estimate here), a knock
on the door wakes me from an erotic dream. "Who's there?" I ask
the nurse in my dream. The knock repeats, replays itself. I put on
a bathrobe and stagger to the door, bumping invisible furniture en
route. "Do you mind my coming to your room?" she asks, stepping in, locking the door behind her. Perhaps she says nothing at
all and the voice I quote is out of that interrupted dream. There is
no time for questions and explanations; there is barely even time
to kiss. Coupling is impersonal and urgent like some natural disaster. "Who's with the children?" I ask later. "Never mind," she
says. "The children are well looked after."

31.

Henry seems unusually jaunty when we meet after work at
O'Neill's for a drink. I am not eager to talk to him, would have
avoided this meeting if I hadn't felt obliged to face him. It takes
him two drinks to get to what's on his mind. "I don't know that I
like what's going on between you and Illana," he says casually and
then again with added weight as if he hadn't heard himself the
first time. "I've always liked Illana," I say. He nods. "She's a
terrific person, and I don't want to see her hurt." Although expecting something like this—Henry is one of the most consciously
moral people I know—I can think of nothing useful to say. "Are
you in love with her?" he asks. "Henry, come on," I say. His face
clenches and for a moment, just for a moment, he is so infuriated
he can barely keep himself together. "I feel very close to Illana,"
he says softly. "I appreciate that," I say. His glass overturns and

the bartender comes over to mop the counter. "It's all right," he says. "I'm not angry with you." The conversation seems to repeat itself. "I don't understand what you're asking," I hear myself say perhaps for the third time. "I don't want to see Illana hurt, that's all," Henry says once again.

"Are you asking me to stop seeing her?"

"I don't think I have the right to ask you that," he says.

32.

Illana seems to call at least once a day, which is all right, though sometimes I wish it were Genevieve, who never calls. One night at her place, she says, "I really want a husband, not a lover."

"You have both," I say.

"I have neither," she says. "Joshua, I'm opposed to disorder."

"I'm not sure it's over with Genevieve," I say.

Illana laughs. "She says it's over. We talk about you on the phone."

That night after the children are in bed and we have made love with our customary hunger, rushing through the act as if it might be taken from us if we waited, I have an odd perception. "You would take Henry back, wouldn't you, if he was ready to come back?"

She thinks about it and thinks about it. "I would," she says finally, "but afterward I'd be sorry."

MY FATHER'S JOKES

PATRICIA ZELVER

Patricia Zelver was born in California, and grew up in Medford, Oregon. She has an M.A. from Stanford and now lives in Portola Valley, California, with her husband and two sons. She has published two novels, *The Honey Bunch* and *The Happy Family,* as well as numerous short stories; a collection of her short stories will be appearing sometime this year. This is her fifth appearance in the O. Henry collection.

The Horrible Hairy Spider was dangling over Cissy's head.

"Jello, again, this is Jack Benny," said Jack Benny.

Cissy was sitting on the rug—the Peck hooked rug, made by our New England great-grandmother on my mother's side; her golden corkscrew curls spilled down her back. Father sat in his faded sprung armchair. A Ryan armchair. Grand Rapids, Mother called it, which meant that it was not an antique, which meant that it was common. I sat on the Peck Boston rocker; I sat very straight, as if I were hanging my head from a string in order not to grow up to be a hunchback. I was eleven; Cissy, six.

Mother? Mother was down with one of her Spells. She often had these Spells, which had something to do with a New England conscience.

"Thank God I don't have a New England conscience," Father used to say.

Was it a disease? I often wondered. If so, would I inherit it?

The Horrible Hairy Spider (revolting, nearly five inches across; fat rubber body with long hairy legs, fifteen cents) dropped lower; it hung menacingly near Cissy's forehead, just above her large, long-lashed baby-blue eyes. Ryan eyes, like Father's. Father's eyes were choirboy blue. They were uplifted, now, toward Heaven. Father was one, once—a choirboy. There was a photograph of him in a lacy robe, holding a candle snuffer—that same sweet, sly expression in his choirboy eyes. That was before he stopped being Catholic.

"It's the only church if you go to church," he sometimes said. "They know how to do things up right," he said, with a touch of vanity in his voice, which aggravated Mother. There was no one, really, less vain than Father. Why, then, I wondered, was he vain about having once been Catholic, when decent people, according to Mother, would be ashamed?

> He only does it to annoy
> Because he knows it teases—

Father loved Mother. On her last birthday he had given her a peek-a-boo blouse and a transparent purple nightie, which hung in her closet, unworn, except when Cissy played Dress Up. Father was also concerned about Mother's Spells. Mother wore her long chestnut hair in a tight bun at the back of her neck. Could it be that she was exerting too much strain upon her scalp? Father asked her. Perhaps, he said, if she let her hair down, let it fall more loosely, it would ease her suffering. His suggestion had no effect. Every year, it seemed, Mother drew her hair tighter; no loose wave nor tendril was permitted to escape. Still, he continued to urge her. Such lovely hair, he said. Hair like yours should be displayed for people to admire.

"Beauty," said Mother, "is as Beauty does."

Father loved Mother, whatever love was. I was not sure. But the absolute token of his affection was that he liked to tease her. Father always teased the people he loved.

He liked to tease Cissy, most of all. He seldom teased me, any more. Did this mean that he loved Cissy more, or did it mean that I had grown too old for most of his jokes? Or, possibly, too dignified? Was love undignified? No. Mother had great dignity, and Mother loved Father.

"We are One," she used to say. "When two people marry, they become One."

Why then did she suffer so? Why did she grieve? Why did she feel that our home, at 43 North Elm, in Norton, was not truly her home, that her marriage had forced her into some sort of awful exile? Why did she never laugh at Father's jokes? It was her pride, her terrible Peck pride. Those were my thoughts, as I watched, with an ill-disguised, adolescent scorn, the descent of the Horrible Hairy Spider.

"Oh yes, they do things up right," Mother said, when Father talked about having been Catholic. "All that mumbo jumbo! It's for people who have nothing else, who want to crawl on their knees in front of the Pope and kiss his feet. Crawl!" she added, with a shudder.

Father's hands were folded, *innocently*, in his lap, in a kind of prayerful attitude. But I knew what was in them. The Secret Control Ring! I tensed my body for what was about to occur.

Another jerk! The Spider dropped, swayed to and fro, in front of Cissy's eyes. Ryan eyes, like Father's. Cissy shrieked. Oh, that shriek! Even though I had prepared myself, it went through me like an electric shock.

Father? Father was looking at Cissy with a deep concern. What dreadful thing can have happened to this little girl? What had caused her to cry out in such an anguished manner? Was she in some sort of awful peril? Oh me! Oh my! Poor Cissy!

Then Cissy caught on. She got it. If she were in the funny papers, a shimmering light bulb would have appeared over her head.

"Oh, Dad—dee!" cried Cissy. She plucked the Horrible Hairy Spider out of the air and examined it; she giggled; she stared at Father with unabashed admiration. "Oh, Dad—dee," she said again.

Father's eyes lost their innocent look; they twinkled. The little laugh wrinkles around his eyes and mouth erupted. His chest, beneath his old coat sweater, heaved, and chuckles exploded out of his mouth—little "heh, heh, heh's," like the "heh, heh, heh's" in the balloons over funny paper people. Father and Cissy were funny paper people. "Did you see *Father and Cissy* today? Wasn't the Spider *funny?*"

"She's the perfect fall guy, isn't she?" said Father, winking at me, as if I were a coconspirator.

I refused to be implicated; I did not acknowledge the wink. I was not a funny paper person, could not have been, even if I tried. I was Emily Peck Ryan, more Peck than Ryan, everyone said.

If Justice ruled the World, which I had, by then, learned it did not, my name would have been Charity Peck Ryan, instead.

> Charity Peck is my name; in peaceful Warren born
> In Sorrow's School my Infant Mind was pierced
>   with a Thorn,
> In Wisdom's Ways, I'll spend my Days,
> Humility be with me
> Should Fortune frown or Friends disown,
> Divine Support can't leave me.

That was the verse Great-Great-Grandmother Charity had embroidered on the Sampler at the age of nine, following the death of her father. Above the verse she had stitched three rows of the alphabet and numbers up to ten in different calligraphic design in order to demonstrate her skill at needlework. Below the verse, a tombstone presided over by a Grieving Angel, such as the one in the Peck Plot in the old IOOF cemetery in Metropolis, which the Reverend Gideon Freeland Peck, owner and publisher of *The Democratic Christian Evangelist* ("Southern Oregon's first newspaper," it said on the historical plaque), had copied from the one he remembered in the Warren cemetery.

Below the tombstone were these lines:

> Phineas Peck departed this life at a
> meeting of the Citizens of Warren on
> July the Fourth, 1831, following the
>   discharge of a cannon.

"Why would a man step in front of a cannon at a Fourth of July celebration?" asked Father, one Sunday afternoon, as he stood in the parlor of my grandmother's house in Metropolis, five miles from Norton, the house where Mother had grown up and which was known by all the right people and even some of the wrong ones as the Old Peck Place. Father was examining the Sampler on the parlor wall. He gazed innocently at Granny, at Aunt Dee, at Uncle Gideon, at Mother. "Unless," he said, "he was perhaps not quite sober?"

Uncle Gideon, who was mixing Granny's before-dinner martini —the most important thing, perhaps the only thing, he learned at

Harvard, Father sometimes said—shook the frosted cocktail shaker more vigorously than usual; Aunt Dee bustled out of the room to see to dinner; Granny, an Abbot, not a Peck, and whose reaction, therefore, did not matter, smiled; Cissy giggled; Mother was silent. A silence fraught with meaning, I thought. I had just learned "fraught." A fraught-with-meaning silence. A silence, meaningfully fraught. This was how so many of Mother's silences were.

"It was only an idle question, to satisfy a point concerning which I have often been curious," said Father.

When I was born, there was already a Charity Peck Ryan, a year older than I, who was now known as Poor Charity; she died, when I was three, of scarlet fever and now lay under the left wing of the angel in Metropolis. Mother's sorrow impaired her delicate Nervous System. Dr. Conroy prescribed warm baths, brisk walks, and no more babies. Both Mother and Father were deeply concerned over Mother's Nervous System; neither would have wilfully disobeyed Dr. Conroy's orders. What had happened? I should never know.

> "Where did you come from Baby dear?
> Out of the Nowhere into the Here.
> Where did you get those eyes so blue?
> God gave them to me, as He did you."

This was how Mother responded when Cissy asked Where She Came From, at an age when she was too little to comprehend. I knew, of course, that babies were the result of the most intimate physical expression of the deepest spiritual love between one man and one woman. Cissy had been told this, now, too, but Heaven only knew if Cissy "got" it. Heaven only knew what went on in Cissy's head. "Out of the Nowhere, into the Here," though hardly a scientific explanation, seemed to me, on the whole, the best explanation for Cissy's existence.

Cissy, by being born in mysterious violation of the Doctor's Orders, had stolen my Rights of Primogeniture, in more ways than one. Being named "Charity," she would inherit the Peck Sampler. Would she spend her days wisely and humbly? Should Fortune frown and Friends disown, would she be able to count on Divine Support? Knowing Cissy, it seemed to me unlikely.

Father and Cissy were a Team. Like Jack Benny and Rochester. Like Edgar Bergen and Charley. Like George Burns and Gracie Allen. John C. Ryan and His Little Daughter, Cissy. John C. Ryan and His Bag of Magical Tricks and Practical Jokes. Little Cissy, the Perfect Fall Guy! Watch her "fall" for all the Tricks, no matter how many times performed.

Father:	"Adam and Eve and Pinch Me Went down to the Water to swim Adam and Eve were drowned-ed And who do you think was saved?"
Cissy:	Pinch Me.
Father:	(pinches Cissy)
Cissy:	(squealing) Oh, Dad—dee!
Father:	I can row a boat, canoe?
Mother:	Oh, John, not again.
Emily:	It's a pun, stupid. A pun on *words*. (One of the lowest forms of humor, despite Shakespeare's use of it, Miss Wilson, her seventh-grade teacher had said.) One of the lowest forms of humor.
Cissy:	Boat! Can-you? I get it! (giggles)
Mother:	Old Mr. Henry died last night in his sleep.
Father:	Mr. Henry is with Barnum and Bailey.
Cissy:	What's Barnum and Bailey?
Emily:	(who knows her History) It was a famous circus, with Buffalo Bill.
Cissy:	Why is Mr. Henry with them?
Emily:	Barnum and Bailey are dead, stupid.
Cissy:	(silence) (giggle) Oh!

Watch Cissy perform, too. A Chip Off the Old Block. Enjoy her Impersonation of Shirley Temple, singing "The Good Ship, Lollypop." A Mimic. A Great Little Trouper. Can really strut her stuff.

Mother:	Not now, Cissy. Judge and Mrs. Blair want to talk.
Judge Blair:	It isn't every day that an old man is entertained by a pretty little girl. Let's hear your song, Sweetheart.

Jack Benny was over. They were playing the Theme Song. Father turned off the Zenith. "I better go look in on poor Mama," he said.

Cissy's response to this was to stand on her head; her dress fell over her shoulders, revealing her pink panties; then she dropped, plop, in a giggling, quivering heap upon the rug.

"When I was a little girl, I always went to bed the moment Jack Benny was over," said Father.

Cissy looked up at Father, blue eyes big. Silence. Then, "Oh, Dad—dee, you were never a little girl!"

Father picked up Cissy and threw her over his shoulder, marched out of the room with a shrieking Cissy, dimpled legs kicking at the air.

I rose and went into the dining room and sat down at the round oak table (Grand Rapids, Ryan) and prepared to begin my seventh-grade Original Research paper.

"Why don't you write about Old Metropolis?" said Miss Emmeline Trowbridge, my friend and head librarian of the Norton Public Library, when I had consulted her about the theme. "After all," she said, "you are a Peck. Your Grandmother and your Uncle Gideon are filled with information. You must pick a particular subject. The journey of your Great-Grandfather from Massachusetts to Metropolis. The Gold Rush. Your Great-Grandfather's Temperance Crusade, the visit of Rutherford B. Hayes—"

I had decided to write about the Railroad. If it had not been for the Railroad, all Pecks would have been rich, today. Not that Pecks cared about material wealth, in itself. It was the respect that went with it.

If it had not been for a man named Norton, who bought up one thousand acres of land in the fertile valley below Metropolis, who bribed the S.P.—

"It was flatter land; it was easier to lay track," said Father.

"He *bribed* them," said Mother, said Uncle Gideon, said Aunt Dee.

History, I sometimes thought, consisted as much, if not more, of what did not happen as what did.

Father was a lawyer in a small Oregon town. John C. Ryan, Atty-at-Law, it said in curly gold-leaf letters on the window of the

Union Building, where he had his office. He had never finished law school; he had gone to World War I, instead. After the war, they made a law that veterans who had left college to enlist could get their degree by passing a formal examination. Father traveled to Salem and was interviewed by the Chief Justice. This is the story he liked to tell concerning the interview:

"The Chief Justice asked me a question, which I wasn't able to answer. Then he asked me another question, which I wasn't able to answer. Then he said, "You are now admitted to the practice of law in the State of Oregon."

Father enjoyed being a lawyer in a small town. He was not ambitious, either for money or fame. You don't have to be if you have the rare privilege of enjoying your work. He was a popular man among people of every social and economic level. He was unassuming, courtly, gentle, genial, honest. He spent little time in court. By temperament, he was a "settler," not a litigator.

Outside of his work and his family, to whom he was devoted, he fished, gardened, and, after age fifty, played gin rummy every Saturday afternoon at the University Club in town. Outside of the Bar Association, this was his only affiliation; he was not a joiner. Once, someone talked him into the Kiwanis Club, because it would be "good for business." He went to one meeting and found it too serious.

He enjoyed his liquor, but drank like a gentleman. He smoked too much; his rumpled clothes were covered with cigarette ash. His other vice—if you can call it that—was his addiction to practical jokes. He kept *The Catalogue of Magical Tricks and Practical Jokes* on top of the toilet tank. The jokes, which he sent away for, were the only things he ever bought for himself, outside of necessities. This story is about my father's jokes.

THE RUBBER POINTED PENCIL
Looks like Lead
Fools and annoys 'em.

Mother: This pencil doesn't work, John. This pencil—Is this one of your *jokes*, John? Will you be so kind as to find me a proper pencil, please?

THE FAKE FLY

Sticks to almost any surface.
Put it on your lapel, on the butter dish.
On Mrs. Social Register's lace tablecloth.
Watch 'em try to brush it off.
Confound your hostess.

Miss Singer: (County Recorder at the Courthouse to Cissy and Emily, who are waiting for Father in her office) Well, if there's anything I can't tolerate, it's a nasty, filthy fly. I tried to brush it off and it wouldn't move. It just —stuck. I should have guessed! He was going all over the courthouse last week with his squirting flower in his buttonhole. Well, we all know your dad! He makes life just a bit brighter for everyone. No, things are never dull when your dad's around!

THE JUMPING SPOON

Greatest Laugh Producer ever invented.
A startling after-dinner trick. The performer
places one of the teaspoons to be found on the
dinner table into an ordinary drinking glass.
In a few seconds, the spoon jumps out of the
glass! This is really surprising and funny.

Mrs. Blair: (wife of Judge Blair)
It was really surprising and funny. I couldn't believe my eyes; it just *jumped* out of the glass!

THE LIVE MYSTERY MOUSE

Miss Jost: (Elevator operator in Union Building. To Cissy and Emily) Going to see your dad?

(The elevator is like an iron cage; through the bars of the cage one sees the cables move past as the elevator rises. Miss Jost has fixed up the interior of the cage like a miniature living room. She sits in an old chintz slipper chair; her knees are covered with a multicolored afghan; her knitting is on her lap. Taped to one of the bars is a photograph of her nephew, Carl, who lost an arm in the service of his country; taped to another bar is a postcard— a pretty rural scene of Denmark, where Miss Jost's par-

ents grew up. Above this, a calendar with a photograph of
the Norton Valley with the pear blossoms in bloom,
courtesy of the Norton Groceteria.)

"Fifth floor, Miss Jost," he says. (Creaking and grinding
of chains, as she pulls the wheel.)

Every morning, every noon—"Fifth floor, please." (The
Union Building only has two floors.) He fooled me with
that mouse of his, last week. "Could that be a *mouse* in
your elevator, Miss Jost?" he says. I looked down and let
out a frightful scream. "Don't worry, Miss Jost, I'll get
the rascal," he says, and he leans down and picks it up
and puts it in his pocket. Very solemnlike. Very calm.
You would think he was accustomed to picking up mice
everyday! Oh, Mr. Ryan, you almost gave me a heart
attack! I said. You really shouldn't, Mr. Ryan!—But you
know your dad. There's no stopping him. Heaven only
knows what he'll think up next!

THE MECHANICAL HAND VIBRATOR
Startle your friends with a "friendly" handshake.

Miss Porter: (Father's stenographer. To Cissy and Emily) My hand
was still tingling in bed that night.

(Miss Porter is Mother's age. An old maid. They knew
each other, *slightly*, at Norton High. Miss Porter lives
very quietly in the Kingscote Arms, with her widowed
mother. She is the only person Emily and Cissy know
who lives "downtown." Miss Porter wears too much
rouge. She has her dyed hair done once a week at the
Fountain of Beauty; every six months she gets a permanent. She plucks her eyebrows to a fine line and dresses
in frilly frocks and sheer silk hose.) "It's a pity someone
can't tell her how to dress suitable for an office," says
Mother. "I'm sure it must give a bad impression when
she meets the Public." Miss Porter is short and plump.
Her freckled flesh is so soft it looks as if it would dent
if you touched her. She has a soft voice and a slight
stammer and is extremely meticulous. Since Mother
doesn't drive—"I don't care to run around like other
women," Mother says—she often asks Emily to phone
the office and give Miss Porter a shopping list for
Father. If Emily says, "One dozen oranges," Miss

Porter will say, "What sort of oranges, dear? Does your mother prefer juice oranges or eating oranges?" This is the part of her meticulousness, which, though appropriate for legal stenography, irritates Mother. (Emily is not sure *why*.) "Miss Porter wants to know if you want juice or eating oranges?" Emily says. "Oh, isn't that just like her! Tell her either kind will do!" Mother's cavalier attitude toward oranges, or, perhaps her cavalier attitude toward Miss Porter, imposes a burden on Emily. "You better say *which*," she tells Mother. "Juice, then! Tell her *juice!*—or, *eating*. Tell her eating! Tell her anything you like." "Juice, please," Emily says. Then Miss Porter inquires after Mother's health. "How is your mother feeling today?" she says. Or, "Is your mother feeling better today?" "Yes, better, thank you," says Emily, no matter how Mother is feeling. She senses that it is not proper to go into more personal details, that neither Miss Porter nor Mother would care for that. Mother, in fact, would prefer that Miss Porter not inquire after her health at all.

Mother never phones, herself, if she can avoid it. Having known Miss Porter, *slightly*, in high school, where they called each other by their first names, it is awkward to phone and say, "This is Mrs. Ryan." On the other hand, it will not do to say, "This is Jean." When it is necessary, for one reason or another to call, herself, Mother says, "Is this Vera?" Then she waits for Miss Porter to recognize her voice, which Miss Porter always does. Miss Porter, recognizing Mother's voice, says, "Oh, how are you?" "Very well, thank you. And you?" says Mother. "I can't complain," says Miss Porter, or, "Chipper, I'm always chipper," she says. Then she says, "I bet you'd like to talk to the Boss." "Yes, please, if he's not occupied," says Mother. "I think I can arrange for you to speak to him," says Miss Porter. "I'll just put a little flea in his ear."

Mother does not care for Miss Porter calling Father, "the Boss," nor does she care for the expression, "a little flea in his ear." But it does solve the awkward social problem for both of them. In all the ten years in which Miss Porter has worked for Father, she has, somehow, managed never to call Mother either Mrs. Ryan, or Jean.)

Miss Porter: That dreadful vibrator! It sent funny little shivers all through me. (She gives Cissy a box of paperclips to make into a chain; she gives Emily a stack of magazines —*The Elks Magazine, Field and Stream,* an old copy of *The Saturday Evening Post,* to entertain them while they wait for Father to drive them home from the dentist's. She opens the drawer of her desk and takes out a small tin box and opens it and offers them hard little white mints called "pastelles.")

Cissy: (listening to the story of the Vibrator, giggles)

Emily: (finds story embarrassing. Why would Father shake Miss Porter's hand, she wonders. That soft plump freckled hand. Sending little shivers through her soft plump body. Making Miss Porter tingle. She does not want to think of Miss Porter in bed. Tingling. She does not want to think of Miss Porter as having any existence at all, outside of her duties as Father's stenographer. She looks up from the *Post* and scowls at Cissy for giggling. Cissy, she thinks, lacks the Peck's innate good taste and proud reserve.)

"Isn't Miss Porter beautiful?" Cissy said one night, when we were in our beds in the upstairs bedroom we shared at 43 North Elm.

"Beautiful?" I said scornfully. "What could possibly make you think she is beautiful?"

But Cissy was already asleep.

Father: (driving our Buick on the way to the Peck House in Metropolis)
                         As I was driving to Salt Lake
                         I met a little rattlesnake
                         I fed it some jellycake,
                         It got a little bellyache,

Mother: (in front seat, holding Father's jacket and tie on her lap; flowers, in a Mason jar, for the Peck Plot, at her feet) Tummy, not belly!

Cissy: (sitting between Mother and Father, because she *claims* to get car sick. Giggles.)

Father: It got a little tummyache, not a bellyache, after all.

Emily: (alone in back seat) It says "belly" in the Bible. (She agrees
          with Mother, but possesses a fund of knowledge she feels
          obliged to demonstrate.)

Mother: The language of the Bible and the language of everyday
          life are two different things altogether.

Father: Your mother is correct, as always. The language of the
          Bible is not appropriate language for everyday speech.

Mother: (ignoring Father) Drive slowly when we go through Me-
          tropolis, so Emily can take notes for her theme.

Cissy: My belly feels fun—ny.

          Consternation! Should they stop? Let Cissy out? Roll down
          the window? Buy her some chewing gum? It is decided to
          drive *fast* through Metropolis and go straight to the Peck
          Plot, where she can run about among the tombstones in
          the fresh air. This, of course, takes precedence over Emily's
          Original Research.

I got an "A" anyhow. "Emily has Literary Tendencies," Mrs.
Wilson wrote across my theme, which I brought home to show to
Mother and Father. They were both proud of me. The phrase:
"Literary Tendencies" was taken up by them, and then by others.

"Emily has Literary Tendencies," people would say. They
didn't mean it, I suppose, but they always made "Literary Tendencies" sound as if it were—not so much a disease, maybe, as a
kind of morbidity, a lack of normal health. They may have been
right. I don't know. Perhaps it was like the New England Conscience, which as it turned out, I did inherit from Mother.

Certainly, Cissy didn't inherit it. The way she climbed upon
gentlemen's laps, for example; climbed up and burrowed in and
snuggled down, as if she were some sort of little animal; made a
nest and curled up, peacefully, as long as she was being cuddled,
patted, stroked—but, should the gentleman reach for a drink or a
cigarette, or, simply pause for a moment, the burrowing and
squirming began again to remind him of his neglect and did not
stop until the neglect was rectified.

"Cissy, don't pester Judge Blair," or, "Cissy, I think Mr.
Hefflinger would be happier if you were to get down at once,"
Mother would say.

"Oh, Cissy's my girl, aren't you, Cissy?"

"It isn't everyday an old codger like myself can hold a pretty blonde on his lap."

The pet names she was called. Cissy. Missy Cissy. Cissy-Pie. Later, scrawled upon the Angel—a famous necking spot for the students at Norton High: "Hot Pants Cissy." This was, fortunately, after Mother's breakdown. Aunt Dee took rubbing alcohol and scrubbed it off.

It was Father's fault. He spoiled her. Mother often said so.

THE DOGGIE DOO DOO
Latex. Fantastically realistic imitation.
Nauseating. Put on your hostess's best rug.
Watch her chide poor Fido.

Mrs. Hefflinger: (mother of Jimmy Hefflinger, with whom Emily is secretly in love, who has invited the Ryan family to visit them at their cabin at the Lake.) Oh, no!

Father: (innocent expression in choir-blue eyes) Is something the matter, Mil?

Mrs. Hefflinger: (to Mr. Hefflinger) Carl!

Father: Perhaps I can be of assistance?

Mrs. Hefflinger: No, no, it's all right. I'm sorry, Bingo's made a mess. Where *is* Bingo? Carl? I'll get paper towels—

Cissy: (looks at Doggie Doo Doo; looks at Father. Giggles.)

Emily: (silent, dying of shame)

Mother: John! John, you didn't—!

Mr. Hefflinger: Well, I guess we better clean it up.

Mrs. Hefflinger: I'll do it. You men take the girls down to the Lake. They want to go out in the boat. I'm afraid Bingo's been a very naughty dog.

Mother: (pale-faced, weakly) John?

Father: I, for one, intend to stay and help Milly. (picks up Doggie Doo Doo, puts it casually in pocket.)

Jimmy Hefflinger: Hey—that's neat. Let's see it!

Emily: Let's go out in the boat!

Cissy: Show it to Jimmy, Daddy.

Mother: John!

Mrs. Hefflinger: (laughing) Oh, John, it's one of your jokes!

Father: You know I never joke, Mil. (takes out Doggie Doo Doo from pocket and hands it, proudly, to Jimmy. Jimmy and Cissy examine Doggie Doo Doo.)

Mrs. Hefflinger: You certainly fooled me this time.

Jimmy: (turning Doggie Doo Doo over in his hand) Hey, this is great. (to Cissy) Where'd your father get it?

Cissy: (giggling, looking up at Jimmy with big blue eyes) He has this catalogue. (coquettishly) I'll show it to you, sometime. It's got lots of neat stuff. Come on, you promised to take us for a boat ride.

Emily: (forever shamed, forever unable to forget her shame when she sees Jimmy Hefflinger at school) I don't think I'll go. I brought a book to read.

(Jimmy and Cissy run off, down to the dock. Mrs. Hefflinger fixes gin fizzes for the adults. Mother declines hers. She has a sudden headache, perhaps it is the run, perhaps she had better lie down for a time with a cool wet washcloth on her forehead. Father fetches a cool wet washcloth, returns from the bedroom. Emily sits down with her book.)

Father: I've been told my—ah—joke—was not in the best of taste.

Mrs. Hefflinger: Nonsense! You wouldn't be John Ryan without your jokes. I'm going to tell her to come back out here.

Father: Better wait a bit, Mil.

Mrs. Hefflinger: Well, you know best. (looks at Emily) Emily is quite a little bookworm, isn't she?

Father: (proudly) Her teacher says she has Literary Tendencies.

SNOW

(7:00 A.M. February morning. Emily is sixteen; Cissy, eleven. Mother, that winter, has "taken to her bed," a phrase of Aunt Dee's, taken up by others. Father sleeps on a cot, in the hallway, in order to be near her in the night. Cissy and Emily are still asleep. Father enters their bedroom.)

Father: Girls! Wake up! We're going to give Mother a nice surprise.

Emily: (always an early riser, already awake, sits up, gets out of bed)

Cissy: (burrows under covers. To Father) Go 'way.

Father pulls covers off Cissy's bed. Cissy shrieks. Both girls follow Father, reluctantly, arms across chests, shivering, in their flannel nighties. Father leads them into Mother's room. Mother is lying on her back, eyes open. She seems to be looking at something beyond, or perhaps through her visitors.)

Father: (to Mother) Surprise! Surprise! We have a little surprise for you this morning. (goes to window, peeps behind drawn curtain; faces Mother again.) Ready? (clears throat, assumes theatrical stance) Presto chango! (pulls curtain) Snow! (Father twinkles, beams)

Mother: (looks at snow, expression does not change; she seems to be looking at something beyond, or perhaps through this sudden Winter Wonderland)

Cissy: (marveling at the magical metamorphosis produced by Father) Oh, Dad—dee!

Father: (to Mother, trying again) Now we see it. (draws curtain) Now we don't. (pulls curtain) Presto chango—Snow!

Mother: It's very nice, but the light hurts my eyes. Would you mind closing the curtain, again, please, John?

In 1949, I returned from Reed College, to attend my mother's funeral. She had taken, it seemed, too many pills all at once. The funeral was private, but Miss Porter showed up, anyhow. Her sobs spoiled the lovely simplicity of the words from the Book of Common Prayer—the service Uncle Gideon had arranged. I considered her presence in the worst of taste.

After the funeral, Father, Cissy, and I sat in the living room at 43 North Elm. Father was pale, solemn, still. The laugh lines in his face were etched more deeply; perhaps they were no longer laugh lines, anymore. He chain-smoked, dropping ashes on the Peck hooked rug. I fetched an ashtray.

Father said, "Well, I guess Mama is with Barnum and Bailey."

Cissy giggled, then burst into tears. Father wept with her. I stood, holding the ashtray—apart, alone, dry-eyed. Being more Peck than Ryan, I could neither laugh nor weep.

This story is about my father's jokes. Father joked. Cissy was his Fall Guy. Mother had her pride. I have Literary Tendencies. I am writing this story. Everyone has his or her way of coping.

THE SMALLEST PART

HERBERT GOLD

Herbert Gold was born and raised in Cleveland, Ohio; he
has lived in New York, Paris, Port-au-Prince, and Detroit,
but has been settled for many years now in San Francisco.
His forthcoming novel is entitled *Slave Trade*.

Their marriage was tender, practical, playful, and finally its body
was obscured to both of them by the birth of their child and the
convulsions of the time. People need freedom, at least I do, she
said. Neither of them had expected this. Their divorce was amicable and mysterious.

She had a vision of herself as a Single Parent, fulfilling her destiny perhaps tragically, in the company of other women harassed
by history and fate. (But now one could choose.) He had a vision
of himself as abandoned by the woman who was once his delight.
Suffering little hemorrhages, the day would suddenly be bloodied
by loneliness for his wife, for his child.

He kept his daughter with him on Sunday, a claustrophobic,
sticky, steamy long day of nonrest. He missed her just as much
Monday morning when she went to school. He visited her on
Tuesday and Thursday at dinnertime.

Since it was amicable, which doesn't mean friendly, he took her
out of her mother's apartment; or if the weather was bad, the
child tired, homework to do, mother permitted that they huddle
together in the child's bedroom. He told stories. Father and
daughter giggled. They used pens, paper, books, records. He liked
this mini game of house with his daughter better than their wandering Sabbaths.

Sometimes his wife—he had trouble saying ex-wife or former
wife—was irritated by the noises they made and would ask him

please, please, why don't you just go out someplace? Ordinarily
she liked to "de-emphasize" sweets, but in her desperation she
even recommended going out for an ice-cream cone. This, he supposed, meant that Single Parent was preoccupied with the reac-
tionary dilemmas of a lover or a nonlover. She became fretful at
such times, sometimes waiting at the telephone, sometimes not
liking the telephone when it rang. Men were a burden to her now,
and she alternated between jeans and boots and defiant, old-
fashioned feminine drag, even to doing her nails and wearing a
long skirt. This English country loveliness gave him a pang when
she greeted him in it, hair brushed, skin glowing, long arms and
legs moving with a grace subtly responsive to the consciousness of
good clothes.

He did not understand her. He could not trace the meaning of
jeans (rump awkwardly bound by studded pockets), boots, hair
awry, against her occasional extravagance of décor. Her behind
wobbled when she hustled up the stairs; then the next week she
glided ahead of him, elegant and proud. She moved too fast. It
was not his business to understand her anymore, especially since
he had done such a poor job of it when it was his business.

He felt a loss of his independence of being as he slipped and
struggled, failed to sleep and failed to wake, passed white nights
and gray days in misery. This misery came of love, and he hated
it. To kill himself—how to do such a thing? with a child he
cherished every day?—was impossible. Yet he found himself wishing for an accident, so that he could not blame himself. Ah, this
was foolish. And so he struggled with himself; it replaced the
struggle with his wife. He fought against love, he fought against
grief, he even fought against anger. They were all linked. He
reminded himself when touched, moved, overwhelmed by the
sight and smell of her, or a sight and smell which recalled her, or
passing their old house or eating their foods or walking on their
streets: don't do this, don't feel. First he succeeded in removing
her from the struggle; he translated it within, to himself, between
himself; then he began to succeed in winning it. He lost love. He
lost anger. She became a limited idea, like a newspaper death notice. He did not lose sorrow entirely, but he chipped away at it:
don't, don't, don't, he would remind himself in the middle of the
night; don't feel; and then dreamlessly he could sleep. Perhaps he
dreamt, but he did not remember the dreams.

When he was with another woman, he was only with that woman. He forgot their names, but he remembered to exist only in what happened then and there. The struggle was still within himself. There was no question of love in the pleasure he often felt, a pleasure like dreamless sleep.

He defended himself against the invasions of love and anger. He paid a price.

It was not neat, and that was okay, too. Probably it shouldn't be neat. That would be too dangerous. And so he allowed himself to feel sorrow at the loss of grief. He named it regret, but it was still sorrow. He took a chance in allowing this, but it was a necessary risk. He could no longer be loving, and he had to pay the price of loss. But he could not entirely give up sorrow in order to survive. That would be too much of a price, even in this cause.

And so, with all these penalties and losses, abandoning the goods of hope and joy, risks of love, risks of anger, thickening memories day by day and year after year, he believed life was now once more worth living. There was the air of early morning. There were certain tastes. He climbed into the newspaper with a certain satisfaction: other lives out there, a nervous large world. He treasured his hours with his daughter. It was interesting, he thought, very interesting indeed, that these things could be enough for a man. In the past he would never have believed it. He had expected something different. This, like the newspaper, constituted very interesting, distracting, objective information.

He read the regret which lay beneath as he read the obituaries in the newspaper. It was not grief, and yet it was still grief. It was merely regret for the disappearing past, rapidly diminishing into itself without his participation.

The chief rule for rescue of himself was not to think about her. That was essential. He began to succeed in this enterprise—not remembering, not imagining, not conjecturing, not taking an imaginary place in her life. He began to succeed. As compensation for this withdrawal from her, he could think more about himself. What might have been a boring vanity seemed to become—an interesting vanity. For example, when he thought about himself, he was surprised at the success with women obtained by a melancholic, bedraggled, preoccupied, recently divorced, gray-flecked man. They liked him! (Some did.) They wanted to help. There is often something agreeable about a disaster. However, he didn't

care about the women with whom he had this success. And this
was probably the reason for it.

Or maybe these women just liked to gather round the disaster
for the fun of it—watching the building crumble and entranced
by how the embers flare up.

Sometimes, when all the conjunctions were right, his wife invited him to sit at the kitchen table, to have dinner with her and
their daughter. He had no pride. When she asked him, he did, although afterward he often felt a new sharp sadness within the
melancholia he carried almost by habit these days. It would be
seasoned for a time by fresh regret. Nevertheless, he had to eat,
didn't he? Even at the butcher-block table they had chosen together one Saturday afternoon in May—didn't he?

Then one day, after such a supper—a Single Parent dinner of
hamburgers and tomatoes and fruit and warmed-over coffee—she
asked if he would like to put their daughter to bed. He would. He
stayed. He wondered if she merely wanted a burden lifted, the one
of good nights, glasses of water, important First Grade gossip, but
no, he smelled fresh coffee, he heard the grinder, she was making
coffee.

She didn't offer him any yet. When he came back from their
daughter's bedroom after the last, final kiss, and the one after
that, and said good night, thanks for the dinner, she asked:
Would you like a glass of wine?

Yes.

She wrestled with the bottle. Would you uncork it?

Yes.

He sank into the deep grandfatherly chair which used to be his.
She sat on the couch and crossed her legs and uncrossed them and
smiled. He thought how long it had been since he had seen her
lips and teeth slightly stained by wine, and how nice it used to be
when they would sit looking at each other, thinking they understood each other without words, not understanding each other
even with words, smiling, loving each other and drinking wine.

She patted the pillow beside her on the couch. Come here.

Obediently, good dog, he came to sit beside her. He asked a
question about their daughter's school. She shook her head stub-
bornly, that was not it at all, and her eyes were also smiling at
him, as she said: Your lips and teeth are pink.

They kissed very lightly. He tasted the wine on her mouth. If it was pink on his mouth, it was red on hers.

During the first months of their separation, almost until their divorce was final, they occasionally made love. At first he would think this a reconciliation and she would fall into a rage about his presumption. Then he would take it only for what it was, as she said he had to take it, but he would grieve and weep when he went home to his own bed afterward, which was where she wanted him to go. A few times, when he was distraught and weak with sorrow, with regret for the lost dream of true love, she would watch him with narrow eyes, how boyish of him, and offer him a sympathy sexing. He accepted this several times. Then, although she never reproached him for it, he learned it was better not to accept it.

Now time had passed, he was familiar with sleeping alone, he was familiar with sleeping with many different women, either was okay, he was used to his life. He could say little more than that he was used to the second half of his life.

So when she, on this autumn evening more than two years after their divorce, in a way he dreamily recalled from the time of separation, decided they should now make love, his thoughts were: Not to be depressed tomorrow. Not to make anything of this. Not to care.

With these negatives in mind, too much freight for fun, he felt somewhat dulled and lacking in energy. But it was easy and comfortable to hold her in his arms, to rock her, to stroke and knead her with his hands, with his fingers, while her arch twisted and her slipper fell off, to kiss her not very much but to breathe on her and let his mouth follow the pleasant paths of her body. Suddenly she jumped up. He waited. Ah. Something she surely had to do with other callers: make sure the child was asleep.

Then she went to the bathroom. When she returned, she was wearing only a robe. You're still dressed? she asked. Come.

He said: No, come here.

He didn't want to go to their bed.

She let him play with her. What he did was not so much make love; he was thinking of other things, even of other women, although with other women he often thought of her; it was not love he was doing with her. He was too dreamy and distant. He was overweighted with negatives. He simply engaged in diddling.

Surely she felt his abstraction.

He thought about the fatigue of driving home after lovemaking, the definition of the bachelor—he comes home from a different direction every morning—and he was in no hurry to leave off the repetitious, gentle, professional gestures he was performing. He could have been a masseur or a doctor. Nevertheless, he remembered her body, and he knew where to go. But he didn't go there. He simply played, in and out, round and about, treading byways, marking out the slim-fleshed skeleton.

He smelled the wine.

He smelled the coffee from the kitchen.

He smelled rich, thick, female smells of pleasure coming from her body. He didn't care. He smelled arousal on himself. He didn't care. Where did you learn that? where did you learn that? Oh, it's good, she said.

He didn't care to answer, but he climbed into the rhythm of what he was doing, let the metronome tick, and he did it and did it, now thinking not about others but about her. But not thinking very much about her. She was just there. He was just there. And they were just making love.

And then it happened. She began to scream and toss and heave her body—thinking of other things, he had moved himself to press against the place which always relieved her toward sleep—and her eyes were open, her mouth was open, her tongue was longer than he had known, now her eyes were squeezed shut and the scream seemed to come from an absence. . . . Shush, he said, you don't want to wake—

Oh, oh, oh.

And then she subsided. When she seemed nearly asleep, he guided her to the bed, her head resting on his shoulder, drowsy, like a little girl too long in the bath, and he tucked her in and said good night. No, he said, he would not stay. She smiled. He went to the kitchen and took a swallow of the cold coffee from the Pyrex pitcher. He left.

Driving home, he took to his old bad habit: ruminating. Figuring it out. He called it thinking, but it was more like an obsessive daydream, the foolish, unquenchable child in the gray-flecked man. She had smiled in relief because he was not staying, because he was not making the mistake of making anything of this. Well, he knew. He might be stupid, but he could be educated.

This time perhaps he really had been thinking.

And so they formed a habit.

Not on every visit ("visitation"), but perhaps once a week, or maybe twice, when it seemed convenient, he would make love to her, he would make a love drill, a love exercise with her, when it seemed convenient, if she had nothing else for the evening, if he had nothing else for the evening. They never discussed it. She seemed deeply grateful at first, not for the lovemaking, of course, which was her due, but for his making nothing more of it than what it was. She was confident in her climaxes—not the little whimpers of their marriage, but howls and thrashings and bitings. She was probably sure he wouldn't do this again and again unless he also wanted to. And of course he did want to, although he was not sure why.

Her slim, lank body began to feel like beef under his fingers, his tongue, his body. He was far from all this, but nevertheless he understood that something new was happening to him, to this person who was far from what was happening to him. He was glad. He was careful not to show too much pleasure. He had liked to laugh and chatter and roar when they made love. Now he said nothing, he tended to business, and at his own climax, he stifled his moans and only his rasping breath could have been recorded. He did not feel it would be polite to give her words of love; not polite to her, not polite to himself.

It was supremely okay. His melancholia was lifting. He enjoyed his girlfriends, and would laugh, chatter, and roar with them when the occasion arose.

He began to feel well at last. In a way, he had a family. The long Sundays with his daughter were filled with adventures—junk food, children's theater, picnics—and he enjoyed them, and enjoyed dropping her back at her mother's house. Once he even took a shower before he made love to his former wife; never, however, would he stay the night afterward.

For that whole autumn she seemed bemused and at rest, and waited with no impatience, not entering into the games, when father and daughter played. When he heard the grinder and smelled fresh coffee, he knew this was one of their evenings. He put the child to bed (good night, good night, sweet thing). He went in to his wife. He liked the smell of the coffee, but if they didn't drink it first, he usually didn't warm it up later.

He was very patient with his wife. He fell into a state of abstraction. He would notice almost with surprise that he was aroused, and that he was very aroused, and that suddenly this was an extreme of pleasure. Sometimes she scratched and clawed at him. Once she lay there shuddering, pulling the blanket up to her chin, and asked if he would like to spend the night, they could cuddle and just sleep—

I'm not tired, he said. I don't think I could sleep. I would disturb you.

That's all right.

It would be confusing for *her* to wake up in the morning and find us . . .

You're right.

When winter came he began to wonder if this would go on forever. It did not interfere with his affairs with other women; at least, he thought it didn't; yet he felt nothing much but laughter or pleasure with the other women. However, that had been the case before, too. And the depression seemed to have lifted. Or at least he thought it had.

Sometimes he wondered what this must be doing to his wife's search. Was she free? Was she free of love and marriage? Was she free to be herself alone? Perhaps she was.

And then one night, eyes flashing, she asked him, as if it were a great joke: Why don't you ever at least take me to the movies?

And he, also joking, said to her: Because I think our marriage is in trouble.

Acknowledging their divorce, they went on making love. He was not sure she meant the joke in the same way he did. Of course, since they never had understood each other, this was in their tradition. And now that he had stopped trying, he too took pleasure, relish, even excitement, in making love to this stranger who, he used to think, was the closest person to him on earth.

Now, of course, their daughter was the dearest person, and as to the closest, there was no one.

One cold late night, as he drove homeward through deserted streets, damp glistening on the streetlights, he found himself uttering a thankful prayer: Not by might nor by power, O Lord, nor by love, does the spirit turn; but by indifference.

And this was the only time during those months when the old sadness returned. This prayer of gratitude brought back all the misery of loss. For the next two weeks he left as soon as he said good night to their daughter.

Why are you so busy these days? Are you in love? she asked him.

No, just busy, he said.

But then they began again. It was like lovers returning to one another after a vacation. And he did not begin on her on the couch and then go to the bedroom. He led her to the bedroom, or she simply walked to the bedroom, dropping her clothes, and he followed, dropping his own clothes in a careless pile near the bed, near the dresser which used to contain his socks, shirts, underwear, and which she now used for all the new things she had bought during her periods of more elaborate décor. He returned naked to that pile of clothes in the dark, dressing rapidly as she slept, slipping down the stairs and out into the cool nighttime street, and then breathing deeply, his face to the sky, before opening his car door.

Let me pursue where love leads me, he thought, so long as it is not love. And this is not a prayer, he thought, it is an observation. He did not want to suffer another episode of sullen grief, when he used to pray for his death, only asking that he not have the responsibility of it. Now he would take the responsibility for following out whatever finally might emerge.

And then he felt the grief. Because there seemed to be no way he could bury it, drown it, stifle it. Why? Why now? Why this time? Because he had loved his wife with the passion of his life. And now he indifferently stroked and played at her body, and waited for her to claw and shudder against him; and then, out of politeness, and also so that he might sleep afterward, he allowed himself the modest shudder of pleasure.

One night, after they had finished, both finished, finished both of them together (this was rare), she did not sink into that famished sleep of hers. She lay awake, her arm askew so that one hand rested on his shoulder, cupping it, and she asked if he was hungry. No. Sleepy? No. Would you like something to eat? Thank you, no. Would you like to stay the night—and her hand tightened on his shoulder to keep him from answering too fast— and have breakfast with both of us?

I don't think that would be a good idea.

His wife fell silent. They had agreed that to raise the hopes of their child would be frivolous. They were serious parents.

She was breathing shallowly, with a catch at the end of each breath, as she started to say something and stopped. Finally she said it. What is all this about?

Nothing, I suppose.

Why are you doing this?

He almost felt angry. That is, he remembered how anger used to feel, the rising flush and turmoil, but of course he did not allow himself to feel this. Why are *we* doing this? he asked. Because we want to.

Because you want to and I do, too, she said.

Okay, if you like.

Is that all? she asked.

He did not like this conversation. It had the pattern of the repetitious explanations of early separation. I admit I want to, he said. We can stipulate that.

But why is that all? Why has it been so good?

Here in the dark, hardly seeing each other's faces, hardly speaking until tonight, trembling and convulsing and sleeping and fleeing, it had been as she said.

Why? she said.

And he answered: Because I don't like you very much, my darling.

But that, of course, was only the smallest part of the truth.

DU CÔTÉ DE CHEZ BRITZ

HENRY VAN DYKE

Henry Van Dyke, of Allegan, Michigan, is author of the
novels *Ladies of the Rachmaninoff Eyes, Blood of Straw-
berries,* and *Dead Piano.* During the Fall 1978 quarter at
Kent State University he was writer-in-residence. Henry Van
Dyke lives in New York City and has just completed a new
novel, *Bitter Chocolate.*

Mrs. Beatrice Britz, the terrible Mrs. Beatrice Britz, has invited
me to dinner and I am afraid to go. Soon, though, I must stop
poking around the edges of Gramercy Park and get up enough
nerve to enter her building. Number Thirty-four. It is eight-thirty.
It is a hot summer night. From a safe shadow, I watch Mae
Browne arrive.

Mae Browne. Mae Browne always went to Mrs. Britz's affairs,
and, I suspect, her complaint about the trouble it took to come all
the way downtown to Gramercy Park was but a cover to hide her
keen anticipation. Perhaps not. Perhaps Mae Browne merely liked
to complain; certainly she had complained about one thing or the
other from the very start. Earlier in the summer, when I first met
her, what had it been? The "e." Yes, the "e." I'd gone down to
her lobby to fetch her mail and when I returned she'd snatched
the letter out of my hands and said, "From Bea Britz, of course."

I watched her rip open the letter.

"I knew it was from Bea," Mae Browne said, explaining that
rarely did anyone—except Bea, naturally—leave off the "e" in her
name. "And she does it on purpose. She always does it on purpose."

First appeared in *The Antioch Review,* Spring 1976, Volume 34, Number
4. Copyright © 1976 by The Antioch Review, Incorporated. Reprinted by permission.

It was perhaps somewhat pretentious to spell her name Mae
Browne when in fact she was born May Brown, but it was, after
all, her privilege, her name, she declared, and she was quite
pleased by the tone and the style the added "e"s gave. Sometimes
Mae Browne, stung by the omission of her "e," felt tempted to
use her married name—de Nagy. She had used it once. After her
husband's death. When she came back to America. For several
years she was known as Mae de Nagy—Madame Mae de Nagy—
but unfortunately she found it difficult playing the black grande
dame in the middle of Harlem with such a name. Aside from the
general flack and occasional derision ("What's a black woman
doing with a name like that?" an impertinent shopkeeper on
135th Street once asked), de Nagy proved taxing even for her al-
lies to pronounce.

However, she did feel Bea Britz of all people could comply with
the desired spelling. Even when Bea Britz would introduce her to
people at parties, Mae imagined Bea was thinking Brown instead
of Browne. But she would go to the party. She always did.

Mae Browne lived in Lenox Terrace on West 135th Street with
only her Doberman pinscher, Pützl, but she'd once lived in the
suburbs of Budapest with horses and servants and candelabras and
Turkish tapestries. She'd dined with princes and counts and
barons. Now, alas, she'd fallen on bad days. Often she thought of
returning home to Boston to die—except she no longer had a
home there.

Once, though—once she was *something*, she often said. As early
as 1934 she was something, having left Boston that year to make
her way as a singer with dance bands in the best of Manhattan's
ballrooms, and as a chanteuse in the smartest of the city's supper
clubs. Lunceford, Basie, Ellington—they all knew her then, she
swore. She'd been a jazz singer of the classiest kind. In fact she
felt she had too much class to forge a top career in America so she
left for Europe in the summer of '36 where she, on talent, and as
an oddity (i.e., a black chanteuse), conquered Paris and Nice,
London, and Rome—not to speak of Lyons, Manchester, Padua,
and Darmstadt. "And I've got clippings to prove it," she'd say
with a querulous little rise in her voice.

Indeed the press clippings, yellowed and worn, now enveloped
in cellophane covers, were part of the source material for her
memoirs-in-progress I was engaged to help her with.

In the late thirties Mae Browne ceased being the toast of Europe and ended her night club career when she married Hermann de Nagy, an Austro-Hungarian baron of dubious lineage but of indubitable income; she traded her life as a glittering chanteuse for a moneyed and sedate life as Madame de Nagy, mistress of a villa between Rakospalota and Gödöllö, outside of Budapest.

She wasn't very nice during those Hungarian years, she readily admitted; she had a tendency, she'd announce with crocodile shame, to act as if she were Catherine the Great. Yet, in spite of her snobbism, her arrogant ruling of the roost as mistress of the villa, and even in spite of her fear and distaste of the Hungarian language ("Darling, I simply wouldn't go near it—even with gloves on—Hermann and I spoke to each other either in German or English"), Mae Browne lived for many years in the villa outside Budapest, and by some miracle survived the Nazis, and nearly survived the communists—Bolsheviki, she called them.

It was this part of her life—her husband's cloak-and-dagger death, her narrow escape from the communists via Athens and North Africa—she skimmed over, preferring to concentrate on her leisurely days and her largesse. One of her hired writers (the fourth one who had good connections with a Boston publisher) had, upon hearing Mae Browne recount her tale of escape from Eastern Europe, said: "Wow! You know, Miss Browne, your story would make one hell of a movie!"

She fired him on the spot. Mae Browne considered herself to be a very serious woman.

Her comeuppance (or misfortune, depending upon one's tolerance of Mae Browne's tarnished grandeur) did seem a bit rough: prepared in life to be only the toast of continents or the mistress of a Hungarian villa, Mae Browne (at sixty-what?) was forced to take a nine-to-five job in central Harlem with a fund-raising organization for impoverished children. She could type a little. She was a regal receptionist—but there was seldom anybody on whom she could shower her regality. She put stamps on envelopes. She answered the phone. She was not, however, without hope: I would write—if not, I, *somebody*—her biography and it would surely sell, she felt, a million copies.

Meanwhile, what would she wear, she kept asking me. She had so few clothes, she claimed. And Pützl. Could she take him?

Mae Browne took her Doberman pinscher along with her to

parties whenever she could. It was not only that she hated leaving him alone, but, sentiment aside, she could also save on dog food bills. ("Do you have a teensy bit of something for dear Pützl?" she'd ask. "Poor dear, I was in such a rush I forgot to feed him.") Mae Browne cut corners whenever she could.

She now got on the phone. "Darling, it's me."

"Lambkin!" Mrs. Britz said. "You got my invitation? You know, you must come, you know. This marvelous man from—"

"Pützl. Can I bring him?"

"Pützl? Well, Mae . . . you remember the last time he nearly knocked over my—"

"It wasn't his fault, Bea Britz, and you well know it. If that silly maid of yours hadn't—"

"All right, all right, for heaven's sake, Mae, bring him if you must. I mean, you know it's not that I *personally* dislike the poor beast, it's just that some of the guests have—"

"I'll bring him. What time?"

"Dear heart, you aren't angry or anything, are you? I *do* like Pützl, I really do. Actually, I adore him."

"What time?"

"Ten-ish. It's an *after*-dinner thing, you know."

"Fine. See you then."

After-dinner. Mae Browne squinted her eyes and looked out into the afternoon sun as if to ask the slanting rays themselves had Bea insinuated that she, Madame de Nagy, mooched?

The relationship between Mrs. Britz and Mae Browne was, I gather, firmer and mutually more satisfying than it appeared; they needed each other. Besides the money, Mae Browne needed a decent place to hold her own salon: she still could command a surprising number of performing artists and musicians she'd known from her years of singing fame. Mrs. Britz loved this; her duplex was nearly always open to Mae Browne, and footing the bill was positively a pleasure if on the next morning the papers declared: "Again last evening in Gramercy Park, the tireless hostess, Mrs. Beatrice Britz . . ."

Pützl, a Doberman pinscher normally of a singularly ill-tempered disposition, decided to console Mae Browne. He stuck his wet nose on her lap. She looked down at the dog, patted him without much interest, and asked again what she could use to spruce up her tired beige frock. Perhaps her butter-yellow scarf?

The cocoa shoes? She ran her fingers through her black hair—still bobbed in a 1930s fashion—and wrinkled her brow (eyebrows also plucked and arched as she'd plucked and arched them since the thirties), and asked, as if I would know, in which drawer had she placed her yellow silk scarf.

Because of her melancholy reverie, I knew there was no use in continuing, that work on her memoirs had ended for the day. I gathered up clippings, notes, index cards, and prepared to leave.

Mae Browne went into the kitchen and made some tea. She put plenty of sugar into the cup. She sat at the kitchen table. She looked out from her fifteenth-floor window into the Harlem sunlight. She cried a little, as she blew into the steaming cup, as she rubbed Pützl's belly with her toe.

The suffocating air of boredom was rife in Mrs. Britz's large drawing room. Nobody seemed to connect. The publishing types (Mrs. Britz's crowd) soon tired of talking shop amongst themselves and only a few editors sought out the aging musicians (Mae Browne's crowd) for gossip and conversation. I passed the time by munching snacks and sipping scotch and trying to sort out Mrs. Britz's chinoiserie: although I'd been told a dozen times, I still could not remember whether the lowboys were from Chungking or Hangchow, the carpets from Chengtu or Kiangsu.

"No . . . no, wells," I heard Mrs. Britz saying. She was wearing something Mandarin. Persimmon. Orange florets decorated her high collar. She was speaking of her dead husband, Sherman, who had done something in oil. "He had no wells and things, mind you," she hastened to explain to the courtiers at her feet, "but he held an awful lot of—" and, as if masticating, she said, "you know —stocks and stocks and stocks."

At ten forty-five, Mae Browne leaned against the highly varnished Pleyel. Her beige dress, her cocoa shoes, and her yellow scarf, picked up these same hues from the elegant instrument. She knew what she was doing. She, too, held court.

Then someone said: "Oh, come on, Mae, sing it." This request came from one of Mae's friends. He was affable enough, although a bit drunk. "Come on, Mae, huh? That old ditty knocks me out."

Mae Browne was not interested in singing for her supper. "No, no," she whispered.

Mrs. Britz leaned forward from her perch on the leather couch as if she were about to make a shrewd chess move. "Oh, we shouldn't ask Mae to do that. Now, really. I mean, her voice isn't at all what—what it used to be—I mean, it's *awfully* unfair to tax her that way." Mrs. Britz shifted in her seat and pushed air away from her lap. Her green eyes turned into crystals. "I do so regret not having any of Mae's old records here. You'd absolutely adore them, I know." The silence was respectful and confused. "Ah, anyway—those were the days, weren't they, Mae dear?"

Without as much as a glance towards Mrs. Britz, Mae Browne sat at the piano and sank her fingers into the keys. She began to sing. One could tell that Mae Browne had once been a singer of great charm, even though her voice was now in its lowest registers, raspy, full of vibrato. Her intonation, her insinuation, her attack, and particularly her phrasing, were indeed praiseworthy. One could also tell, watching her perform, that she'd been an unusually attractive woman with her thinly proportioned features, her bobbed hair, and especially her large black eyes. Sardinian grapes they were. One could well believe she'd been the toast of a couple of continents. She might have been, as she'd often claimed, something.

Finally, around two-fifteen, the last guests began to leave. In the foyer, someone attempted to pat Pützl, who had been let out of the utility room. (He'd been locked away not so much because of the guests—although he was exceedingly anti-social—but rather because Mrs. Britz feared he'd knock over and smash the two ceramic pots standing in the hallway. The pots weren't Chinese, but they looked Chinese, and they were expensive). But Pützl could not abide fawning, and he found patting distasteful. He backed away from the human paws.

"He's sweet," some woman lied in her teeth to Kitty, the maid, as Kitty helped the woman put on her smart raincoat. She did, the woman, something clever in advertising. "What's his name?"

Kitty, thin and blond, who had spent most of her life in Ireland, blushed faintly and said, "It's Miss Browne's dog. She calls it Poot-zol, I think." Kitty, like most people, could not pronounce Pützl's name.

"Odd," said the advertising woman. "How's it spelled?"

Kitty didn't know.

The woman's escort, who had just stopped shaking goodbye-hands, turned. He, perhaps because of his German extraction, spelled it and pronounced it perfectly. But the woman wouldn't believe her escort; she, in any case, had been disagreeing with him the entire evening. "I'll ask Mae Browne," she said, traipsing back into the drawing room. "Mae, your cute dog—how exactly do you say his name? Is it German?"

Mae Browne enjoyed giving instructions on the correct pronunciation of her dog's name. Indeed she may have named him Pützl for that very reason. "Pützl," she said, tapping the woman's shoulder with a good deal of élan. "Make your mouth into a shape as if you were about to say 'o'—as in—as in 'low.' Go on, do it. Okay. Now, keep that position but pronounce 'e' instead. Try it. You'll feel your tongue pushing forward." Mae Browne's Sardinian grape eyes glowed with delight at her pupil's wonderment. "Start to say 'o' but pronounce 'e' instead."

"May Browne and her bloody 'e' again," Bea Britz said loudly enough for Mae Browne to hear. I felt that particular sally was unfair, for the umlaut sound *was* made in the manner Mae Browne had demonstrated.

Mae Browne whirled around and said sharply, "Leave my 'e' alone!"

"Your 'e', indeed . . . it's all such small beer, anyway," Bea Britz muttered, as if to dismiss the matter. "You should have named the little monster 'Rover' and been done with it."

The advertising woman, having provoked a fuss, fled.

"Miss! Miss!" Kitty chased after the fleeing woman. "Your bag. This is your bag, isn't—"

The awful crash froze Kitty's tongue. Pützl, in chase, had knocked over and broken one of the ceramic pots in the foyer.

Mrs. Britz closed her eyes.

Kitty fell upon the smithereens, her dress a shroud upon the precious pieces. She let out a Celtic wail.

Bea Britz, in the center of her drawing room, was curiously serene. She stared at the broken ceramic Kitty was sweeping from the floor. I wasn't sure, but I thought I saw her suppress a smile. Then, quite calmly, she said, "Well, you do, you must admit, you *do* insist upon that 'e' nonsense to the extreme. You have—you have positively a fetish for it."

Mae Browne stood alone on the Chengtu carpet (Kiangsu?); she was almost in tears. "Don't think, don't think for a red hot

minute I didn't hear the way you introduced me to—to—what's
his name?—to a lot of people that way. May Brown. As May
Brown."

"You're tired, dear. You only imagined that. I said, as I always
say, 'Mae Browne.' I know I did."

"You said 'May Brown.'"

"Let's—let's don't argue, Mae." Bea Britz cast a green crystal
eye over the far nooks and crannies of the room, up to the top of
her stairs. "We still have guests to attend to—or do we?" (The
"we," to include Mae Browne, was calculated to placate, which it
did. Or seemed to.)

"Good night, good night," I called out, preparing to leave with
a magazine editor I'd met earlier in the evening. I heard just
before we left: "Well, in any case," Bea Britz said to Mae
Browne, "*you're* staying right here. I'll not have you going up to
Harlem at this time of night." The hall clock, as if taking up its
cue, struck two-thirty. "So. That's settled."

As Mae Browne acquiesced silently, without even a nod of her
head, I began to suspect that the Mae-Bea squabble had an aspect
to it I'd overlooked: they were enmeshed in a charade of Mandarin complexity; they were locked together in a syndrome of an
order I'd grossly underrated; Mrs. Britz, the terrible Mrs. Britz,
loved to tyrannize, and she was paying Mae Browne (if not exactly in cash) for the privilege. They needed each other, those
two.

Nine days later, on Saturday afternoon, Mae Browne said, "*Es
ist Freitagmorgen sieben Uhr im—*"

"Mae, Mae," I interrupted. Sometimes she did that—drifted off
into German while dictating. She'd done it often today. She
wasn't concentrating.

"I know," she said. "It's no use. Let's knock it off, okay?"

I began sorting bits and pieces of notes so that I could dash
downtown to my place in the Village. "Are you coming to Mrs.
Britz's party tonight?"

"*Am* I?" Mae burst into hoarse giggles. "Darling, nothing could
stop me from going down there tonight. Nothing."

Or any other night, I wanted to add, but said instead, "Why?
What's so special about tonight?"

Mae bounced twice on the sofa and ran her ringed fingers

through her bobbed hair. "Come, come," she said, patting the cushion beside her. "I'll die if I don't tell somebody. I'll simply die."

"What—what's the—"

"Come, come, honeybunch. Sit. Sit."

I knew I was in for something, but I wasn't prepared for the Byzantine madness which somersaulted from her lips. When she'd finished (with an asthmatic solicitation for my approval), I asked her to start all over again—slowly.

From what I gather, Mae Browne had not been pleased about the turn of events nine days ago at Mrs. Britz's party: granted, it was late that night and taxis to Harlem were hard to come by, and she furthermore *liked* staying overnight in Mrs. Britz's guest room and being pandered to by Kitty at breakfast in the morning, but the demand to remain there was, Mae Browne felt, just another example of the artillery Mrs. Britz would use whenever the two of them were engaged in a contretemps. In short, Bea Britz, Mae Browne declared, won that round with condescending beneficence. However, throughout a long, slow, breakfast the next morning, gentility reigned. They talked of Parke-Bernet, of a sale at Bloomingdale's, of the possibility of Pützl seeing a veterinarian for his hind paw—or at least *she* talked, Bea did; Mae said she was thinking, thinking what her next move would be. It was about that time the matter of the invitations came up. Of course she would be delighted to post them, Mae told Bea. Of course she'd do it the very second she got out of the cab. Of course at the time she had every intention of doing so, Mae said, as if I would think her lack of malice aforethought would—if not exactly excuse— mitigate the heinous nature of her crime.

"Look, lovey. Look." Mae Browne sprang up from the sofa and skipped across her carpet to fetch a handsome cloisonné box. Carefully she lifted out the unmailed invitations. Saturday sun slid over her stained teeth. She squinted her eyes with exquisite malice, and her scent, which I had theretofore believed to have been merely Shalimar, hung in the air as if it were the vapors of evil itself.

"But Mae—it's, it's a sit *down* thing for eight. I mean, it'd be different if it were—"

"All the better, my dear, all the better." She tapped on her chin

the chalk-gray invitations that were addressed in Mrs. Britz's or-
nate handwriting. "Oh, there'll be four of us," she assured me. "I
sent Cessy's." Then she began pouring schnapps into fragile
glasses to celebrate no doubt her one-upmanship, her victory, and,
I suspect, the toast she proposed was a gesture of relief as well; the
enactment of evil, like a charitable bequest, loses its zest without
a witness.

Mae had extracted my vow not to tell. She knew very well I
wouldn't, for she could in a flash wipe me out of the memoir-
project, even if Mrs. Britz did foot the bill. (My honor, alas, is
limited.) Four of us, she'd said. Mae. Mrs. Britz. I would come,
sworn to silence. And Cessy? "Mae, who is Cessy?"

"Cessy? Cessy Leghorne. God only knows. Some young thing
who does stuff with films. Documentaries, I think."

Chosen, I figured, as a fresh ear to listen to Mae's interminable
stories of her years of Hungarian largesse. And Pützl, I bet—surely
he'd be there. "Where is he, anyway?"

"Who?"

"Pützl."

"Oh. Kitty took him to the vet." She glanced at the wall clock
over the red-leather volumes of Walter de la Mare. "Goodness,
though, they ought to be back by now. Hmm. Well . . ." She
snatched up the decanter of schnapps and put it back on the liquor cabinet. "Now. I've got my face and hair to fix. And my nails.
Lordy, lordy, what on earth will I wear?"

Her last remark was rhetorical for she was already in the bathroom dumping Givenchy bath granules into the tub and I'd earlier seen, carefully laid out across her bed, a lavender blouse, an
ash-gray linen suit, some sort of rhinestone-looking beads. "Honeybunch," she shouted between phrases of some ancient love song,
"be sure to fix the latch when you go out."

The dinner party was a brilliant disaster. Mrs. Britz finally gave
up hope for the appearance of the four other guests and we sat
down in front of piles and piles of sweet-and-sour-something-
Chinese. (Pützl will adore this, I imagined Mae thinking as her
large black eyes—now fixed with kohl—surveyed the food atop the
silver platters.)

The gaiety was so false and the glittering table was so sadly in vain that Mae, with a lapse into compassion, made an effort to contribute as much to the conversation as she could. She even paid compliments to Mrs. Britz on her crêpe de chine tunic. Then she managed to get around to nuclear disarmament, which led her to NATO, which led her to Hungary, where she stayed. Bea sighed.

So did I, for I, too, had been on that trip before. I occupied myself with chewy meat and snow peas and wondered what vicarious kick Mae was getting out of it all. And I wondered who had been the seedy Chinaman Mrs. Britz ushered out (with embarrassment?) when I arrived for dinner. And why was Kitty's sister, Myrna, serving dinner instead of Kitty? There'd been mutterings about Pützl having badly scratched Kitty and mutterings about leaving Pützl at the vet's but Mrs. Britz couldn't reach Kitty's home by phone nor did anyone answer at the animal hospital. Equally unsatisfactory was Mrs. Britz's explanation of the seedy Chinaman's presence in her foyer—he'd brought up some condiments from Mott Street, she'd said. And who in the publishing world had been invited I'd have been interested in meeting? And the evening—it was boring, boring, boring. Damn Mae.

All the way up to dessert (a vile little pudding number) Mae spoke to Cessy Leghorne about her days in Hungary, interspersing now and then, for the sake of variety, comments on her singing career in Europe. Mrs. Britz finally broke into Mae's monologue and asked Mae: "Some Pudding Nam Tso, dear?"

"No pud. No pud for me, thanks."

Cessy Leghorne's spoon slowed down; it was in the middle of it, in the middle of the Pudding Nam Tso. The woman's eyes, shuttered by her lids, slid sideways.

Mae continued, right where she left off, about her life in her villa outside of Gödöllö.

Once, and then very briefly, I thought I saw Cessy Leghorne nod.

Mrs. Britz stood up. "Let's have coffee and brandy in the drawing room."

"Oh, goody," Cessy Leghorne said, getting up rather quickly. Mae followed so that she could finish her story but Mrs. Britz snapped on the television and said, "You—you won't mind, will you? I want to catch the news."

"Oh, no, no," Cessy Leghorne said, eagerly waiting for Mrs. Britz to adjust the picture.

Mrs. Britz turned channel after channel. No news. At last she found a program about soil erosion on the Eastern seacoast. She put her glasses on. She listened to everything the commentator had to say. So did Cessy Leghorne. Myrna, Kitty's sister, brought in Black Russians and brandy.

"*Es ist hier drinnen kalt?*" Mae asked in the middle of the reporter's comments on soil erosion on the Eastern seacoast.

No one turned a head. The thunderstorm had indeed brought the temperature down considerably but it was far from being cold.

When the eleven o'clock news came on, Cessy Leghorne said, "Gracious me, I'd no idea it was so late. I really must—where is your—"

"At the top of the stairs, dear," Mrs. Britz said. "To your left."

There were no earthquakes. No hijacks. No assassinations. We paid attention to the news anyway.

"Lovely, simply lovely," Cessy Leghorne said as she came downstairs. "Where did you get that heavenly Tiffany? On the desk. The one in the study."

"Ah-ha, my dear," Mrs. Britz said. "I have my sources. Oh, I have my sources." Then, with a kiss on the cheek, she bid Cessy Leghorne good night.

The moment the woman left, Mae said: "Bea? You have a new Tiffany? You didn't tell me."

"I was going to, lambkin, I was going to. It was to be a surprise."

Mae clattered upstairs to inspect it.

Mrs. Britz sat. She folded her arms. A sinister tranquility settled in her eyes. I then knew something was wrong. My soporific state quickened into anxiety, curiosity. I heard my heart pounding when I caught sight of Mae—ashen, drawn, aged—descend the stairs. In silence, she took her jacket from the hall rack and slowly walked out of the apartment.

Mrs. Britz's face was immobile. She still sat there, her arms folded.

I went upstairs to the study. The lamp was there. Attractive enough. A Tiffany lamp. I was about to leave when my eye caught a smudgy five-by-seven card on the table beneath the lamp. I came closer. It was a recipe.

Sweet and Sour Doberman

Pre-heat deep fryer to 375 degrees.
Cut into half-inch squares two pounds boned Doberman loin, toss with:
    Three teaspoons soy sauce
    Three tablespoons flour.
Fry in deep fat until squares come to surface and float.
When crisp and golden brown, drain on absorbent paper.
Have ready and simmering the following sauce.
Mix: One and a half teaspoons cornstarch.
Heat: Two tablespoons lard.
Sauté until golden: One very small chopped onion.
Add: Six tablespoons sugar
      One-half cup water
      One-quarter finely chopped garlic clove
      One tablespoon soy sauce
      One-quarter cup vinegar
      One-half cup Chinese sweet and sour pickle and the cornstarch
mixture. Cook and stir for one minute. Add the meat and heat. Ladle
over rice.

Serves eight.

I sat down. In the study I sat down near the Tiffany lamp that
summer evening du côté de chez Britz.

After a lot of brandy, and a good deal of pleading, I managed
to get Mrs. Britz to talk. When she did, she spat out a barrage of
bullets: she said that people were far too sentimental about dogs,
that people ate turtles didn't they, that people ate rabbits didn't
they, that people ate deer, that people ate birds (meaning squab),
that people ate goldfish, that people ate things like snails, eels, chit-
terlings, that no one could say for *certain* it had been Sweet-and-
Sour Pützl, that she was collecting all sorts of exotic recipes for a
new cookbook, that Mr. Wong was aiding her, that Pützl might
be at the vet's that very minute, that he might have been stolen,
that people often stole pets in New York, that in any case nobody
on God's earth could prove Mr. Wong killed Pützl in his shop on
Mott Street and that she served him over rice. Nobody.

After even more brandy, and more haggling and prying, Mrs.
Britz relented and said she'd been sick and tired of Mae's dog
breaking things in her house and that she really hadn't had him
killed; she had him impounded for a few days.

Impounded? Her elaborate charade did not make sense—or did it? It then occurred to me that the possibility of evil, like the idea of danger, was for her more pleasurable than the actuality. I suddenly remembered Mae tapping on her chin the unmailed invitations, smelling of cologne. I took another brandy and shut up.

Again, Mrs. Britz has invited me to dinner. I am afraid to go. I poke around the edges of Gramercy Park. I watch Mae Browne arrive in a yellow cab. It is eight-thirty.

I cross the street. I enter Number Thirty-four.

MRS. DARCY MEETS THE BLUE-EYED STRANGER AT THE BEACH

LEE SMITH

Lee Smith was born in Grundy, Virginia, in 1944. She has
had three novels and various stories published; a new novel,
Black Mountain Breakdown, was recently completed. Married, with two sons, she lives in Chapel Hill, North Carolina.

It was cocktail time. The sun, which had been in and out all day,
now found a crack in the piles of gray cloud and shone brilliantly,
falsely, down the length of the beach, even though thunder rolled
on in the distance. The ocean was full of whitecaps. Its color went
from a mean gray, far out near the horizon under those clouds, to
steely blue patches closer in where the sun hit it. The tide was
coming in, running about a foot higher than usual, eating up the
beach, bunching the people on the beach closer and closer together. It was unreliable, irritating weather, typical of August. A
strong wind had come up after the most recent shower, blowing
straight in from the ocean over the waves. This wind was perfect
for kites and kites had sprung up everywhere, flown mostly by
grandchildren who tangled their strings or let them get caught on
TV antennaes and then had to have another one, immediately,
from El's Hardware Store on the mainland. It was this day, August 25, nearing sunset, cocktail time in kite weather, when Mrs.
Darcy received her first vision.

Below the house, Mrs. Darcy's daughters had arranged themselves together on the beach. Tall, graceful women like flowers,
they leaned delicately toward one another and sipped their gin
and tonics and shouted into the wind. Their family resemblance
was noticeable, if not particularly striking: the narrow forehead,
the high cheekbones, the dark eyes set a fraction of an inch too

228   LEE SMITHLEE SMITH

close together; the long straight nose, rather imperious, aristocratic, and prone to sinus. They were good-looking women.

Yet try as she might—and she had tried, all their years of growing up—Mrs. Darcy was unable to find anything of herself in them. Mrs. Darcy was short, blond, and overweight, with folds of flesh that dangled like dewlaps from her upper arms. She had been a pretty girl once, but she had never been a thin girl, or a fashionable girl, or a fashionable young woman. These girls took after their father; they had his long, thin hands. Inside the house, Mrs. Darcy leafed through the pile of craft books that Trixie had brought her, and looked down at her daughters on the beach. Craft books! Mrs. Darcy thought. Craft books. What does she know? Wrapping her robe about her, Mrs. Darcy moved to stand at the door.

"What was she doing when you came out?" Trixie asked. Trixie was the oldest, with three teenagers of her own. Her close-cut hair was streaked with gray, and her horn-rimmed glasses sat squarely on her nose. "What was she *doing?*" Trixie asked again, over the wind.

Maria, the middle sister, shifted her position on the quilt. "Not much, I think. Puttering around in the kitchen."

"Well, there's nothing to do for supper," Trixie pointed out. "It's already done."

"I don't know," said Maria, who always deliberated, or gave the impression of deliberating, before she spoke. "I think some of the children had come in and gotten a drink or something."

"I tried to get her to help cook," Trixie said. "Remember how she used to cook?"

"You know what really drove me mad?" Ginny said suddenly. "I was telling my shrink this the other day. I mean, whenever I think of Mama, you know what I think of her doing? I think of her putting leftovers in a smaller container. Like, say, we've had a roast, right? and if it were *me*, I'd leave the roast in the pan it was in. But oh no. After dinner, she had to find a smaller pan, right? For the refrigerator. Tupperware or something. The Tupperware pot-roast container. Then somebody makes a sandwich maybe, and one inch of the roast is gone, so she had to find another container. Then another, then another, then another. She must have gone through about fifteen containers for every major thing she fixed. That's all I can remember of childhood." Ginny had been leaning forward intensely, sucking on a Salem in the wind. Now she stabbed the cigarette out in the sand and flung herself back flat and her long black hair fanned out on the quilt.

"You're feeling very angry about this," Maria said in her precise, well-modulated voice. Maria was a psychologist, married to another psychologist, Mark, who sat some thirty yards behind the sisters on the deck at the back of the house, observing things through his binoculars. "Your anger seems oddly out of proportion to the event," Maria remarked.

"No kidding," Ginny said.

One of Maria's children, Andrew, came up to get his shoe tied. "Why can't we buy any firecrackers?" he wailed, and then ran off, a blur of blue jean legs, without waiting for the answer.

"Now, then," Trixie said. The wind had died down, it was possible to talk and Trixie liked to get right to the heart of the matter. "It does seem to me, as I wrote to both of you, that a certain amount of—er—*aimlessness* is understandable under the circumstances. But as I said before, when I went to Raleigh last month, I just couldn't believe it. I couldn't believe the way she was living. Dust on everything, and you know how she always was about dust. She was drinking Coca-Colas. Hawaiian Punch. Frozen pizza in the refrigerator—*pizza*, can you imagine?"

Maria smiled at the idea of pizza, the mere mention of it so incongruous with their childhood dinners in Raleigh. She remembered the long shining expanse of mahogany, the silver, the peacocks on the wallpaper, the crimson-flowered oriental rug. "Pizza!" Maria said softly. "Pop would have died."

"He did," Ginny pointed out.

"Really!" Trixie said.

"I think there has to be a natural period of mourning," Maria said, not meaning to lecture. "It's absolutely essential in the cycle of regeneration."

"But it's not mourning, exactly," Trixie said. "It's just being not interested. Not interested in anything, that's the only way I can describe it. Lack of interest in life."

"I can understand that," Ginny said.

"That could be a form of mourning," Maria said. "No two people mourn alike, of course."

"Different strokes for different folks," Ginny said. They ignored her.

"But you know how she used to keep herself so busy all the time," Trixie said. "She always had some craft project going, always. She was always doing volunteer work, playing bridge, you know how she was."

"She wore spectator heels and stockings every day," Ginny said in a passing-judgment voice.

"Yes, well, that's what I mean," Trixie went on. "And now what is she wearing? Rubber flip-flops from Woolco. She's let Lorene go, too. Lorene only comes in once a week now and does the bathrooms and the floors."

"I can't imagine that house without Lorene," Maria said. Lorene had been a central figure in their girlhood, skinny as Olive Oil in her starched white uniform.

"Well, Lorene is just as worried about Mama as she can be," Trixie said. "As you might well imagine. I went over to see her in the projects and gave her some money and I wrote down my number for her, at home, and told her to call me up any time. Any time she goes over there to clean and anything worries her."

"That's a good idea, Trixie," Maria said.

"Well," Trixie said. Trixie saw her two daughters, tan leggy Richmond girls, far down the beach, walking toward them in the foaming line of surf. "I'll tell you what I told Mother," Trixie continued. "I said, 'Why don't you start going to church again? Why don't you join one of these retirement clubs in town? They have all sorts of them now, you wouldn't believe it. They go to the mountains and they go to New York to see plays and everything is all arranged for them ahead of time. Why, we saw a group of them at Walt Disney World in Florida, having a perfectly wonderful time!'"

"I can't see that," Ginny said.

"Of course you can't, you're twenty-seven years old," Trixie snapped. Sometimes she felt as though Ginny were her daughter instead of her sister.

"Still, she did show some interest in coming down here," Maria pointed out. "Surely that's something."

"Interest but no initiative," Trixie said. "I suggested it, I picked her up."

"Aren't you something?" Ginny said.

"Ginny, I realize that you're going through a difficult period of adjustment yourself, but that is no excuse, no excuse at all for childish behavior. I think we have to start thinking in terms of a nursing home, is what I think. Caswell agrees, incidentally. Of course that would involve selling the Raleigh house; it would all be quite complicated. But I do see that as a distinct possibility."

"There's Margaret, why don't you ask her what she thinks?" Maria said. "She came over to see Mama this morning."

"When?" Trixie asked sharply.

"Oh, about ten o'clock. You were at the Hammock Shop, I think."

"Gotcha!" Ginny said.

Margaret Dale Whitted, who had divorced one husband and buried two, made her slow majestic way across the sand. A white caftan billowed about her and she carried a martini balanced carefully in one hand. "Cheers!" Margaret said when she reached them, steadying herself with a hand on Trixie's shoulder. "My God, dears, it's not worth it, is it? Nature, I mean." Margaret's voice was raspy and decisive, the voice of someone who has always had money. She had known their mother for forty summers more or less, since the time when Lolly and Pop had built their house, the Lollipop, next to Margaret's Sand Castle. There had been nothing, almost nothing, on the south end of the island then. They had been pioneers.

"Margaret, how are you?" Ginny asked. Ginny had always liked Margaret.

"Oh, there's some life in the old girl yet." Margaret gave her famous wink. "I'm having some trouble, though, just between us girls, with this shoulder. I fell, you know, in March."

They didn't know.

Margaret sipped her martini and stared out to sea, breathing heavily. Ginny stood up and dusted the sand off her jeans. Margaret's gold medallion winked in the fitful sun.

"We wanted to ask you about Mama. What you think, I mean," Trixie said. Trixie noticed how her own daughters had seated themselves just far enough away so that no one could connect them with her at all.

"Mama, Mama, it's all tangled up," wailed Christy, Maria's six-year-old daughter.

"Take it to Daddy," Maria said. "He'll have to cut some string."

Trixie and Maria stood up.

"Well," Margaret rasped. "I'll tell you what, girls. It's hell to get old." Margaret laughed and steadied herself on Trixie's elbow. The wind blew Margaret's huge white skirt about their legs, entwining them. Suddenly Ginny dashed off after a frisbee, got it, and threw it back to Bill, Trixie's son. Maria picked up the quilt, shook it, and walked back up toward the Lollipop, the deck, her husband. Through the binoculars, he stared toward the ocean, with his red beard curled around his pipe. The screen door of the Lollipop opened and Mrs. Darcy came slowly out, blinking in the sun.

Down on the beach, Margaret raised her silver cup aloft. "Cheers, honey," she said to Trixie.

"Look, Mama, look!" Christy and Andrew started up a howl. "Look, Mama, a rainbow, a rainbow!"

Maria nodded to them, with exaggerated gestures, from the deck.

"How's it going, honey?" Mark asked without lowering the binoculars. "Getting everything worked out?"

"Oh, it's just so difficult." Maria put the quilt over the rail and sat down in a chair. "Ginny is so difficult, for one thing. I hate these whole-family things, I always have. There are so many things to work through. So many layers of meaning to sort out."

"Actually there's a great deal to be said for the nuclear family structure," said Mark, focusing his binoculars on the sight he had been viewing for some time now, Ginny's breasts moving beneath her pink T-shirt as she played frisbee with his nephew.

But Ginny stopped playing frisbee then and turned to stare out at the ocean and Bill did too, as all movement stopped along the beach.

"Mama, Mama, Mama!" Christy screamed.

"I'll be damned," Mark said, putting the binoculars down. "A double rainbow." Mark put an arm around his wife and they stood together on the deck, nuclear and whole, like a piece of architecture against the wind.

"All the summers we've been here, I've never seen one of those," Trixie remarked to Margaret.

A giant rainbow shimmied above the horizon, pink and blue

and yellow and blue again, above the mass of clouds, and as they all watched, the clouds parted and a second rainbow—almost iridescent at first, the merest hint of color—arched across the sky beneath the first, spreading color until the rainbows seemed to fill the sky. The children on the beach, caught in motion as definitely as if they had been playing statues, broke up with a whoop and began to cavort madly, whirling around and around in all directions. Sand and frisbees flew. Up on the porch, behind Maria and her son-in-law, Mrs. Darcy moved hesitantly at first, in an oddly sidewise, crablike fashion, further out into the afternoon. Mrs. Darcy wore her flip-flops and a flowered housecoat. She raised her arms suddenly, stretching them up and out toward the rainbows. "Ai-yi-yi!" she wailed loudly. "Yi-yi-yi!" Mrs. Darcy stood transfixed, then fell forward onto the sandy deck in a dead faint.

The next morning dawned clear and beautiful. The joggers were at it early, pounding the road from one end of the island to the other. Fishermen lined the bridge over the sound to the mainland, dropping their lines straight down into the outgoing tide. Marsh grass waved in the wind and strange South Carolina birds flew overhead. Somebody caught a blowfish. Along the road beside the biggest houses, white-uniformed maids came out to dump the bottles and trash from the night before, getting their houses ready for the day, lingering to gossip in the sun. Children ran out onto the piers that protruded far into the marsh, checking crab traps, squealing at the catch.

At the far south end of the island, Ginny prowled the beach for sand dollars, watching the shifting tide pools as the tide rushed out to sea. She remembered getting on her raft in the sound at about the middle of the island, drifting lazily through the marsh grass past all the piers, gaining speed as the tide picked up, rocketing around the south end of the island finally, right here, jetting out to sea to be knocked back at last by the waves. Ginny remembered the final, absolute panic each time in the rush to the sea, how strong the current was. In this memory she seemed to be always alone. Maria never wanted to do it, Trixie had been too old, off at school or something. But there had been friends every summer. Ginny remembered the Mitchells from Columbia, whose house had been sold five years ago. Johnny Bridgely, her first beau. The Padgetts who always had birthday parties with piñatas.

Ginny sat in a tide pool and played with the hermit crabs. The water was so clear you couldn't tell it was there sometimes. She could feel the sun, already hot on her shoulders, and nothing seemed worth the effort it took.

At the Lollipop, Mrs. Darcy lay back on a day bed in the big rustic living room, surrounded by children and friends who urged her back each time she attempted to rise.

"I still think, Mama, that it would be very silly—I repeat, very silly—for you not to let us take you right up to the doctor in Myrtle Beach. Or down to Georgetown if you prefer. But you cannot just ignore an attack like this," Trixie said.

"I wonder if this might not be some sort of ploy," Maria whispered to Mark in the kitchen. "An attention-getting thing. Unconscious, of course."

"It's possible," Mark said. "Or she might have had a slight stroke."

"A stroke!" Maria said. "Do you think so?"

"No, but it's possible," Mark said. Mark got a cup of coffee and went out onto the beach. His nieces, already oiled, lay on their stomachs reading books from their summer book list. His own children were making a castle in the wet sand further out.

"I think I'll scramble some eggs," Mrs. Darcy said, but the lady from across the street, Susie Reynolds, jumped up and began doing it for her.

There was something new about Mrs. Darcy, something ethereal, this morning. Had she had a brush with death? a simple fall? or what? Why did she refuse to see the doctor? Mrs. Darcy looked absurdly small lying there on the rather large daybed, surrounded by pillows. She still wore the flowered housecoat. Her small fat ankles stuck out at the bottom, the bare feet plump and blue-veined, with a splotch or two of old red nail polish on the yellowed toenails. Her arms were folded over her stomach, the hands clasped. Her hair curled white and blond in all directions; but beneath the wild hair, her wrinkled face had taken on a new, luminous quality, so that it appeared to shine.

Trixie, looking at her mother, grew more and more annoyed. Trixie remembered her mother's careful makeup, her conservative dress. Why couldn't she be reasonable, dress up a little, like the other old ladies out on the beach? Even Margaret, with her mar-

tinis and her bossiness, was better than this. *Life does go on,*
Trixie thought.

Mrs. Darcy smiled suddenly, a beatific smile which traveled the
room like a searchlight, directed at no one in particular.

"She seems a little better, don't you think?" Mrs. Reynolds said
to Trixie from the kitchen door. Mrs. Reynolds brought in the
plate of scrambled eggs and toast.

"Oh, I don't know," Trixie said. "I've been so worried, I just
can't tell."

"Well, I think she looks just fine," Mrs. Reynolds said. "I'll go
on back now. Call me if you need me, honey."

Mrs. Darcy sat up and began to eat. Maria, book in hand,
watched her silently from the wicker armchair. Morning sun came
in the glass doors, and a crossbreeze ruffled the pages of the magazines on the table. Bill came back for his flippers and mask. The
volume of children rose from the beach. "How do you feel now?"
Maria asked carefully.

Mrs. Darcy's watery blue eyes seemed to darken in color as she
looked at her middle daughter. "When I saw the rainbow," she
said in her soft Southern voice, "why, it was the strangest thing!
All of a sudden I felt this, this *presence*, I can't tell you what it
was like, it just filled me up until I was floating. Then I saw
him."

"*Saw who?*" Maria put down the book and leaned forward in
her chair. In the kitchen, Trixie dropped a coffee cup with a clatter and came to sit at the end of the day bed.

"Why, I don't know!" Mrs. Darcy said in a wondering sort of
way. "I just don't know!" She began to eat heartily.

"Mother, I don't believe I quite understand," Maria said
calmly. "Do you mean that you saw a stranger, some strange man,
on the deck? Or did he come into the house from the front?"

"Oh no," Mrs. Darcy said airily, waving her fork. "Oh no, nothing like that. I went out on the porch, I was looking at the rainbow, I felt this overwhelming presence everywhere, oh, I just can't
tell you what it was like! Then I saw him." She beamed at them.
"Trixie, honey, could you bring me some salt?" she asked.

Trixie rose automatically, was stopped by the sight of her son
Bill standing in the kitchen door, flippers and mask in hand, staring at his grandmother. "Go on down to the beach," Trixie said
to him. "Go!" He went. Trixie got the salt, came back and gave it

to her mother who sat placidly munching toast and dropping crumbs all down the front of her housecoat.

"Could you be a little clearer, Mother?" Maria asked. "I'm still not sure who this man was."

"But I don't *know!*" Mrs. Darcy said. "Thank you, dear," she said to Trixie, and sprinkled salt liberally on her eggs. "He had long hair, he wore a long white thing, sort of like Margaret's dress as a matter of fact, you know the one I mean, and he had the most beautiful blue eyes. He looked at me and stretched out his arms and said, 'Lolly.' Just like that, just my name."

"Then what?" Maria said.

"Then I went to him, of course." Mrs. Darcy finished her breakfast and stood up. "I may have a swim," she said.

"Oh, I wouldn't," Trixie said quickly.

Mrs. Darcy seemed not to hear. Training her new smile upon each of them in turn, she went into her bedroom and softly closed the door. The sisters stared at each other.

"That beats everything I've ever heard!" Trixie said. "You see why I brought up the nursing home?" Under the brown thatch of her hair, Trixie's face looked nearly triumphant, causing Maria to reflect fleetingly upon the strange accident of birth, the fact that if the woman facing her had not happened to be her sister, they would have had nothing in common at all. Nothing! Maria thought.

"I think we have to proceed very carefully here," she told Trixie. "Let me go and discuss this with Mark."

Trixie went upstairs to lie down, thinking, as she climbed the stairs, that Caswell had been right after all. They should have gone to Sea Island by themselves.

Ginny had joined the others on the beach, standing with Mark at the water's edge to watch the children swim.

"Let me put some of this on your back," Mark said, holding up a bottle of suntan oil.

"No, thanks," Ginny said. "Please. Not any more."

Mark put the top back on the bottle. "Well, what happened with Don, then?" he asked. "You want to talk about it?"

"No," Ginny said. "I don't."

"Mark, Mark!" Maria came running toward them. She arrived; she told them everything. Ginny began to laugh.

Bill came dripping up out of the water, followed by the girls.

"There's a real strong undertow," he yelled to everybody. When they didn't answer he came closer, pushing the face mask up. "Grandma's going batty, isn't she?" he said to his uncle and aunts.

"Is that true?" the girls demanded. "Is she going to go in a nut house?"

"Of course not," Ginny said.

"What's a nut house?" Christy asked.

Ginny was laughing and laughing.

"This will take some thought," Mark said, pulling at his beard.

Slowly and daintily, Mrs. Darcy made her way past the whole group of them and stood at the edge of the ocean to adjust her red rubber bathing cap. Her skin was so white that she looked startling among the sun-browned children in the surf. She turned once, waved, before she walked straight out into the waves until they were hip-high. Then she raised her hands and dove.

"You know I don't believe I've ever seen your mother swim before," Mark said to Maria.

Maria stood openmouthed. "She doesn't," she finally said. In years past, her mother's beach routine had never varied: up around nine, a walk perhaps, some shopping, drinks with friends, but never—never—had she actually gone for a swim. Maria burst into tears. "She needs help," Maria said.

"Oh, come on," Ginny said. "We all do. Look, I'll drive all the kids up to the trampoline for a while, OK?"

Before them, just beyond the breakers, Mrs. Darcy's red bathing cap bobbed like a cork in the gentle rise and fall of the waves.

Three days passed, all of them sunny and blue, calm and idyllic. Caswell arrived. The Lollipop settled into the old routine of summers past. Plans were made and carried out, menus were planned, groceries were bought and cooked. Caswell and Mark chartered a boat out of Murrell's Inlet and took Bill fishing. Maria was always amazed at how well Caswell and Mark got along; she couldn't imagine what they had to say to each other. Trixie's girls found some nice boys from Charleston to date. Old friends came and went. Margaret took Mrs. Darcy to lunch at Litchfield Plantation. Pop was mentioned often, casually and affectionately, and Mrs. Darcy seemed not to mind. She did not mention the "presence" or the blue-eyed stranger again. She continued to pad about the house in her flip-flops and housecoat, but she showed some inter-

est in the cooking and she played checkers with Christy and Andrew.

By Thursday morning, Trixie had begun to relax. She thought
it was time to interest her mother in Shrink-Art. Trixie had
brought all the materials with her, and now she unpacked them
and brought them into the kitchen and spread them out. The
others had gone crabbing up at Huntington Beach State Park.
"Now, Mother," Trixie said, "let's do a little bit of this. It's really
fun, really easy, and you'll just be amazed at what you can make."

"Maybe a little later, dear," Mrs. Darcy said. Mrs. Darcy sat in
the wicker armchair, looking out at the beach.

"No," Trixie said firmly. "Now is the time. They'll be back before long, then we'll have to make sandwiches. Now look, Mother,
all you do is trace designs onto this clear plastic, using these permanent markers. Or you can make your own designs, of course.
Then you cut them out and bake them for three minutes and—"

"*Bake* them?" Mrs. Darcy echoed faintly.

"Sure!" Trixie said. "Then they turn into something exactly
like stained glass. They're really lovely. You can make jewelry,
Christmas ornaments, whatever. They make lovely Christmas ornaments."

"But how would you hang them up?" Mrs. Darcy came to
stand beside her daughter at the table.

"Oh, you punch a little hole before you put them in the oven,"
she said. "I've got the hole-puncher right here."

Trixie spread out the plastic sheets, the designs, the permanent
pens. She turned the oven on to 300. "OK," she said. "All set.
Which one do you want to try?"

"Maybe this," Mrs. Darcy said. She placed a sheet of clear plastic over a design involving a bunch of tulips stuck into a wooden
shoe. Trixie was mildly surprised by the choice, more surprised by
her mother's easy acquiescence. Everything seemed so much better since the weather had cleared. Perhaps things were not so complicated, so serious as they had thought. Still, it was reassuring
that Mark and Maria had arranged treatment for Mother back in
Raleigh. A most competent doctor by all accounts, highly recommended. Trixie felt sure that Mother would agree to see him. The
teakettle began to whistle. Trixie got up to make the iced tea. The
pitcher, old heavy brown pottery, had been at the beach house
ever since she could remember. Out of the corner of her eye,

Trixie watched Mother biting her tongue a bit and gripping her marker tightly, like a small, pudgy, dutiful child. Trixie added lemon and sugar to the tea.

"There now," Mrs. Darcy said, sitting back in the chair, her round wrinkled face rather flushed. She looked at Trixie hopefully. "Now what?"

"Now you cut it out," Trixie said, "and punch a hole, and we put it in the oven for three minutes."

Mrs. Darcy cut the design out carefully, using some old round-tipped scissors that Trixie had found way back in a kitchen drawer. Trixie took the design from her, somewhat distressed to find that Mother had colored the tulips blue. Still, it would not do to appear disparaging. "This is so pretty, Mother," Trixie said. "Now you can watch it shrink if you want to." Mrs. Darcy turned her chair, so that she could peer through the oven's glass door.

The kitchen door burst open at that moment and there they were suddenly, all of the rest of them, with two coolers full of scrambling crabs and the children all talking at once.

"Just leave those on the porch," Trixie directed. "Go on, take them right back out this instant. Right now. Go on. Bill, what do you mean, tracking in here this way? Go take off those shoes on the porch."

"Bill fell in, Bill fell in!" Andrew danced up and down, still holding his piece of twine with the rock and the chicken neck tied to the end.

"You're so excited, darling," Maria said.

"Well, I'm starving." Still wearing her black bikini, Ginny came barefooted into the kitchen, so that she was the closest one to her mother, the only one who actually saw Mrs. Darcy's face as she watched her tulips shrink, and shrink, and shrink before her eyes. Ginny stopped, caught in the oddest sensation: it might have been her face before her, it might have been her own voice which began to scream.

A fine drizzle fell all day Sunday, jewelling the surface of things. They left for hours, it seemed, and their leavetaking took up most of the day. Lolly knew that they had been up far into the night, deciding what to do about her. She realized that she had created a problem by her refusal to leave. But she did not *want* to leave yet, and she had never created a problem before—not ever, for anyone. So. She remained stubborn and went to bed early, leaving them to deal with her as best they could.

As they told themselves over and over, the others had to go. There was no question. Caswell had to fly straight up to Washington for a conference. The children's schools were beginning again, and Trixie had to buy school clothes for the girls. Maria and Mark had faculty meetings, workshops, classes. It was hard to believe that Christy would be in the first grade.

"Look," Ginny had surprised them all by saying. "Look, I'll stick around for a week or so. OK? You all go on. I'll bring her back to Raleigh before long." It was so unlike Ginny to be responsible that Maria had stared at her with considerable interest.

"I'd like to know why you're doing this," Maria said.

"Why not?" Ginny had answered.

And they had left, Trixie and Caswell and their large children in the long sleek car, Maria and Mark in their van. Christy and Andrew waved madly from the rear window as long as they stayed in sight. Lolly stood on the rainswept back porch, looking across the road to see the rising mist over the marsh. She traced designs in the drops of water that clung to the sides of the water heater. Each little drop seemed singular and profound, seemed to hold some iridescence of its own, or perhaps it was just the reflection from passing cars.

"Mama," Ginny said for the third time. Ginny stood in the kitchen door wearing white slacks, a windbreaker. She looked Lolly in the eye. "Listen, Mama, I'm driving up to Long Beach to have dinner with a friend, OK? The number is by the telephone. I might be back tonight, or I might be back tomorrow. There's a pizza in the freezer. OK?"

"OK." Lolly smiled at Ginny and watched her leave too, running lightly down the steps, slamming into her little car.

Lolly went back in the house. The silence wrapped her up like soft cotton. She got a Coke from the refrigerator, poured it, and sucked off the foam. She smiled to herself, turned on some lights. After a while she went to the telephone and called Margaret and in a little while Margaret came, bringing the friend she'd told Lolly about.

This friend was a wealthy widow of their own age, from Norfolk. "The doctor can't seem to find any explanation for it," she said. "Some sort of damaged nerve. It's just this intense pain, right here." She lifted her forearm so that the heavy bracelets jangled like wind chimes. "Sometimes the pain is so intense I just can't seem to go out at all. I can't even get out of bed."

"I know," said Lolly. Her pale eyes darkened and focused, she smiled. "Lie down," Lolly said, indicating the daybed, and she took the stringy manicured hand of Margaret's friend in her own soft white ringless fingers.

"That's right, dear," Margaret rasped from the wicker armchair. "Don't be nervous, dear. This is exactly the way she fixed my shoulder. I was lying just like that on my own chaise longue. The green one. Remarkable. Now just do exactly what Lolly says. Close your eyes, dear. Relax. That's right. Relax."

Later, healed and radiant, Margaret's friend wanted to pay Lolly, to make some contribution at least to the charity of her choice. Lolly declined, and they all had a glass of sherry.

"Really, how do you do it?" Margaret's friend asked. "Really, if you only knew how much money I've spent on doctors. Why, I even tried a chiropractor at Virginia Beach."

"It's nothing," Lolly said.

"Listen to that!" Margaret hooted. "Ha!" Margaret blew out a great puff of smoke which hung blue in the comfortable glow of the lamps.

"It's not me at all," Lolly told them. "I'm just an agent, you might say. An intermediary."

"Do you do much work with arthritis?" Margaret's friend asked. "I have a friend who's in the most terrible pain."

"I could give it a try," Lolly said.

When they had gone, she heated up the pizza and drank a glass of milk, leaving all her dishes in the sink. She took a bath. She put on a faded terry housecoat. Opening the doors to the ocean, Lolly went out on the deck. Out here everything was cold and clean-smelling and a sharpness bit through the air, signaling summer's end. There were few lights along the beach; most of the summer people and renters had gone. Beyond Lolly, out in the darkness, waves crashed onto the sand. She could taste their salt on her lips. Lolly was not even cold. She seated herself in a damp deck chair and leaned back. "Now," she said into the night.

THE DERBY HOPEFUL

ANTHONY CAPUTI

> Born and raised in Buffalo, New York, Anthony Caputi has
> taught in the English Department at Cornell for many years.
> He has published books, anthologies, and articles on drama,
> especially Renaissance drama. A novel, *Loving Evie*, was
> published by Harper & Row. Currently he lives in the coun-
> try, where he is working on a second novel and a collection
> of short stories; he enjoys the theater and horse races.

I saw him before he saw me, standing under the green awning of
the Army Surplus Store, his gaze idling from the suntans and
shoepacs in the window to the sun-blanched street. From the
side and rear he looked the same. Delicate jaw and slender shoulders, wispy butt in loose, faded jeans, high-heeled boots run down
at the side, draggly-sleeved blue shirt and broad-brimmed straw
hat. The same tentative grace, like a pitcher fingering the ball before winding up. And then he turned and saw me, blue eyes
awash with innocence.

"I knew it!" he exploded. "I knew it. I told Dad this morning
you'd be back. 'Clyde won't miss the Trial, you'll see,' I said." He
swallowed hard and pumped my hand.

We had gone to school together, hunted and fished together,
and most of all gone to the races together. We had walked hots
and watched Sonny Claiborne gallop his string and school them
to the gate. We had worked all summer on the farms near Decatur to go to Keeneland in the fall, every day, betting every race, X-
raying the past performance sheets in every waking hour, in the
end losing it all, or most of it, bleary-eyed with content, exhausted
with the weight of things learned. At fifteen we had found this in

each other, and it had obliterated all differences. Now he seemed little changed, maybe a touch sturdier and duller—older.

In Decatur everyone is a little nuts about horses. Only forty miles from Lexington and the glamour horse fans and Keeneland, and only sixty-five from Louisville and Churchill Downs, Decatur has racing in its air and water and midsummer dust. Everyone, except the very poor, has either owned a horse, or a piece of one, or is going to. In those days when the season was on at Keeneland, half the town moved in with relatives in Lexington, sleeping on sofas in the living room or on swings on the screened porch, wearing fresh cottons for four days and pomading their hair. They never looked so good in church.

"What did I tell you? Didn't I say he'd be back?" Jesse was shouting at a smaller, fiftyish man easing out of the Surplus Store. He had a large, flat paper bag in one hand, and his washed-out flannel shirt was buttoned up to his neck.

"Well, if it ain't Clyde Simmons. A sight for sore eyes." He smiled, lips tight, creasing his bronzed cheek, as if he had just sold a dog that would be dead by morning. We shook hands, his hard and dry, then for want of something to say looked at blond, red-faced Jesse, who had now hooked his fingers in his belt loops as if there were going to be something to watch. "Jesse's looking fine," I said. "Family well?"

"Course. Nothing can hurt us." The remark took in Mrs. Tompkins and Edna, the daughter just younger than Jesse. There had been an older daughter who had run away with one of the Tompkins' many hired men, but they never talked about her. "Are you back for the Trial?" He asked the question as if he were sharing a confidence.

"Wouldn't miss it."

"Where you been at school?"

"Michigan State. In Lansing, Michigan."

"Do they have a track there?"

"Not there. The nearest is in Chicago. They've got three there."

"That so?" He may not have believed me. "Well, the Derby crowd doesn't look like much this year. Wide open, I'd say. Any one of six or seven could do it."

"Oh tell him, Dad. For cryin' out loud, tell him." All at once Jesse was jerking and twisting out of control. His father leveled cool brown eyes at me, in no hurry, shifted the paper bag to his other hand and waited, as if I were supposed to say something.

"When can you come out to the place?" He glanced at Jesse as if scratching an itch. "I've got something I want to show you."

"What is it?" I asked. Jesse stamped out into the street and back to the curb.

"You come out to the place." He touched the peak of his straw hat with Randolph Scott grace and moved away. Jesse hesitated, protesting with his eyes and finally pulling his hat down over his brow, then darted after him across Independence Street, striding choppily to adapt his loping gait to his father's low charging stride. About fifty yards up the street stood the bleached, battered pickup which had changed many times over the years, yet always remained the same.

Since I'd become a Research Associate at Michigan State, my trips home had been less frequent. Christmas, once for a couple of weeks during the summer, then for the Trial at the end of April. I might see the Tompkinses during the summer visit or at Christmas, but I always saw them for the Trial. It was a holdover from boyhood, when we used to drive up to Lexington for the Sales and a couple of days of racing with the Trial on Thursday the highlight. In those days Mr. Tompkins had a chicken and egg business which his father had left him, and it was still good enough that he had a car and would take a half-dozen reserved seats at Keeneland for the racing days. In Lexington we stayed with his sister, the wife of a Baptist minister who disapproved of racing and, I think, disapproved of Mr. Tompkins. But we didn't let him bother us. We'd read the *Racing Form* at the breakfast table and have supper in hotel dining rooms downtown. And at least once Mr. Tompkins would drop Jesse and me off at a movie while he went off alone, we used to think to a burlesque show, and we'd all get in after the minister and Jesse's aunt were in bed.

It was an understanding which didn't have many years to run, I knew, but in 1948 and for a few more it was still holding fine. By then the chicken and egg business had dribbled away, as almost everything had a way of doing with Mr. Tompkins, and we no longer went up for the Sales or stayed with the minister and Jesse's aunt because they had moved to Memphis. But we still went up for two days, leaving early enough Wednesday morning to catch the ring, then staying over at the YMCA and driving back after the last race on Thursday. Despite the YMCA Mr. Tompkins still had reserved seats at Keeneland, on Trial day no mean feat.

The day after our meeting in Independence Street I borrowed my brother's motorcycle and went out to the Tompkins' farm. In all the years I had been going out there I had never seen an improvement. The barn was the same faded red from the days when Jesse and I had gone fishing in the creek down back, the barn doors had gradually fallen off and now were held in place by a fence post and the tongue of an ancient wagon. The fences around the pasture were a patchwork of wire and old pieces of barn sheeting and discarded doors, and inside, looking sick at heart if cows can ever look sick at heart, were the four survivors of the Tompkins' once numerous herd. It all looked sagging, sloping, feeling for the ground, looking for a place to sit and sleep after an exhausting day of free enterprise. Even the name "Twin Sycamores" printed in sticks tacked to a plank over the mailbox at the road had fallen off to "Twin ycamores" when the "S" had been lost.

I pushed the cycle up on its stand and started toward the garden, where I could see Jesse leaning on a hoe. The house beyond the barn looked closed, perhaps unoccupied; even the windows and doors behind the torn screens were shut. I looked carefully, however, because I thought Mrs. Tompkins or Edna might look out. Mrs. Tompkins had been very beautiful when Jesse and I were boys, with thick black hair and elegant hips and breasts. And her girls were like her. But there was no movement at the windows.

As I crossed the empty pasture, I called out and Jesse shaded his eyes and said something to a shady place under a peach tree. In a few steps I could make out Mr. Tompkins sitting against the tree, fanning the flies away with his hat.

"That your bike, Clyde?" He was chewing a blade of stiff grass, smiling and squinting up at me through the filtered light.

I explained that it wasn't, that as a Research Associate I didn't earn enough to have one. He looked at Jesse as if to say "What did I tell you?"

"There's no money in schools." He broke it to me gently, because as an old, simpleminded friend I had to be told.

"I guess not."

"You got to get into business, selling. A smart boy like you. Why'nt you get into one of them big laboratories? Invent something. That's where the money is."

"After a couple of more years I probably will. Go into industry, I mean. But not yet."

He waited for me to go on, and, when I didn't, he looked at Jesse as if admitting that there wouldn't be any more hoeing for a while and pushed himself to his feet and beat the dust from his overalls. Jesse had begun to roll himself a cigarette, all thumbs, smiling slyly as the tobacco escaped from the paper shell, waiting. The hoe was still leaning against his hip.

"Well, what is it? What have you got to show me?"

He leveled me with his agate eyes and took a deep breath of pleasure. He must have been past fifty-five, but his jaw was smooth and his dark skin tight on his cheeks and straight nose. A handsome man if it weren't for the shifty angle of his neck and sleepy glitter in his eyes. He looked more like Jesse's brother than his father, trim, hardly a gray hair in his close-cropped head. He took the hoe in one hand and fingered it with a hand used to milking, then let it drop.

"We've got something to show you." He started across the garden, stepping over the rows where beans and peas had begun to show, and headed for the creek. Jesse squealed, let the cigarette paper flutter to the ground and followed.

The route was familiar, past the garden through a stand of crowded beech, through a hayfield already knee-high, toward the uneven row of willows in the bottom land. Jesse and I had come this way hundreds of times when we had gone fishing, picking our path carefully because in the spring the creek usually flooded and even in high summer the land near it was soggy. I asked Jesse if he had been fishing yet, and he shook his head as if I had said something funny.

"No time. Ain't been time for anything this spring."

When we came to the last drainage ditch in the hayfield, I could see that the bottom land was, as usual, dark brown in mud. But Mr. Tompkins had already found one of the ridges of loose stone, so we followed without slowing down. About thirty yards from the creek he stopped and straightened up to look toward a copse of pussywillows.

"See him?"

I looked but saw only the pussywillows and the ragged trees beyond. We pushed on. As we entered the cluster of bushes, he stopped again. Then forty yards farther on, standing in mud up to his knees, was a small, chestnut horse on a tether.

"We've got us a mudder," Mr. Tompkins announced with hissing exhilaration.

What he meant was instantly clear: they had a horse, a race horse, and he had been bred and they planned to raise him to excel in the mud. A mudder: that phenomenon among runners that is ten lengths better when the track is like wet cement, that follows other horses happily every sunny, dry day of his life to metamorphose into a flyer when the temperature drops and the heavens open and the ducks flee for cover in the bushes along the edges of the infield lake. The Tompkinses had had horses before, never more than one at a time and never anything better than a cheap claimer. Once they had had a so-so gelding named Speedy Mushroom, whom they still talked about, but the Mushroom had caught a bad cold over the winter between his third and fourth years and had never again made it to the races. Then a long, five or six year gap until now.

Jesse was spinning off his pedigree. Kentucky stock for generations. Blue Larkspur in the male line and Man of War somewhere in the mare's. A sire that had won five, all of them on muddy tracks, and a mare that had never raced but that was famous for rolling in every puddle on Seth Whittaker's farm. Speed, toughness, and a fondness for running best when everyone else was running worst. They were going to call him Marvin's Tip. Mr. Tompkins' name was Marvin.

We stood watching him for more than an hour, and he watched us. Short in the body and wiry through the shoulder, he shook his head up and down and swished his straw-colored tail to shake off flies. He was an inch thick in yellow mud and dust that day. When Mr. Tompkins tried to rouse him, he backed off a step, seeming to sulk. Finally, Mr. Tompkins threw a clump of mud at his flanks and he galumped around in a circle in mild panic.

"When you going to put him in training?" I asked, though I didn't really expect them to have a plan for so small a two-year-old.

"What'd you say if I said he was in training already?" Mr.

Tompkins said this while looking away from me toward the creek
and a flight of birds lighting near it.

"Here?"

He turned, his face creased in the grin of a winner. "He's more
growed up than you'd think. He's pretty far along, in fact. He'll
never be big. Don't need it. What'd you say if I said we'd been
galloping him for six weeks?"

"Where?"

"Right there." He pointed a crusty finger toward the flat, still
wet verges of the creek running with only an occasional bush for a
quarter of a mile in each direction. "I gallop him myself." He
waited for the enormity of the project to sink in. "Come out and
see for yourself."

"You should see him move, Clyde." Jesse could barely control
himself.

"He gets a kick out of it, I swear he does," Mr. Tompkins added.

"Come out and see for yourself." Jesse's eyes popped with blue,
so different from Mrs. Tompkins', and even Edna's. "He's a real
good one. You'll see. You never seen more natural ability. The
Mushroom was a claimer to him."

I couldn't bring myself to point out that the Mushroom was, in
fact, a claimer—$4,500 on his best day, and no takers.

"We're going to do the real work here," Mr. Tompkins was
conspiratorial now, speaking fast for him, "gallop him and breeze
him in this till it's first nature, then we'll go to Keeneland or
River downs to break him to the gate and such. But only when
we're ready. We're breezing him quarters already." His dark eyes
disappeared in a squint.

"And don't you say a word to anyone. This time we got one, I
tell you."

I swore myself to secrecy as we walked back. Mr. Tompkins
tried to send Jesse up to the house to get Mrs. Tompkins to give
us some lemonade, but Jesse said he knew better than that and
didn't go. I thanked them just the same and started toward the
motorcycle with the promise that I'd be back the next morning.
The house was still closed tight, sinking toward the snowball
bushes along the near side. A half dozen towels and a cotton
wrapper flapped on the line at the back.

At six-thirty the following morning I borrowed the bike again
and rode out. They were already down on the bottom land when I

arrived, and Marvin's Tip was already saddled. Jesse was leading him at a fast walk through the wettest places in the dew-sodden field. After about twenty minutes of this Mr. Tomkins was boosted onto his back, and he walked him up the creek.

It was true: he looked better under tack and with someone on his back, and he did step with a gingerly poise that was reassuring. But there was no disguising that he was very small and very dirty, and Mr. Tompkins sat such an awkward seat, his back curved and his head angled to the side, that you thought of a cow pony instead of a runner. They were far up the creek now. Jesse and I sat on our haunches at a high, gravelly place to watch.

"Here he comes." Jesse leaned forward and snatched at a dry reed. Up the creek the horse bunched into a run and moved toward us, low and smooth.

"See how he loves it!" Jesse gasped as Marvin came toward us. "No strain; like a fish in water." And, in fact, when they passed, he was going easily, not very fast, but in an easy breeze, without fuss. Mr. Tompkins took him another two hundred yards up the creek, then drew up and started walking him back.

"He's a good one, Clyde. He'll beat the best on the right day. You see if he don't." Jesse was jogging now to intercept them. He and his father exchanged squeals, and Mr. Tompkins dismounted, winded. Jesse walked the horse to the creek's edge and then in the large circle.

"In a couple of weeks we should have him ready for Keeneland, then in a month or so for the races." Mr. Tompkins was breathless. "By July we should be at River Downs. Break his maiden and take down one allowance race or two. Have to pick them carefully. We're in no hurry. And mud is the name of the game. When everyone else wants to stay in the barn. Then back here for the winter. Start galloping him in February, bringing him up slowly again, lay a good foundation, so that when Keeneland opens we're ready. A race, maybe two, then the Trial."

"The Trial?"

"Why not? And if he does well there, why not the Derby? Do you know how many Trials and Derbies have turned up muddy? They're run in the spring remember."

"The Derby?"

His dark eyes widened by now to reveal the white all around them. Normally slow of speech and tight-lipped, he spoke like

someone talking as he ran. Jesse tried to listen from where he was
walking Marvin, and once or twice said again, "He's a good one,
Clyde."

I said nothing. But as we started across the soggy bottom land
again and fell silent, I realized my chest was tight. I almost
believed.

The following Wednesday we drove up to Keeneland. All the
way up and all the way back the next day they talked about Marvin, about how they found him on Seth Whittaker's farm standing in a puddle while the other five or six of Seth's small crop
were rolling in the grass on higher ground. He had cost next to
nothing; Seth admitted he was eager to get rid of him.

"A narrow man, Seth. He's got no imagination." Jesse made the
comment, but you could hear in it that Mr. Tompkins had made
it before.

"It's a whole different thing. They're different horses in the
mud. How would you like to run in the slop?"

"Not much."

"See there."

When they dropped me off, I promised to see them again on
my summer visit. But I didn't see them when I was home for ten
days in August, though I heard that they still had not taken Marvin to the races. Sometime in September, I learned later, they
finally entered him in a maiden race at River Downs, and then in
another and another. He didn't win until his seventh outing in
maiden claiming company; but he won by six lengths that day on
a very muddy track.

By the following April he had won two races out of thirteen,
both in the mud, and Jesse and Mr. Tompkins were giving all
their time to him, driving him back to the farm to save their ex-
penses away from home, selling what little they had in junk
around the place to buy feed and pay riders' bills. They hadn't
planted a garden, and the cows had been sold the previous November. Mrs. Tompkins and Edna had gone to Louisville to live
with Mrs. Tompkins' stepmother when the cows went.

Spring was early and unusually warm that year, in a great rush
to get to summer. When I pulled up at the Tompkins' place in
the secondhand Buick my brother had bought over the winter, the
weeds around the barn were already hip-high and the former garden was thick with blue and white field flowers. The house looked

abandoned, as if, after years of trying, the owners had finally walked away to let it sink into the bushes gone wild and the seedling maples. The old Ford tractor, tilted forward because its front wheels were gone, was already nosing into the earth. In fact, Jesse and Mr. Tompkins had moved out of the house and into the barn, "to make it easier," as they explained. I found them on the lower level among the stanchions trying to wire the front corner support of a ramshackle horse trailer.

As planned, Marvin was to run on Trial Day, but in an earlier race than the big one, a $6,500 claiming affair at seven furlongs.

"He's got to go, even though it ain't rained in three weeks. We can't lose his peak. He's got to go," Jesse pouted. "We've got to take what we can get."

Mr. Tompkins looked up, his face tight from holding the corner of the trailer up while Jesse wired. He grunted something as he hefted the corner pieces up on his legs, and when I asked him what he had said, he shouted, "Sharp as a copperhead's tooth!" He sounded angry. The Trial that year was thought to be a gambol for a three-year-old freak named Citation.

We left early the day before the Trial to take our time with the trailer, Jesse and Mr. Tompkins cursing the sun all the way. About halfway we had a flat and took Marvin out of the rig while Jesse walked the wheel to a garage. I led Marvin into the shade of a pine grove where we waited together; at the road Mr. Tompkins paced and talked to himself and twice kicked the good tire on the trailer. Marvin tensed at the flies in the summery shade, seemed to consider some more violent reaction, then thought better about it and blinked a vacuous eye in my direction. Finally, Jesse came back, slapping the tire to keep it rolling. We missed only the first two races.

On Trial Thursday the weather forecast said there was a possibility of showers, but I could see when I came out of the Tourist Home that it would be hot and dry all day. At the track I found Jesse and Mr. Tompkins already shaved and wearing the threadbare suits they always wore on the big day. They had slept on the seat of the pickup and the floor of the trailer and had risen early to get Marvin ready for the hot-walker they had hired to look after him till post time so they could watch the races. As we started away from the stall toward the grandstand, Jesse mumbled something about "He'll eat 'em up" and fell over a water tub that had not been put away.

Keeneland never looked better. The infield glistened with the newness of the year, falling away gracefully to the wooded hollow on the far side that made the backstretch seem a little off the ground. The combed straight leading from the starting chute always looked, and it did that day, as if waiting for fabled events, epic runners to drive through the golden air.

But Jesse and Mr. Tompkins seemed somewhere else, stiff and subdued on either side of me. I tried to talk to them about the first few races, but they hadn't even looked at the Form. I offered to get them hot dogs and drinks, but they weren't hungry. When I caught the winner of the first race, a longshot that got up in the last jump and paid $22.40, they stood with me to scream him in, but their faces were drawn and vacant and they didn't even curse that they had let it go. When we all had the winner of the second, a $5.20 favorite that led all the way, they sent me to cash the tickets, saying they had to get Marvin ready. I watched the third race alone and lost it.

Marvin ran in the fourth, and Jesse and Mr. Tompkins returned to their places just in time to rise with the crowd at the prayer-like "They're off!" Marvin stumbled slightly as he came out of the gate. Jesse sagged on my right; Mr. Tompkins lowered his ancient field glasses as if they had suddenly become very heavy. But in a dozen strides Marvin recovered and raced back into the middle of the second flight, and by the stretch turn he seemed to be moving: at least he passed a couple of horses by dropping in along the rail, and he wasn't losing the leaders. Anyhow, as they turned into the straight—Jesse started to shout, then didn't—another horse, a gray, moved in front of him, and that was that. He finished fifth in a ten-horse field, about six lengths behind the winner. Mr. Tompkins screamed "Foul," pointing his field glasses at the gray, and then went to lodge an official claim of interference. But it was disallowed. Jesse, oddly bent in his ill-fitting suit, slouched off to receive Marvin and fit him for cooling off. They didn't come back until after the sixth race.

In the Trial, Citation won by ten lengths in what looked for him to be a lazy gallop. The Tompkinses watched him glide home like convicts witnessing an execution. They stared into the track and the returning horses and the milling stablehands and lingered on the presentation ceremony long after it was over. Even I missed appreciating, as I saw all of this, that I was watching one of the great runners.

We didn't wait for the last race. We put Marvin in the trailer and jammed the tack and pails in a box on the side and started back.

For the first half hour no one spoke. Jesse hunched over the steering wheel and chewed his lip. I sat in the middle. On my right Mr. Tompkins cocked his knees against the pickup's dashboard and stared out the side window. Evening was coming on soft and cooler. To ease the strain I remarked, "With a little luck Marvin might have won that race." Both men sat straight up.

"Won it? He'd have run away with it." Suddenly Mr. Tompkins was shouting. "He lost two lengths at the start, then about five when the horse moved in front of him and checked his action. God, he wanted to fly today. I'm just sorry we didn't try him against better."

"And that was on a dry track. Think what he'd 'a done in the mud." Jesse's eyes were wild, as if he had just been in a furious fight. I had to point to the road ahead to remind him of his driving.

"It's my fault." Mr. Tompkins drove his fist into his thin thigh. "I began to lose faith. He won that race as far as I'm concerned. Won it easy."

"He'd 'a been tough in the Trial," Jesse added. "He would have, I tell you." They were talking to each other now, two sides of one mind answering each other.

"Tough? If it had turned up mud?" Mr. Tompkins exploded with laughter. "Why what did that leggy colt win in? A mile and an eighth in 1:48 flat? And Marvin's seven furlongs went in 1:24.1. So figure about six lengths back Marvin went it in 1:25.2. All right."

"But then Marvin lost two lengths at the start and at least five when he was blocked. That's seven lengths." Jesse was talking now, and again I had to point to the road. "Marvin would 'a won in 1:24 flat, easy."

"Then give him ten lengths for the mud," Mr. Tompkins went on. "Ten lengths is fair. The mud makes that much difference. Ten lengths, two full seconds. In the mud the Trial wouldn't have gone in less than 1:50, and even that would be good. All Marvin had to do was gallop out the last quarter mile in less than .26. He'd 'a done it easy, I tell you. Why he's a full second better than Citation."

"Woo-ee!" Jesse gasped and wheezed at the same time. "A full second."

They fell silent and for the next five minutes only the rattle of the old pickup could be heard over their breathing. The sun set, washing the fields of bluegrass in muted gold. The tall grass, the trees in the rolling fields, the bushes along the road stood motionless.

"We'll bring him back next week." You could almost hear Mr. Tompkins calculating. "By God, we'll sell the twenty acres across the road. Frank Conway's had his greedy eyes on that piece for years. We'll get a good price. An allowance race this time, at Churchill. Then we'll take him to Arlington. Another allowance race—move him up steadily. By August we'll be ready for the handicaps and stakes. God damn, it's too bad I dropped him from the Derby list. Damn! Damn! But by fall he'll be ready for the big end-of-season races. All we need is mud, by God! First we'll try the American Derby, then . . ."

I settled back between them and tried not to listen. Ahead, the road pointed murkily into darkness.

ROUGH STRIFE

LYNNE SHARON SCHWARTZ

Lynne Sharon Schwartz was born in New York City, where she presently lives. Her fiction has appeared in *Redbook*, *Ploughshares*, *The Smith*, *Transatlantic Review*, and many other magazines, as well as in anthologies (most recently *Banquet: 5 Short Stories*, published by Penmaen Press). Ms. Schwartz has taught English at Hunter College in New York City, and reviews regularly for *The Saturday Review*, *MS.*, the Chicago *Tribune*, and other periodicals.

> Now let us sport us while we may;
> And now, like am'rous birds of prey
> . . . tear our pleasure with rough strife
> Through the iron gates of life.
> —*Andrew Marvell*

Caroline and Ivan finally had a child. Conception stunned them; they didn't think, by now, that it could happen. For years they had tried and failed, till it seemed that a special barren destiny was preordained. Meanwhile, in the wide spaces of childlessness, they had created activity: their work flourished. Ivan, happy and moderately powerful in a large foundation, helped decide how to distribute money for artistic and social projects. Caroline taught mathematics at a small suburban university. Being a mathematician, she found, conferred a painful private wisdom on her efforts to conceive. In her brain, as Ivan exploded within her, she would involuntarily calculate probabilities; millions of blind sperm and one reluctant egg clustered before her eyes in swiftly transmuting geometric patterns. She lost her grasp of pleasure, forgot what it could feel like without a goal. She had no idea what

Ivan might be thinking about, scattered seed money, maybe. Their passion became courteous and automatic until, by attrition, for months they didn't make love—it was too awkward.

One September Sunday morning she was in the shower, watching, through a crack in the curtain, Ivan naked at the washstand. He was shaving, his jaw tilted at an innocently self-satisfied angle. He wasn't aware of being watched, so that a secret quality, an essence of Ivan, exuded in great waves. Caroline could almost see it, a cloudy aura. He stroked his jaw vainly with intense concentration, a self-absorption so contagious that she needed, suddenly, to possess it with him. She stepped out of the shower.

"Ivan."

He turned abruptly, surprised, perhaps even annoyed at the interruption.

"Let's not have a baby any more. Let's just . . . come on." When she placed her wet hand on his back he lifted her easily off her feet with his right arm, the razor still poised in his other, outstretched hand.

"Come on," she insisted. She opened the door and a draft blew into the small steamy room. She pulled him by the hand toward the bedroom.

Ivan grinned. "You're soaking wet."

"Wet, dry, what's the difference?" It was hard to speak. She began to run, to tease him; he caught her and tossed her onto their disheveled bed and dug his teeth so deep into her shoulder that she thought she would bleed.

Then with disinterest, taken up only in this fresh rushing need for him, weeks later Caroline conceived. Afterwards she liked to say that she had known the moment it happened. It felt different, she told him, like a pin pricking a balloon, but without the shattering noise, without the quick collapse. "Oh, come on," said Ivan. "That's impossible."

But she was a mathematician, after all, and dealt with infinitesimal precise abstractions, and she did know how it had happened. The baby was conceived in strife, one early October night, Indian summer. All day the sun glowed hot and low in the sky, settling an amber torpor on people and things, and the night was the same, only now a dark hot heaviness sunk slowly down. The scent of the still-blooming honeysuckle rose to their bedroom window. Just as she was bending over to kiss him, heavy and quivering with heat like the night, he teased her about something, about a mole on her leg, and in reply she punched him lightly on the shoulder. He grabbed her wrists, and when she began kicking, pinned her feet down with his own. In an instant Ivan lay stretched out on her back like a blanket, smothering her, while she struggled beneath, writhing to escape. It was a silent, sweaty struggle, interrupted with outbursts of wild laughter, shrieks and gasping breaths. She tried biting but, laughing loudly, he evaded her, and she tried scratching the fists that held her down, but she couldn't reach. All her desire was transformed into physical effort, but he was too strong for her. He wanted her to say she gave up, but she refused, and since he wouldn't loosen his grip they lay locked and panting in their static embrace for some time.

"You win," she said at last, but as he rolled off she sneakily jabbed him in the ribs with her elbow.

"Aha!" Ivan shouted, and was ready to begin again, but she quickly distracted him. Once the wrestling was at an end, though, Caroline found her passion dissipated, and her pleasure tinged with resentment. After they made love forcefully, when they were covered with sweat, dripping on each other, she said, "Still, you don't play fair."

"I don't play fair! Look who's talking. Do you want me to give you a handicap?"

"No."

"So?"

"It's not fair, that's all."

Ivan laughed gloatingly and curled up in her arms. She smiled in the dark.

That was the night the baby was conceived, not in high passion but rough strife.

She lay on the table in the doctor's office weeks later. The doctor, whom she had known for a long time, habitually kept up a running conversation while he probed. Today, fretting over his weight problem, he outlined his plans for a new diet. Tensely she watched him, framed and centered by her raised knees, which were still bronzed from summer sun. His other hand was pressing on her stomach. Caroline was nauseated with fear and trembling, afraid of the verdict. It was taking so long, perhaps it was a tumor.

"I'm cutting out all starches," he said. "I've really let myself go lately."

"Good idea." Then she gasped in pain. A final, sickening thrust, and he was out. Relief, and a sore gap where he had been. In a moment, she knew, she would be retching violently.

"Well?"

"Well, Caroline, you hit the jackpot this time."

She felt a smile, a stupid, puppet smile, spread over her face. In the tiny bathroom where she threw up, she saw in the mirror the silly smile looming over her ashen face like a dancer's glowing grimace of labored joy. She smiled through the rest of the visit, through his advice about milk, weight, travel and rest, smiled at herself in the window of the bus, and at her moving image in the fenders of parked cars as she walked home.

Ivan, incredulous over the telephone, came home beaming stupidly just like Caroline, and brought a bottle of champagne. After dinner they drank it and made love.

"Do you think it's all right to do this?" he asked.

"Oh, Ivan, honestly. It's microscopic."

He was in one of his whimsical moods and made terrible jokes that she laughed at with easy indulgence. He said he was going to pay the baby a visit and asked if she had any messages she wanted delivered. He unlocked from her embrace, moved down her body and said he was going to have a look for himself. Clowning, he put his ear between her legs to listen. Whatever amusement she felt soon ebbed away into irritation. She had never thought Ivan would be a doting parent—he was so preoccupied with himself. Finally he stopped his antics as she clasped her arms around him and whispered, "Ivan, you are really too much." He became unusually gentle. Tamed, and she didn't like it, hoped he wouldn't continue that way for months. Pleasure lapped over her with a mild, lackadaisical bitterness, and then when she could be articulate once more she explained patiently, "Ivan, you know, it really is all right. I mean, it's a natural process."

"Well I didn't want to hurt you."

"I'm not sick."

Then, as though her body were admonishing that cool confidence, she did get sick. There were mornings when she awoke with such paralyzing nausea that she had to ask Ivan to bring her a hard roll from the kitchen before she could stir from bed. To move from her awakening position seemed a tremendous risk, as if she might spill out. She rarely threw up—the nausea resembled vi-

olent hunger. Something wanted to be filled, not expelled, a peril-
ous vacuum occupying her insides. The crucial act was getting the
first few mouthfuls down. Then the solidity and denseness of the
hard unbuttered roll stabilized her, like a heavy weight thrown
down to anchor a tottering ship. Her head ached. On the mornings when she had no classes she would wander around the house
till almost noon clutching the partly eaten roll in her hand like a
talisman. Finishing one roll, she quickly went to the breadbox for
another; she bought them regularly at the bakery a half dozen at a
time. With enough roll inside her she could sometimes manage a
half cup of tea, but liquids were risky. They sloshed around inside
and made her envision the baby sloshing around too, in its cloudy
fluid. By early afternoon she would feel fine. The baby, she imagined, claimed her for the night and was reluctant to give up its
hold in the morning: they vied till she conquered. She was willing
to yield her sleeping hours to the baby, her dreams even, if necessary, but she wanted the daylight for herself.

The mornings that she taught were agony. Ivan would wake her
up early, bring her a roll, and gently prod her out of bed.

"I simply cannot do it," she would say, placing her legs cautiously over the side of the bed.

"Sure you can. Now get up."

"I'll die if I get up."

"You have no choice. You have a job." He was freshly showered
and dressed, and his neatness irritated her. He had nothing more
to do—the discomfort was all hers. She rose to her feet and
swayed.

Ivan looked alarmed. "Do you want me to call and tell them
you can't make it?"

"No, no." That frightened her. She needed to hold on to the
job, to defend herself against the growing baby. Once she walked
into the classroom she would be fine. A Mondrian print hung on
the back wall—she could look at that, and it would steady her.
With waves of nausea roiling in her chest, she stumbled into the
bathroom.

She liked him to wait until she was out of the shower before he
left for work, because she anticipated fainting under the impact of
the water. Often at the end she forced herself to stand under an
ice cold flow, leaning her head way back and letting her short fair

hair drip down behind her. Though it was torture, when she emerged she felt more alive.

After the shower had been off a while Ivan would come and open the bathroom door. "Are you O.K. now, Caroline? I've got to go." It made her feel like a child. She would be wrapped in a towel with her hair dripping on the mat, brushing her teeth or rubbing cream into her face. "Yes, thanks for waiting. I guess this'll end soon. They say it's only the first few months."

He kissed her lips, her bare damp shoulder, gave a parting squeeze to her toweled behind, and was gone. She watched him walk down the hall. Ivan was very large. She had always been drawn and aroused by his largeness, by the huge bones and the taut legs that felt as though he had steel rods inside. But now she watched with some trepidation, hoping Ivan wouldn't have a large, inflexible baby.

Very slowly she would put on clothes. Selecting each article seemed a much more demanding task than ever before. Seeing how slow she had become, she allowed herself over an hour, keeping her hard roll nearby as she dressed and prepared her face. All the while, through the stages of dressing, she evaluated her body closely in the full-length mirror, first naked, then in bra and underpants, then with shoes added, and finally with a dress. She was looking for signs, but the baby was invisible. Nothing had changed yet. She was still as she had always been, not quite slim yet somehow appearing small, almost delicate. She used to pride herself on strength. When they moved in she had worked as hard as Ivan, lugging furniture and lifting heavy cartons. He was impressed. Now, of course, she could no longer do that—it took all her strength to move her own weight.

With the profound sensuous narcissism of women past first youth, she admired her still-narrow waist and full breasts. She was especially fond of her shoulders and prominent collarbone, which had a fragile, inviting look. That would all be gone soon, of course, gone soft. Curious about how she would alter, she scanned her face for the pregnant look she knew well from the faces of friends. It was far less a tangible change than a look of transparent vulnerability that took over the face: nearly a pleading look, a beg for help like a message from a powerless invaded country to the rest of the world. Caroline did not see it on her face yet. From the tenth to the fourteenth week of her pregnancy she slept, with brief intervals of lucidity when she taught her classes. It was a strange dreamy time. The passionate nausea faded, but the lure of the bed was irresistible. In the middle of the day, even, she could pass by the bedroom, glimpse the waiting bed and be overcome by the soft heavy desire to lie down. She fell into a stupor immediately and did not dream. She forgot what it was like to awaken with energy and move through an entire day without lying down once. She forgot the feeling of eyes opened wide without effort. She would have liked to hide this strange, shameful perversity from Ivan, but that was impossible. Ivan kept wanting to go to the movies. Clearly, he was bored with her. Maybe, she imagined, staring up at the bedroom ceiling through slitted eyes, he would become so bored he would abandon her and the baby and she would not be able to support the house alone and she and the baby would end up on the streets in rags, begging. She smiled. That was highly unlikely. Ivan would not be the same Ivan without her.

"You go on, Ivan. I just can't."

Once he said, "I thought I might ask Ruth Forbes to go with me to see the Charlie Chaplin in town. I know she likes him. Would that bother you?"

She was half-asleep, slowly eating a large apple in bed and watching "Medical Center" on television, but she roused herself to answer. "No, of course not." Ruth Forbes was a divorced woman who lived down the block, a casual friend and not Ivan's type at all, too large, loud and depressed. Caroline didn't care if he wanted her company. She didn't care if he held her hand on his knee in the movies as he liked to do, or even if, improbably, he made love to her afterwards in her sloppy house crawling with children. She didn't care about anything except staying nestled in bed.

She made love with him sometimes, in a slow way. She felt no specific desire but didn't want to deny him, she loved him so. Or had, she thought vaguely, when she was alive and strong. Besides, she knew she could sleep right after. Usually there would be a moment when she came alive despite herself, when the reality of his body would strike her all at once with a wistful throb of lust, but mostly she was too tired to see it through, to leap towards it, so she let it subside, merely nodding at it gratefully as a sign of dormant life. She felt sorry for Ivan, but helpless.

Once to her great shame, she fell asleep while he was inside her. He woke her with a pat on her cheek, actually, she realized from the faint sting, a gesture more like a slap than a pat. "Caroline, for Christ's sake, you're sleeping."

"No, no, I'm sorry. I wasn't really sleeping. Oh, Ivan, it's nothing. This will end." She wondered, though.

Moments later she felt his hands on her thighs. His lips were brooding on her stomach, edging, with expertise, lower and lower down. He was murmuring something she couldn't catch. She felt an ache, an irritation. Of course he meant well, Ivan always did. Wryly, she appreciated his intentions. But she couldn't bear that excitement now.

"Please," she said. "Please don't do that."

He was terribly hurt. He said nothing, but leaped away violently and pulled all the blankets around him. She was contrite, shed a few private tears and fell instantly into a dreamless dark.

He wanted to go to a New Year's Eve party some close friends were giving, and naturally he wanted her to come with him. Caroline vowed to herself she would do this for him because she had been giving so little for so long. She planned to get dressed and look very beautiful, as she could still look when she took plenty of time and tried hard enough; she would not drink very much—it was sleep-inducing—and she would not be the one to suggest going home. After sleeping through the day in preparation, she washed her hair, using something she found in the drugstore to heighten the blond flecks. Then she put on a long green velvet dress with gold embroidery, and inserted the gold hoop earrings Ivan bought her some years ago for her twenty-fifth birthday. Before they set out she drank a cup of black coffee. She would have taken No-Doze but she was afraid of drugs, afraid of giving birth to an armless or legless baby who would be a burden and a heartache to them for the rest of their days.

At the party of mostly university people, she chatted with everyone equally, those she knew well and those she had never met. Sociably, she held a filled glass in her hand, taking tiny sips. She and Ivan were not together very much—it was crowded, smoky and loud; people kept moving and encounters were brief—but she knew he was aware of her, could feel his awareness through the milling bodies. He was aware and he was pleased. He deserved more than the somnambulist she had become, and she was pleased to please him. But after a while her legs would not support her for another instant. The skin tingled: soft warning bells rang from every pore. She allowed herself a moment to sit down alone in a small alcove off the living room, where she smoked a cigarette and stared down at her lap, holding her eyes open very wide. Examining the gold and rose-colored embroidery on her dress, Caroline traced the coiled pattern, mathematical and hypnotic, with her index finger. Just as she was happily merging into its intricacies, a man, a stranger, came in, breaking her trance. He was a very young man, twenty-three, maybe, of no apparent interest.

"Hi. I hear you're expecting a baby," he began, and sat down with a distinct air of settling in.

"Yes. That's quite an opening line. How did you know?"

"I know because Linda told me. You know Linda, don't you? I'm her brother."

He began asking about her symptoms. Sleepiness? Apathy? He knew, he had worked in a clinic. Unresponsive, she retorted by inquiring about his taste in music. He sat on a leather hassock opposite Caroline on the couch, and with every inquisitive sentence drew his seat closer till their knees were almost touching. She shifted her weight to avoid him, tucked her feet under her and lit another cigarette, feeling she could lie down and fall into a stupor quite easily. Still, words were coming out of her mouth, she heard them; she hoped they were not encouraging words but she seemed to have very little control over what they were.

"I—" he said. "You see—" He reached out and put his hand over hers. "Pregnant women, like, they really turn me on. I mean, there's a special aura. You're sensational."

She pulled her hand away. "God almighty."

"What's the matter? Honestly, I didn't mean to offend you."

"I really must go." She stood up and stepped around him.

"Could I see you some time?"

"You're seeing me now. Enjoy it."

He ran his eyes over her from head to toe, appraising. "It doesn't show yet."

Gazing down at her body, Caroline stretched the loose velvet dress taut over her stomach. "No, you're right, it doesn't." Then, over her shoulder, as she left their little corner, she tossed, "Fuck you, you pig."

With a surge of energy she downed a quick scotch, found Ivan and tugged at his arm. "Let's dance."

Ivan's blue eyes lightened with shock. At home she could barely walk.

"Yes, let's." He took her in his arms and she buried her face against his shoulder. But she held her tears back, she would not let him know.

Later she told him about it. It was three-thirty in the morning, they had just made love drunkenly, and Ivan was in high spirits. She knew why—he felt he had her back again. She had held him close and uttered her old sounds, familiar moans and cries like a poignant, nearly-forgotten tune, and Ivan was miraculously restored, his impact once again sensible to eye and ear. He was making her laugh hysterically now, imitating the eccentric professor of art history at the party, an owlish émigré from Bavaria who expounded on the dilemmas of today's youth, all the while pronouncing "youth" as if it rhymed with "mouth." Ivan had also discovered that he pronounced "unique" as if it were "eunuch." Then, sitting up in bed cross-legged, they competed in making up pretentious scholarly sentences that included both "unique" and "youth" mispronounced.

"Speaking of 'yowth,'" Caroline said, "I met a weird one tonight, Linda's brother. A very eunuch yowth, I must say." And giggling, she recounted their conversation. Suddenly at the end she unexpectedly found herself in tears. Shuddering, she flopped over and sobbed into her pillow.

"Caroline," he said tenderly, "please. For heaven's sake, it was just some nut. It was nothing. Don't get all upset over it." He stroked her bare back.

"I can't help it," she wailed. "It made me feel so disgusting."

"You're much too sensitive. Come on." He ran his hand slowly through her hair, over and over.

She pulled the blanket around her. "Enough. I'm going to sleep."

A few days later, when classes were beginning again for the new semester, she woke early and went immediately to the shower, going through the ritual motions briskly and automatically. She was finished and brushing her teeth when she realized what had happened. There she was on her feet, sturdy, before eight in the morning, planning how she would introduce the topic of the differential calculus to her new students. She stared at her face in the mirror with unaccustomed recognition, her mouth dripping white foam, her dark eyes startled. She was alive. She didn't know how the miracle had happened, nor did she care to explore it. Back in the bedroom she dressed quickly, zipping up a pair of slim rust-colored woollen slacks with satisfaction. It didn't show yet, but soon.

"Ivan, time to get up."

He grunted and opened his eyes. When at last they focused on Caroline leaning over him they burned blue and wide with astonishment. He rubbed a fist across his forehead. "Are you dressed already?"

"Yes. I'm cured."

"What do you mean?"

"I'm not tired any more. I'm slept out. I've come back to life."

"Oh." He moaned and rolled over in one piece like a seal.

"Aren't you getting up?"

"In a little while. I'm so tired. I must sleep for a while." The words were thick and slurred.

"Well!" She was strangely annoyed. Ivan always got up with vigor. "Are you sick?"

"Uh-uh."

After a quick cup of coffee she called out, "Ivan, I'm leaving now. Don't forget to get up." The January air was crisp and exhilarating, and she walked the half mile to the university at a nimble clip, going over her introductory remarks in her head.

Ivan was tired for a week. Caroline wanted to go out to dinner every evening—she had her appetite back. She had broken through dense earth to fresh air. It was a new year and soon they would have a new baby. But all Ivan wanted to do was stay home and lie on the bed and watch television. It was repellent. Sloth, she pointed out to him more than once, was one of the seven deadly sins. The fifth night she said in exasperation, "What the hell is the matter with you? If you're sick go to a doctor."

"I'm not sick. I'm tired. Can't I be tired too? Leave me alone. I left you alone, didn't I?"

"That was different."

"How?"

"I'm pregnant and you're not, in case you've forgotten."

"How could I forget?"

She said nothing, only cast him an evil look.

One evening soon after Ivan's symptoms disappeared, they sat together on the living-room sofa sharing sections of the newspaper. Ivan had his feet up on the coffee table and Caroline sat diagonally, resting her legs on his. She paused in her reading and touched her stomach.

"Ivan."

"What?"

"It's no use. I'm going to have to buy some maternity clothes."

He put down the paper and stared. "Really?" He seemed distressed.

"Yes."

"Well, don't buy any of those ugly things they wear. Can't you get some of those, you know, sort of Indian things?"

"Yes. That's a good idea. I will."

He picked up the paper again.

"It moves."

"What?"

"I said it moves. The baby."

"It moves?"

She laughed. "Remember Galileo? *Eppure, si muove.*" They had spent years together in Italy in their first youth, in mad love, and visited the birthplace of Galileo. He was a hero to both of them, because his mind remained free and strong though his body succumbed to tyranny.

Ivan laughed too. "*Eppure, si muove.* Let me see." He bent his head down to feel it, then looked up at her, his face full of longing, marvel and envy. In a moment he was scrambling at her clothes in a young eager rush. He wanted to be there, he said. Caroline, taken by surprise, was suspended between laughter and tears. He had her on the floor in silence, and for each it was swift and consuming.

Ivan lay spent in her arms. Caroline, still gasping and clutching him, said, "I could never love it as much as I love you." She wondered, then, hearing her words fall in the still air, whether this would always be true.

Shortly after she began wearing the Indian shirts and dresses, she noticed that Ivan was acting oddly. He stayed late at the office more than ever before, and often brought work home with him. He appeared to have lost interest in the baby, rarely asking how she felt, and when she moaned in bed sometimes, "Oh, I can't get to sleep, it keeps moving around," he responded with a grunt or not at all. He asked her, one warm Sunday in March, if she wanted to go bicycle riding.

"Ivan, I can't go bicycle riding. I mean, look at me."

"Oh, right. Of course."

He seemed to avoid looking at her, and she did look terrible, she had to admit. Even she looked at herself in the mirror as infrequently as possible. She dreaded what she had heard about hair falling out and teeth rotting, but she drank her milk diligently and so far neither of those things had happened. But besides the grotesque belly, her ankles swelled up so that the shape of her own legs was alien. She took diuretics and woke every hour at night to go to the bathroom. Sometimes it was impossible to get back to sleep so she sat up in bed reading. Ivan said, "Can't you turn the light out? You know I can't sleep with the light on."

"But what should I do? I can't sleep at all."

"Read in the living room."

"It's so cold in there at night."

He would turn away irritably. Once he took the blanket and went to sleep in the living room himself.

They liked to go for drives in the country on warm weekends. It seemed to Caroline that he chose the bumpiest, most untended roads and drove them as rashly as possible. Then when they stopped to picnic and he lay back to bask in the sharp April sunlight, she would always need to go and look for a bathroom, or even a clump of trees. At first this amused him, but soon his amusement became sardonic. He pulled in wearily at gas stations where he didn't need gas and waited in the car with folded arms and a sullen expression that made her apologetic about her ludicrous needs. They were growing apart. She could feel the distance between them like a patch of fog, dimming and distorting the relations of objects in space. The baby that lay between them in the dark was pushing them apart.

Sometimes as she lay awake in bed at night, not wanting to read in the cold living room but reluctant to turn on the light (and it was only a small light, she thought bitterly, a small bedside light), Caroline brooded over the horrible deformities the baby might be born with. She was thirty-one years old, not the best age to bear a first child. It could have cerebral palsy, cleft palate, two heads, club foot. She wondered if she could love a baby with a gross defect. She wondered if Ivan would want to put it in an institution, and if there were any decent institutions in their area, and if they would be spending every Sunday afternoon for the rest of their lives visiting the baby and driving home heart-broken in silence. She lived through these visits to the institution in vivid detail till she knew the doctors' and nurses' faces well. And there would come a point when Ivan would refuse to go any more—she knew what he was like, selfish with his time and impa-tient with futility—and she would have to go alone. She wondered if Ivan ever thought about these things, but with that cold mood of his she was afraid to ask.

One night she was desolate. She couldn't bear the loneliness and the heaviness any more, so she woke him.

"Ivan, please. Talk to me. I'm so lonely."

He sat up abruptly. "What?" He was still asleep. With the dark straight hair hanging down over his lean face he looked boyish and vulnerable. Without knowing why, she felt sorry for him.

"I'm sorry. I know you were sleeping but I—" Here she began to weep. "I just lie here forever in the dark and think awful things and you're so far away, and I just—"

"Oh, Caroline. Oh, God." Now he was wide awake, and took her in his arms.

"You're so far away," she wept. "I don't know what's the mat-ter with you."

"I'm sorry. I know it's hard for you. You're so—everything's so different, that's all."

"But it's still me."

"I know. I know it's stupid of me. I can't—"

She knew what it was. It would never be the same. They sat up all night holding each other, and they talked. Ivan talked more than he had in weeks. He said of course the baby would be per-fectly all right, and it would be born at just the right time, too, late June, so she could finish up the term, and they would start their natural childbirth group in two weeks so he could be with her and help her, though of course she would do it easily because she was so competent at everything, and then they would have the summer for the early difficult months, and she would be feeling fine and be ready to go back to work in the fall, and they would find a good person, someone like a grandmother, to come in, and he would try to stagger his schedule so she would not feel overburdened and trapped, and in short everything would be just fine, and they would make love again like they used to and be close again. He said exactly what she needed to hear, while she huddled against him, wrenched with pain to realize that he had known all along the right words to say but hadn't thought to say them till she woke him in desperation. Still, in the dawn she slept contented. She loved him. Every now and then she perceived this like a fact of life, an ancient tropism.

Two weeks later they had one of their horrible quarrels. It happened at a gallery, at the opening of a show by a group of young local artists Ivan had discovered. He had encouraged them to apply to his foundation for money and smoothed the way to their success. Now at their triumphant hour he was to be publicly thanked at a formal dinner. There were too many paintings to look at, too many people to greet, and too many glasses of champagne thrust at Caroline, who was near the end of her eighth month now. She walked around for an hour, then whispered to Ivan, "Listen, I'm sorry but I've got to go. Give me the car keys, will you? I don't feel well."

"What's the matter?"

"I can't stop having to go to the bathroom and my feet are killing me and my head aches, and the kid is rolling around like a basketball. You stay and enjoy it. You can get a ride with someone. I'll see you later."

"I'll drive you home," he said grimly. "We'll leave."

An awful knot gripped her stomach. The knot was the image of his perverse resistance, the immense trouble coming, all the trouble congealed and solidified and tied up in one moment. Meanwhile they smiled at the passers-by as they whispered ferociously to each other.

"Ivan, I do not want you to take me home. This is your event. Stay. I am leaving. We are separate people."

"If you're as sick as you say you can't drive home alone. You're my wife and I'll take you home."

"Suit yourself," she said sweetly, because the director of the gallery was approaching. "We all know you're much bigger and stronger than I am." And she smiled maliciously.

Ivan waved vaguely at the director, turned and ushered her to the door. Outside he exploded.

"Shit, Caroline! We can't do a fucking thing any more, can we?"

"You can do anything you like. Just give me the keys. I left mine home."

"I will not give you the keys. Get in the car. You're supposed to be sick."

"You big resentful selfish idiot. Jealous of an embryo." She was screaming now. He started the car with a rush that jolted her forward against the dashboard. "I'd be better off driving myself. You'll kill me this way."

"Shut up," he shouted. "I don't want to hear any more."

"I don't care what you want to hear or not hear."

"Shut the hell up or I swear I'll go into a tree. I don't give a shit any more."

It was starting to rain, a soft silent rain that glittered in the drab dusk outside. At exactly the same moment they rolled up their windows. They were sealed in together, Caroline thought, like restless beasts in a cage. The air in the car was dank and stuffy.

When they got home he slammed the door so hard the house shook. Caroline had calmed herself. She sank down in a chair, kicked off her shoes and rubbed her ankles. "Ivan, why don't you go back? It's not too late. These dinners are always late anyway. I'll be O.K."

"I don't want to go any more," he yelled. "The whole thing is spoiled. Our whole lives are spoiled from now on. We were better off before. I thought you had gotten over wanting it. I thought it was a dead issue." He stared at her bulging stomach with such loathing that she was shocked into horrid, lucid perception.

"You disgust me," she said quietly. "Frankly, you always have and probably always will." She didn't know why she said that. It was quite untrue. It was only true that he disgusted her at this moment, yet the rest had rolled out like string from a hidden ball of twine.

"So why did we ever start this in the first place?" he screamed.

She didn't know whether he meant the marriage or the baby, and for an instant she was afraid he might hit her, there was such compressed force in his huge shoulders.

"Get the hell out of here. I don't want to have to look at you."

"I will. I'll go back. I'll take your advice. Call your fucking obstetrician if you need anything. I'm sure he's always glad of an extra feel."

"You ignorant pig. Go on. And don't hurry back. Find yourself a skinny little art student and give her a big treat."

"I just might." He slammed the door and the house shook again.

He would be back. This was not the first time. Only now she felt no secret excitement, no tremor, no passion that could re-shape into lust; she was too heavy and burdened. It would not be easy to make it up—she was in no condition. It would lie between them silently like a dead weight till weeks after the baby was born, till Ivan felt he could reclaim his rightful territory. She knew him too well. Caroline took two aspirins. When she woke at three he was in bed beside her, gripping the blanket in his sleep and breathing heavily. For days afterwards they spoke with strained, subdued courtesy.

They worked diligently in the natural childbirth classes once a week, while at home they giggled over how silly the exercises were, yet Ivan insisted she pant her five minutes each day as instructed. As relaxation training, Ivan was supposed to lift each of her legs and arms three times and drop them, while she remained perfectly limp and passive. From the very start Caroline was excellent at this routine, which they did in bed before going to sleep. A substitute, she thought, yawning. She could make her body so limp and passive her arms and legs bounced on the mattress when they fell. One night for diversion she tried doing it to Ivan, but he couldn't master the technique of passivity.

"Don't do anything, Ivan. I lift the leg and I drop the leg. You do nothing. Do you see? Nothing at all," she smiled.

But that was not possible for him. He tried to be limp but kept working along with her; she could see his muscles, precisely those leg muscles she found so desirable, exerting to lift and drop, lift and drop.

"You can't give yourself up. Don't you feel what you're doing? You have to let me do it to you. Let me try just your hand, from the wrist. That might be easier."

"No, forget it. Give me back my hand." He smiled and stroked her stomach gently. "What's the difference? I don't have to do it well. You do it very well."

She did it very well indeed when the time came. It was a short labor, less than an hour, very unusual for a first baby, the nurses kept muttering. She breathed intently, beginning with the long slow breaths she had been taught, feeling quite remote from the bustle around her. Then, in a flurry, they raced her down the hall on a wheeled table with a train of white-coated people trotting after, and she thought, panting, No matter what I suffer, soon I will be thin again, I will be more beautiful than ever.

The room was crowded with people, far more people than she would have thought necessary, but the only faces she singled out were Ivan's and the doctor's. The doctor, with a new russet beard and his face a good deal thinner now, was once again framed by her knees, paler than before. Wildly enthusiastic about the proceedings, he yelled, "Terrific, Caroline, terrific," as though they were in a noisy public place. "O.K., start pushing."

They placed her hands on chrome rails along the table. On the left, groping, she found Ivan's hand and held it instead of the rail. She pushed. In surprise she became aware of a great cleavage, like a mountain of granite splitting apart, only it was in her, she realized, and if it kept on going it would go right up to her neck. She gripped Ivan's warm hand, and just as she opened her mouth to roar someone clapped an oxygen mask on her face so the roar reverberated inward on her own ears. She wasn't supposed to roar, the natural childbirth teacher hadn't mentioned anything about that, she was supposed to breathe and push. But as long as no one seemed to take any notice she might as well keep on roaring, it felt so satisfying and necessary. The teacher would never know. She trusted that if she split all the way up to her neck they would sew her up somehow—she was too far gone to worry about that now. Maybe that was why there were so many of them, yes, of course, to put her back together, and maybe they had simply forgotten to tell her about being bisected; or maybe it was a closely guarded secret, like an initiation rite. She gripped Ivan's hand tighter. She was not having too bad a time, she would surely survive, she told herself, captivated by the hellish bestial sounds going from her mouth to her ear; it certainly was what her students would call a peak experience, and how gratifying to hear the doctor exclaim, "Oh, this is one terrific girl! One more, Caroline, give me one more push and send it out. Sock it to me."

She always tried to be obliging, if possible. Now she raised herself on her elbows and, staring straight at him—he too, after all, had been most obliging these long months—gave him with tremendous force the final push he asked for. She had Ivan's hand tightly around the rail, could feel his knuckles bursting, and then all of a sudden the room and the faces were obliterated. A dark thick curtain swiftly wrapped around her and she was left all alone gasping, sucked violently into a windy black hole of pain so explosive she knew it must be death, she was dying fast, like a bomb detonating. It was all right, it was almost over, only she would have liked to see his blue eyes one last time.

From somewhere in the void Ivan's voice shouted in exultation, "It's coming out," and the roaring stopped and at last there was peace and quiet in her ears. The curtain fell away, the world returned. But her eyes kept on burning, as if they had seen something not meant for living eyes to see and return from alive.

"Give it to me," Caroline said, and held it. She saw that every part was in the proper place, then shut her eyes.

They wheeled her to a room and eased her onto the bed. It was past ten in the morning. She could dimly remember they had been up all night watching a James Cagney movie about prize-fighting while they timed her irregular mild contractions. James Cagney went blind from blows given by poisoned gloves in a rigged match, and she wept for him as she held her hands on her stomach and breathed. Neither she nor Ivan had slept or eaten for hours.

"Ivan, there is something I am really dying to have right now."

"Your wish is my command."

She asked for a roast beef on rye with ketchup, and iced tea. "Would you mind? It'll be hours before they serve lunch."

He bought it and stood at the window while she ate ravenously. "Didn't you get anything for yourself?"

"No, I'm too exhausted to eat." He did, in fact, look terrible. He was sallow; his eyes, usually so radiant, were nearly drained of color, and small downward-curving lines around his mouth recalled his laborious vigil.

"You had a rough night, Ivan. You ought to get some sleep. What's it like outside?"

"What?" Ivan's movements seemed to her extremely purposeless. He was pacing the room with his hands deep in his pockets, going slowly from the foot of the bed to the window and back. Her eyes followed him from the pillow. Every now and then he would stop to peer at Caroline in an unfamiliar way, as if she were a puzzling stranger.

"Ivan, are you O.K.? I meant the weather. What's it doing outside?" It struck her, as she asked, that it was weeks since she had cared to know anything about the outside. That there was an outside, now that she was emptied out, came rushing at her with the most urgent importance, wafting her on a tide of grateful joy.

"Oh," he said vaguely, and came to sit on the edge of her bed. "Well, it's doing something very peculiar outside, as a matter of fact. It's raining but the sun is shining."

She laughed at him. "But haven't you ever seen it do that before?"

"I don't know. I guess so." He opened his mouth and closed it several times. She ate, waiting patiently. Finally he spoke. "You know, Caroline, you really have quite a grip. When you were holding my hand in there, you squeezed it so tight I thought you would break it."

"Oh, come on, that can't be."

"I'm not joking." He massaged his hand absently. Ivan never complained of pain; if anything he understated. But now he held out his right hand and showed her the raw red knuckles and palm, with raised flaming welts forming.

She took his hand. "You're serious. Did I do that? Well, how do you like that?"

"I really thought you'd break my hand. It was killing me." He kept repeating it, not resentfully but dully, as though there were something secreted in the words that he couldn't fathom.

"But why didn't you take it away if it hurt that badly?" She put down her half-eaten sandwich as she saw the pale amazement ripple over his face.

"Oh, no, I couldn't do that. I mean—if that was what you needed just then—" He looked away, embarrassed. "Listen," he shrugged, not facing her, "we're in a hospital, after all. What better place? They'd fix it for me."

Overwhelmed, Caroline lay back on the pillows. "Oh, Ivan. You would do that?"

"What are you crying for?" he asked gently. "You didn't break it, did you? Almost doesn't count. So what are you crying about. You just had a baby. Don't cry."

And she smiled and thought her heart would burst.

OH, JOSEPH, I'M SO TIRED

RICHARD YATES

Richard Yates lives in Boston. He is the author of six books, including *Revolutionary Road* and *A Good School*. This is the third time his work has appeared in the *O. Henry Awards*.

When Franklin D. Roosevelt was President-elect there must have been sculptors all over America who wanted a chance to model his head from life, but my mother had connections. One of her closest friends and neighbors, in the Greenwich Village courtyard where we lived, was an amiable man named Howard Whitman who had recently lost his job as a reporter on the New York *Post*. And one of Howard's former colleagues from the *Post* was now employed in the press office of Roosevelt's New York headquarters. That would make it easy for her to get in—or, as she said, to get an entrée—and she was confident she could take it from there. She was confident about everything she did in those days, but it never quite disguised a terrible need for support and approval on every side.

She wasn't a very good sculptor. She had been working at it for only three years, since breaking up her marriage to my father, and there was still something stiff and amateurish about her pieces. Before the Roosevelt project her specialty had been "garden figures"—a life-size little boy whose legs turned into the legs of a goat at the knee and another who knelt among ferns to play the pipes of Pan; little girls who trailed chains of daisies from their upraised arms or walked beside a spread-winged goose. These fanciful children, in plaster painted green to simulate weathered bronze, were arranged on homemade wooden pedestals to loom around her studio and to leave a cleared space in the middle for the modeling stand that held whatever she was working on in clay.

Her idea was that any number of rich people, all of them gracious and aristocratic, would soon discover her: they would want her sculpture to decorate their landscaped gardens, and they would want to make her their friend for life. In the meantime, a little nationwide publicity as the first woman sculptor to "do" the President-elect certainly wouldn't hurt her career.

And if nothing else, she had a good studio. It was, in fact, the best of all the studios she would have in the rest of her life. There were six or eight old houses facing our side of the courtyard, with their backs to Bedford Street, and ours was probably the showplace of the row because the front room on its ground floor was two stories high. You went down a broad set of brick steps to the tall front windows and the front door; then you were in the high, wide, light-flooded studio. It was big enough to serve as a living room too, and so along with the green garden children it contained all the living-room furniture from the house we'd lived in with my father in the suburban town of Hastings-on-Hudson, where I was born. A second-floor balcony ran along the far end of the studio, with two small bedrooms and a tiny bathroom tucked away upstairs; beneath that, where the ground floor continued through to the Bedford Street side, lay the only part of the apartment that might let you know we didn't have much money. The ceiling was very low and it was always dark in there; the small windows looked out underneath an iron sidewalk grating, and the bottom of that street cavity was thick with strewn garbage. Our roach-infested kitchen was barely big enough for a stove and sink that were never clean, and for a brown wooden icebox with its dark, ever-melting block of ice; the rest of that area was our dining room, and not even the amplitude of the old Hastings dining-room table could brighten it. But our Majestic radio was in there too, and that made it a cozy place for my older sister Edith and me: we liked the children's programs that came on in the late afternoons.

We had just turned off the radio one day when we went out into the studio and found our mother discussing the Roosevelt project with Howard Whitman. It was the first we'd heard of it, and we must have interrupted her with too many questions because she said "Edith? Billy? That's enough, now. I'll tell you all about this later. Run out in the garden and play."

She always called the courtyard "the garden," though nothing grew there except a few stunted city trees and a patch of grass that never had a chance to spread. Mostly it was bald earth, interrupted here and there by brick paving, lightly powdered with soot and scattered with the droppings of dogs and cats. It may have been six or eight houses long but it was only two houses wide, which gave it a hemmed-in, cheerless look; its only point of interest was a dilapidated marble fountain, not much bigger than a birdbath, which stood near our house. The original idea of the fountain was that water would drip evenly from around the rim of its upper tier and tinkle into its lower basin, but age had unsettled it; the water spilled in a single ropy stream from the only inch of the upper tier's rim that stayed clean. The lower basin was deep enough to soak your feet in on a hot day, but there wasn't much pleasure in that because the underwater part of the marble was coated with brown scum.

My sister and I found things to do in the courtyard every day, for all of the two years we lived there, but that was only because Edith was an imaginative child. She was eleven at the time of the Roosevelt project, and I was seven.

"Daddy?" she asked in our father's office uptown one afternoon. "Have you heard Mommy's doing a head of President Roosevelt?"

"Oh?" He was rummaging in his desk, looking for something he'd said we might like.

"She's going to take his measurements and stuff here in New York," Edith said, "and then after the Inauguration, when the sculpture's done, she's going to take it to Washington and present it to him in the White House." Edith often told one of our parents about the other's more virtuous activities; it was part of her long, hopeless effort to bring them back together. Many years later she told me she thought she had never recovered, and never would, from the shock of their breakup: she said Hastings-on-Hudson remained the happiest time of her life, and that made me envious because I could scarcely remember it at all.

"Well," my father said. "That's really something, isn't it?" Then he found what he'd been looking for in the desk and said "Here we go; what do you think of these?" They were two fragile perforated sheets of what looked like postage stamps, each stamp bearing the insignia of an electric light bulb in vivid white against a yellow background, and the words "More light."

My father's office was one of many small cubicles on the twenty-third floor of the General Electric Company building. He was an assistant regional sales manager in what was then called the Mazda Lamp Division—a modest job, but good enough to have allowed him to rent into a town like Hastings-on-Hudson in better times—and these "More light" stamps were souvenirs of a recent sales convention. We told him the stamps were neat—and they were—but expressed some doubt as to what we might do with them.

"Oh, they're just for decoration," he said. "I thought you could paste them into your schoolbooks, or—you know—whatever you want. Ready to go?" And he carefully folded the sheets of stamps and put them in his inside pocket for safekeeping on the way home.

Between the subway exit and the courtyard, somewhere in the West Village, we always walked past a vacant lot where men stood huddled around weak fires built of broken fruit crates and trash, some of them warming tin cans of food held by coat-hanger wire over the flames. "Don't stare," my father had said the first time. "All those men are out of work, and they're hungry."

"Daddy?" Edith inquired. "Do you think Roosevelt's good?"

"Sure I do."

"Do you think all the Democrats are good?"

"Well, most of 'em, sure."

Much later I would learn that my father had participated in local Democratic party politics for years. He had served some of his political friends—men my mother described as dreadful little Irish people from Tammany Hall—by helping them to establish Mazda Lamp distributorships in various parts of the city. And he loved their social gatherings, at which he was always asked to sing.

"Well, of course, you're too young to remember Daddy's singing," Edith said to me once after his death in 1942.

"No I'm not; I remember."

"But I mean really remember," she said. "He had the most beautiful tenor voice I've ever heard. Remember 'Danny Boy'?"

"Sure."

"Ah, God, that was something," she said, closing her eyes. "That was really—that was really something."

When we got back to the courtyard that afternoon, and back into the studio, Edith and I watched our parents say hello to each other. We always watched that closely, hoping they might drift into conversation and sit down together and find things to laugh about, but they never did. And it was even less likely than usual that day because my mother had a guest—a woman named Sloane Cabot who was her best friend in the courtyard, and who greeted my father with a little rush of false, flirtatious enthusiasm.

"How've you been, Sloane?" he said. Then he turned back to his former wife and said "Helen? I hear you're planning to make a bust of Roosevelt."

"Well, not a bust," she said. "A head. I think it'll be more effective if I cut it off at the neck."

"Well, good. That's fine. Good luck with it. Okay, then." He gave his whole attention to Edith and me. "Okay. See you soon. How about a hug?"

And those hugs of his, the climax of his visitation rights, were unforgettable. One at a time we would be swept up and pressed hard into the smells of linen and whiskey and tobacco; the warm rasp of his jaw would graze one cheek and there would be a quick moist kiss near the ear; then he'd let us go.

He was almost all the way out of the courtyard, almost out in the street, when Edith and I went racing after him.

"Daddy! Daddy! You forgot the stamps!"

He stopped and turned around, and that was when we saw he was crying. He tried to hide it—he put his face nearly into his armpit as if that might help him search his inside pocket—but there is no way to disguise the awful bloat and pucker of a face in tears.

"Here," he said. "Here you go." And he gave us the least convincing smile I had ever seen. It would be good to report that we stayed and talked to him—that we hugged him again—but we were too embarrassed for that. We took the stamps and ran home without looking back.

"Oh, aren't you excited, Helen?" Sloane Cabot was saying. "To be meeting him, and talking to him and everything, in front of all those reporters?"

"Well, of course," my mother said, "but the important thing is to get the measurements right. I hope there won't be a lot of photographers and silly interruptions."

Sloane Cabot was some years younger than my mother, and strikingly pretty in a style often portrayed in what I think are called Art Deco illustrations of that period: straight dark bangs, big eyes, and a big mouth. She too was a divorced mother, though her former husband had vanished long ago and was referred to only as "that bastard" or "that cowardly son of a bitch." Her only child was a boy of Edith's age named John, whom Edith and I liked enormously.

The two women had met within days of our moving into the courtyard, and their friendship was sealed when my mother solved the problem of John's schooling. She knew a Hastings-on-Hudson family who would appreciate the money earned from taking in a boarder, so John went up there to live and go to school, and came home only on weekends. The arrangement cost more than Sloane could comfortably afford, but she managed to make ends meet and was forever grateful.

Sloane worked in the Wall Street district as a private secretary. She talked a lot about how she hated her job and her boss, but the good part was that her boss was often out of town for extended periods: that gave her time to use the office typewriter in pursuit of her life's ambition, which was to write scripts for the radio.

She once confided to my mother that she'd made up both of her names: "Sloane" because it sounded masculine, the kind of name a woman alone might need for making her way in the world, and "Cabot" because—well, because it had a touch of class. Was there anything wrong with that?

"Oh, Helen," she said. "This is going to be wonderful for you. If you get the publicity—if the papers pick it up, and the newsreels—you'll be one of the most interesting personalities in America."

Five or six people were gathered in the studio on the day my mother came home from her first visit with the President-elect.

"Will somebody get me a drink?" she asked, looking around in mock helplessness. "Then I'll tell you all about it."

And with the drink in her hand, with her eyes as wide as a child's, she told us how a door had opened and two big men had brought him in.

"Big men," she insisted. "Young, strong men, holding him up

under the arms, and you could see how they were straining. Then you saw this *foot* come out, with these awful metal braces on the shoe, and then the *other* foot. And he was sweating, and he was panting for breath, and his face was—I don't know—all bright and tense and horrible." She shuddered.

"Well," Howard Whitman said, looking uneasy, "he can't help being crippled, Helen."

"Howard," she said impatiently, "I'm only trying to tell you how *ugly* it was." And that seemed to carry a certain weight. If she was an authority on beauty—on how a little boy might kneel among ferns to play the pipes of Pan, for example—then surely she had earned her credentials as an authority on ugliness.

"*Any*way," she went on, "they got him into a chair, and he wiped most of the sweat off his face with a handkerchief—he was still out of breath—and after a while he started talking to some of the other men there; I couldn't follow that part of it. Then finally he turned to me with this smile of his. Honestly, I don't know if I can describe that smile. It isn't something you can see in the newsreels; you have to be there. His eyes don't change at all, but the corners of his mouth go up as if they're being pulled by puppet strings. It's a frightening smile. It makes you think: This could be a dangerous man. This could be an evil man. Well anyway, we started talking, and I spoke right up to him. I said 'I didn't vote for you, Mr. President.' I said 'I'm a good Republican and I voted for President Hoover.' He said 'Why are you here, then?' or something like that, and I said 'Because you have a very interesting head.' So he gave me the smile again and he said 'What's interesting about it?' And I said 'I like the bumps on it.' "

By then she must have assumed that every reporter in the room was writing in his notebook, while the photographers got their flashbulbs ready; tomorrow's papers might easily read:

GAL SCULPTOR TWITS FDR
ABOUT "BUMPS" ON HEAD

At the end of her preliminary chat with him she got down to business, which was to measure different parts of his head with her calipers. I knew how that felt: the cold, trembling points of those clay-encrusted calipers had tickled and poked me all over during the times I'd served as model for her fey little woodland boys.

But not a single flashbulb went off while she took and recorded the measurements, and nobody asked her any questions; after a few nervous words of thanks and goodbye she was out in the corridor again among all the hopeless, craning people who couldn't get in. It must have been a bad disappointment, and I imagine she tried to make up for it by planning the triumphant way she'd tell us about it when she got home.

"Helen?" Howard Whitman inquired, after most of the other visitors had gone. "Why'd you tell him you didn't vote for him?"

"Well, because it's true. I *am* a good Republican; you know that."

She was a storekeeper's daughter from a small town in Ohio; she had probably grown up hearing the phrase "good Republican" as an index of respectability and clean clothes. And maybe she had come to relax her standards of respectability, maybe she didn't even care much about clean clothes anymore, but "good Republican" was worth clinging to. It would be helpful when she met the customers of her garden figures, the people whose low, courteous voices would welcome her into their lives and who would almost certainly turn out to be Republicans too.

"I believe in the aristocracy!" she often cried, trying to make herself heard above the rumble of voices when her guests were discussing communism, and they seldom paid her any attention. They liked her well enough: she gave parties with plenty of liquor, and she was an agreeable hostess if only because of her touching eagerness to please; but in any talk of politics she was like a shrill, exasperating child. She believed in the aristocracy.

She believed in God, too, or at least in the ceremony of St. Luke's Episcopal Church, which she attended several times a year. And she believed in Eric Nicholson, the handsome middle-aged Englishman who was her lover. He had something to do with the American end of a British chain of foundries: his company cast ornamental objects into bronze and lead. The cupolas of college and high school buildings all over the East, the lead-casement windows for Tudor-style homes in places like Scarsdale and Bronxville—these were some of the things Eric Nicholson's firm had accomplished. He was always self-deprecating about his business, but ruddy and glowing with its success.

My mother had met him the year before, when she'd sought help in having one of her garden figures cast into bronze, to be "placed on consignment" with some garden-sculpture gallery from which it would never be sold. Eric Nicholson had persuaded her that lead would be almost as nice as bronze and much cheaper; then he'd asked her out to dinner, and that evening changed our lives.

Mr. Nicholson rarely spoke to my sister or me, and I think we were both frightened of him, but he overwhelmed us with gifts. At first they were mostly books—a volume of cartoons from *Punch*, a partial set of Dickens, a book called *England in Tudor Times* containing tissue-covered color plates that Edith liked. But in the summer of 1933, when our father arranged for us to spend two weeks with our mother at a small lake in New Jersey, Mr. Nicholson's gifts became a cornucopia of sporting goods. He gave Edith a steel fishing rod with a reel so intricate that none of us could have figured it out even if we'd known how to fish, a wicker creel for carrying the fish she would never catch, and a sheathed hunting knife to be worn at her waist. He gave me a short ax whose head was encased in a leather holster and strapped to my belt—I guess this was for cutting firewood to cook the fish—and a cumbersome net with a handle that hung from an elastic shoulder strap, in case I should be called upon to wade in and help Edith land a tricky one. There was nothing to do in that New Jersey village except take walks, or what my mother called good hikes; and every day, as we plodded out through the insect-humming weeds in the sun, we wore our full regalia of useless equipment.

That same summer Mr. Nicholson gave me a three-year subscription to *Field and Stream*, and I think that impenetrable magazine was the least appropriate of all his gifts because it kept coming in the mail for such a long, long time after everything else had changed for us: after we'd moved out of New York to Scarsdale, where Mr. Nicholson had found a house with a low rent, and after he had abandoned my mother in that house—with no warning—to return to England and to the wife from whom he'd never really been divorced.

But all that came later; I want to go back to the time between Franklin D. Roosevelt's election and his Inauguration, when his head was slowly taking shape on my mother's modeling stand.

Her original plan had been to make it life-size, or larger than life-size, but Mr. Nicholson urged her to scale it down for economy in the casting, and so she made it only seven or eight inches high. He persuaded her too, for the second time since he'd known her, that lead would be almost as nice as bronze.

She had always said she didn't mind at all if Edith and I watched her work, but we had never much wanted to; now it was a little more interesting because we could watch her sift through many photographs of Roosevelt cut from newspapers until she found one that would help her execute a subtle plane of cheek or brow.

But most of our day was taken up with school. John Cabot might go to school in Hastings-on-Hudson, for which Edith would always yearn, but we had what even Edith admitted was the next best thing: we went to school in our bedroom.

During the previous year my mother had enrolled us in the public school down the street, but she'd begun to regret it when we came home with lice in our hair. Then one day Edith came home accused of having stolen a boy's coat, and that was too much. She withdrew us both, in defiance of the city truant officer, and pleaded with my father to help her meet the cost of a private school. He refused. The rent she paid and the bills she ran up were already taxing him far beyond the terms of the divorce agreement; he was in debt; surely she must realize he was lucky even to have a job. Would she ever learn to be reasonable?

It was Howard Whitman who broke the deadlock. He knew of an inexpensive, fully accredited mail-order service called The Calvert School, intended mainly for the homes of children who were invalids. The Calvert School furnished weekly supplies of books and materials and study plans; all she would need was someone in the house to administer the program and to serve as a tutor. And someone like Bart Kampen would be ideal for the job.

"The skinny fellow?" she asked. "The Jewish boy from Holland or wherever it is?"

"He's very well educated, Helen," Howard told her. "And he speaks fluent English, and he'd be very conscientious. And he could certainly use the money."

We were delighted to learn that Bart Kampen would be our tutor. With the exception of Howard himself, Bart was probably our favorite among the adults around the courtyard. He was twenty-eight or so, young enough so that his ears could still turn red when he was teased by children; we had found that out in teasing him once or twice about such matters as that his socks didn't match. He was tall and very thin and seemed always to look startled except when he was comforted enough to smile. He was a violinist, a Dutch Jew who had emigrated the year before in the hope of joining a symphony orchestra, and eventually of launching a concert career. But the symphonies weren't hiring then, nor were the pit orchestras of Broadway theaters, so Bart had gone without work for a long time. He lived alone in a room on Seventh Avenue, not far from the courtyard, and people who liked him used to worry that he might not have enough to eat. He owned two suits, both cut in a way that must have been stylish in the Netherlands at the time: stiff, heavily padded shoulders and a nipped-in waist; they would probably have looked better on someone with a little more meat on his bones. In shirtsleeves, with the cuffs rolled back, his hairy wrists and forearms looked even more fragile than you might have expected, but his long hands were shapely and strong enough to suggest authority on the violin.

"I'll leave it entirely up to you, Bart," my mother said when he asked if she had any instructions for our tutoring. "I know you'll do wonders with them."

A small table was moved into our bedroom, under the window, and three chairs placed around it. Bart sat in the middle so that he could divide his time equally between Edith and me. Big, clean, heavy brown envelopes arrived in the mail from The Calvert School once a week, and when Bart slid their fascinating contents onto the table it was like settling down to begin a game.

Edith was in the fifth grade that year—her part of the table was given over to incomprehensible talk about English and History and Social Studies—and I was in the first. I spent my mornings asking Bart to help me puzzle out the very opening moves of an education.

"Take your time, Billy," he would say. "Don't get impatient with this. Once you have it you'll see how easy it is, and then you'll be ready for the next thing."

At eleven each morning we would take a break. We'd go downstairs and out to the part of the courtyard that had a little grass. Bart would carefully lay his folded coat on the sidelines, turn back his shirt cuffs, and present himself as ready to give what he called airplane rides. Taking us one at a time, he would grasp one wrist and one ankle; then he'd whirl us off our feet and around and around, with himself as the pivot, until the courtyard and the buildings and the city and the world were lost in the dizzying blur of our flight.

After the airplane rides we would hurry down the steps into the studio, where we'd usually find that my mother had set out a tray bearing three tall glasses of cold Ovaltine, sometimes with cookies on the side and sometimes not. I once overheard her telling Sloane Cabot she thought the Ovaltine must be Bart's first nourishment of the day—and I think she was probably right, if only because of the way his hand would tremble in reaching for his glass. Sometimes she'd forget to prepare the tray and we'd go into the kitchen and fix it ourselves; I can never see a jar of Ovaltine on a grocery shelf without remembering those times. Then it was back upstairs to school again. And during that year, by coaxing and prodding and telling me not to get impatient, Bart Kampen taught me to read.

It was an excellent opportunity for showing off. I would pull books down from my mother's shelves—mostly books that were the gifts of Mr. Nicholson—and try to impress her by reading mangled sentences aloud.

"That's wonderful, dear," she would say. "You've really learned to read, haven't you."

Soon a white and yellow "More light" stamp was affixed to every page of my Calvert First Grade Reader, proving I had mastered it, and others were accumulating at a slower rate in my arithmetic workbook. Still other stamps were fastened to the wall beside my place at the school table, arranged in a proud little white and yellow, thumb-smudged column that rose as high as I could reach.

"You shouldn't have put your stamps on the wall," Edith said.

"Why?"

"Well, because they'll be hard to take off."

"Who's going to take them off?"

That small room of ours, with its double function of sleep and learning, stands more clearly in my memory than any other part of our home. Someone should probably have told my mother that a girl and boy of our ages ought to have separate rooms, but that never occurred to me until much later. Our cots were set foot-to-foot against the wall, leaving just enough space to pass alongside

them to the school table, and we had some good conversations as
we lay waiting for sleep at night. The one I remember best was
the time Edith told me about the sound of the city.

"I don't mean just the loud sounds," she said, "like the siren
going by just now, or those car doors slamming, or all the laughing and shouting down the street; that's just close-up stuff. I'm
talking about something else. Because you see there are millions
and millions of people in New York—more people than you can
possibly imagine, ever—and most of them are doing something
that makes a sound. Maybe talking, or playing the radio, maybe
closing doors, maybe putting their forks down on their plates if
they're having dinner, or dropping their shoes if they're going to
bed—and because there are so many of them, all those little
sounds add up and come together in a kind of hum. But it's so
faint—so very, very faint—that you can't hear it unless you listen
very carefully for a long time."

"Can you hear it?" I asked her.

"Sometimes. I listen every night, but I can only hear it sometimes. Other times I fall asleep. Let's be quiet now, and just listen. See if you can hear it, Billy."

And I tried hard, closing my eyes as if that would help, opening
my mouth to minimize the sound of my breathing, but in the end
I had to tell her I'd failed. "How about you?" I asked.

"Oh, I heard it," she said. "Just for a few seconds, but I heard
it. You'll hear it too, if you keep trying. And it's worth waiting
for. When you hear it, you're hearing the whole city of New
York."

The high point of our week was Friday afternoon, when John
Cabot came home from Hastings. He exuded health and normal-
ity; he brought fresh suburban air into our bohemian lives. He
even transformed his mother's small apartment, while he was
there, into an enviable place of rest between vigorous encounters
with the world. He subscribed to both *Boys' Life* and *Open Road
for Boys*, and these seemed to me to be wonderful things to have
in your house, if only for the illustrations. John dressed in the
same heroic way as the boys shown in those magazines, corduroy
knickers with ribbed stockings pulled taut over his muscular
calves. He talked a lot about the Hastings high school football
team, for which he planned to try out as soon as he was old

enough, and about Hastings friends whose names and personalities grew almost as familiar to us as if they were friends of our
own. He taught us invigorating new ways to speak, like saying
"What's the diff?" instead of "What's the difference?" And he
was better even than Edith at finding new things to do in the
courtyard.

You could buy goldfish for ten or fifteen cents apiece in Wool-
worth's then, and one day we brought home three of them to
keep in the fountain. We sprinkled the water with more Wool-
worth's granulated fish food than they could possibly need, and
we named them after ourselves: "John," "Edith," and "Billy." For
a week or two Edith and I would run to the fountain every morning, before Bart came for school, to make sure they were still alive
and to see if they had enough food, and to watch them.

"Have you noticed how much bigger Billy's getting?" Edith
asked me. "He's huge. He's almost as big as John and Edith now.
He'll probably be bigger than both of them."

Then one weekend when John was home he called our attention to how quickly the fish could turn and move. "They have
better reflexes than humans," he explained. "When they see a
shadow in the water, or anything that looks like danger, they get
away faster than you can blink. Watch." And he sank one hand
into the water to make a grab for the fish named Edith, but she
evaded him and fled. "See that?" he asked. "How's that for speed?
Know something? I bet you could shoot an arrow in there, and
they'd get away in time. Wait." To prove his point he ran to his
mother's apartment and came back with the handsome bow and
arrow he had made at summer camp (going to camp every summer was another admirable thing about John); then he knelt at
the rim of the fountain like the picture of an archer, his bow
steady in one strong hand and the feathered end of his arrow tight
against the bowstring in the other. He was taking aim at the fish
named Billy. "Now, the velocity of this arrow," he said in a voice
weakened by his effort, "is probably more than a car going eighty
miles an hour. It's probably more like an airplane, or maybe even
more than that. Okay; watch."

The fish named Billy was suddenly floating dead on the surface,
on his side, impaled a quarter of the way up the arrow with part
of his pink guts dribbled along the shaft.

I was too old to cry, but something had to be done about the shock and rage and grief that filled me as I ran from the fountain, heading blindly for home, and halfway there I came upon my mother. She stood looking very clean, wearing a new coat and dress I'd never seen before and fastened to the arm of Mr. Nicholson. They were either just going out or just coming in—I didn't care which—and Mr. Nicholson frowned at me (he had told me more than once that boys of my age went to boarding school in England), but I didn't care about that either. I bent my head into her waist and didn't stop crying until long after I'd felt her hands stroking my back, until after she had assured me that goldfish didn't cost much and I'd have another one soon, and that John was sorry for the thoughtless thing he'd done. I had discovered, or rediscovered, that crying is a pleasure—that it can be a pleasure beyond all reckoning if your head is pressed in your mother's waist and her hands are on your back, and if she happens to be wearing clean clothes.

There were other pleasures. We had a good Christmas Eve in our house that year, or at least it was good at first. My father was there, which obliged Mr. Nicholson to stay away, and it was nice to see how relaxed he was among my mother's friends. He was shy, but they seemed to like him. He got along especially well with Bart Kampen.

Howard Whitman's daughter Nancy, a sweet-natured girl of about my age, had come in from New Rochelle to spend the holidays with him, and there were several other children whom we knew but rarely saw. John looked very mature that night in a dark coat and tie, plainly aware of his social responsibilities as the oldest boy.

After a while, with no plan, the party drifted back into the dining-room area and staged an impromptu vaudeville. Howard started it: he brought the tall stool from my mother's modeling stand and sat his daughter on it, facing the audience. He folded back the opening of a brown paper bag two or three times and fitted it onto her head; then he took off his suit coat and draped it around her backwards, up to the chin; he went behind her, crouched out of sight, and worked his hands through the coat-sleeves so that when they emerged they appeared to be hers. And the sight of a smiling little girl in a paper-bag hat, waving and gesturing with huge, expressive hands, was enough to make everyone laugh. The big hands wiped her eyes and stroked her chin and pushed her hair behind her ears; then they elaborately thumbed her nose at us.

Next came Sloane Cabot. She sat very straight on the stool with her heels hooked over the rungs in such a way as to show her good legs to their best advantage, but her first act didn't go over.

"Well," she began, "I was at work today—you know my office is on the fortieth floor—when I happened to glance up from my typewriter and saw this big old man sort of crouched on the ledge outside the window, with a white beard and a funny red suit. So I ran to the window and opened it and said 'Are you all right?' Well, it was Santa Claus, and he said 'Of course I'm all right; I'm used to high places. But listen, Miss: can you direct me to number seventy-five Bedford Street?' "

There was more, but our embarrassed looks must have told her we knew we were being condescended to; as soon as she'd found a way to finish it she did so quickly. Then, after a thoughtful pause, she tried something else that turned out to be much better.

"Have you children ever heard the story of the first Christmas?" she asked. "When Jesus was born?" And she began to tell it in the kind of hushed, dramatic voice she must have hoped might be used by the narrators of her more serious radio plays.

". . . And there were still many miles to go before they reached Bethlehem," she said, "and it was a cold night. Now, Mary knew she would very soon have a baby. She even knew, because an angel had told her, that her baby might one day be the saviour of all mankind. But she was only a young girl"—here Sloane's eyes glistened, as if they might be filling with tears—"and the traveling had exhausted her. She was bruised by the jolting gait of the donkey and she ached all over, and she thought they'd never, ever get there, and all she could say was 'Oh, Joseph, I'm so tired.' "

The story went on through the rejection at the inn, and the birth in the stable, and the manger, and the animals, and the arrival of the three kings; when it was over we clapped a long time because Sloane had told it so well.

"Daddy?" Edith asked. "Will you sing for us?"

"Oh, well, thanks, honey," he said, "but no; I really need a piano for that. Thanks anyway."

The final performer of the evening was Bart Kampen, persuaded by popular demand to go home and get his violin. There was no surprise in discovering that he played like a professional, like something you might easily hear on the radio; the enjoyment came from watching how his thin face frowned over the chin rest, empty of all emotion except concern that the sound be right. We were proud of him.

Some time after my father left a good many other adults began to arrive, most of them strangers to me, looking as though they'd already been to several other parties that night. It was very late, or rather very early Christmas morning, when I looked into the kitchen and saw Sloane standing close to a bald man I didn't know. He held a trembling drink in one hand and slowly massaged her shoulder with the other; she seemed to be shrinking back against the old wooden icebox. Sloane had a way of smiling that allowed little wisps of cigarette smoke to escape from between her almost-closed lips while she looked you up and down, and she was doing that. Then the man put his drink on top of the icebox and took her in his arms, and I couldn't see her face anymore.

Another man, in a rumpled brown suit, lay unconscious on the dining-room floor. I walked around him and went into the studio, where a good-looking young woman stood weeping wretchedly and three men kept getting in each other's way as they tried to comfort her. Then I saw that one of the men was Bart, and I watched while he outlasted the other two and turned the girl away toward the door. He put his arm around her and she nestled her head in his shoulder; that was how they left the house.

Edith looked jaded in her wrinkled party dress. She was reclining in our old Hastings-on-Hudson easy chair with her head tipped back and her legs flung out over both the chair's arms, and John sat cross-legged on the floor near one of her dangling feet. They seemed to have been talking about something that didn't interest either of them much, and the talk petered out altogether when I sat on the floor to join them.

"Billy," she said, "do you realize what time it is?"

"What's the diff?" I said.

"You should've been in bed hours ago. Come on. Let's go up."

"I don't feel like it."

"Well," she said, "I'm going up, anyway," and she got laboriously out of the chair and walked away into the crowd.

John turned to me and narrowed his eyes unpleasantly. "Know

something?" he said. "When she was sitting in the chair that way I could see everything."

"Huh?"

"I could see everything. I could see the crack, and the hair. She's beginning to get hair."

I had observed these features of my sister many times—in the bathtub, or when she was changing her clothes—and hadn't found them especially remarkable; even so, I understood at once how remarkable they must have been for him. If only he had smiled in a bashful way we might have laughed together like a couple of regular fellows out of *Open Road for Boys*, but his face was still set in that disdainful look.

"I kept looking and looking," he said, "and I had to keep her talking so she wouldn't catch on, but I was doing fine until you had to come over and ruin it."

Was I supposed to apologize? That didn't seem right, but nothing else seemed right either. All I did was look at the floor.

When I finally got to bed there was scarcely time for trying to hear the elusive sound of the city—I had found that a good way to keep from thinking of anything else—when my mother came blundering in. She'd had too much to drink and wanted to lie down, but instead of going to her own room she got into bed with me. "Oh," she said. "Oh, my boy. Oh, my boy." It was a narrow cot and there was no way to make room for her; then suddenly she retched, bolted to her feet, and ran for the bathroom, where I heard her vomiting. And when I moved over into the part of the bed she had occupied my face recoiled quickly, but not quite in time, from the slick mouthful of puke she had left on her side of the pillow.

For a month or so that winter we didn't see much of Sloane because she said she was "working on something big. Something really big." When it was finished she brought it to the studio, looking tired but prettier than ever, and shyly asked if she could read it aloud.

"Wonderful," my mother said. "What's it about?"

"That's the best part. It's about us. All of us. Listen."

Bart had gone for the day and Edith was out in the courtyard by herself—she often played by herself—so there was nobody for an audience but my mother and me. We sat on the sofa and

Sloane arranged herself on the tall stool, just as she'd done for telling the Bethlehem story.

"There is an enchanted courtyard in Greenwich Village," she read. "It's only a narrow patch of brick and green among the ir- regular shapes of very old houses, but what makes it enchanted is that the people who live in it, or near it, have come to form an enchanted circle of friends.

"None of them have enough money and some are quite poor, but they believe in the future; they believe in each other, and in themselves.

"There is Howard, once a top reporter on a metropolitan daily newspaper. Everyone knows Howard will soon scale the journal- istic heights again, and in the meantime he serves as the wise and humorous sage of the courtyard.

"There is Bart, a young violinist clearly destined for virtuosity on the concert stage, who just for the present must graciously ac- cept all lunch and dinner invitations in order to survive.

"And there is Helen, a sculptor whose charming works will someday grace the finest gardens in America, and whose studio is the favorite gathering place for members of the circle."

There were several more pages like that, introducing other char- acters, and toward the end she got around to the children. She de- scribed my sister as "a lanky, dreamy tomboy," which was odd—I had never thought of Edith that way—and she called me "a sad- eyed, seven-year-old philosopher," which was wholly baffling. When the introduction was over she paused a few seconds for dra- matic effect and then went into the opening episode of the series, or what I suppose would be called the "pilot."

I couldn't follow the story very well—it seemed to be mostly an excuse for bringing each character up to the microphone for a few lines apiece—and before long I was listening only to see if there would be any lines for the character based on me. And there were, in a way. She announced my name—"Billy"—but then instead of speaking she put her mouth through a terrible series of contor- tions, accompanied by funny little bursts of sound, and by the time the words came out I didn't care what they were. It was true that I stuttered badly—I wouldn't get over it for five or six more years—but I hadn't expected anyone to put it on the radio.

"Oh, Sloane, that's marvelous," my mother said when the read- ing was over. "That's really exciting."

And Sloane was carefully stacking her typed pages in the way she'd probably been taught to do in secretarial school, blushing and smiling with pride. "Well," she said, "it probably needs work, but I do think it's got a lot of potential."

"It's perfect," my mother said. "Just the way it is."

Sloane mailed the script to a radio producer and he mailed it back with a letter typed by some radio secretary, explaining that her material had too limited an appeal to be commercial. The radio public was not yet ready, he said, for a story of Greenwich Village life.

Then it was March. The new President promised that the only thing we had to fear was fear itself, and soon after that his head came packed in wood and excelsior from Mr. Nicholson's foundry.

It was a fairly good likeness. She had caught the famous lift of the chin—it might not have looked like him at all if she hadn't—and everyone told her it was fine. What nobody said was that her original plan had been right, and Mr. Nicholson shouldn't have interfered: it was too small. It didn't look heroic. If you could have hollowed it out and put a slot in the top, it might have made a serviceable bank for loose change.

The foundry had burnished the lead until it shone almost silver in the highlights, and they'd mounted it on a sturdy little base of heavy black plastic. They had sent back three copies: one for the White House presentation, one to keep for exhibition purposes, and an extra one. But the extra one soon toppled to the floor and was badly damaged—the nose mashed almost into the chin—and my mother might have burst into tears if Howard Whitman hadn't made everyone laugh by saying it was now a good portrait of Vice President Garner.

Charlie Hines, Howard's old friend from the *Post* who was now a minor member of the White House staff, made an appointment for my mother with the President late on a weekday morning. She arranged for Sloane to spend the night with Edith and me; then she took an evening train down to Washington, carrying the sculpture in a cardboard box, and stayed at one of the less expensive Washington hotels. In the morning she met Charlie Hines in some crowded White House anteroom, where I guess they disposed of the cardboard box, and he took her to the waiting room outside the Oval Office. He sat with her as she held the naked head in her lap, and when their turn came he escorted her in to the President's desk for the presentation. It didn't take long. There were no reporters and no photographers.

Afterward Charlie Hines took her out to lunch, probably because he'd promised Howard Whitman to do so. I imagine it wasn't a first-class restaurant, more likely some bustling, no-nonsense place favored by the working press, and I imagine they had trouble making conversation until they settled on Howard, and on what a shame it was that he was still out of work.

"No, but do you know Howard's friend Bart Kampen?" Charlie asked. "The young Dutchman? The violinist?"

"Yes, certainly," she said. "I know Bart."

"Well, Jesus, there's *one* story with a happy ending, right? Have you heard about that? Last time I saw Bart he said 'Charlie, the Depression's over for me,' and he told me he'd found some rich, dumb, crazy woman who's paying him to tutor her kids."

I can picture how she looked riding the long, slow train back to New York that afternoon. She must have sat staring straight ahead or out the dirty window, seeing nothing, her eyes round and her face held in a soft shape of hurt. Her adventure with Franklin D. Roosevelt had come to nothing. There would be no photographs or interviews or feature articles, no thrilling moments of newsreel coverage; strangers would never know of how she'd come from a small Ohio town, or of how she'd nurtured her talent through the brave, difficult, one-woman journey that had brought her to the attention of the world. It wasn't fair.

All she had to look forward to now was her romance with Eric Nicholson, and I think she may have known even then that it was faltering—his final desertion came the next fall.

She was forty-one, an age when even romantics must admit that youth is gone, and she had nothing to show for the years but a studio crowded with green plaster statues that nobody would buy. She believed in the aristocracy, but there was no reason to suppose the aristocracy would ever believe in her.

And every time she thought of what Charlie Hines had said about Bart Kampen—oh, how hateful; oh, how hateful—the humiliation came back in wave on wave, in merciless rhythm to the clatter of the train.

She made a brave show of her homecoming, though nobody was there to greet her but Sloane and Edith and me. Sloane had fed us, and she said "There's a plate for you in the oven, Helen," but my mother said she'd rather just have a drink instead. She was then at the onset of a long battle with alcohol that she would ultimately lose; it must have seemed bracing that night to decide on a drink instead of dinner. Then she told us "all about" her trip to Washington, managing to make it sound like a success. She talked of how thrilling it was to be actually inside the White House; she repeated whatever small, courteous thing it was that President Roosevelt had said to her on receiving the head. And she had brought back souvenirs: a handful of note-size White House stationery for Edith, and a well-used briar pipe for me. She explained that she'd seen a very distinguished-looking man smoking the pipe in the waiting room outside the Oval Office; when his name was called he had knocked it out quickly into an ashtray and left it there as he hurried inside. She had waited until she was sure no one was looking; then she'd taken the pipe from the ashtray and put it in her purse. "Because I knew he must have been somebody important," she said. "He could easily have been a member of the Cabinet, or something like that. Anyway, I thought you'd have a lot of fun with it." But I didn't. It was too heavy to hold in my teeth and it tasted terrible when I sucked on it; besides, I kept wondering what the man must have thought when he came out of the President's office and found it gone.

Sloane went home after a while, and my mother sat drinking alone at the dining-room table. I think she hoped Howard Whitman or some of her other friends might drop in, but nobody did. It was almost our bedtime when she looked up and said "Edith? Run out in the garden and see if you can find Bart."

He had recently bought a pair of bright tan shoes with crepe soles. I saw those shoes trip rapidly down the dark brick steps beyond the windows—he seemed scarcely to touch each step in his buoyancy—and then I saw him come smiling into the studio, with Edith closing the door behind him. "Helen!" he said. "You're back!"

She acknowledged that she was back. Then she got up from the table and slowly advanced on him, and Edith and I began to realize we were in for something bad.

"Bart," she said, "I had lunch with Charlie Hines in Washington today."

"Oh?"

"And we had a very interesting talk. He seems to know you very well."

"Oh, not really; we've met a few times at Howard's, but we're not really—"

"And he said you'd told him the Depression was over for you because you'd found some rich, dumb, crazy woman who was paying you to tutor her kids. Don't interrupt me."

But Bart clearly had no intention of interrupting her. He was backing away from her in his soundless shoes, retreating past one stiff green garden child after another. His face looked startled and pink.

"I'm not a rich woman, Bart," she said, bearing down on him. "And I'm not dumb. And I'm not crazy. And I can recognize ingratitude and disloyalty and sheer, rotten viciousness and *lies* when they're thrown in my face."

My sister and I were halfway up the stairs, jostling each other in our need to hide before the worst part came. The worst part of these things always came at the end, after she'd lost all control and gone on shouting anyway.

"I want you to get out of my house, Bart," she said. "And I don't ever want to see you again. And I want to tell you something. All my life I've hated people who say 'Some of my best friends are Jews.' Because *none* of my friends are Jews, or ever will be. Do you understand me? *None* of my friends are Jews, or ever will be."

The studio was quiet after that. Without speaking, avoiding each other's eyes, Edith and I got into our pajamas and into bed. But it wasn't more than a few minutes before the house began to ring with our mother's raging voice all over again, as if Bart had somehow been brought back and made to take his punishment twice.

". . . And I said '*None* of my friends are Jews, or ever will be . . .'"

She was on the telephone, giving Sloane Cabot the highlights of the scene, and it was clear that Sloane would take her side and comfort her. Sloane might know how the Virgin Mary felt on the way to Bethlehem, but she also knew how to play my stutter for laughs. In a case like this she would quickly see where her allegiance lay, and it wouldn't cost her much to drop Bart Kampen from her enchanted circle.

When the telephone call came to an end at last, there was silence downstairs until we heard her working with the ice pick in the icebox: she was making herself another drink.

There would be no more school in our room. We would probably never see Bart again—or if we ever did, he would probably not want to see us. But our mother was ours; we were hers; and we lived with that knowledge as we lay listening for the faint, faint sound of millions.

TRAVELLING

MARY BUNKER PETERSON

Mary Bunker Peterson, whose home town is Cambridge, Minnesota, studied writing at the University of New Hampshire and the Iowa Writer's Workshop. She has published fiction in the *North American Review, South Dakota Review, Fiction International,* and *Ploughshares*; a story appeared in the 1978 *Pushcart Prize III: Best of the Small Presses*. At present she lives in Maine and teaches writing at the University of New Hampshire.

In April when she drove away he looked at his hands. They were oily from the boat's engine, from the garage. But what a thing to notice. He turned and saw the children, who were watching from the steps, and wondered what she had given him now.

The day before she left they discovered something wrong with the Volkswagen. He swore it was running on only three cylinders, but she refused to take it to the shop. "It runs," she said. "That's all."

"But it won't get you there."

"It will."

Yet when she started it, the engine coughed and died. Warmed up, it raced too fast and he could hear her coming home a half mile down the road, sounding crazy, like a car without a muffler, a car with a problem. He didn't want her to leave that way. He wanted to trust the machine. That was the reason he did the premature tune-up and the oil change himself. And, too, it was the reason he urged a sleeping bag on her, in the trunk, although nights were warm. He wanted her to be safe.

When she had first brought up a trip alone he sensed she'd been thinking about it a long time and waited for the right moment. The time when she would tell, and not ask. In the last year he'd learned to expect statements from her rather than questions. Now she usually asserted what she would do. It was left for him to complain or to let it be.

And usually he said nothing.

In the thirteen years of their marriage they had hardly argued. When they did it was startling and important, reminding him of the time in Rockport when they were first engaged. He was captain and she was crew in the interclub races. She knew what the boat was for him. Respected it, too. It put an edge on him to prepare for a race. The night before one, he never slept. Yet, even knowing, she had risen up in the boat like a witch or an apparition when he ordered her to tack. Had risen up and said, "You won't use that voice with me! Sail the damned thing yourself!"

They were heading out and surrounded with sailboats, and the whole harbor heard. The whole harbor watched.

"What do you mean?" he shouted. "Ready about!"

"The hell!" she screamed.

They had fallen upon each other in the cockpit right there, in the middle of the race, rolling and grappling like scrappy dogs while the boats sailed on past them. He was a mild man. He couldn't believe this had happened. She was all fire but he couldn't believe it happened.

Afterward he told her what she already knew: the town of Rockport wondered what he was doing with this girl.

But she loved him and she would marry him on the condition that they leave Rockport. It wasn't the race. Only that as long as he was bound by his family and the town, he could be no husband to her. Did he care that much?

When they married and left, people said he was making a great mistake.

If loving her was a mistake it was one he wanted to make. They moved to Maine where he worked as a county psychologist. The first years were hard and slow, and she was restless. But the children transformed her. She had an instinct for being a mother, responding to the world as half a child herself. He watched her feeling he was attending a great mystery.

And they didn't stop being lovers. She was small and alert; he was reed-tall and gentle. He made love to her carefully in the beginning, teaching her as he himself had been taught by a woman while he was still young. She was as ardent as he had been.

So they had grown together, but apart too. He sensed in her, always had, an urgency that the marriage did not address. Or a need. He told himself her childhood did it. She was her father's daughter, and the man had raised her to be wild and intense and loving and desperate. Her nature was like a continual accident. She seemed as surprised by herself as he was. But she told him she couldn't be other than she was.

When she first said she was going to Nova Scotia alone, he didn't know what to answer. Rushing ahead of him, she said how at nineteen she'd planned to go to Alaska with some college kids. Alaska seemed a great adventure. To go so far, she said, was like running out to the end of something and teetering, balancing, looking dead-on into mystery. Her mother had opposed the trip, but the arguments did no good. Finally she told her daughter she thought the group leaders were lesbians and it wouldn't be safe, travelling with them.

She had not gone.

But the idea rankled in her, oppressed her, all these years afterward. She said her instincts were to go; said that to argue it her mother had craftily run instinct backwards into fear. And it worked. But left her feeling fundamentally failed. Something, she said, was stolen from her then. She couldn't name it. She wanted it back.

"It's because I have to do it," she said, turning that familiar look on him, her eyes so utterly blue they reminded him of the hearts of glaciers.

"Yes," he said. Just the word.

Leaning over the fireplace she talked until he better understood, or thought he did. When she went down the long driveway, the Volkswagen engine racing and exploding, one arm out the window waving goodbye, he understood less.

"I'm getting to know the kids better," he said when she phoned on the third night.

"Daddy plays ball with us," Paul said. "And he's good, Mom."

"He makes hamburgers better than McDonald's," Elisabeth said, pride in her voice.

"We miss you," he said, taking the phone again. He held it balanced against his ear, looked at the kitchen mess, cat food smeared on the floor.

"I miss you too, darling."

She said she was staying at a wonderful hotel directly on the ocean, and she would probably spend the whole remaining time there. Said she was fighting the impulse to go antiquing. That she had found a painter who did wonderful risky things with color and shape, and if his smaller pieces weren't too costly she'd bring one home. "Imagine a royal blue sky!" she told him. "The color of Elisabeth's jumper! Can you see it?"

During the day he went to work and the clinic felt the same as it had. His patients—but he preferred to call them clients—were unchanged by the change in his immediate life, and he listened to them closely, sorted their confessions and fears as if he were scrying a very precious object. But what he wanted to read in them was the form of his own life.

At night when he came home the children were there and waiting. He announced the meals would be community business and they would all take a hand at cooking. Elisabeth made a banana cake with food-color blue frosting. Paul made hot dogs, carried them proudly into the dining room. Some nights they all cleaned up together. Other times, dishes from two days stood in the sink. It was not that unusual—she didn't do dishes faithfully either. When she cleaned, it was always with a violent activity that left nothing motionless: chairs, books, lamps, his mother's bone china. Elisabeth and Paul instructed him in their mother's routines and he tried to follow them, or adapt them for himself.

And he saw how generous his children were. Wondered what part of it was his own doing, what part hers. In their conversations over dinner he asked them questions which they answered more honestly than he would have thought possible. They were original, these children. At nine and ten they had an essential goodness about them. And they were fair. Old enough that perhaps they would carry these qualities into adulthood. He felt a pride that was embarrassing, even uncomfortable.

She sent post cards in the mail: "Dear Everybody. I love you and miss you all. The weather is perfect. When I eat alone I think of you hard. That's the worst time."

He never doubted, even for a single moment, that he wanted her to return to him.

When she was back, she did not seem much changed. For a few days she talked eagerly about things she'd seen, the thrill and fear of being alone in a strange place. But matters of the children, of the house, pressed them both into familiar patterns. Before long he expected dinner at night again, drinks before it. Paul and Elisabeth stopped asking him to play softball with them.

He felt a warmth with the children that wasn't there before, as if they shared a secret. But he reminded himself the secret was only their privacy and the small things they'd learned while she was gone.

They discovered they were lovers still, as if they had doubted it. He learned again the good security of being in bed with her. The third night she was home, when they lay in the dark looking at the window, he searched for a way to tell her. She was warm against him.

"There was a man in Nova Scotia," her voice came from the silence.

He waited, listening.

"He bought me dinner, and a drink. Took out all the pictures of his wife and kids. Even one of the family Doberman, for Christ's sake." She sat up and turned to face him in the dark, intent, like a Buddha. He couldn't see her face.

"I thought, why is he paying attention to me?" Then she laughed girlishly. "Then I knew why it was."

His question was in his silence.

"I told him I was tired." She leaned forward in the dark and he imagined her face, what it had. What did a face hold? Only more information, to help along a conclusion. Still the reality was that when they were apart, they were separate beings.

"He tried to convince me for another drink," she said. "I was flattered. He wanted me to stay with him."

He cleared his throat, thick from so much silence. "You're an attractive woman . . ."

"Middle-aged," she said. "They don't treat you that way anymore, at my age."

He realized he hadn't expected this, or feared it either. "I'll never know what happened to you, really," he said, as much to himself as to her.

"But nothing," she said too soon. "Really, just nothing."

It seemed to him they didn't spend enough time together. When he came home from work and they sat with gin and tonics, their conversation was good, encouraging, but not . . . he wasn't sure. Only that when she described her talks with Barbara, with Amy, they sounded more interesting. There was an energy that he seemed to miss, keep missing. As though she had things for these women she didn't have for him.

It came down to the boat, finally. Last summer they had bought a twenty-six-foot sloop with savings—it was that or work on the house. Now, their second summer, he was eager for them to be a family on the boat. The children were no problem. Elisabeth was a good sailor, a natural. Paul, though he was often sick on board, refused to leave even during the worst times.

It was different with her. She loved the boat, she said, but not as he did. Said she would cruise with the family but not just go out and sail in the harbor as he liked to do. That was dull. She had other things. He didn't need her company always. Couldn't he understand?

No, he could not understand. Beyond that, she should know. She'd seen him fool with the engine all winter. Seen him drive to the marina when the boat was in dry dock, just to look at it.

She said she understood he needed to unwind. He needed these weekends. But she needed her time too, and when he took the children to the boat she had her chance for privacy, for quiet . . . They were good enough words, and he thought he believed them. Their force carried him all the way to the harbor. Yet when he rowed out and climbed on board, prepared to get underway, he felt only that she belonged there with him.

So he argued. First he said he missed her. Then, when she wouldn't hear this, he said the other men with boats wondered about them. Other wives sailed. "People will think something's off in our marriage," he said. He was unable to keep the accusation from his voice.

"People will think!" she exploded. "Damn them, let them think what they want!"

"What do you have that's so important," he asked her.

The look on her face was like the one before she'd announced her trip alone. As though if he didn't understand, he should not ask. As if asking was the worst insult.

But he wanted to know.

If they were a family, if she was his partner, he reasoned, then they should be together on the boat. She had her days alone.

But those were for children and housework. It was the other

time, private time, that she needed. She reminded him that the boat made her seasick.

He reminded her that she behaved like a perfect fool on board, eating sardines and corn chips and drinking beer; taking Dramamine that only made her dizzy. "It's in your head," he said. "Psychosomatic."

The arguments silenced her to a point where she went grudgingly to the boat sometimes, whole-heartedly others. Still she accused him of an internal logic that tangled himself with the boat, her love of him with sailing. It wasn't so. She could separate these things, and God knew she wanted to. Couldn't he see she needed time for herself, after the pressures of family, of the town?

He caught himself wondering if there was another man. Stopped himself from wondering it.

In August they had planned a whole weekend on board, but she refused to go.

"This can't be," she said, pacing the length of the front windows. She stopped and looked out at the pine woods. "I'm lying to myself. To you. Sometimes I like sailing, but not so often as you. You can't force me to."

He looked at her standing there, her arms folded.

"The boat's become an issue," she said.

"Anything would be."

"But this is the one for us."

"I don't understand," he said.

She said she didn't expect understanding, but only tolerance. She wouldn't be pressured any more—"bullied," she called it. She accused him of failure of imagination. How could he want her on board, when she hated it?

"You won't give it a chance," he said.

"Damn it, what have I been doing all summer?"

When she left he sat in his brown leather chair and the house, his own house, felt like a stranger's. He was as uncomfortable there as an intruder. He reasoned with himself that their problem was an inability to live with differences. She was right, he couldn't understand her distaste for sailing. But he was right, too, in wanting to share what he loved most, with her.

He found her in bed, lying face down. It hurt him to see her bent, tense shoulders. He felt the loneliness and distance coiled in himself around the hollow it was making, had made. He didn't like feeling this way. "I'm going to the boat," he said.

She murmured something into the pillow.

He crossed the room and got his jacket, came back and sat on the edge of the bed to change his shoes. "I'll spend the night there."

"All right," came her voice from the pillow.

"It's not an argument," he said.

"I know."

"Just . . . something."

She didn't sit up. He stood, and with the jacket over his arm, bent and kissed her hair. He wanted to say more, but he was afraid of the words. They might become something he didn't mean.

It was a clear night, and the air was soft. He drove with the window rolled all the way down, feeling the air on his face. The moon was almost full and there were thin clouds around it. On the River Bridge he could see the harbor lights, and the stars as well. There was smoke coming from the factory.

What do I feel? he wondered, checking himself for feeling.

Down Kittery Point Road toward the harbor, he drove slowly looking at the houses with their lights and their dark lawns.

There were no other cars in the rental lot. As he walked along the dock with the oars on his shoulder, he listened to the bell buoy ringing out in the harbor. Water slapped on the dinghies and bumped them against one another. Their boat was moored quite far out, but he could see its beamy shape from where he stood.

The water was calm, and in the quiet, feeling the tug of the oars against the tide, he felt himself almost to be a trespasser. Still the secret feeling was a good one. Even in the dark, this was a world he knew.

Their boat rocked in the night like a seed pod, moonlight on her decks. When he crawled on board and tied up the dinghy, he felt something hard and tense let go inside him. The boat was an island and he was safe on it. He knew everything, here. If anyone came, he would hear the creak and groan of their oars in the locks. Even she would have to come that way.

As he unlocked the cabin, pulling the boards from its opening, he thought how privacy was what he'd wanted. He wondered if she understood that. Not to get away from her, or from the chil-

dren either. Just to go to what he knew. The boat was the best
place. All the work of painting and repairing, he had done himself. The damned winches had had to be ordered from England
since the boat was English in design—made for the Channel—and
he'd done that too. He smiled. He had done all that.

He sat and lit a cigarette, wondering what she thought now.
Imagining her, he found in himself a smugness that was surprising. He had been thinking: now you will understand how it felt,
to stand on the lawn and watch you drive off to Nova Scotia. To
leave us. He had been thinking it all the way to the harbor, his
arm out the window. That she was getting hers, now.

That was detestable. It said things he didn't want. Said how
much he was hurt by her travelling without him. More than that,
how resentful. But the worst thing it said, was that he wanted to
punish her. He hadn't known that, didn't want to know it now.

He felt the boat rocking. Usually the harbor sounds relaxed
him. All the noises of water, metal, and wood. And over his shoulder, the rotating beam of the Coast Guard Lighthouse. He liked
all of it. But like wasn't enough. Loved it, by God. It was home to
him. And she didn't love it.

The resentment was gone, not because he'd wished it but only
because it was worn away. That was a small part anyhow, not substantially true of his feeling for her.

He wondered what was true, then. The emptiness he had felt
when he looked at her lying on the bed? Yes. The hollowness?
That too. Not only true, but growing in the last year. She was
changing. More of her was secret to him than had ever been. Her
fire had always been a mystery, but a wonderful one. And now
there was this . . .

So a man had to wonder what to do. He thought of the children. In the last year he'd loved them not less, but more.

He tossed the cigarette into the water. It made a curve of red
light, then it was gone.

Do I want a woman? he asked himself. But he knew the answer. They were different, she and he, but he loved her. Perhaps
even more for the way she pointed up their differences.

He thought that maybe for him it was this night alone on the
boat, just as for her it was that time in Nova Scotia. Well, if that
was so, she had courage then. He had to admire her courage.
What else could it be, to risk him and the children, to drive off

alone such as no woman her age ever did, certainly nobody in
town? The risks of middle age were less dramatic, but then the
stakes were higher. He was alone, now. Still, he thought, in going
to what we love, we don't deny anything. When he looked, the
boat had shifted in the tide so that the main mast seemed about
to pierce the moon.

XMAS

THOMAS M. DISCH

Thomas M. Disch was raised in Minnesota, and now lives
in New York City. A collection of stories, *Getting into
Death*, was published by Alfred A. Knopf; a novel, *On
Wings of Song*, has just appeared.

It was December 12 and the Christmas coming up looked like it
was going to be the worst yet, a catastrophe. He began to get in
more and more of a state about it. The Geritol jingle from the Six
O'Clock News formed a tape-loop in his head and played itself
over and over. Make every day count. Do what you really want to
do. Every day every day every day.

Partly the problem was being stuck here in the heart of the
woeful Midwest, the American Siberia. Because he was divorced,
the company considered him more deployable than his married
colleagues. He'd been posted to four branches in as many years.
Each new posting represented a step up the ladder but even so.
This time at least he was returning somewhere, and if it wasn't
anywhere he'd have *chosen* to return to, he could take comfort
that it wasn't as alien as Anchorage, which had been one of the alternatives. Here there were faces he could recognize, names he
could remember, addresses still extant in his address book.

That was the other part of the problem. None of these names
and faces bore thinking of. He had run out of friends. Not just
here but everywhere, in the whole creation. Practically speaking
he'd become a misanthrope. Certainly he'd never intended to, and
he had no theory to back up his spontaneous dislike of the people
he knew. It had just sneaked up on him gradually over the years,
like baldness.

Last Christmas it had reached the point where he'd received only a single present that could be considered a gift of friendship, and in the ensuing year the friend who'd given it to him had totaled his new Buick and himself in a collision on the Santa Monica freeway. This Christmas, therefore, there would be no booty under the tree, no stuffing in his stocking, nobody in the whole world to care. It was gross to make such reckonings, it was embarrassing, but it was true. Christmas was coming at him like the searchlight in pursuit of an escaped convict, ready to expose the mess he'd made of his life.

It wasn't fair. At almost any other time he was rather contented, not to say smug, with the shape that his life—meaning, his career—had taken. He liked his work, he did it well, and he was making good money. But all through Advent his success had a distinct aftertaste of ashes. Better an underling and swaddled in love than a vice president and alone for the holidays. If he'd wanted to build a crèche, it would have represented not the stable in Bethlehem but Herod's palace, with lots of little plaster statuettes of Herod's staff and secretaries.

It shouldn't have made such a difference. Other people in his position seemed to glide by Yuletide with just a few bahs and humbugs. It shouldn't but it did. He'd been the oldest child in a large family, and the drama of gathering the various branches and generations together for solemn unwrappings around the Christmas tree had been a major one. It wasn't just getting; it even transcended the slightly less suspect pleasure of giving, for he could be aroused by the wholly impersonal tableau of his cousin Dolly opening presents from people he'd never heard of. And then, the next morning, there'd been the ever-lovely fiction of presents from Santa, a pretense he'd maintained well into adolescence for the sake of his younger brothers. That golden age was gone, irretrievably. His parents had died, and his brothers had chosen to contest a will that had given him a firstborn's (or lion's) share, including the house. His lawyers had won the case, and he'd sold the house to a developer for a spitefully low price, with the result that there was no chance, now or ever, of flying back home to horn in on his brothers' festivities. The house had become a Methadone clinic.

It was the twelfth and then the thirteenth and every store window in this frozen city's lamentable downtown reproached him for not being part of the human race. Santa's elves hammered with manic, unflagging industry in the windows of Evans & McDowell's, while in the rival department store across the street a ballerina performed a perpetual pirouette, touching with her gilded wand gift after gift after gift whose sweet mysteries he would never see unveiled. A pair of gloves? Stereo earphones? A deluxe edition of Monopoly? Whatever, they were not for him and he would never know.

He thought of buying presents for himself but that smacked too patently of self-pity and, what was worse, futility.

Still, there was one little charity he might perform that would not go unappreciated. He stopped at his liquor store on the way home and asked for a bottle of Chivas Regal and one of Cordon Bleu.

"I'm afraid we're out of Christmas boxes for the Chivas," the clerk said.

He assured him it would be all right, that he'd use his own gift wrap, and at the stationery shop next door he did buy a long tube of their most expensive gold-foil wrap and two big stick-on bows of simulated red ribbon.

At home he wrapped the two boxed bottles carefully and put them away in the hall closet. He meant to unwrap them and drink them on Christmas Eve.

On the fifteenth he bought a gigantic Scotch pine. Mrs. Lurkey, the super's wife, seeing him wrestle it into the elevator, thanked him for his check and wished him a merry Christmas.

"The same to you," he shouted, just as the doors chomped together on the lowest branches of his twenty-dollar pine.

He was up till after midnight decorating the thing. Balls, lights, garlands, tinsel, and an antique Art Deco angel on the top.

When he was done he sank back on his recliner and thought: "There, that does it. I've exorcised Christmas. *I'm* in control."

But he lay awake that night remembering past Christmases in obsessive detail—the presents he'd got and the presents he'd given, the different turkeys and the single underdone goose.

He was forty-three years old. Every day did *not* count. He did *not* do what he really wanted to. Every day every day every day.

Next morning on the way into the office and altogether against his principles he dropped ten dollars into a Salvation Army pot. He thought it might help.

His secretary had sorted his mail, as requested, into actual business and seasons greetings, of which there were twelve, eight from underlings, three from superiors, and one from his opposite number in the Cincinnati office. He read the texts that various employees of Hallmark and Norcross and UNICEF had written to print on the blank insides of their cards. Harley Krueger wished him:

> A wonderful world of
> good wishes for the
> HOLIDAY SEASON.

Mrs. Palmer, of Accounting, offered this thought:

> Every gift of love to our neighbors
> is a gift of peace to our world.

And Ted and Vita Milstein saluted him with a multilingual:

> Seasons Greetings
> Meilleurs Voeux
> Felices Fiesta
> C HoBblm Toaom.

They all went into his attache case, and that night he propped them up under the tree, a little paper fortress to guard him from his doom.

On the evening of the eighteenth, with Christmas only a week away, he began to imagine friends, friends who would (if they'd been real) have given him the presents he wasn't going to get, friends who cherished his good qualities and forgave his faults. This required, in order to formulate such friends with any exactness, that he ask himself what his good qualities and his faults were.

He couldn't think of any, in either category.

Wasn't it, he wondered, a fault in itself that he didn't like other people more than he did? In college he'd had lots of friends. He'd been a pre-med and palled around with other pre-meds. Then, in his senior year, someone, he never found out who, sabotaged a crucial organic chemistry experiment, and someone else (he suspected his roommate) had swiped all his notebooks a week before the finals. He didn't get into med school. (In fairness it must be said that even without treachery his would have been a borderline case.) After that, working at this job and that job, he'd formed a few tentative friendships, although he tended to think of Ralph and Bob and Terry even then more as "acquaintances" or at best "colleagues." He'd had a wife, and a mistress, sort of, both very beautiful and both rather limited intellectually, putting it kindly. Such love as he'd felt for them was of the obsessive, grabbing kind. He'd never thought of women as potential friends, understanding and understood, but rather as mysterious bosomy embodiments of Otherness.

He was lonely. Of course. But he'd come to think of loneliness as a necessary attribute of manhood, the moral corollary of being clearheaded. Being clearheaded, he couldn't help being aware that the people he knew were shits. There might be people elsewhere in the world who were not. He had no theoretical reason for supposing that there weren't. But he had yet to meet them.

As to the propriety or sanity of inventing his own alternatives, that gave him no concern. From his earliest years, when he had governed the complex fates of two families of multicolored bowling pins, his fantasy life had been hyperactive. In later years his unreal friends had usually been females who differed from each other chiefly with respect to their sexual proclivities, but at least he'd kept in practice, and even then he was capable of daydreaming long James Bondish adventures on which blond Trina or even raven-haired Rebecca would accompany him, adventures in which sex figured only peripherally. He had no qualms: it could be done.

The first friend to be hypothesized was John Bartram Hall, who was now seventy and living in retirement in Savannah, Georgia, with two Negro servants and a stamp collection of exceptional rarity. Hall would have been his first boss, assuming he'd gone to work at Meinhard-Commercial, as he'd seriously considered doing in his last weeks of grad school. His real-life bosses had been little more than rednecks in business suits, true believers in football, Goldwater, and flying saucers. Their only merit had been a coarseness of wit so genuine that they never knew till much too late when they'd been outmaneuvered in the brushes and skirmishes of middle-management politics. John Bartram Hall, by contrast, was a man of culture, a bon vivant, a gentleman. He was solicitous of his protégé in an avuncular way and anxious to remedy the defects of his false-genteel suburban upbringing and an education topheavy with science and math. He selected his shoes and censored his ties and helped him get an American Express card when his first application had been refused. He bullied him into reading grown-up books and made him sit down and listen to the three M's—Mozart, Monteverdi, and Mahler. They talked about important things. They were friends. Once (to mark his retirement) Hall took him on a four-day holiday to Las Vegas where he proceeded to lose a bundle with the most gentlemanly aplomb.

There was something uneasy-making about this first friendship, a distinct undercurrent of something latent and unmentionable, that prompted him to fashion, perhaps too hastily, an Eve for his Adam. He called her Weena Jessel, after Weena of *Green Mansions* and Mary Jessel whom he'd lusted after uselessly all through eleventh grade. Weena was an ex-callgirl who now worked as a beautician and dealt dope. He'd first met her, or would have, late in '68, as his marriage was breaking up. Weena was Venus the goddess of Love, manic and langorous, all-accommodating yet fiercely independent, a centerfold come to life. Through her he'd discovered his own deepest feelings. Through him she'd found the strength to leave her life of degradation. Basically, Weena was Jane Fonda in *Klute*, minus the dialogue. It wasn't so much that she was stupid (though she would accuse herself of that from time to time) but rather that she was overprotective of her tenuous, never entirely expressible thoughts. Occasionally, in an odd remark or in one of the sad little watercolors she painted of doll-faced modistes and pink ballerinas, he could glimpse the possibility of a finer Weena trapped inside this one, a Weena, alas, lost forever in a haze of drugs.

He became fascinated with the way his fantasy, like a hooked fish invisible beneath his boat, seemed to have a life of its own. Deliberately he let it run with his line. Weena (it developed) was really rather dull! It was all very well to respect her potentialities but in the here and now, except when they had sex, Weena was about as interesting as a dead TV screen. Trying to carry on a conversation with her was like trying to talk to seaweed. It was like being married all over again.

One night, the nineteenth of December, he arranged to meet

her at the diner across from the beauty shop where she worked. He never showed up. Weena waited two hours and then slowly, sadly, walked home through the snow.

It's hard to make friends, even imaginary friends, and harder still to keep them. Something, his reality principle or his death-wish, kept intruding, like a vengeful witch cursing each newly fledged friend with warts and foibles and fatal flaws of character. Lolah Silverberg was his most painful disappointment in this respect, for she had seemed at first the most promising of his creations, virtually a new direction for his hopes to move in, a Grail to go off in quest of.

Lolah was the polar opposite of Weena. She was homely, but homely, like George Eliot or Virginia Woolf, in a manner associated with abundance of character. Not Venus but gray-eyed Athena. Not only could you talk to her, you could listen. She had ideas, beliefs, a sense of humor. What's more, she could cope. After years of teaching she was now an assistant principal in one of the city's toughest junior high schools. Like himself, she was divorced. By mutual unspoken agreement they never discussed their ex's. She lived with her two teenaged daughters, Alice and Emma, in the same apartment building on a higher floor. Often he'd go up the firestairs late at night to play long, guilty games of Monopoly with them, till two or three in the morning. They were happy just being together. He began to wonder (in his fantasy) if he were in love.

If so, that love was not returned, for suddenly Lolah began to avoid him, suddenly she was always in a hurry somewhere else. Once, on Adams Street, she'd seen him approaching from the opposite direction and—obviously to avoid the chance encounter—had stooped down, pretending to lace a shoe. (That had happened to him in real life, in Omaha.) Her daughters would answer the phone and say that Lolah wasn't there and could they take a message. He knew they were lying and that they were under orders to. What had he done to deserve it? Was it because he'd criticized her for letting Alice and Emma subscribe to an astrology magazine? Because he made jokes about her affecting to be part Cherokee? Could she be so petty? In any case he'd sent her an imaginary letter apologizing for these slights. It was more basic: he had begun to bore her. No, it was something still worse and more serious, something rooted in his nature, something he couldn't imagine.

He'd known from the very start that the last of his friends, Peter Snyder, was a son-of-a-bitch. A thin, red-haired parrot of a man, vain as a mirror, Peter considered himself a kind of Count of Monte Cristo with a score to settle against the world at large. He wrote (this much was a fact) the movie reviews for the *Evening Star-Courier*, as intemperate and mean-spirited a column as one could find this side of John Simon. Through all of 1975 the only movie he had anything good to say about was *Jaws*. There were people (he was one) who took the *Star-Courier* just for the spectacle of Snyder's savage tongue. He was also a sponge: of food, of booze, of books, of whatever he could wangle. He would even make jokes about it, as though to show that he was on your side, after all.

They'd met at a party that Lolah had taken him to, and over the next weeks he'd graduated from being one of the admiring throng to the status of an old pal thanks to an apparently ungrudging willingness to provide all the flattery and the free drinks that Snyder required. The quid for this quo was that he got to be a witness to the man's kamikaze assaults on other subjects than the movies. Watergate, naturally, had been his heyday, but with half a bottle of B.&L. under his belt (Snyder was not, bless him, picky about labels) there was nothing that wasn't grist for his mill. He would assassinate the characters of his friends or complain about the weather or ridicule the pretensions of the restaurant he was being taken to, all with an equanimity that was equal to his eloquence.

He was not such a fool as to suppose that Peter Snyder *liked* him, or that he liked Snyder. He thought of him rather as a cellmate in the world's prison, one who made the time pass better than most, but a criminal essentially, a person not to be trusted.

If there was anything worse than being Peter Snyder it was being Peter Snyder's sycophant, and that's what he'd become.

At this point he stopped inventing imaginary friends.

It was the night before Christmas. Besides the liquor and the Christmas cards there were four presents under the tree: a present from John Bartram Hall, a present from Weena Jessel, a present from Lolah Silverberg, and a present from Peter Snyder. They were wrapped in gold foil paper but they lacked bows. Weena's was the smallest, about the size of a box of Anacin, and Peter's the largest, the size of a brick.

Not yet, he told himself. Later.

He broke out the Chivas and put on a record from his album of Handel's *Messiah*. "Oh, we like sheep!" the chorus announced cheerily. "Oh, we like sheep!" He'd made a mistake. Instead of the opening Nativity section he'd hit the Crucifixion. But it sounded pretty in a tinkly way that suited the occasion just as well, even when the chorus was laughing Christ to scorn. "Oh, we like sheep! Oh, we like sheep!" The lights on the tree seemed to blink on and off in time to the music. He drank a toast to George Frederick Handel.

The phone rang.

He turned down the volume and answered it by the third ring. A woman wished him a merry Christmas. Her name was Janet, and she'd dialed a wrong number. He tried to keep her on the phone with small talk but she grew uneasy. He proposed marriage and hung up.

When he turned the volume back up, the tenor was just starting the recitative that goes, "He was cut off out of the land of the living. . . ." And even that Handel made to seem halfway cheerful.

The record played over and over. He'd neglected to lower the arm of the changer.

At midnight he thought, "Now's the time to open the presents."

But next morning they were still intact underneath the big red wool stocking hanging limply from the arm of the recliner. Oddly, he did not feel hungover. He'd only dozed off for four hours, so maybe he was still drunk. Half of the brandy was left and a smidgeon of scotch. He put off opening the presents till later and watched a non-denominational church service while he soaked in the tub. Children in red choir robes walked about with candles, singing shrill carols.

He made a very simple stuffing for the turkey, nothing but breadcrumbs, butter, celery, onion, and seasonings. It weighed twelve pounds and it went into the oven at ten-thirty. That meant, according to Fanny Farmer, that it should come out at two-thirty or three.

The pie came from a local bakery. He could pop it in the oven when the bird came out. Nothing else required much in the way of preparation. There would be instant mashed potatoes, yams from a can, and frozen peas, all of which could be done at the last minute. Simple but sufficient. The important thing was to uphold tradition.

There was nothing but dreck on the television, and he still didn't feel like opening the presents, so he occupied the time by doing his next year's taxes.

All the while it had cooked it had smelled terrific, but now, sitting there on the table, and sitting there himself before it, he had no appetite at all. He'd put on the *Messiah* again, careful this time to start with side One. He just sat there like a marble allegory of Abundance all through "Comfort ye my people (saith your God)" without lifting the carving knife or looking up from the poinsettias on his paper napkin.

He felt iniquitous and utterly cast down.

Was there no way to combat Christmas? Must it make him wretched over and over all through his life?

Or, as the countertenor put it, rather more pointedly: Who may abide the day of His coming? Who shall stand when He appeareth?

Slowly and reverently, in strict time to the contralto's joyful air ("O thou that tellest good tidings to Zion"), he began to stab the golden turkey in its moist, plump breast.

Later, after he'd cleaned up most of the mess, and feeling cleansed himself and radiant and free, he fed the scraps of his sacrifice into the incinerator. Along with it went the presents from his four imaginary friends. He'd never opened them and he would never know how they had meant to surprise him.

THE GIRL ACROSS THE ROOM

ALICE ADAMS

Alice Adams grew up in Chapel Hill, North Carolina, and
graduated from Radcliffe; since then she has lived mostly
in San Francisco. Her third novel, *Listening to Billie*, was
published by Knopf in January 1978; a collection of stories,
Beautiful Girl, appeared in January 1979. This is her ninth
O. Henry inclusion.

Yvonne Soulas, the art historian, is much more beautiful in her
late sixties than she was when she was young, and this is strange,
because she has had much trouble in her life, including pancreatic
cancer, through which she lived when no one expected her to.
Neither her doctor nor her husband, Matthew Vann, the musicol-
ogist-manufacturer, thought she would make it, such a small, thin
woman. Make it she did, however, although she lost much of her
hair in the process of treatment. Now, seated with Matthew on
the porch of an inn on the northern-California coast, her fine, precise features framed in skillfully arranged false white waves, she is
a lovely woman. In the cool spring night she is wearing soft pale
woollen clothes, a shawl, and Italian boots, daintily stitched.

Matthew Vann is also a handsome person, with silky white hair
and impressive dark eyes, and he, too, wears elegant clothes. His
posture is distinguished. Yvonne has never taken his name, not for
feminist reasons but because she thinks the combination is
unaesthetic: Yvonne Vann? Matthew looks and is considerably
more fragile than Yvonne, although they are about the same age:
that is to say, among other things, of an age to wonder which of
them will outlive the other. The question is impossible, inadmis-
sible, and crucially important. Matthew *is* frailer, but then,
Yvonne's illness could recur at any time.

They have been married for a little over thirty years, and they
live, these days, in San Francisco, having decided that the rigors
of New England winters and the overstimulation of Cambridge
social life were, in combination, far too much for them. Trips to
Europe, also, formerly a source of much pleasure, now seem, really, more strenuous than fun. And so Yvonne and Matthew have
taken to exploring certain areas of California, beginning with the
near at hand: Yosemite, Lake Tahoe, and now this extraordinarily
beautiful stretch of coast at Mendocino, where rivers empty into
the sea between sheer cliffs of rock.

They are sitting at the far end of the white-railed porch that
runs the length of the building in which they are lodging. They
have had an early dinner, hoping for quiet, and they are tired
from a day of exploring the town and the meadows high above
the vibrating sea. The other guests are almost all golfing people,
since there is a course adjacent to the inn. They are people in late
middle age, a little younger than Yvonne and Matthew, mostly
overweight, tending to noise and heavy smoking and excessive
drink. Not pleasant dinner companions. And Yvonne and
Matthew were successful: they finished a quiet dinner of excellent
abalone before the boisterous arrival of the golfing group. There
was only one other couple in the dining room. That other couple
had also been distinctly not a part of the golfing group, and they
were as striking, in their way, as Yvonne and Matthew were in
theirs. Yvonne had been unable not to stare at them—the girl so
young and perfectly controlled in all her gestures, the man much
older than the girl, so clearly and happily in love with her. It
won't end well, Yvonne had thought.

Everything is fine, as they sit now on the porch. This place to
which they have come is very beautiful. The walks through wild
flowers and the views back to the river mouth, the beaches, the
opposite banks of green are all marvellous. Everything is fine, except for a nagging area of trouble that has just lodged itself somewhere near Yvonne's heart. But the trouble is quite irrational, and
she is an eminently sensible woman, and so she pushes it aside
and begins a conversation with Matthew about something else.

"A thing that I like about being old," she observes to him, at
the same time as she reflects that many of their conversations
have had just this beginning, "is that you go on trips for their own
sake, just to see something. Not expecting the trip to change your

life." Not hoping that the man you are with will want to marry you, she is thinking to herself, or that Italy will cure your husband of a girl.

"Ye-e-es," drawls Matthew, in his vague New Hampshire way. But he is a good listener; he very much enjoys her conversation. "Yvonne is the least boring person in the world," he has often said—if not to her, to a great many other people.

"When you're young, you really don't see much beyond yourself," Yvonne muses.

Then, perhaps at having spoken the word "young," thinking of young people, of herself much younger, the trouble increases. It becomes an active heavy pressure on her heart, so that she closes her eyes for a moment. Then she opens them, facing it, admitting to herself: That girl in the dining room reminded me of Susanna, in Cambridge, almost thirty years ago. Not long after we were married, which of course made it worse.

What happened was this:

In the late forties, in Cambridge, Yvonne was viewed as a smart, attractive, but not really pretty Frenchwoman. A widow? Divorced? No one knew for sure. She had heavy dark hair, a husky voice, and a way of starting sentences with an "Ah!" that sounded like a tiny bark. Some people were surprised to find her married to Matthew Vann, a glamorous man, admired for having fought in Spain as well as for his great good looks, a man as distinguished as he was rich. Then a beautiful young Radcliffe girl who wanted to become a dancer, and for all anyone knew eventually became one —a golden California girl, Susanna—fell in love with Matthew, and he with her. But Yvonne wouldn't let him go, and so nothing came of it. That was all.

Thus went the story that circulated like a lively winter germ through the areas of Cambridge adjacent to Harvard Square, up and down Brattle Street, Linnaean, Garden Street, and Massachusetts Avenue, and finally over to Hillside Place, where Yvonne and Matthew then were living.

But that is not, exactly, how it was. It went more like this:

"You won't believe me, but I think a very young girl has fallen in love with me," Matthew said to Yvonne one night, near the end of their dinner of *lapin au moutarde*, a specialty of Yvonne's which she always thenceforward connected unpleasantly with that night, although she continued to make it from time to time. (Silly not to, really.) Then Matthew laughed, a little awkward, embarrassed. "It does seem unlikely."

"Not at all." Yvonne's tone was light, the words automatic. Her accent was still very French. "You are a most handsome man," she said.

"You might remember her. We met her at the Emorys'. Susanna something, from California. I've kept seeing her in Widener, and now she says she wants to help me with my research." He laughed, more embarrassed yet.

Yvonne experienced a wave of fury, which she quickly brought under control, breathing regularly and taking a small sip of wine. Of course she remembered the girl: long dark-gold hair and sunny, tawny skin; bad clothes, but not needing good clothes with that long lovely neck; a stiff, rather self-conscious dancer's walk; lovely long hands, beautifully controlled. Anyone would fall in love with her.

In those days, while Yvonne did her own work at the Fogg, Matthew was combining supervision of the factory he had inherited, in Waltham, with the musicologist's career that he had chosen. The research he had mentioned was for his book on Boccherini, for which they would later spend a year in Italy. They had married after a wildly passionate affair, during which Yvonne had managed to wrest Matthew away from poor Flossie, his alcoholic first wife, now long since dead in Tennessee.

And, thinking over the problem of Susanna, one thing that Yvonne said silently to her rival was: You can't have him, I've already been through too much for Matthew. Also, in her exceptionally clearheaded way, Yvonne *knew* Matthew, in a way that violent love can sometimes preclude. She knew that he would not take Susanna to bed unless he had decided to break with Yvonne —this out of a strong and somewhat aberrant New England sense of honor, and also out of sexual shyness, unusual in so handsome, so sensual a man. Yvonne herself had had to resort to a kind of seduction by force. But a young, proud girl could not know of such tactics.

Yvonne was right. Matthew did not have an affair with Susanna; he probably never saw her outside of Widener, except for an intense cup of coffee at Hayes-Bickford, where they were noticed together. However, Matthew suffered severely, and that was how Yvonne treated him—like someone with a serious disease. She was affectionate and solicitous, and very slightly distant, as though his illness were something that she didn't want to catch.

One March evening, after a bright, harsh day of intermittent sun, rain, and wind, Matthew came home for dinner a little late, with a look on his face of total and anguished exhaustion. Handing him his gin—they were in the kitchen; she had been tasting her good lamb stew, a *navarin*—Yvonne thought, Ah, the girl has broken it off, or has given him an ultimatum; such a mistake. She thought, I hope I won't have to hear about it.

All Matthew said during dinner was "The Boccherini project is sort of getting me down. My ideas don't come together."

"Poor darling," she said carefully, alertly watching his face.

"I should spend more time at the factory."

"Well, why don't you?"

As they settled in the living room for coffee, Yvonne saw that his face had relaxed a little. Perhaps now he would want to talk to her? She said, "There's a Fred Astaire revival at the U.T. tonight. I know you don't like them, but would you mind if I go? Ah, dear, it's almost time."

Not saying: You unspeakable fool, how dare you put me through all this? Are you really worth it?

Alone in the crowded balcony of the University Theatre, as on the screen Fred and Ginger sang to each other about how lovely a day it was to be caught in the rain, Yvonne thought, for a moment, that she would after all go home and tell Matthew to go to his girl, Susanna. She would release him, with as little guilt as possible, since she was indeed fond of Matthew. *Je tiens à Matthew.*

Tenir à. I hold to Matthew, Yvonne thought then. And she also thought, No, it would not work out well at all. Matthew is much too vulnerable for a girl like that. He is better off with me.

Of course she was right, as Matthew himself must have come to realize, and over the summer he seemed to recover from his affliction. Yvonne saw his recovery, but she also understood that she had been seriously wounded by that episode, coming as it did so early in their life together. Afterward she was able to think more sensibly, Well, much better early than later on, when he could have felt more free.

That fall they left for Italy, where, curiously, neither of them had been before—Yvonne because her Anglophile parents had always taken her to the Devon coast on holidays, or sometimes to Scotland, Matthew because with drunken Flossie any travel was impossible.

They settled in a small hotel in Rome, in a large romantically alcoved room that overlooked the Borghese Gardens. They went on trips: north to Orvieto, Todi, Spoleto, Gubbio; south to Salerno, Positano, Ravello. They were dazed, dizzy with pleasure at the landscape, the vistas of olive orchards, of pines and flowers and stones, the ancient buildings, the paintings and statuary. The food and wine. They shared a mania for pasta.

A perfect trip, except that from time to time Yvonne was jolted sharply by a thought of that girl, Susanna. And, looking at Matthew, she wondered if he, too, thought of her—with sadness, regret? The question hurt.

She would have to ask Matthew, and deliberately she chose a moment of pure happiness. They were seated on a vine-covered terrace, at Orvieto, across the square from the gorgeously striped cathedral, drinking cool white wine, having made love early that morning, when Yvonne asked, "Do you ever wonder what happened to that girl, Susanna?"

Genuine puzzlement appeared on Matthew's distinguished face, and then he said, "I almost never think of her. I don't have time."

Knowing Matthew, Yvonne was sure that he spoke the truth, and she wryly thought, I undoubtedly think more often of that girl, that episode, than Matthew does.

And so she, too, stopped thinking of Susanna—or almost, except for an occasional reminder.

Leaving Rome, they travelled up to Florence, then Venice, Innsbruck, and Vienna—where Boccherini did, or quite possibly did not, murder his rival, Mozart.

That was the first of a succession of great trips.

Yvonne and Matthew remained, for the most part, very happy with each other, and over the years their sexual life declined only slightly. Then, in her late fifties, Yvonne became terribly sick, at first undiagnosably so. Surgery was indicated. On being told the probable nature of her illness—she had insisted on that—Yvonne remarked to her doctor, one of the chief surgeons at Massachusetts General, "Well, my chances are not exactly marvellous, then, are they?"

He looked embarrassed, and gazed in the direction of the Charles, just visible from his high office window. "No, not marvellous," he admitted.

After surgery, oppressively drugged, Yvonne was mainly aware of pain, which surged in heavy waves toward her, almost overwhelming her, and very gradually receding. She was aware, too, of being handled a great deal, not always gently, of needles inserted, and tubes, of strong hands manipulating her small body.

Sometimes, half conscious, she would wonder if she was dreaming. But at least she knew that she was alive: dead people don't wonder about anything, she was sure of that.

The first face that she was aware of was her surgeon's: humorless, stern, seeming always to be saying, No, not marvellous. Then there was the face of a black nurse, kind and sad, a gentle, mourning face. At last she saw Matthew, so gaunt and stricken that she knew she had to live. It was that simple: dying was something she could not do to Matthew.

"She's got to be the strongest woman I've ever seen, basically," the dubious surgeon remarked later on to Matthew, who by then could beamingly agree.

Chemotherapy worked; it took most of her hair but fortunately did not make her sick. Yvonne very gradually regained strength, and some health, and with a great effort she put back on a few of the many lost pounds. Matthew learned to make a superior *fettuccine*, and he served it to her often.

After her illness and surgery, they did not make love anymore; they just did not. Yvonne missed it, in a dim sad way, but on the other hand she could sometimes smile at the very idea of such a ludicrous human activity, to which she herself had once devoted so much time. She was on the whole amused and a little skeptical of accounts of very sexually active seventy- and eighty-year-olds: why did they bother, really?

While she was recuperating, Yvonne finished a study of Marie Laurencin that she had been working on for years, and her book had considerable acclaim, even reasonably good sales. Matthew did not finish his Boccherini study, but from time to time he published articles in places like the *Yale Review*, the *Virginia Quarterly Review*.

A year ago, they left Cambridge and moved to the pleasant flat on Green Street, in San Francisco.

Now, on the porch in Mendocino, thinking of the girl across the room at dinner, and remembering Susanna, all that pain, Yvonne has a vivid insight as to how it would have been if she had abandoned Matthew to Susanna all those years ago. Matthew would, of course, have married the girl—that is how he is—and they would have been quite happy for a while. He would have gazed dotingly upon her in restaurants, like the man in the dining room, with his Susanna. And then somehow it would all have gone bad, with a sad old age for Matthew, the girl bored and irritable, Matthew worn out, not understanding anything.

But what of herself? What would have happened to her? The strange part is that Yvonne has never inquired into this before. Now, with perfect logic, she suddenly, jarringly sees just what would have happened: for a while, considerable unhappiness for her, a slow recovery. And then she would have been quite herself again, maybe a little improved. She would have remarried—amazing, she can almost see him! He is no one she knows, but a man much younger than herself, very dark. In fact, he is French; they have many intimate things in common. He might be a painter. He is very unlike Matthew. Would she still have had her great illness? She is not sure; her vision ends with that man, her marriage to him.

Something in her expression, probably, has made Matthew ask a question never asked between them, a question, in fact, for adolescent lovers: "What were you thinking about, just now?"

And he is given, by Yvonne, the requisite response: "I was thinking, my darling, of you. At least in part."

The air on the porch is perceptibly chillier than when they first came out from dinner. Time to go in, and yet they are both reluctant to move: it is so beautiful where they are. In the distance, gray-white lines of foam cross the sea, beneath a calm pale evening sky; closer to hand are the surrounding, sheltering pines and cypresses.

Then, from whatever uncharacteristic moment of strong emotion, Matthew says another thing that he has not said before. "I was thinking," he says, "that without you I would not have had much of a life at all."

Does he mean if they had never met? Or does he mean if he had left her for that girl, for fair Susanna? Or if she had died? It is impossible to ask, and so Yvonne frowns, unseen, in the gathering dusk—both at the ambiguity and at the surprise of it. And she, too, says something new: "Ah, Matthew, what an absolute fool you are." But she has said it lightly, and she adds, "You would have got along perfectly well without me." She knows that out of her true fondness for Matthew she has lied, and that it is still necessary for her to survive him.

MAGAZINES CONSULTED

Antaeus
Ecco Press—1 West 30th Street, New York, N.Y. 10001
Antioch Review
P. O. Box 148, Yellow Springs, Ohio 45387
Ararat
Armenian General Benevolent Union of America, 628 Second Avenue, New York, N.Y. 10016
Arizona Quarterly
University of Arizona, Tucson, Ariz. 85721
Ark River Review
c/o Anthony Sobin, English Department, Wichita State University, Wichita, Kan. 67208
Ascent
English Department, University of Illinois, Urbana, Ill. 61801
The Atlantic
8 Arlington Street, Boston, Mass. 02116
Bachy
11317 Santa Monica Boulevard, Los Angeles, Calif. 90025
Bennington Review
Bennington College, Bennington, Vt. 05201
Berkeley Poets Collective
P. O. Box 459, Berkeley, Calif. 94701
Boston University Journal
704 Commonwealth Avenue, Boston, Mass. 02215
California Quarterly
100 Sproul Hall, University of California, Davis, Calif. 95616
Canadian Fiction Magazine
P. O. Box 46422, Station G, Vancouver, B.C., Canada V6R 4G7
Canto
11 Bartlett Street, Andover, Mass. 01810
Carleton Miscellany
Carleton College, Northfield, Minn. 55057

Carolina Quarterly
    Box 1117, Chapel Hill, N.C. 27515
The Chariton Review
    Division of Language & Literature, Northeast Missouri State
    University, Kirksville, Mo. 63501
Chicago Review
    Faculty Exchange, Box C, University of Chicago, Chicago,
    Ill. 60637
Christopher Street
    60 West 13th Street, New York, N.Y. 10011
Colorado Quarterly
    Hellums 134, University of Colorado, Boulder, Colo. 80309
Confrontation
    English Department, Brooklyn Center of Long Island Uni-
    versity, Brooklyn, N.Y. 11201
Cornell Review
    108 North Plain Street, Ithaca, N.Y. 14850
Cosmopolitan
    224 West 57th Street, New York, N.Y. 10019
Crucible
    Atlantic Christian College, Wilson, N.C. 27893
Cumberlands
    Pikeville College, Pikeville, Ky. 41501
December
    P. O. Box 274, Western Springs, Ill. 60558
The Denver Quarterly
    Dept. of English, University of Denver, Denver, Colo. 80210
Descant
    Dept. of English, TCU Station, Fort Worth, Tex. 76129
Epoch
    254 Goldwyn Smith Hall, Cornell University, Ithaca, N.Y.
    14853
Esquire
    488 Madison Avenue, New York, N.Y. 10022
The Falcon
    Bilknap Hall, Mansfield State College, Mansfield, Pa. 16933
Fantasy and Science Fiction
    Box 56, Cornwall, Conn. 06753
The Fault
    33513 6th Street, Union City, Calif. 94538

Fiction
    c/o Dept. of English, The City College of New York, N.Y.
    10031
Fiction International
    Dept. of English, St. Lawrence University, Canton, N.Y.
    13617
Fiction*Texas
    College of the Mainland, Texas City, Tex. 77590
The Fiddlehead
    The Observatory, University of New Brunswick, P. O. Box
    4400, Fredericton, N.B., Canada E3B 5A3
Forum
    Ball State University, Muncie, Ind. 47306
Four Quarters
    La Salle College, Philadelphia, Pa. 19141
GPU News
    c/o The Farwell Center, 1568 N. Farwell, Milwaukee, Wis.
    53202
Georgia Review
    University of Georgia, Athens, Ga. 30602
The Great Lakes Review
    Northeastern Illinois University, Chicago, Ill. 60625
Green River Review
    Box 56, University Center, Mich. 48710
The Greensboro Review
    University of North Carolina, Greensboro, N.C. 27412
Harper's Magazine
    2 Park Avenue, New York, N.Y. 10016
Hudson Review
    65 East 55th Street, New York, N.Y. 10022
Iowa Review
    EPB 453, University of Iowa, Iowa City, Iowa 52240
Kansas Quarterly
    Dept. of English, Kansas State University, Manhattan, Kan.
    66506
Ladies' Home Journal
    641 Lexington Avenue, New York, N.Y. 10022
The Literary Review
    Fairleigh Dickinson University, Teaneck, N.J. 07666

The Little Magazine
 P. O. Box 207, Cathedral Station, New York, N.Y. 10025
The Louisville Review
 University of Louisville, Louisville, Ky. 40208
Mademoiselle
 350 Madison Avenue, New York, N.Y. 10017
Malahat Review
 University of Victoria, Victoria, B.C., Canada
The Massachusetts Review
 Memorial Hall, University of Massachusetts, Amherst, Mass. 01002
McCall's
 230 Park Avenue, New York, N.Y. 10017
Michigan Quarterly Review
 3032 Rackham Bldg., The University of Michigan, Ann Arbor, Mich. 48109
Midstream
 515 Park Avenue, New York, N.Y. 10022
Mother Jones
 607 Market Street, San Francisco, Calif. 94105
The National Jewish Monthly
 1640 Rhode Island Avenue, N.W., Washington, D.C. 20036
New Boston Review
 Boston Critic, Inc., 77 Sacramento Street, Somerville, Mass. 02143
New Directions
 333 Sixth Avenue, New York, N.Y. 10014
New Letters
 University of Missouri–Kansas City, Kansas City, Mo. 64110
The New Renaissance
 9 Heath Road, Arlington, Mass. 02174
New Voices
 P. O. Box 308, Clintondale, N.Y. 12515
The New Yorker
 25 West 43rd Street, New York, N.Y. 10036
The North American Review
 University of Northern Iowa, 1222 West 27th Street, Cedar Falls, Iowa 50613
Northwest Review
 129 French Hall, University of Oregon, Eugene, Ore. 97403

The Ohio Journal
> 164 West 17th Avenue, Columbus, Ohio 43210

Ohio Review
> Ellis Hall, Ohio University, Athens, Ohio 45701

The Ontario Review
> 6000 Riverside Drive East, Windsor, Ont., Canada N8S 1B6

Paragraph: A Quarterly of Gay Fiction
> Box 14051, San Francisco, Calif. 94114

The Paris Review
> 45-39–171st Place, Flushing, N.Y. 11358

Partisan Review
> Rutgers University, New Brunswick, N.J. 08903

Perspective
> Washington University, St. Louis, Mo. 63130

Phylon
> 223 Chestnut Street, S.W., Atlanta, Ga. 30314

Playboy
> 919 North Michigan Avenue, Chicago, Ill. 60611

Ploughshares
> Box 529, Cambridge, Mass. 02139

Prairie Schooner
> Andrews Hall, University of Nebraska, Lincoln, Nebr. 68588

Prism International
> Dept. of Creative Writing, University of British Columbia, Vancouver, Canada V6T 1WR

Quarterly Review of Literature
> 26 Haslet Avenue, Princeton, N.J. 08540

Quarterly West
> 312 Olpin Union, University of Utah, Salt Lake City, Utah 84112

Quartet
> 1119 Neal Pickett Drive, College Station, Tex. 77840

Redbook
> 230 Park Avenue, New York, N.Y. 10017

Rolling Stone
> 625 Third Street, San Francisco, Calif. 94107

The Saturday Evening Post
> 110 Waterway Boulevard, Indianapolis, Ind. 46202

Sequoia
> Storke Student Publications Bldg., Stanford, Calif. 94305

The Sewanee Review
    University of the South, Sewanee, Tenn. 37375
Shenandoah
    Box 722, Lexington, Va. 24450
The Smith
    5 Beekman Street, New York, N.Y. 10038
The South Carolina Review
    Dept. of English, Clemson University, Clemson, S.C. 29631
The South Dakota Review
    Box 111, University Exchange, Vermillion, S.D. 57069
Southern Humanities Review
    Auburn University, Auburn, Ala. 36830
Southern Review
    Drawer D, University Station, Baton Rouge, La. 70803
Southwest Review
    Southern Methodist University Press, Dallas, Tex. 75275
Story Quarterly
    220 Myrtle Street, Winnetka, Ill. 60093
The Tamarack Review
    Box 159, Postal Station K, Toronto, Ont., Canada M4P 2G5
Transfer
    San Francisco State University, San Francisco, Calif. 94132
Tri-Quarterly
    University Hall 101, Northwestern University, Evanston, Ill. 60201
University of Windsor Review
    Dept. of English, University of Windsor, Windsor, Ontario, Canada N9B 3P4
U. S. Catholic
    221 West Madison Street, Chicago, Ill. 60606
Vagabond
    P. O. Box 879, Ellensburg, Wash. 98926
The Virginia Quarterly Review
    University of Virginia, 1 West Range, Charlottesville, Va. 22903
Vogue
    350 Madison Avenue, New York, N.Y. 10017
West Coast Review
    Simon Fraser University, Vancouver, B.C., Canada

Western Humanities Review
  Bldg. 41, University of Utah, Salt Lake City, Utah 84112
Wind
  RFD Route 1, Box 809, Pikeville, Ky. 41501
Yale Review
  250 Church Street, 1902A Yale Station, New Haven, Conn. 06520
Yankee
  Dublin, N.H. 03444